FULTON COUNTY

BY JAMES GOLDMAN

FICTION

Waldorf
The Man from Greek and Roman
Myself as Witness

PLAYS

They Might Be Giants
Blood, Sweat and Stanley Poole
(with William Goldman)
The Lion in Winter

MUSICALS

A Family Affair
(with John Kander and William Goldman)
Follies
(with Stephen Sondheim)

SCREENPLAYS

The Lion in Winter
They Might Be Giants
Nicholas and Alexandra
Robin and Marian
White Nights
(with Eric Hughes)

TELEPLAYS

Evening Primrose
(with Stephen Sondheim)
Oliver Twist
Anna Karenina
Anastasia: The Mystery of Anna

FULTON COUNTY

A NOVEL

James Goldman

WILLIAM MORROW AND COMPANY, INC.
NEW YORK

Library of Congress Cataloging-in-Publication Data

Goldman, James.
  Fulton County.

  I. Title.
PS3513.0337F85 1989   813'.54   88–33035
ISBN 0–688–08815–5

Printed in the United States of America

First Edition

1 2 3 4 5 6 7 8 9 10

BOOK DESIGN BY NICOLA MAZZELLA

FULTON COUNTY

1

BEAVER COUNTY, PENNSYLVANIA, lies on the Ohio border to the north and west of Pittsburgh. It is intersected by the Turnpike, the Ohio River wanders through it, but it has no cities, not to speak of, and no industry worth noting. Traces of the Alleghenies make it difficult to farm and hard to live on. It is poor and it is rural; rocky fields and scattered towns and shabby villages at crossroads. Route 251, a state road two lanes wide with narrow shoulders, passes north of Beaver Falls and then goes twisting westward through deserted hills and valleys on its way to nowhere in particular. It is not an easy road to do at sixty-five, not in a twenty-four-foot van with half a billion miles on it.

Talker shifted down to take the curve. The old truck bucked and rattled. There was no oncoming traffic, not this late, but there were scraps of mist, the turns were poorly banked, on top of which he didn't know the road. Below him, in the valley, pricks of light were moving on the Fairgrounds; roughies taking down the rides and loading up the trucks. The town itself, of course, was dark. There was no life in Pittsfield after midnight. Or before it, Talker thought as he came off the curve and picked up speed. They'd given him an hour to clear the county and he had some twenty minutes left. He wasn't certain where the border was, but ten miles, give or take, should see him well across it.

"Talker?"

She was sitting there across the cab, legs tucked up on the seat. He glanced at her. She looked about eleven in the dim light from the dashboard; pale and boyish. From the first time he had seen her, she'd reminded him of Peter Pan.

Wind whistled in through rolled-up windows, chilling her. She hunched her shoulders, jammed her hands into her jacket pockets, looked at him. His cheek was swollen and his lip was cut.

"Are you O.K.?"

It was the first thing she had said since she had helped him to the truck. "I'm fine," he said, and grinned to prove it. Truth to tell, all things considered, nothing really hurt. His arms and shoulders would be sore tomorrow, they had taken all the punishment. Or most of it. Eventually, he had gone down, of course. There were, he knew, few absolutes in life, but there were some he lived by: you don't drive or gamble when you're drunk, you do not fuck your buddy and you never, ever hit a cop.

She grinned back at him, not certain what to say, what course to take. She scarcely knew him. Friends were hard to come by, and she needed him to be one. "I thought you were great," she said. "I mean it. Just terrific. I was kind of scared there for a while, you know."

He knew. She hadn't been the only one, and if the Sheriff hadn't come around and called his boys off, God knows how it might have ended. He'd been lucky. Maybe finding Annie was a turning point. He slowed down for a patch of mist. She spoke again as they went through it.

"Talker?"

"Yeah?"

She had a lot of questions. Did he really think that she could make it? Could she trust him? He had told her that she didn't have to put out: she could do it if she wanted to—or not. Could she believe him? And the other girls, what were they like, how would they treat her? Endless questions. She picked out an easy one.

"Where are we going to?"

"Ohio."

"I mean where, exactly."

"I don't know." He shrugged. He'd never seen Ohio, but that didn't trouble him; like Scarlett, he would deal with it tomorrow. Half the time you never knew where you were going next. You played a lot of towns by chance. "Every county has a fair. We'll find one. It's no problem."

"I was only wondering, that's all." Then she smiled. "Besides, I don't care where we end up. Any place beats Pittsfield."

Spoken from the heart. She meant it. If you didn't count one trip to Erie, she had never been away from home. She'd always known that she was going. There was more to life than mucking out the barn or mending clothes and tidying the henhouse. She was not about to settle with some farmer and produce a line of chinless dimwits. Maybe that was good enough for Aunt Maria who, if wedding pictures didn't lie, was glum and dumpy to begin with. Maybe listening to the soaps and never making love and wearing clothes from J. C. Penney was a hoot for her. But not for Annie. Some days, when she had the time, she'd settle in the library at school, all seven hundred books of it, and read about the world. She liked the way it sounded and she knew it was for her. She had to see it. She had even tried to once, when she was fourteen, but good old Uncle Emil called the cops and they had caught her out here, on this very road.

It was a valuable lesson. Taking off when you're a minor gets you nowhere. Kids are runaways but young adults are people. So she waited, did her chores, fought off the boys, passed English which was easy and Biology, which wasn't. Secretly, she sent away for travel pamphlets, signing Susie's name—her best and one-and-only friend—and had them mailed to Susie's house. She sneaked them home, devoured them in bed at night and saved her money. Eighteen was the thing she had to be, and when it happened to her, finally, at last, she packed her bag and hid it in the cedar chest beneath the blankets. That was on the seventh day of August, just three weeks ago.

The bag was on the floor, between her feet. She looked down at it, picked it up and put it on her lap. No reason; she just felt like holding it. She'd packed it carefully and it held all her precious things: the travel pamphlets and two pairs of jeans with studs, some socks and T-shirts, makeup, forty-seven dollars, toilet articles, her party dress, last year's *World Almanac,* sunglasses, and the only photograph she had of Mom and

Dad. It showed them in the front yard, holding hands, the summer they had gone away and had the car crash.

Annie turned and looked at Talker as the old truck groaned and shuddered up a hill. He was a big man, strong and solid, with a funny kind of face, a bit lopsided and uneven. Like a sort of Richard Boone, or Lincoln if he hadn't been so thin and tall. You couldn't call him handsome, and besides, she didn't think of him that way. How could she? He was twice her age, she guessed; or maybe even more, which made him old enough to be her father.

It was just four days ago that she had met him. Wednesday afternoon. The day was steaming hot and she had driven into town with Uncle Emil and his three sons, Ignace, Jan, and Emil, Jr. They had brought these pigs in to exhibit, hoping for some ribbons, fat chance, and she'd helped them in the Swine Shed for a while before she slipped away.

She loved the Fair. It was the high point of her year. She didn't care that much about the rides or games and she could take the food or leave it—all those things cost money. What she loved was all the people. There were hundreds of them, some days even thousands, come from all across the county. There were kids she knew from school and folks from town, but she avoided them. It was the strangers who attracted her. New faces. She collected faces; scraps of conversation, too. It was like making movies. Later, she would play them back and make up stories all about them. She was always in the stories. Sometimes she would have a big part, sometimes not. It didn't matter; either way, the fun was in the playing.

She was listening to an argument: some man was jealous of his wife and she was threatening to leave him. It was not a story she was fond of, so she turned them off and stepped away, and that was when she saw the crowd.

There must have been a hundred people clustered all around some show or other on the hillside up above. She started toward it, pausing briefly to record two children who had gotten lost. She was about to help them when their mother came, and it was then she heard the voice. Some man connected with the show was talking to the crowd. She couldn't understand the words but there was something in the voice that caught her. In the sound. She couldn't name it, but she hurried up the hill, slipped past the people at the crowd's edge, squeezed around two big men who were blocking off her view, and there, in all its glory, was the Moulin Rouge.

And Talker. He was standing on a narrow stage. Behind him was a curtained doorway that was set into a wall of life-size paintings, in the brightest colors she had ever seen, of women dressed in daring clothes. She stood there, scarcely breathing, listening to him speak. His voice was like a TV anchorman's, except it wasn't phony. He could make it rough or smooth or hard, and he could make the crowd do anything he wanted to. They laughed when he said something funny; when he whispered, they were still as mice.

The show was just for men and he was telling them about the miracles of femininity inside and how, for just two dollars, they could have an unforgettable experience. Then music started, Talker turned, moved to the curtain, drew it back, and out this lady came. She had long hair and she was tall and twenty-five at least. She wore an evening gown that fit her everywhere, all shiny and rich yellow, like spun gold.

The lady stood there for a moment as if she were all alone and there was no one watching. Then she smiled a secret smile, her hips began to move, one hand reached slowly up to touch her breasts, and Annie's breath caught in her throat.

At home, at Uncle Emil's place, there was one bathroom for the six of them. It had the only full-length mirror in the house and sometimes when she couldn't sleep, when it was very late at night, she'd tiptoe down the hall and slip the bolt. Then she would turn the light on, take her top and bottoms off and stand there looking at herself. She liked her body, kind of. It was nice enough, but skinny, nothing like the girls in *Playboy*.

Some nights, all she did was stand there. She might smile her secret smile—she had one, too—but that was all she did. And some nights she would take one finger, put it in her mouth and then, when it was very wet, eyes on the mirror all the time, she'd touch her nipples with it, rubbing gently. As a rule, she'd feel a pleasant feeling, nothing more. But sometimes it would make her gasp, and when that happened, she would stand there while the hand went slowly down and she would watch it touch herself. Not every night, but some nights, there was nothing she could do to stop the hand. The first time this had happened, she had watched it all. Not anymore She didn't want to see the things her body did or what was on her face.

Someone bumped into her. The lady on the stage was gone, the men around her, most of them, were moving toward the ticket booth and Talker, still on stage, was saying "Show time, show time, show time." She felt dizzy, just a little, so she stood there till it passed and then went off and bought a Coke.

Five minutes later, she was back. The crowd was gone and there was no one out in front except for Talker and the gray-haired lady in the ticket booth. The sun was low now but the day was hot as ever. She had made her mind up, and she walked across the dry grass, walked right up to them and spoke.

"Hey, mister?"

"In a minute, kid." He went on talking to the lady, so she stepped back like a good girl, waiting to be spoken to. The show was going on inside. Sounds drifted out: rock music from the sixties mixed with shouts and whistles, sudden silences. She wondered what the girls were doing.

"O.K., kid, what is it?"

He was looking down at her. The sun was on his face and he was squinting. Annie couldn't see his eyes.

"I'm looking for a job," she said.

"What kind of job?"

What did he think? "I want to be a dancer in the show."

He shook his head. "Come back in three years."

"I'm eighteen and I can prove it. I'd be good. I sing and dance. You want to see?" He shook his head again. "Come on, give me a chance. At school we did *The King and I*. You have a minute, I can show you all the steps."

"What's your name, kid?"

"Annie."

"Annie, you know what a strip show is?"

She nodded briskly. "Sure I do. Who doesn't?"

"Have you ever seen one?"

"Lots of times. I've been around. Don't let the work boots fool you. I've seen plenty." He was grinning. Didn't he believe her? "All the girls do is, they move around some and they take their clothes off. I could do that, it's no trick."

"Uh-huh."

"Look, mister, where I live, there's four men and one

bathtub. They've been sneaking looks at me since I was ten. I don't exactly love it, but it doesn't hurt."

He shook his head, reached out and put his big hand lightly on her shoulder. "Annie," he said softly, "go on home."

Her eyes filled up; she felt as if he'd slapped her. "Why? What's wrong with me? You think I'm not that much to look at? I don't, either. I'm no beauty, you don't have to tell me."

"You're a pretty girl."

"Come off it." She knew soft soap when she heard it. "Mister, you can take your show and stuff it. All I know is, one way or another, I am getting out of Pittsfield if it kills me."

She turned sharply, started off. Her ears were ringing and she almost didn't hear him say, "Hey, Annie." She turned back.

"I'm going for a beer," he said. "You want one?"

Annie didn't like beer, but she nodded.

It would have to be a quick one, he was pressed for time, and as they walked downhill together, past the fortune teller and the pizza stand, he wondered why he'd stopped her. She'd be trouble, she was far too inexperienced, too fragile; she would go to pieces on him. On the other hand, the fact was, they were short one girl. Babette had left the show in Uniontown, three weeks ago. She always used to say that what she wanted out of life was love and marriage. Talker half suspected it was what all his girls dreamed of, and sometimes it actually happened to them. Babette's man turned out to be a pharmacist; he wrote prescriptions in some drugstore. He was short and forty, but he owned his home and drove an Oldsmobile. Babette adored him. Talker had been present at the wedding. He had given her away.

The beer was freezing. Talker let it trickle down his throat, then took the plunge. Her face lit like a pumpkin when you light the candle.

"There's a job? You mean it, mister? There's a place for me?"

He nodded and began to fill her in about the Moulin Rouge. He wanted her to know the downside, what the life was like. She cut him off. She didn't care.

"Just tell me when I start, that's all."

"That's up to Norma. All I do is run the show. She owns it."

"Right. Where's Norma?"

Talker shook his head. "We're here till Saturday, there's lots of time. What you do is, you go home and you think about it. I don't want you crapping out on me next week. It's not a free ride, Annie." It was said to shake her up. He thought it did.

"O.K." She paused. "I guess you're right. Besides, if I went off with you, they'd never take me back." She looked down at her beer. "There's one thing; it's a stupid question, really dumb. You mind?" He shrugged and shook his head. She licked her lips. "The thing is, mister, do I have to do it?"

"Do it?"

Annie's eyes went up to his, then quickly down again. She nodded, mumbled, "You know. Do it."

Was she queer? He didn't think so. "What's the matter? Don't you like it?"

"I don't know yet."

Talker blinked. He'd worked with every kind of girl there was, from necrophiles to needle freaks, but this was something new. A first. He felt a pang for her, no reason why. "No, you don't have to. It's a strip show, not a cat house."

"Honestly?"

He nodded. Strictly speaking, it was true enough. Eventually, of course, all Talker's girls put out. For love or money, reassurance, boredom; for one reason or another. But that didn't make them hookers. No, sir. Any more than Alex Karras was an actor. You could put him in a movie, you could pay him for it, he was still a football player. These distinctions were important. Even so, it didn't sit right. What else could he tell her?

She was smiling, thanking him. He cut her off. "Look, Annie, when you're sure, and I mean damn sure, you come back, meet Norma and the girls, and see the show. If everything works out, you've got a job. O.K.?"

"O.K."

Enough said. He had more important things to do. The show was ending, they did three an hour, and he had to get back to his bally stage and rustle up a crowd. He nodded to her. "So long, Annie."

He was turning when she stopped him. "What's your name?" she asked. He told her. "That's a funny name. Thanks, Talker." Then she grinned, stretched up on tiptoe, kissed his cheek and skipped away. He watched her till she disappeared around the Bingo tent.

He had a hunch he'd seen the last of her. If getting out of town was really what she wanted, there were better ways to do it; and if she had any sense, she'd find one. When she didn't turn up Thursday, he forgot her, more or less. Besides, he had his hands full with the girls. It never failed, nor did it ever stop surprising him. He had gone talking every summer now for fourteen years, he had seen highs and lows with fifty girls at least, and they could sail through ugliness and troubles, things that really got to him, without a blink. And then, let something come along like Babette getting married, and they'd all go straight to pieces.

So for days now, he'd been pouring coffee into Skipper, who was either up on pills or down on booze. And Laurel, bright and clever, funny when she felt good and a real bitch when she didn't, was impossible to deal with. And Pauline, who tended to be bovine at the best of times, had gone completely cowlike and for hours on end would lie there mooning at the ceiling. It was not a lot of fun, and Norma, who could generally be counted on at times like this, had troubles of her own.

He had come close to packing up on Friday. Nothing all that bad had happened, nothing special. It was just a mood, that's all it was. Still, more and more all summer, he'd begun to wonder why he came back every year. He loved the life, no doubt about it. Maybe Pennsylvania was the problem. Coming west had been his bright idea. The Moulin Rouge had always played New England: Rutland, Auburn, Greenfield, Maine to Massachusetts. He was comfortable up there, he knew the territory; but when business started drying up, what else was there to do?

You couldn't rave about the business on a Friday night in Pittsfield, either. Thin. Slim pickings. Maybe twenty heads a show, and it was uphill making twenty. Half of them were drunk, that happened on the weekends, and his spiel was even raunchier than usual. It had to be, you had to give them pussy once a sentence or you'd lose them. He was sweating. Though the rain had lifted, it was cold and damp, and he had half a mind to close things down and call it quits when he saw Annie. She was standing way back, near the doughnut vendor, in a little pool of light. He almost didn't recognize her.

She had spent a long time fretting over how to look. All day, in fact. There weren't a lot of choices in her closet and it wasn't hard to settle on the white blouse and the yellow skirt with flowers on it. As for jewelry, she had nothing but her mother's wedding ring, which somehow didn't seem appropriate. Her hair and face, though, were another matter. She had stood for hours, bolted in the bathroom, done her hair half a dozen different ways, and put on all the makeup she could think of. In the end, she'd scrubbed her face and let her hair just hang straight down her back. She never wore it loose, she lived in pigtails. Kid stuff: and tonight of all nights, what she had to look was older.

Every summer at the Fair, there was a Demolition Derby Friday night. The boys were going. It was all they talked about all year, they ate it up, and they were giving her a lift. So she had raced through dinner and the dishes, hurried to her room, put on the pantyhose she'd borrowed yesterday from Susie, then her Sunday shoes, the skirt and blouse, let loose her hair and she was ready. She was sure that Emil and Maria wouldn't notice she was all dressed up, and she was right; they didn't.

All the way to town, she felt like whistling. Annie never sang when she was happy; whistling was more private somehow, you could do it softer. Often she made up the tunes, and sometimes they had words. But not tonight. She couldn't put what she was feeling into words. So she just sat there in the old DeSoto as the sun went down, hands folded primly in her lap, wind drifting through her hair, and listened to the music in her head.

The parking field was full of cars and people, and the ground was muddy from the rain. She bought her ticket with her own two dollars, turned to tell the boys where she would meet them later on. She had a story ready if they asked where she was going, but they hadn't waited for her, they were pushing through the crowd that eddied toward the grandstand.

So she turned and started uphill, past the stands and rides and games and all the people with their stories, but she wasn't tuning in tonight. A bunch of screeching kids ran past her, and some local yokel offered her a drink. She scarcely noticed. Nothing mattered but the Moulin Rouge and being part of it. She wondered what the other girls were like; and Norma, too, whoever Norma was. She'd find out soon enough. One thing for sure: they'd been around, they'd seen a lot. She hoped they'd like her and she'd do her best to get along, but that was frosting on the cake. To land a job that took her out of town and let her stand on stage in golden dresses—hell, for all that, she'd put up with anything.

She hadn't seen the Moulin Rouge at night before. She stopped dead. There, above the stage where Talker stood, were blinking lights, three rows of them—red, white, and blue. And spotlights from below lit up the paintings of the girls. His voice was mingled with the music and the noises from the crowd. Then it was show time and the men were buying tickets, grinning, joking with each other as the women who were with them giggled, waved and drifted off. She waited. Hadn't Talker seen her there? Had he forgotten? Then he put his mike down, looked at her and beckoned.

The ground felt slippery as she crossed it. He stayed on stage, crouching, looking down at her. She squinted up into the lights and smiled. "Hi," she said.

He nodded, saying nothing, then jumped down beside her, took her lightly by the elbow, led her to the ticket booth. The gray-haired lady sat there with a cash box, counting money.

"Norma?"

"Just a sec."

Her voice was soft and raspy, like a whiskey voice. She went on counting. Annie watched her. She had big hands. She was big all over, large and bosomy and way past fifty, even older than Maria. She wore glasses, round ones with old-fashioned-looking wire rims. She finished counting, took them off, looked up and shook her head.

"Some Friday."

Talker nodded. "Norma, this is Annie."

Norma's eyes were blue and faded, like a work shirt. Annie smiled and held her hand out. "Pleased to meet you, M'am."

"So you're the girl who wants the job."

"That's me."

"You're pretty." Norma's hand, on hers now, felt as strong and smooth as leather. "Even prettier than Talker said. We don't get all that many cute ones. Are you clean?"

What was the woman asking? "Sure, I guess so."

"No VD, no drugs, no record?" Annie shook her head. "Don't lie to me."

"I'm not."

"How old are you?"

"Eighteen." Annie had come prepared for this one. "Here," she said, whipping out her driver's license from the pocket of her skirt. "I've got more, there's my ID card from Beaver High. You want to see it?"

Norma nodded, put her glasses on. Her lips moved when she read; not much but just a little. Annie watched, then turned, looked up at Talker, wanting something from him. Had she been O.K. so far, how was she doing, did she look all right? A ton of questions and he hadn't said a word so far, he'd hardly even looked at her. He wasn't looking at her now.

Then Norma stood, gave back the cards, picked up the cash box. "All right, honeybuns," she said, "let's go." She left the ticket booth and led them through the canvas archway just beyond. There was an aisle here with walls of paintings, naked girls, on both sides. Up ahead, Annie saw the entrance to the tent. You couldn't see it from in front, the paintings were too high, and just then shouts and whistles went up from the men inside. The show was starting. Annie felt excited; they were taking her to see it. She'd spent hours imagining what it was like: the faces of the men, the look their eyes had as they watched, the movements of the girls who danced, the clothes they wore, or didn't wear. She couldn't wait.

A bit before the entrance, Norma stopped and turned. There was an opening, a narrow space between the paintings. She moved through it. Annie followed just behind, and there, of all things, was a truck. A big one, like a moving van. The back of it, the loading door, was just in front of them. Attached to it, along one side, she saw the stage where Talker worked. The tent was roped on to the other side, so that the truck was at the center, in between. Some steps led to the loading door. Norma climbed them, slid the door back and went in.

Annie followed. It was not what she expected. She was backstage, but it wasn't like the one at school. The light seemed very bright. She saw some beds, all messed up, piled with clothes and paper bags. There were some folding chairs and wooden tables, and the TV set was on. A girl sat watching it, all huddled in a blanket. In a corner, propped up on a bed, there was another girl, the one who wore the golden dress. She had a bathrobe on and she was reading from a big book. Both of them looked up at her.

She felt uneasy, kind of scared; why had they taken her in here, what did they want? The air was warm and stuffy. Talker closed the van door, Norma sat down on a chair, took out a cigarette and, as she struck the match, said, "O.K., let's look at you."

For just a moment, Annie didn't understand her. Then she nodded. "Sure. Here goes." She knew exactly what was wanted, and she knew she mustn't hesitate or seem embarrassed. It was nothing, it was easy, she could do it.

Talker watched her take her clothes off. He had been through this God knows how many times. It was a useful exercise; not every girl felt comfortable about exhibiting her pussy, and the ones who didn't were to be avoided, weeded out. They almost always drank too much, they needed to be blind to strip, and life was hard enough without him playing nursemaid to some alcoholic. There was nothing wrong with booze, they all got stoned from time to time, himself included; but a lush was something different, and he didn't like to see it happen to his girls. Not that he felt responsible or guilty; he just didn't like it.

Annie didn't seem to mind. No hesitation as she took her skirt off, put it neatly on a chair. Off came the blouse without a blink. She wouldn't look at anyone, she kept her eyes averted; otherwise, you would have thought she did this every day. It wasn't till the pantyhose came down and she was reaching for her bra that she showed anything at all, a moment's hesitation, nothing more. Then off it came.

She stood there in that wretched truck, amongst the bowls of cigarette butts, coffee cups and empty bags of junk food as if she were standing on a pedestal. She held her head high and her shoulders back. Her skin looked silky, ivory-colored; cool and warm at once. She seemed transformed without her clothes; the boyish look was gone, and Talker felt his chest go tight. Not from desire; God no. He had met a lot of sexy women in his time and bedded his fair share of them, but this was different. There was something in the lines of Annie's body, in the curves and hollows of her flesh, that shook him up. He couldn't name the feeling. She seemed made for sunlight, open fields, and for a moment he imagined her stark naked in a woodland, running free against the green. His lips were dry. He licked them.

"O.K., honey." It was Norma. "You can put your things on." Annie didn't seem to hear her. Then she nodded, bent, picked up her pantyhose, and Talker turned at last and looked away. Business was business.

"Well?" he said to Norma.

"Tell her how the money works and what the deal is. If she wants to, she can start tomorrow."

"Right." He nodded. Laurel went back to her reading, Norma stood and left the truck, Pauline returned to watching *Kojak* on the tube. He lit a cigarette and then, while Annie finished dressing, crossed the truck to check the show.

He drew the curtain back a crack. The tent was quarter full. The crowd was fairly orderly, considering how drunk most of them were. The two cops—Talker called them Pat and Mike, all assholes looked alike to him—stood at the back, on duty, drinking beer. All eyes were glued on Skipper. She was working strong, which meant that she was sauced again, she never did it sober. Annie had to see this. It was only right; she had to know what she was getting into, even if she never worked like Skipper did. He was about to turn and call her over when he felt her touch his shoulder.

"Talker?" Annie's eyes were shining at him. "Can I really start tomorrow? Can I?"

"If you want to, sure." He stepped back from the curtain. "Would you like to see the show?"

"You mean from here, from backstage?" He nodded.

Annie stepped up to the curtain. She felt breathless and her hand was shaky as she drew it back a little, just an inch or so, and looked through. It was hard to see at first. Some lights were shining toward her from the back part of the tent. Then she began to see the faces of the people. There were some she recognized. Like Anton Gerber. An old friend of Uncle Emil's, he was leaning on the tent pole, holding it with one hand and the other hand was in his pocket, moving back and forth. She couldn't see his face too well; she didn't really want to, anyway.

The faces of the men down front were lit by stage lights; they were clear. John Hedricks, Marvin Dove, he ran the grocery store, Pete Parker, Stevie Gooberman from high school, and a lot of men she didn't know. Their heads were tilted back so they could look up at the stage. They had the same expression, every one of them. Their skin looked chalky-gray and slack, their eyes were flat and glassy, and their mouths hung open just a little. It was not a look she'd seen before; she didn't like it, so she turned and saw the girl on stage.

She wasn't dancing. She had short red hair, a strong back, she looked firm and solid and she had no clothes on. Nothing but some high-heeled shoes and she was sitting on her haunches with her knees apart as wide as they could go. She was just inches from the men up front, and they could see her. They could see. That's what they all were looking at.

Then suddenly, the girl moved. She went down on stage flat on her back and kicked her legs up, straight up, wide apart into a V. And then the man in front of her, the closest one, leaned forward, put his face down. He was licking her, the man was licking her down there, and then the men around him started moving, pushing at each other. They were getting into line.

Annie shut her eyes. It didn't help, it only made her dizzy. She felt cold and damp and there was a taste of acid in her mouth. She turned and bolted, bumped into a corner of a table, kept on going, found the handle to the loading door and got it open. She forgot the stairs. She fell, went twisting to the ground. She couldn't stay there, not where anyone could see her. It was dark beneath the truck. She got up on her hands and knees, on all fours, and she crawled. She made it to the shadows. Then she lay down on her side, tucked up her knees and vomited.

Talker closed the loading door. He stood there on the steps and listened to the retching sounds. He knew what she was going through. Even Skipper, now and then, still got upset; a lot of girls were like that, and what puzzled him was why they did it. Working strong was never something you were asked or told to do; it was a personal decision and if getting eaten out in public made you sick, why do it to yourself?

He thought of telling Annie something, like so long or have a good life, but why bother? He had known from the beginning that she couldn't cut it. She was wrong, she'd never fit in, she'd be trouble; nothing but. The grind was rough enough, he didn't need her on his back. He turned away and left her there.

He saw her when she came out, maybe half an hour later.

He was on stage, arousing the rustics, when she moved through the entrance, walking stiffly, passing Norma in the ticket booth without a glance, then moving down the hill. If anything, he felt relieved.

The rear wheels skidded on the turn, on sand or something, and he almost lost the road. It made no sense to press it, there was no one chasing him. He'd had a bellyful of Pennsylvania, that was all. He slowed down, cursed himself.

"What's wrong?"

He must have sworn aloud. He looked at her and shrugged. She held a candy bar, half-eaten, in one hand. She held it out. "You want some?"

"No, thanks."

Kids were something; they could always eat. He wasn't certain how he felt about her being with him. When she hadn't shown for work that afternoon, he'd been relieved. And, to be honest, slightly disappointed. She had something going for her. What it was, he'd never know. Saturday was it for Pittsfield, he had seen the last of Annie—and then, she'd turned up just in time to see him getting his ribs kicked in.

The trouble started just as they were wrapping up. It was a little short of midnight and the last of the Saturday night crowd was shuffling from the tent. They had a long day's drive tomorrow, they were leaving early, and he had some roughies waiting, three of them, to help him take the stages down, fold up the flats and strike the show. The girls were dressing in the van. As soon as they were finished, he could start to load.

So he was waiting with his roughies, outside by the bally stage, when Norma called him. She was standing by the ticket booth. The lights were off, and in the dimness she looked tired.

"What's up?" he asked.

Her voice was low. "We've got a little problem."

"Tell me."

"It's those two cops."

"Pat and Mike?"

She nodded. "Yeah. They want a late show."

Late shows were the pits. He shook his head. "To hell with them." Those cops were bought and paid for. Every time he checked into a Fair, he greased the local Sheriff and asked for a cop or two. They helped keep order in the tent, they made you look legitimate. They cost a hundred bucks a night; and worth it. Only sometimes, usually on closing night when you were leaving town, they wanted something extra. Talker didn't care much what girls did on their own, they could turn all the tricks they wanted to. But not against their will; no, not if he could help it. There were several courses open to him. He went through them, picked the safest.

"O.K., Norma. Here's the thing." He told her what to do. It wasn't difficult, not from her end. She listened closely, then she nodded.

"Right," she said. "We'll meet you there."

"Don't worry if I'm late."

"I'll worry if I want to." Then she turned. "Good luck."

He hoped he didn't need it. "Thanks." He watched her hurry off; then, hands in pockets, looking casual, he sauntered toward the entrance to the tent.

The two of them sat sprawled on folding chairs, ties loose and jackets open, cans of beer in hand. They must have weighed five hundred pounds between them. Talker put his leer on.

"Hiya, fellas. How's it going?"

"Want a beer?"

They both had six-packs. Talker nodded. "Norma's told me what you want." He paused. Their eyes were on him. "It's no problem, nothing to it. I'll go set it up." He took the beer, moved forward, vaulted to the stage, called out. "Hey, Skip."

She moved in through the curtain, dressed for town: skirt, blouse and jacket, low-heeled shoes. "Yeah? What is it?"

"How about another show?" He leered again. "A big one for the boys."

She groaned. "You're fucking kidding. Jesus Christ—"

He cut her off. "I want all three of you. We're going to do this right. You got me?"

Skipper let her shoulders slump. "I got you."

"O.K., go and change."

She nodded, shuffled off back through the curtain. Talker figured Pat and Mike would be a good five minutes catching on. And then, with any luck, they'd curse him out and go on home.

He was half right. Five minutes later, give or take, Pat started grumbling, what was taking them so long, for Chrissake? Talker shrugged; the girls were beat, that's all it was, but maybe he could get things moving. And besides, he had the truck to load, he'd be there half the night. So, grumbling, he went back on stage and stuck his head in through the curtain.

"What the hell?" He turned to face them, shook his head. "They've gone, they've taken off. How do you like that? I'll be damned."

They didn't like it. They were on their feet and moving toward him. There was still a chance to keep things cool. "Look, fellas, you know what these girls are like. They're drunk or crazy half the time, you can't control them." It was pointless. Talker set himself as they climbed up on stage. They were as slow as they were big and he could take them both, he knew he could, he still had fast hands. One of them was shouting at him, words like pimp and motherfucker. They had worked this way before, two against one; they split up on the tiny stage, came at him from both sides. He shot between them, vaulted to the tent floor; there was more room to maneuver.

It was then that he saw Annie. She was standing at the entrance, travel bag in hand. He yelled at her, "Get out of here!" She spun around and bolted.

Then it started. They were on him, both at once. He watched their eyes, potato eyes set in potato faces. Fairly soon, things got a little blurry, there was ringing in his ears. Then he was on the tent floor, but he didn't stay there; he got up again. He couldn't see them very well. They got behind him, started kicking at him, but it didn't hurt much. Then, somehow, he was down again and it was roughly at this point he heard the voice. A big voice, it was guttural and deep and it was shouting. Suddenly, the kicking stopped.

He thought of sitting up, decided not to, frowned and brought things into focus. There was Annie, and beside her was a big man. Talker placed him: Sheriff Hocker, Blocker, Crocker, something like that. He was giving Pat and Mike a reaming. Then he turned on Talker and evicted him from Beaver County.

"Hey. Hey, Talker." It was Annie. She was pointing at the road ahead. There was a sign; he'd seen it, too. The border. Norma and the girls were waiting somewhere up ahead, a mile or two, he'd find them. Annie took his hand and squeezed it. She was grinning. "Here we go" was what she said.

The sign was close enough to read now.

GREETINGS FROM THE BUCKEYE STATE.

RESPECT OUR LAWS.

PROTECT OUR CHILDREN.

WELCOME TO OHIO.

2

EVERY HOUSE ON Sunset Crescent had at least three acres. Van and Marcie's house had four.

The Crescent, twenty-seven homes in all, had been developed in the sixties with the help of Akron money. Quiet and secluded, it stood like an outpost, isolated from the rest of Fulton, just inside the township line. The grounds of Longview Country Club lay slightly to the east. But there was nothing else nearby; for to the north and west lay vacant land, and to the south the farms began.

There was a dinner-dance at Longview every Saturday. They were the highlights of the summer. There were special decorations, an elaborate buffet, and dancing on the terrace to the music of Ben Burbidge and His Boys from nine till midnight. Everybody went.

If Marcie ever wondered why, she never dwelt on it. One dinner-dance was like the next, all carbon copies. It was reassuring. Marcie nodded; that was it. There was, God knows, enough uncertainty in life to go around.

Her dressing room was cool—Van liked to keep the house at 65 exactly, you could hang meat in the hallways—and there was, she knew, no moisture on her forehead but she wiped it anyway, then zipped the dress up, fluffed her hair and turned to check the net effect.

Not bad, but not a triumph, either. She was conscious of

her looks—not vain, just conscious. She could see herself objectively, and on a scale of ten she was an eight to eight-point-five, depending. Pretty, but not beautiful. She shrugged. To change or not to change? The dress was two years old, maybe the time had come to put it out to pasture, give it to the thrift shop for the tax deduction.

"Marcie?"

It was Van, from downstairs, calling. Waiting always made him anxious, so she hurried to the bedroom door and called down, "In a minute."

It would have to be a minute or she'd lose him for the evening. Van was under pressure these days, and he wasn't good at pressure. She was. So she hurried back, surveyed her jewelry, took the pearls, checked out the end result, shrugged, grabbed her purse, and flicked the lights off.

When she came down, Van was in the family room with Betsy. There were fabric swatches everywhere, pinned on the curtains and the sofa. It was time to do the room again. Van cared about these things, but it was her profession, sort of, and she usually knew exactly what she wanted.

"Well, don't you look nice," Van told her.

Betsy looked up from her book. "You really do, Mom."

Betsy rarely said things if she didn't mean them. Marcie smiled, then bent to kiss her cheek. "We may be late."

"That's O.K. Have a good time."

Betsy watched them go. They made a handsome couple, like the ones you saw on *The Love Boat;* simpy people for the most part, and she instantly felt guilty. Betsy loved them. Couldn't talk to them, but kids of fourteen never could talk to their parents. She stretched out on the sofa and went back to *Crime and Punishment.* Some of it was difficult, but she could catch the drift.

The air outside was stultifying. Nothing stirred. The temperature hung in the 90's, no rain or relief in sight. Small patches of the lawn were browning out. They took Van's car and drove. It wasn't far. Just past the Kohlers' and the Jacksons' to the Fallsburg Road, then left for half a mile.

She wondered what to say to him. They weren't alone together much these days. No reason why, except they led such busy lives, and by the time they went upstairs to bed, it was too late for anything but sleep. There was a lot they ought to talk about: Dee's coming home and what if anything it meant to them; the Agency; the Fair; Betsy and the Redding boy. The trouble was, these subjects all had consequences. Marcie thought of something safe.

"Well, how'd it go this afternoon?"

He looked blank for a moment. "Oh. You mean the golf?"

She nodded. Van was serious about his game, and he had played a match that afternoon against Jack Abbott in an early round of the Calcutta.

"Six and five, I beat him, but it's not a lot of fun. You've got to watch him all the time."

"What for?"

"He cheats."

"He doesn't." Marcie grinned. Jack Abbott was a CPA.

"He whiffs the ball and calls it practice."

"Don't you love it?"

"It's not funny when you're playing with him."

By the time they turned onto the Club grounds, Van was laughing. It was going to be a pleasant evening. Longview, with its portico and Doric columns, looked vaguely antebellum, and when Marcie was a little girl, it used to make her think of Tara. It had been her home-away-from-home back then. In summer, every morning, she and Dee would take their bikes and race each other all the way. When they got old enough, they came in their convertibles.

She fiddled with her necklace as Van pulled up at the entrance. There was valet parking in July and August—college boys, their white shirts sticking to them in the heat. Van left the engine running. One boy slipped behind the wheel, another leaned to help her out.

"Good evening, M'am."

She let him take her hand. It used to bother her when they tried peeping up her skirt as she got out. It didn't anymore. Where was the harm? She thanked him with a smile.

"Well, shall we?"

It was Van. He offered her his arm and in they went. As always, the reception desk was unattended; no one ever tried to crash the Club and strangers never came. They passed by cases filled with trophies, photos of Past Presidents. Her dad had been the second one. She glanced up at him. He looked so young, and she could not remember him like that; but then, it had been thirty years ago, when she was only eight.

The Paddlewheel was mobbed. It always was on Saturdays. The room had been the Men's Grill when the Club went up, and it was still a mannish place. The dress code—some things had to change—seemed wrong to Marcie. It was backwards: women in pastels and whites, the men like peacocks, stripes and plaids, lime green, canary yellow, shocking pink, electric blue.

Van raised his voice above the noise. "You see the folks anyplace?"

She looked around. They alternated company on Saturdays, one with their own friends and the next with Dad and Mother. "There they are." She beamed and waved. Van leading, they began to wedge their way between the tables. Marcie did a lot of smiling, much of which was genuine. She liked the Clarkes and Kembles, and if Nancy Brinker wanted to be bitchy, Marcie would give tit for tat. But not tonight. Some other time.

Edgar Steuben—5'6", but everybody called him Big Ed—rose and flung his arms out. Marcie hugged him.

"How's my Princess?"

"Great," she told him, turned, looked straight into her mother's china-blue eyes, bent and kissed her perfect cheek. "You're looking lovely." Which was true. No signs of fading beauty and she'd just turned sixty-four.

"You, too, dear. I grow fonder of that dress each time you wear it."

Marcie smiled, said thank you like a good girl. Mother could be like that, she was either tart or sweet, a compliment or not, you never knew. She was about to sit when Pam and Jerry paused to say hello. Marcie knew a life buoy when she saw one. "You're both having dinner with us." It was not a question.

The Leggetts were her closest friends. Pam was her partner in the shop, and Jerry was an angel, she had known him all her life. He was a doctor, and the only man in town, not counting Van, whose right it was to kiss her on the lips.

They sat and ordered drinks. She had a lot to talk to Pam about. The Fair brought people into town from all across the county, and the week ahead, not counting Christmastime, could be the biggest of the year. She didn't need the money any more than Pam did, but it mattered to them both to show a profit. Otherwise, it was a hobby, not a business, and they might as well be working for the Garden Club.

There was a second round, more pleasant small talk. Then Ed, whose glass was empty, asked who cared to join him in another.

"After dinner, dear," said Harriet. And it was time for the Buffet.

The chef was new this year and very controversial. He had worked in San Francisco, and on weekdays unfamiliar things began appearing on the menu. But the Saturday Buffet was sacred. Nothing changed, not ever. Ribs and roast beef, jello molds and salads, steam trays filled with creamed corn, peas with baby onions.

The desserts, all homemade at the Club, were Marcie's downfall. She had been plump as a child, a chubby little girl, and to this day it made her feel uneasy when the childhood photographs came out. As if that round face with the curly hair belonged to someone else.

They had Kahlúa with their coffee, by which time Ed was busy gunning at his favorite topic: politics. The Democrats were meddlers, crackpots, always fixing things that worked: the country hadn't been the same since FDR. The Republicans were better—but not much. He'd voted for them all his life, their hearts were in the right place, they had good intentions, but they always screwed things up.

"Who gave us the Depression? Hoover. And now look at what we've got. You want to tell me how we'll ever get this country out of debt?"

Van shrugged and shook his head. He'd heard this speech before. They all had.

"Listen, son." Ed tapped his arm. "You know what's great about America? Nothing kills it. The Democrats can give away the store, the Republicans can send it into bankruptcy, those clowns in Washington can do their worst—and what it means is squat." He smiled. He knew it worried Van. "What's down comes up, what's up comes down. We're doing fine. I'm a believer."

Everybody nodded, even Van, who knew it wasn't true. There was a pause, and Marcie seized it. "Let's go dance," she said.

The air felt good to Marcie when they reached the terrace. She was slightly buzzed, as were they all. The night was clear, the paper lanterns threw the kind of glow that made your skin look seventeen. Pale candles flickered on the table-tops, and everyone was dancing.

Marcie liked the way Ben Burbidge played. He was a fixture. Ever since she could remember, he had driven all the way from Akron every Saturday. He wore a hairpiece now.

"Van?"

He turned to her and nodded. Dancing was one thing that they did beautifully together. Van was light and very graceful. Sometimes other dancers stopped to watch them. Marcie let her eyes half close, imagining the way they looked. Van would be forty soon, and time was being kind to him. He was, no doubt of it, a handsome man, and getting more so all the time.

The Leggetts had a table in a corner of the terrace. Drinks were waiting. Ed and Harriet were circulating, touching base; Ed was a natural salesman and he loved to work the room. The conversation quickly turned to children. Pam and Jerry had a pair; twin boys, eleven and a handful. There were always funny stories. Marcie, listening with half an ear, made sure to smile when everybody else did. Then the first mosquito of the evening buzzed around her head and something in the distance caught her eye.

The terrace overlooked the eighteenth green, and Marcie, who was seated facing out, had seen a light. A bright light but a small one, just a pinpoint in the distance out beyond the sixteenth hole. The course was bone-dry. Even so, it was a little late for someone to be watering the greens. Or was it? Van would know. She might have asked him, but the light went out.

Or rather, as it happened, disappeared; for when she looked again, the light was brighter, closer, moving toward them with some speed. She frowned, reached out and touched Pam's shoulder.

"Look at that."

Pam looked, then turned back. "It's a light."

By then the light had reached the eighteenth hole, and it was racing up the fairway, weaving left and right, from side to side. It was a car. It had to be.

She stood up. "Van, for godsake, someone's got a car out there."

Van spun around, then bolted to his feet. His chair fell over. "Crazy bastard."

She could see it now, an open pickup truck with one dead headlight. It seemed out of all control, careening wildly through the rough, just missing trees, then back into the clear again. Next thing she knew, Van took off. He was running downhill, racing toward the green, arms waving, shouting at the truck.

She found herself in motion, running after him, her high heels sinking in the grass. She bent to kick them off, and when she looked up, Van was on the green, caught squarely in the headlight's glare. The truck was curving, rushing toward him. Marcie froze. What was the driver doing, was he blind? Van crouched, then pivoted and leaped away just as the driver threw the brakes on and the truck began to skid. It slewed across the green on two wheels, dropped into a sand trap, reappeared a moment later, moving slowly till it bumped into the drinking fountain.

It struck her funny for a moment: all that peril for a bump. She may in fact have giggled. Then she noticed someone running past her. Jerry. He was racing toward the truck. She started after him.

He got there first, of course. He had the cab door open and was leaning inside, doing doctor things. She stepped up on the running board. The cab smelled like a brewery, there were beer cans everywhere. The driver had no shirt on. He lay sprawled against the wheel, unconscious, naked to the waist. Across from him, there was a girl. A pretty girl—no breeding or intelligence, but very pretty nonetheless. She looked at Marcie glassy-eyed, and smiled.

"Hi," she said.

Then Jerry moved the driver from the wheel, asked Marcie for a hand, and, very carefully, they got him out and moved him forward toward the headlight, laid him gently on the grass. By this time, Van was there.

"He could of killed me. What's the matter with him?"

Jerry, on his knees beside the boy—he was a boy, still under twenty—shrugged. "Not much, I think. Just shit-faced. Crazy farm kids, shit-faced every weekend."

"Mister?"

They looked up. It was the girl. They hadn't seen her

leave the cab, and she was standing near them, weaving slightly. Marcie thought she looked sixteen.

"Is Marvin hurt much?"

Jerry stood up. "He'll be fine. Let's look at you."

He sat her squarely in the headlight's beam. Her blouse had been unbuttoned. Marcie, who was sitting by the boy, could see her breasts. She watched as Jerry checked her eyes, then expertly, hands moving swiftly, touched her here and there.

"No broken bones. You're going to live." He grinned at her, got up, then sat Van down beside her. "I don't want her moving. Understand?" Van nodded. "That goes double for the boy." He looked at Marcie. "If he comes to, keep him still, O.K.?"

"O.K."

Then Jerry turned and took off at a trot to get his bag. By that time, people from the terrace were starting down. She watched as Jerry, on his way by, stopped them, turned them back. A few of them stayed where they were, just looking.

Marcie glanced at Van. He seemed so tense. "Are you all right?"

He shrugged. "A little shaken up, that's all. I thought I'd had it when that thing came at me."

"So did I."

"What gets into these kids? Why can't they stay in Fallsburg, where they belong?"

She nodded, though she'd done some crazy things when she was twenty. So had Van, but now was not the time to bring it up. The band kept playing. She was conscious of the music and the cricket sounds, the buzz of the mosquitoes. They were everywhere. She brushed one from her arm, then looked down at the boy. There were mosquitoes on his chest. He had a good chest, full and firm, no bulging muscles. Marcie was repulsed by muscle men; they seemed distorted, artificial. Farm boys' bodies were another matter. Swimmers, too; they had the same look. Marcie watched the chest go up and down. Then lightly, barely touching with her fingertips, she moved her hand across it, brushing the mosquitoes off.

The skin felt smooth and soft, like living velvet. He would be like that all over. Marcie let her eyes half close. She saw him standing in a field, between tall rows of ripened corn. The scene played like a movie; quick cuts, close-ups, not the whole boy ever, only parts of him. He had a farmer's tan; brown forearms, but the rest was white. Dead white. His bottom, like two vast breasts pressed together. Then the flatness of his stomach just above where all the hair began. Then thighs. And in between them, there it was. She moved her tongue across her lower lip.

It was then she heard Van speak. His voice was so soft, just a whisper.

"No," she heard him say. "Don't even think of it."

Her heart stopped and her eyes flew open. There was Van, perhaps six feet away, one arm around the girl. She had dozed off or passed out and she lay against him heavily, unbuttoned blouse and all. Van's face seemed gray beneath its tan, and on it was a look of anguish. It was then, and only then, that Marcie saw his eyes were closed. He had been talking to himself.

She almost giggled with relief. He couldn't read her mind. Besides, thoughts didn't count; the sin was in the deed. She clasped her hands together, put them primly in her lap.

And only then did it come home to her. Not once since she had met him had she ever doubted Van or wondered what he did or where he went. She knew him, she was certain he belonged to her completely. Van, who never flirted, never looked at other women—was it possible he had a life apart from her? Or longed for one? Perhaps it hadn't happened yet. It didn't matter. Either way, she had to wonder now; and watch him, search for signs. It made her sad and angry, both. Mistrust was like a parasite, it grew inside and wriggled, and she didn't want to live with it. Her plate was full enough, thanks very much.

Then Jerry came back with his bag, the girl woke up, the boy came to. Jerry checked him out, found nothing, but you couldn't be too careful. So he called an ambulance, and paramedics carted them away to County General.

By which time, police were on the scene. Ed was with them on the eighteenth green when Van and Marcie got there, looking at the gash the tires had made across the creeping bent. The marks looked like a knife wound, dark and ragged. Charges would be filed, of course; for drunken driving, trespassing, and damages. Things like this didn't happen, not in

Fulton. Marcie, Van and Jerry talked while two policemen took their stories down.

They reached home after midnight, went upstairs and got undressed: Van in his dressing room, Marcie in hers. Then teeth were brushed, and so to bed.

Van fluffed up his pillow.

"You want to talk about it?" Marcie asked.

"What's there to say? I wish it hadn't happened."

"So do I."

Van kissed her cheek and turned his light out. Marcie left hers burning.

"You're not sleepy?" Van asked.

"No, not yet."

"I've got a killer of a day tomorrow."

Marcie watched him settle on his side. "Some night," she heard him say. She nodded, listened as his breathing deepened, then lay back and tried to summon happy thoughts. Like Dee. Her Dee was coming home tomorrow. First time in how many years? And then the Fair. So much to do. The Fair was fun, and there was nothing to compare with being busy.

Marcie sighed. It often happened that they both had trouble sleeping. As a rule, it didn't happen on the same night; they were rarely up together. So she drew the sheet back softly, eased her body from the bed. Then—God forbid she wake him up—she tiptoed to the bathroom, found the Seconal, took two, crept back to bed, turned out the light.

The clock said one.

3

THE BLUE LAGOON had been the third motel they'd passed since crossing the Ohio line. At each one, Talker braked the van down while they scanned the parking lot. This time, his car, a bright red Thunderbird, was parked close to the highway, where they couldn't miss it.

Talker drove in the van, killed the engine, cut the lights. She watched him wipe a hand across his eyes, then open up the cab door. He was halfway out before he looked back.

"Bring your things," was all he said.

She got down from the cab. Her legs felt shaky and her throat was dry. The air, which had been nice enough while they were moving, weighed a ton, all hot and sticky, as if somehow they had come a million miles from Beaver Falls. She reached in for her bag and when she turned, she saw a motel door come open. Light poured out.

Norma was in the doorway, looking big and shapeless in her bathrobe. Talker moved up to her. Annie hung back in the shadows, watching while they talked. Then Norma handed him a room key and a whiskey bottle. Talker took them, turned and beckoned to her.

Annie moved into the light. She looked at Norma. "Hi," she said. It came out sounding funny, so she cleared her throat. "Thanks for the job."

"That's O.K., honey. Get some sleep."

Her door closed, she was gone, and Talker was moving toward a doorway, key in hand.

"Come on, kid."

Annie watched him slip the key in. That was when it hit her; they were rooming two by two, just like the Ark. She stood there rooted while the door came open. Then he stepped in, flicked the lights on, disappeared. Maybe she could sleep with Norma, on the floor or something, only how for godsake would that look, her first night out? She shook her head and crossed the threshold, stopped just inside the door.

She squinted in the sudden light. The room was small: two beds, a table in between, an armchair, not much else. The walls were painted green, the air smelled awful. Talker was across the room, crouched by the air conditioner. He got it going, straightened up and headed for the nearest bed.

"You want to close the door?" he said.

"O.K." She closed it as he sat and let his shoulders slump.

"You want to lock it, too?"

"Sure thing." She turned and slipped the bolt. When she looked back, he had the bottle open, halfway to his lips.

"You going to stand there by the door all night?"

"Who, me?" She moved a few steps, put her bag down by the armchair while he drank. The beds looked awfully close together; you could sit on one and touch the other.

Talker wiped his lips. "The bathroom's yours," he said.

She had a cotton nightgown with her, but she wasn't going to wear it, not tonight. Her clothes were on and staying on. "I'll wash up later, thanks."

He had the bottle to his lips again. She watched him drink. The air conditioner was making clonking noises, but the room was getting cooler. There was no way she could go on standing there forever. And besides, he had the other girls to screw around with. Three of them; what did he need her for?

She took the long walk to the bed. The springs creaked— they were old and broken—and the mattress sagged. His bottle looked at least a quarter empty by the time he put it down.

"You want a cigarette?" He held the pack out.

"No, thanks."

"Drink?"

"Uh-uh."

He lit up, took a deep drag, and began unbuttoning his shirt. He moved with care. The whiskey wasn't helping much, at least not yet, and what he needed was a shower. Steaming hot. He loved to steam out, there was nothing like a good sweat for the curing of what ailed you. He bent forward to unlace his boots. His back was agony.

"Are you all right?"

He must have made a face. "I'm fine." He kicked the boots off, stood and started to take off his pants. His hand was on the zipper when he saw her turn away. He almost felt a pang. A week from now, she'd be a different girl.

He left the zipper where it was. "I'll be a while, O.K.?"

"O.K."

He padded to the bathroom, closed the door, turned on the shower, stripped, and waited for the steam to build. His eyes caught something in the bathroom mirror: it was him. His face. The way he felt, another week was just about all he could handle. He would bring it up to Norma in the morning. Usually, they played September out before they closed up the show for the winter. Why not cut it short this year? He figured Norma wouldn't mind.

As for the girls, they'd be all right. If they had saved their pay, they each had maybe twenty thousand tax-free dollars. Laurel would go back to college, Skipper and Pauline would do whatever, drift around till next year. Even Annie came out well ahead. She'd have her portion of the take from Labor Day, and she was off and running, out of Beaver Falls.

He stepped into the shower. It was very heaven. Who had said that? He collected quotes, he liked remembering good lines, you could never tell when they'd be useful. Once the show was closed, he'd follow Norma down to Lauderdale. He always did that, he liked knowing she was safe. He grinned. She was a funny woman. Half the year she was a lady, living in a condo full of widows on Galt Ocean Drive. She told them she had children in the North, and every spring when she took off to run the show again, they all thought she was visiting her kids. She was the envy of the building.

He took in a lungful of the steam. And after Lauderdale, then what? New Orleans? There was always action in the Quarter, girls and go-cups, brunch at Brennan's, all that jazz. Or Santa Fe. Some years he'd take a job there, honest work. He didn't have to, he could float through on summer money, but it helped to pass the time. Or maybe catch the beach at Malibu, drift down to Baja, and when that got boring there was always somewhere else. Not home, though. Never home. It was a great life. Slice it any way you liked, who wouldn't want it?

He bent to get the soap, and when he straightened up, his ears were ringing. He felt dizzy. Suddenly, the walls began to tilt. He floated, then he landed hard. It didn't hurt. The booze had hit him, that was all; the beating and the steam and half a bottle. No harm done. In fact, it felt nice sitting in the bathtub with the water running over him. The thing to do was stay there for a while, until the room slowed down.

Somebody yanked the shower curtain. It was Annie.

"Jesus Christ, what happened?" She reached in, turned off the water. "Are you all right?"

He felt a little foolish, so he grinned. "I'm fine."

"You're sure?"

He nodded. "Absolutely."

"Can you stand up?"

"Now?" He thought about it. "I don't know."

"I'll help."

He watched her bend and reach out toward him, felt her hands go underneath his arms.

"You ready?"

"Any time." Her strength surprised him. He was standing. "Thanks," he said, then sagged against her. "Sorry."

"That's O.K. Just lean on me."

She helped him to the toilet, kicked the seat down, eased him onto it, then turned and got a towel. The room was slowing down.

"Are you all right now? Can you dry yourself?"

For one mad moment, he was tempted to say no. The image of her standing stripped, those curves and hollows, flashed across his mind. He cleared his throat. "Go on," he said. "I'll be out in a minute."

Annie closed the bathroom door and leaned against it. She had handled drunks before, most notably Ignace and Uncle Emil, but they'd always had their clothes on. She had tried to keep her eyes averted, tried and failed. Her cheeks felt hot. She hoped he hadn't seen her staring. His was not the first one she had seen, not with one bathroom in the house, but his was different. His, God help her, God forgive her, his was pretty. Not enormous, nothing huge or scary. Just plain pretty. She imagined, for a moment, how it might look standing up.

She heard him moving in the bathroom, so she headed back to bed, turned off her light and waited. Talker came in with his pants on. She sat up and watched him, looking pale but fairly steady, as he made it to his bed. He sat down heavily, then leaned back.

"Thanks again," he said.

"How are you feeling?"

"Beat."

"Same here."

He flicked his light off. "See you in the morning."

"Yeah." She settled on her side and listened to his breathing. Deep and steady. She was sure he was asleep. He wasn't.

"Annie?" It was just a whisper.

"Uh-huh?"

"Go back home."

"Go home?"

"You heard me. Get out while the going's good."

She felt like crying. "Not me. I'm not ever going back."

The sign outside of Fallsburg promised country eggs, fresh home-baked pies, and air-conditioned comfort. The diner actually had none of the above, but Annie didn't care. She wasn't hungry, couldn't eat, she hadn't slept much, and the girls weren't talking to her. Norma, either.

She had thought at first they didn't like her, but the truth was they weren't being rude or anything; they just weren't up and moving yet. Too early for them. After ten, the best part of the morning gone, and they were staring into space and drinking coffee.

Annie shifted on the bench and looked around the diner. Things were quiet. It would fill up, if it ever did, when Church was over. There were two old farmers at the counter, and except for Talker in the phone booth, that was it. There was a Fair this week in Fulton—they'd seen signs all over town—and he was making calls, going through the county weekly, hunting for a place to stay. He looked like he was feeling better, but she had a hunch he wasn't. She had seen the bruises where those goons had kicked him; just last night, that's all it was.

She looked up as the diner's door banged open and three boys about her age came in. Farm boys, just like the meatheads who lived down the road back home. Big hands and little foreheads; she could spot them in the dark. They had their Sunday clothes on. Church was over.

Talker watched them from the phone booth as they took his girls in, nudging one another as they settled at the counter. Then he shifted, wiped his forehead, listening as the dry voice on the line said, "Yessir, we can take you, but you're lucky, I can tell you."

It was time he had some. He'd begun by trying Fulton. All of its motels were full up. He'd found single rooms in boarding houses, but it was dangerous to split his girls up. There was no controlling them. He needed space for six.

The *Fulton County Plainsmen* had a solid page of ads for trailer parks and camping sites. Not his idea of heaven, and this place was in the boondocks. "CARTHAGE LAKE," the ad read, "5 mi. NE of Fallsburg on SR 17, then 2 mi. W on CR 7. Family camping in a Christian atmosphere. 100 sites with sewer. Swim in spring-fed lake, good fishing, laundry, gas, propane, store, modern restrooms, Bingo, horseshoes, hiking trails, church services. Some cottages for rent."

He looked up from the ad and grinned. *The Moulin Rouge Does Carthage Lake;* that was a show he'd pay to see. "How much?" he asked.

"Four cottages from now through Labor Day? That's . . ."

Talker waited while the math was done, then closed the deal and left the booth. Across from him, the boys were moving from the counter, drifting toward his girls. It never failed. The locals always buzzed around, like honeybees or flies to sugar; even when his girls looked half-dead, which they did.

He took a twenty from his wallet, put it on the tabletop among the coffee cups. The boys were looking at him. He ignored it. "O.K., ladies?"

"Hold on, mister."

Talker turned. The biggest of the three had spoken. He had sideburns and a wispy moustache and no chin to speak of. Talker smiled. "Sorry, fellas, but we gotta go."

"You're in a hurry, mister, you should take yourself a walk."

As Talker well knew, there were several ways of handling

this, but Skipper did it for him. "Jesus Christ, why don't you creeps give us a break? Get lost."

"Screw you."

"Aw, kiss my ass." She stood and started for the door.

"You heard the lady," Talker said.

There was some mumbling as the boys backed off.

When Talker pulled out of the parking lot, he saw them in his rearview mirror. They were standing just outside the diner, watching. Country towns were all alike, the East was full of Fallsburgs. Ten years back, he'd had some good times hanging out; the beer was cheap, the girls were easy. Either times had changed or he had.

He shifted into second, took the turn, and headed north toward Carthage Lake.

4

MATTHEW LARKIN COULD not see his congregation very clearly. Even with his spectacles, which he disliked and rarely wore, the details of his life had come to be distinctly blurred about the edges. It was not, he felt convinced, a liability; for sight was one thing, wasn't it, and vision something else again.

In any case, he knew his Church by heart; each beam and floor peg, all the carving. It was his Church more than anyone's, except for God, of course. His great-grandfather, age eighteen, a former drummer boy and veteran of Gettysburg, had come to Fulton as a carpenter's apprentice and had helped to lay the floor. The Church looked very much today as it did then. He took full credit, for the funds required to restore it far exceeded building something new, and he had raised them. That was long ago, before most people recognized that Fulton had a history worth preserving. Now, today, most every book about Ohio landmarks had a picture of the Barrow Lane United Methodist, established 1866.

As for his congregation, all those out-of-focus shapes still shifting, settling in their places, they were known to him in intimate detail. Old families, like his own: the spine of the community. That's not to say they didn't have their faults and desperate secrets; all men did. But he was careful not to judge them. They were not his children. No, indeed. They were his fellow travelers through the Vale: the Steubens and the Reddings and the Brinkers, Clarkes, and Oberlanders, they were all his fellow travelers.

Matthew put his notes down on the lectern. The Church bell—forged in Masillon, Ohio, when the Barrow Lane was built, and just as clear and true today as ever—finished ringing out the hour. It was time to start. He turned and nodded to his right, where Charlie Spofford, the custodian, was watching from behind the curtain. Charlie nodded back and, moments after that, the air-conditioning went off. The whirring of the fans and motors made it difficult for Matthew to be heard; for he'd be eighty Easter next, please God, and his projection wasn't what it was.

The temperature outside was well into the 90's, and the stained-glass windows, of which Reverend Larkin was so proud, had not been made to open. Marcie wondered, as the heat built up, if she was going to make it. She had overslept, her head felt leaden from the pills and Betsy had been difficult, if not impossible. Already she could see a film of moisture on her arms.

She shifted on the hardwood bench. She knew its bumps and hollows; it had always been her place. Each family had its pew. It wasn't formalized, there were no written rules, and you could pray from where you liked. It was a choice that no one exercised. So there was Mother on the aisle; then Dad beside her on her right, Van on her left, and Betsy at the end. It was a little like a royal line, succession to the throne. One day, she would be sitting where her mother sat.

She tuned in briefly to the sermon—anything beat thinking—but it wasn't any use. The old man gave the same one every year the Sunday just before the Fair, and she knew parts of it by heart. "For fairs are harvest festivals, a time for giving thanks to God for all His bounty. This may seem a worn and simple lesson, yet it needs repeating. It is easy to forget."

She took a Kleenex from her purse and wiped her forehead. Was it possible to die of boredom? Reverend Larkin was a dear man, he'd officiated at her wedding and her parents' wedding, he was probably responsible for joining every couple in the Church. She grinned—he had a lot to answer for. She was as much for continuity as anyone, but there were limits. It was time for him to go.

She glanced at Van. No signs of sweat. He seemed both comfortable and interested. A stranger would have sworn that he was listening. She knew better. He was miles away. She wondered where. Last night, who was he seeing in his mind's eye, with that drunken farm girl leaning on him, all unbuttoned? She had large, full breasts, that was the hell of it, and Marcie didn't. Van never minded, or at least he always said so. He had liked hers from the first time he had seen them.

That was back at Denison. A Friday at the end of April of her junior year. She had been all of twenty. It was Dee who introduced them; that's what lifelong friends are for.

The two of them had roomed together all four years. Dee worked in Theater, she had a knack for acting, she could cry at will; and Marcie was an English major. She had been in bed that fatal morning, reading *Middlemarch,* when Dee sailed in.

"Get up, get up."

"What for?"

There followed a cascade of talk about a boy named Van. He was a friend of Dennis Bradley, her companion of the moment, and the four of them were going to spend the day together. "He's your type," Dee told her as she stripped to change. "He's nice. You'll like him."

Marcie had her doubts. For one thing, Dee's idea of nice was too elastic to be trusted. For another, it meant leaving *Middlemarch,* which she was quite enjoying, though the central conflict of the heroine, the choice of love or money, seemed an easy one: for money could be made—"Who steals my purse steals trash"—but love was precious.

In the end, she gave in, threw on a skirt and blouse, grabbed a jacket, and went flying downstairs after Dee and out the side door to the parking lot. The boys had cars, of course—in Granville you were dead without one—but the girls both had convertibles. The day was gorgeous, so they took the tops down and, Dee leading, tailed each other up the long hill toward Frat Row.

It was a good school, Denison; not great like Oberlin or Kenyon where the brains went, but it was the kind of place where decent kids from decent homes could get a decent education, which was all that Marcie wanted. On the downside, it was rural with a big *R.* You could travel twenty miles in all directions and not find a band to dance to or a restaurant with tablecloths; and as for culture, you could get some up in Cleveland, if a seven-hour drive, round trip, appealed to you.

They pulled up at the Sigma House and hurried in. It was

just minutes after noon, but from the look of things the day
had started early. Drinking was the major weekend sport, state
laws on liquor notwithstanding. Music blasted from the club
room, and the air already smelled of cigarettes and beer. As
they moved in, two boys looked up with sloppy grins and
"hiyas," and a moment later, Dennis Bradley came to greet
them.

"Ladies." Glass in hand, he bowed extravagantly, spilling
nothing. He was studying directing. Dee was certain he was
talented. She curtsied in response, gave him her hand to kiss,
and let him hold it while he led them to the club room.

Marcie looked around. No girls to speak of yet, they
would come drifting in all afternoon; but there were lots of
boys, all clustered by the bar. There were some faces Marcie
knew, not many; Sigmas didn't mix much with the arts crowd.
She was reaching for a cigarette, about to ask Dee where her
date was, when she heard a voice from just behind her.

"Marcie Steuben?"

Marcie turned and nodded. "Van?"

She liked him right away. He was good-looking, even
handsome, though good looks in men were not important to
her. She had passed that phase in high school. True, nice features didn't hurt, but what she liked most in a man were
things like personality and scope and depth of feeling.

There was beer or there was gin and grapefruit juice. She
opted for the gin, as usual. She never liked the taste at first,
but it got better after one or two. His name, it turned out, was
Maurice. Maurice Van Buren. Everybody called him Van except his mother, who had hung Maurice on him in the first
place. He was twenty-one, a senior majoring in business with a
minor in philosophy, and he thought Denison was great although he'd only been there one semester, having transferred
in from Michigan to be near home because his father wasn't
well.

"I'm sorry," Marcie said.

"It isn't all that serious. He'll be O.K."

"Where's home?"

They had another drink. Home was in Wooster and his
father sold insurance, but Van wanted something different.
"There are better things to do, you know."

She knew. She longed to be a writer, she got "A"'s in
Composition, and she'd even had a story printed in the lit

mag. It was nothing great and she had no illusions, but it never hurt to dream. The story was about a little girl who had a speech impediment, and Marcie was at the point of telling Van about it when Dee tapped her on the shoulder.

"O.K., troops, let's hit the road."

They took both cars and zoomed off, heading north of town, just looking for a quiet place where they could sit around and talk. The day was perfect for it. Marcie liked to drive; it made her feel good. She imagined how she looked to Van, wind whipping through her long hair as the sun streamed down. She knew that she was pretty. Not like Dee, of course. Dee wasn't pretty; she was beautiful. But Marcie never envied her; just being pretty was enough, thanks. You got noticed, you were popular, the girls weren't jealous and the boys felt comfortable about approaching you. Like Van. She had a feeling he was shy with girls, and there he was, relaxed and smiling, telling her about his life. He was an only child, too.

She slowed down as Dee braked and signaled. She was turning. Marcie followed. They went bouncing down a dirt road, fallow fields on both sides. It was warmer, driving slowly, and the air smelled sweet.

"Where are we going?"

"I don't know."

"Does Dee?"

"I doubt it." Marcie grinned. "It's an adventure."

They were passing by a hill when Dee pulled over on the shoulder. Marcie drew alongside. Dee was pointing toward the hilltop.

"There," she said. "Come on."

"What's up there?"

"Trust me."

From the hilltop, you could see for miles. It was thrilling: trees with young leaves, new grass, rolling fields and, far away, small farms with tiny silos sticking up. They settled on the ground as Dennis made drinks from the gin and juice he'd taken from the Sigma House. He would be graduating soon, along with Van, and he was going out to Hollywood. He had some friends there he could room with, though he'd rather work in theater, who wouldn't, but the theater was dead. Dee didn't think so.

Marcie listened to them argue as she drained her paper cup. It didn't taste of gin at all, not anymore. The sun felt warmer and she was, she thought, the least bit buzzed, but she could handle that. Some girls got loosened up by alcohol, but all she ever did was fall asleep. Besides, she felt so safe with Van. She stretched and took her jacket off.

They all had refills, and talked about important things: the future, grades, the Beatles, where they'd been when Kennedy was shot. The memory must have made her cry, because Van put his arm around her. It occurred to her to wonder what would happen if she kissed him, so she did. His lips were soft and gentle, not like other boys'.

A while later, when she looked up, Dee and Dennis had moved off a little. They were kissing, too. Dee's blouse was open, Dennis had one hand inside it. Marcie looked away. She knew they'd spend the evening shacking up somewhere. She didn't really disapprove; she loved Dee, and she was no prude herself. She'd even let Bob Drake undress her once: no touching, she'd just let him look. That didn't make her purer or more virtuous than Dee. It only meant she thought a girl should wait for marriage. Or at least until it really mattered.

What she did feel was a sudden, desperate need to pee. There were some trees and bushes on the hillcrest not too far away. She turned to Van, excused herself, stood up and started off. She didn't feel unsteady, and it quite surprised her when the earth began to tilt. She made it to the trees and leaned against one for a minute. Clearly, she should think twice about having more to drink. She left the tree and moved on past some bushes till she found an open space. She looked back. Van was out of sight. All clear. It felt delicious, squatting in the out-of-doors and making wee-wee on the grass. She hadn't done it for a million years, not since she used to play with Dee when they were five or six, out in the woods behind the house on Blanchard Street.

She finished, stood, tugged up her panties, started back. Somehow, she must have gotten turned around. She passed a bush she hadn't passed before and stopped dead.

Dee and Dennis had no clothes on. They were locked together, writhing. Doing it. The beast with two backs. Shakespeare knew what he was saying. It was bestial. Dee, her lovely Dee, was like an animal. Unrecognizable. Contorted. And the sounds she made—not human. Marcie stood there, rooted. It was awful, like a nightmare, Rodin's *Gates of Hell*.

She turned away, went past the trees and out into the sunshine. Van was moving on the hillcrest, coming toward her. Why? How long had she been watching? Ages?"

"Van."

"What's wrong?"

She let him hold her, let her body sag against him. "I don't know what's wrong." Her voice was strange, all raw and shaky. Then she kissed him, and next thing the two of them were on the grass. She felt him taking off her bra. She didn't care, she even helped him.

"Oh," he said, "they're beautiful."

She let him kiss them. Then her hands moved, they were moving everywhere, all over him, like someone else's hands. Not hers. It wasn't Marcie's hand between his legs. It couldn't be.

She felt him through his trousers. He lay back while she unzipped him. Then she watched her hand slip in. She'd never touched a man before. It felt so hard and very hot, much hotter than she'd ever thought. She pulled it out so she could look at it. She bent close and her lips came open. There it was.

Her head was spinning. "Oh," she said. "Oh, Van." At which point, she passed out cold.

At least, that's what Van told her later. She remembered nothing till she woke up with a shiver. She felt chilled, her head ached and her lips were dry. She lay still, scarcely breathing, as disjointed fragments of the afternoon came back to her. Clear images, in hideous detail. She felt humiliated, drenched with shame.

She willed her eyes to open. It was twilight. Van was lying there beside her, sound asleep. His pants were zipped; at least he hadn't left it out there, lying in the open. What in God's name could she say to him? What must he think of her? She saw him smirking, talking to the boys. "You want an easy lay? Just pour some gin in Marcie Steuben."

Tears were starting down her cheeks when out of nowhere came a sudden pang of hope. The first time was supposed to hurt. She wasn't sore. Holding her breath, she spread her thighs, reached down and touched herself. Intact. He hadn't done it. Nothing really bad had happened. She began to sob. It woke him.

"Are you O.K.?"

She nodded, she was too choked up to speak. He took her

hand and held it. She felt overwhelmed by tenderness and
gratitude. She wondered if he ached; she knew boys did, a lot
of dates had told her so. She owed him something—didn't
she?—for all the things he hadn't done. The question was,
how would he take it if she offered to relieve him?

"If you're sure you want to, Marcie."

She felt sure. With steady hands, she brought it out.
That's all it took. One touch and it went off. It took her by
surprise. She held on, she was fascinated.

"Princess?"

Marcie blinked. Her dad was looking at her, smiling.
Church was over. People all around were rising, talking, moving to the aisles. She felt soaked, bathed in perspiration, and
her thighs seemed stuck together. What she needed was a
minute, just to be alone.

"Let's get some air," she heard Van saying. He was standing, reaching for her hand. She let him take it, and, for just a
flash, she wanted him. Right then and there. It didn't happen
often; it was not her style, or his. They tended to be
thoughtful and polite about their sex. They knew it was important, and they treated it with due respect. When times
came, as they sometimes did, when contacts were too few or
far between, it was no problem to relieve herself. She didn't
know what Van did when—or if—he felt that way. She never
asked.

It felt better to be outside. The lane was shaded by great
rows of elms that spread above it like a canopy. There was a
murmur of low voices in the air. Some people lingered, passing time in little clusters. Others drifted off. She watched
while Betsy gave quick hugs to Gram and Gramps, then
turned and bounded off to spend her Sunday with the Redding boy. They had been dating for a year or more, they were
inseparable. He was a nice boy. Marcie liked him, and the
Reddings were as rich as God, which didn't hurt, but they
were much too young to be so close. What did they do together, all day every day? She wondered and she worried, just
as any mother would, but when she tried to talk to Betsy, she
got stony looks or bursts of temper. Van was no help; all he
ever said was, "You were fourteen once, remember."

"Marcie?"

It was Dee's voice calling. She'd forgotten Dee was home.

Her heart skipped as she turned and saw Dee moving toward her down the narrow sidewalk. She looked just as beautiful as ever.

Marcie opened up her arms and ran. Dee felt the way she always did, both soft and strong. "Oh God, Dee," Marcie said, "it's good to see you."

5

FINDING CARTHAGE LAKE had been a snap. It really was on SR 17, 2 mi. W on CR something, and you couldn't miss the sign. But what the ad had failed to say was that the camp was in the woods. Deep in. The entrance drive, unpaved and rutted, wove its narrow way through brush and shrubs.

"It looks nice," Annie told him as he turned his T-bird up the cowpath, hoping not to scrape the muffler, wincing when he did. The van with Norma at the wheel was right behind him, bashing into branches as it chugged along. Laurel's Olds brought up the rear.

They passed some campsites on the way in, just a few, off in the woods. Then one sharp turn and they could see the lake. There were a lot of tents along the shore, pitched close together, bikes and beach balls, barbecues and camp chairs, swimsuits hung to dry.

"Where is everybody?" Annie asked.

He shrugged as they went by a clearing. In it were rows of wooden benches jammed with people. Up front was a sort of pulpit made of birchwood with a cross on top. Church services, for godsake. They were singing: ". . . as the little brown church in the vale . . ."

Talker grinned and shook his head. "It's going to be a long week."

Up ahead, there was a store, as advertised. He knew because the sign said STORE. It was a little clapboard structure. There were others near it, all with signs: REST ROOM, LAUNDRY, REC HALL, OFFICE. And beyond them, strung along the lake; were maybe half a dozen cottages.

Talker pulled up by the office. "Bring your gear," he said to Annie, by which time a man was heading toward them. Fiftyish, pale, thin and balding, with his Sunday suit on, he looked harried, in a hurry.

"Yessir, can I help you?"

Talker recognized his voice. "You're Mr. Lovell, right?"

"That's me."

"We spoke a while ago, about some cottages."

"I got 'em for you, there they are." He turned and pointed. "First four on the left. It's good you got here, I'm just on my way to Fulton." Then he frowned. "You said you needed room for six."

"They're coming." You could hear the van now, grinding up the drive. They watched it pull in, Laurel right behind it.

"Mister?"

Talker turned to Lovell. "Yes?"

"You plan to keep that truck here, do you?"

It was not a friendly question. Talker smiled. "Just for tonight, if that's O.K."

"Well, maybe. I mean, it don't look right, not to me. You understand?"

He was beginning to. "We'll move it in the morning." By that time, the girls were out and coming toward them. Skipper's high heels kept on sinking in the grass, and Laurel had the smile she wore when she'd been drinking. Pauline had her teddy bear, and Norma brought up the rear, carrying the cash box.

Talker's full attention was on Lovell. He was ready for the question when it came.

"Are you folks here to do some camping?"

"Camping?" Talker let it sound surprised.

"That's all we do here. Nothing else goes on. You got me, mister?"

Talker felt like walking, but they had no place else to go. He kept his voice calm. "Mr. Lovell, we'll be working at the Fair. I want those cabins for a week, and you can have your money now, up front, so either take it or forget it."

Lovell took it, turned to go.

"Hold on a sec. Don't we need keys?"

"We don't believe in locks here. Honest folk is all that comes." He nodded, got into his Plymouth, drove off.

Norma chuckled. "Five'll get you ten he goes for teenage pussy."

Talker helped them settle in. As always, Skipper roomed with Laurel, Norma had her cottage, he had his, so Annie got Pauline. The cottages were a surprise, dead plain but neat and very clean. Even the walls looked freshly scrubbed.

"Oh God," Pauline said. "How'm I going to live here?"

Annie rather liked the place. "What's wrong?"

"There's no TV. I'll lose my mind."

"Don't worry," Talker told her. "There's no chance of that." The line got a giggle from Pauline, she loved it when he teased her. Time to go. He headed for the door. "I'll see you."

Annie hurried after him. "Where are you going, can I come?"

"You stay and get to know Pauline. She may have half a deck, but she's a good kid."

Annie smiled for him. "Sure thing."

When she turned, Pauline was sitting, arms around her bear. It wasn't going to be easy. "What's your bear's name?"

"Dumbo."

Annie started to unpack her things.

Coming home was hard for Dee. It always was. Sometimes it puzzled her. She had loved growing up in Fulton; rich, by local standards anyway, and good to look at. When you're ten or fifteen, even twenty, popularity is hard to knock. These days, if it weren't for Eleanor—she never called her mother Mother—Dee supposed she'd never come. Except for Marcie. Marcie meant a lot.

Eight years had slipped by since they'd been together. Separations called for new beginnings, touching base again was delicate. They rarely wrote, and phone calls made them both feel awkward, so they spoke on birthdays, Christmastime, and that was that.

It hadn't always been this way. When Dee first took off for New York, there had been visits now and then. Sometimes Van came with Marcie, sometimes not, and though they all tried very hard, it hadn't worked. The problem wasn't personal. New York and the Van Burens didn't mix. The answer lay in joint vacations, going off wherever for a week or two, but either Betsy had the mumps or Dee was on the road or Van was busy; there was always something.

After Marcie's hug of greeting, things had been a little stilted. Small talk, it was only natural, and Dee wondered what the big surprise was as they hurried down East Liberty. It used to be, still was, the nicest shopping street in town. The Carters' shoe store on the corner, Nu-Mode Frocks, then Hammond Jewelers, where her first gold watch had come from. Daddy's graduation gift. From eighth grade. He had always been too generous, he spent himself too freely; dead at forty-seven. She still missed him.

Marcie stopped and pointed to a shop front. On display were quilts and samplers, ironstone and brassware. Tasteful window lettering in gold read: JOHNNY APPLESEED— ANTIQUES, INTERIORS

"Well?"

"I'll bite," Dee said. "Well, what?"

"It's mine. I started it. With Pam. Pam Leggett. You remember her?"

"Oh, sure."

"So tell me true, what do you think?"

Dee cocked her head to one side. "Johnny Appleseed?"

"Too cute? I thought so, too, but what the hell. You want to look around?"

Dee nodded. "Show me everything."

The two girls stood among the clutter. Some of it, Dee knew, was first-class repro, some was real; and here and there—the Shaker desk, the Amish rocker—were serious pieces. Dee said so.

Marcie pointed to the rocker. "See the date?"

Dee nodded. "Eighteen twenty-three."

"I picked it up for fifty dollars."

Dee looked impressed. What happens to our dreams? she thought, as if she didn't know. Where was the Marcie who read *Middlemarch* and wrote things for the lit mag? "Fifty dollars," Dee said. Then she risked it. "What in God's name got you into this?"

"Sheer desperation."

That was all it took. The questions poured out. How was life with Van? Like living with a loving uncle, lots of politesse and tedium. How was Dee's life in theater? Distinctly mezz-a-mezz. Off-Broadway mostly. There was nothing on the Great White Way worth doing, but you never knew, one break was all it took.

"How long are you in town for?"

Last time, when she'd come home for her thirtieth, she'd toughed it out for ten days. "I don't know. Till after Labor Day at least."

"That's just a week."

"I'm flexible."

"How's private life?"

"Is there a man, you mean?" Dee shrugged. She had been married once. A writer—Bill or something. He'd been either self-destructive or infatuated with himself. Dee knew it sounded contradictory. Anyway, it hadn't worked. "You know the story; all the nicest ones are gay or married."

"Maybe I can fix you up. Or both of us."

"You shock me." Dee was grinning.

Sheriff Weller had a long fuse and a short one. Once his wick was lit, you never knew when he'd go off, or even if he would. And truth to tell, he wasn't sure of it himself. On some occasions, he'd put Job to shame; on others, like the hand of God, he'd come down through your roof, and pow. Compassionate or vengeful, that was Harry Weller, and he knew it.

Liked it, too. It was an asset, and he kept his county clean and decent. No corruption. Actually, except for keeping order at the Fair, it was an easy job. The folks in town were law-abiding; drank too much sometimes, but they could handle it. The farmers, on the other hand, would frequently get liquored up on weekends, and there could be nasty accidents at country crossroads.

He had a mild case of that this morning, two kids plowing up the Country Club. It didn't seem like much to him—no harm done, no one hurt. But charges had been filed, and the people who belonged to Longview carried weight. He couldn't let it pass.

He looked across his desk. "I don't know, Mr. Steuben. It's a tough call."

"Not to me. Drunk as skunks on private property." He glanced at Van. "They damn near ran him over, let alone they tore the green to pieces."

"Do you want to put a price on that and let it go—or throw the book at them?"

Ed turned to Van. "What do you think?"

Van shrugged. He hated making trouble. "I don't know. The money doesn't come to much." He chaired the Greens Committee. "Say, five hundred dollars, give or take."

"That's heavy-duty for some people. Think about it." Weller picked up his phone. "Send 'em in."

Barney Lovell came in first, a firm hand on his daughter's arm. Then Marvin and his father. Both kids looked contrite and scared. Lucy's eyes were red from crying, and her blouse was buttoned to her neck now. Marvin's eyes were on the floor.

Weller snapped the words out. "You kids have a lot to answer for. You see that man?"

They looked at Van, and Marvin mumbled, "Yessir."

"You damn near killed him last night. What the hell did you think you were doing?"

Marvin sounded wretched. "I dunno. I'm sorry."

"Sorry gets you nowhere." Weller turned to Ed. "Any questions, Mr. Steuben?"

Ed was frowning, eyes on Lovell. "Don't I know you?"

"Bet you do, sir." Lovell smiled. "I bought my Plymouth from you. Ten years back. She's parked outside this minute, still runs like a dream."

Ed nodded. "Once I see a face, I don't forget it. Like a dream, you say? How many miles on her?"

"Hundred thousand, maybe more."

"There's nothing like a car from Chrysler."

In the end, they settled on a fine.

Outside the office, Marvin's dad, Walt Greener, turned to Barney Lovell. "Jee-sus Kee-rist. Five hundred bucks."

"They think we're made of money?"

Walt was livid. "God damn stinking rich, five hundred don't mean shit to them."

"I'll kill my kid when we get home."

"Same here."

They meant it.

The pool house at the Redding place looked like Williamsburg with changing rooms. Red brick, white columns on the outside, airy chambers inside, each with sauna, shower, vanity, thick carpet, mirrors. Betsy stood in one of them, undressing.

The Redding place: that's how the house was known. No one in Fulton called the home a mansion. It stood just outside of town on countless acres, hundreds of them. Denny's great-grandfather, Clendennon Redding—Denny was Clendennon IV—had been in partnership with Harry Studebaker in the early days. That's where the money started. How it got to be so big, Bets didn't know. And didn't ask.

She slipped the bottom of her swimsuit on. She'd bought it on the sly, with baby-sitting money. Mother didn't know, and Denny hadn't seen it yet. You couldn't call it a bikini, not exactly, but it left a lot of her exposed. She liked the way it made her look. She knew he'd like it, too.

The two of them were so close. They had met when they were six, in first grade. Both of them were problem children— it takes one to know one—and that bond was never broken.

There were times when it was strained. According to their teachers, Beech Street Grammar School had not seen brains the size of theirs since Reconstruction. Betsy loved to read, particularly books too old for her. And Denny had a knack with numbers. Feed him anything, including fractions, and he'd snap the answer back.

Did they compete? For years, it was a question of who got more "A"'s, who knocked the teachers dead the most. In eighth grade, as Betsy's hips began to curve and Denny's voice got lower, marks mattered less and less.

But quite aside from brains and growing up, the tie that, from the start, had made them close was loneliness. They both were popular enough. But Denny's folks loved travel, they were always somewhere else, and since you couldn't count the governess and eight in staff, he lived alone. He never let his feelings show, except to Betsy. And vice versa. Betsy knew Dad loved her, and Mom tried, she did her level best. But Betsy was an alien inhabiting an empty space; that's how she felt. It wasn't anybody's fault.

So here they were, fourteen, inseparable and not a brother-sister act, not anymore. Her breasts were pretty. Betsy quite approved of them, and so did Denny. She'd let him touch them once or twice through bra and sweater, God knows why he liked it so. Through all that stuff, what could he feel?

But it was summer now, and much more difficult for both of them. They hugged and kissed a lot, not deep or drastic, but the day was coming and they both knew they were still too young.

She put the bra on, checked her hair, and darted out into the sun.

Denny's heart jumped when he saw her. Bets was more than beautiful. Tall, slim, so graceful, eyes that went from here to there; like Audrey Hepburn used to be, except with boobs. Her looks went through him like a knife. His mouth felt dry. He stood there tongue-tied, not his usual condition. What to say? It came out kid stuff. "Come on, Bets, I'll race you to the pool."

They dived in, started doing laps, four, five, six, ending at the shallow end. He hadn't said a word about her suit. She stood up, put the bra in place, and looked him in the eye. "No comment?" Betsy asked.

"Oh, it'll do." He kissed her lightly on the lips. And then again. He felt his organ rising. So would she, she had to if he didn't step away. He turned and sat down on the pool's edge, put his legs together so the fool thing wouldn't show. "What do you feel like doing now?"

She burst out laughing. "Golly, Denny, that's a tough one."

"What I meant—" Then he was laughing, too. When it began to hurt, he stopped and wiped his eyes. She moved close, took his hand. "Oh, Bets . . ."

"I know, I know." They stayed like that a long time, looking at each other.

Then he stood up. It was standing, too. What could he say? "I'm going to take a shower, good and cold."

How close she came to saying, 'Want some company?' he'd never know.

There had been farmland, nothing but, for miles. When the city limits came, Talker nearly missed it, he'd been listening to the tape. He shifted down, flicked off the Stones, and looked around; he always paid attention to details.

It was a different world across the city line. There were

some handsome houses, big ones, on his left; and to his right, what had to be the Country Club. He checked his speed. The sign said thirty-five, and he was in a sports car with Rhode Island plates.

His back ached. What he wanted more than anything was sleep, a month of it. He'd almost stayed at Carthage Lake and sacked out, like the girls were doing. If it weren't for all the money to be made on this week, he'd be in bed instead of driving to the grounds and renting space. The right space made a difference; you could count it in the thousands.

There were Fairgrounds signs on almost every other phone pole. They were leading him around the edge of town. He made a note to check out Fulton later, drive around and see what they had gotten into. It was nothing like the East, that much he couldn't miss; and checking out the local scene, getting a sense and feel of things, could make a difference.

There were trucks ahead now, blocking out the view, and when he got his first look at the Fairgrounds, what he did was whistle. He had played some major fairs, life wasn't always Beaver Falls, but this was something else again. Like Danbury in Connecticut used to be: right out of Norman Rockwell.

There was the customary holdup at the entrance. Talker waited, lit a cigarette. Then, moving slowly, making sure to nod and smile at the cop on duty—you never knew, the guy could end up on the payroll—he drove in.

The place was busy, which was only natural; it was opening tomorrow night. He headed for the grandstand. There were vehicles all over: cars and carts and wagons, trucks and tractors, anything with wheels. Slow going. Two kids with a cow were waiting for a chance to cross the road. He stopped and waved them on.

As usual, there was an open field beside the grandstand. Talker parked and started walking; the main entrance would be on the far side. There were posters, neatly mounted on the walls, announcing what was coming up this week. Loretta Lynn was singing Tuesday, opening night; there was a Demolition Derby and the Tournament of Thrills, whatever that might be, and Johnny Cash was on for Friday. Stars, real big ones, worked these places. And they made real money for it, maybe thirty grand a night. He looked up at the stands. Ten thousand seats, three bucks a throw; it added up.

He found the entrance, moved into the dimness underneath the stands. There were a lot of people, mainly farmers, in to register their animals and produce, talking, drifting, sweating in the heat. Some fellow nodded to him, so he nodded back. As always, there were signs directing you to Maintenance or Registration. He was looking for Concessions.

The office was as large as it was airless. There were bulletin boards covered with notices and stands with stacks of pamphlets, copies of the Fair Rules. He'd been smart to check in early. Judging by the mob scene, all the best space could be gone already. Easily a dozen men were in two lines at the counter, and another dozen at the tables, filling forms out. Like the Moulin Rouge, they'd folded up last night wherever they were playing. Doughnut men and pizza vendors, guys who ran the rides and games and souvenir booths, they'd be checking in all afternoon.

Talker sat down at a table, took a form and scanned it: Name of Concessionaire, Permanent Address, Type of Concession. All of it was standard, he could do it in his sleep, but better safe than sorry, and besides, he wasn't under oath. Taking all the time he needed, he began to fill it out.

Marcie wiped her forehead, looked around the office. She had Harriet to thank for this. "Dear, we're shorthanded." Like a dope, she'd said O.K., dragged Dee along, and their relief was overdue. She glanced at Dee who sat behind her, working phones. Dee grinned.

Then Marcie turned and looked across the counter. "Can I help you?"

Talker hadn't seen her. He'd been reading, checking out his form. He looked up. Did he stare? He didn't think so. "Yes, thanks."

She began to take him through it, starting from the top. "Name of Concessionaire is Norma Cusak?"

"That's right."

"Are you Mr. Cusak?"

"No, M'am. She's the owner, I'm the manager, that's all."

"Your name, please?"

There were several names he used from time to time. He chose a nice one. "Paul McBride." He watched her write it down. Her hands were beautiful.

She raised her eyes. "Is Boston your address?"

"No, M'am; it's Mrs. Cusak's."

"Yours is . . . ?"

Anyplace; it didn't matter. "Tampa. Tampa, Florida."
"Is there a street?"
"There's just a P.O. box. You want the number?"
"Please."
He gave one to her. She had brown eyes, golden brown, just like the rest of her. He took out a cigarette.
"Would you mind not smoking? It's so close in here."
"I'm sorry."
"Thank you." She glanced down. "The name of your concession is the Moulin Rouge?"
He nodded. She pronounced it like the French did, with that nasal sound and funny *r*. It sounded nice.
She looked up with a puzzled frown. "And you put on a show of ethnic dancing?"
"Right." He usually wrote down "Exotic."
"Could you tell me what that is, exactly?"
Was she serious or joking? Either way, he had to play it straight. "It's folk dance. You know, like they do in foreign countries: Greece or Turkey or the South Seas. It's a nice show."
"Are you in it?"
"No, M'am. We've got girls who do the dancing. I'm the talker."
He could feel her eyes, but was she looking at or through him? If they met again tomorrow, would she know she'd ever seen him? Would she nod and smile? Or pause, or even blink? A man could hope.
He was careful not to look at her too closely after that. She told him Fulton didn't get a lot of shows, especially with dancing girls; she had some trouble finding him a space, deciding where to put him. When he paid her, she said thank you. So did he.
It gnawed at him. What did she have that made her so special? He had slept with women just as beautiful. Or just as upper crust and educated; she was both. He couldn't label what it was.
He crossed the office. Pausing at the door, he turned for one last look at her. He hunted for the word. It came to him.
She was a lady.

The three of them were sitting on the terrace by the swimming pool. The light was blue. It glowed up from the bottom of the pool, only to die out well before it reached the mass of trees and shrubs that walled the large backyard and hid it from its neighbors and the fields beyond.

Van couldn't answer for the girls, but it was nearly midnight now, and he was beat. Sundays, on a scale of ten, could range from zero up to seven; never higher. This had been a two or three. First, Church, or was it sauna; then the circus in the Sheriff's office, after which he'd lost an easy golf match with a double bogey on the final hole. Then home to serve up charcoal steaks for everyone and listen to his in-laws. They were something, Harriet and Ed, like the Jack Spratts licking clean the platter. Sometimes Marcie was the platter, sometimes he was. Sometimes both.

He let his eyes come open, looking at the two girls, listening to the murmur of their voices, not the words. Was there something in the way they sat and how they touched each other when they talked, hands resting lightly here and there? Van wondered, without meaning to, how far they went. What kinds of things had gone on all those years ago when they had roomed together? Van had no use for unnatural things. He swept the thought away.

"That's it for me, girls." He stood up, put down his empty glass, and stretched. "I'm all day at the Fair tomorrow."

Marcie nodded. "Aren't we all." She watched him move across the terrace. Come next month, they'd celebrate their seventeenth. Dee had been her maid of honor. Where did all the time go?

Dee leaned back. Though it was cooler, everything she touched felt sticky. *Summertime.* She let the song play, listening to the lyrics: ". . . daddy's rich . . . hush, little baby . . ." It was late and she should go soon; Eleanor would be up, waiting for her.

"Dee? You want another?" Marcie's glass was empty.

"If I'm out much longer, Eleanor will kill me."

"What the hell, she'll kill you anyway."

They got up, moving slowly to the bar. Dee stood there gazing at the pool and listened to the ice cubes dropping in the tumblers. One by one.

"Dee?"

"Ummm?" She turned as Marcie poured the gin.

"Just wondering, did you see that guy this afternoon?"

"What guy?"

"The one who had the dancing girls."

"You're kidding. Dancing girls?"

"Uh-huh. He told me they did ethnic dancing. Did you see him?"

"I don't know. What did he look like?"

"Nothing much."

"That's some description."

Marcie shrugged. "Forget it." She bent down to get the tonic. When she straightened, Dee was taking off her blouse. "What are you doing?"

"Going swimming."

"Are you serious?"

Dee stood there, naked to the waist. "Why not?"

"I'll get some suits."

"What for?"

"Good question."

In a moment, both of them were standing there with nothing on but their panties. They looked at one another, hesitating. They had seen each other's bodies all of their lives, from playing doctor after nursery school through gym at Fulton High and all the time at Denison. But that was years ago, so long, and they stood for a moment, feeling shy with one another.

Marcie broke the silence. "What the hell." She bent, took off her panties. By the time she straightened, Dee was naked, too. They giggled, for no reason, stepped across the terrace to the blue light, paused to dive. They did it cleanly, slicing in, then started swimming side by side. With pretty strokes; they'd learned to swim at Longview, daily lessons from the high-school coach who taught there in the summers, twenty years ago.

Van watched them from the bedroom window. He had heard them dive in. There they were, their buttocks just below the water, moving smoothly. Should he stay and see what happened? For a moment, he was tempted; but if something did, he didn't want to know.

Dee stood up at the shallow end, a little breathless, water to her waist. She felt another giggle coming up. "You had enough?" she asked.

"Have you?"

The giggle burst. "O.K., Steuben, stand up and defend yourself."

"You asked for it."

They set themselves and for the longest time they stood there water-fighting, splashing, scooping handfuls, losing balance, tumbling, laughing. Van could hear the laughter. He crammed his pillow round his head, he felt himself grow hard, then he started humming, anything to block out the sound.

In the end, the girls collapsed, exhausted, in the shallow water, sitting there too spent to speak, just grinning at each other. By the time Marcie came upstairs to bed, Van was asleep.

6

ALL THE CABINS had cute names, like Dewdropinn or Kwitchergrowlin. They had picnic tables out in front, and open hearths for cooking.

Annie had been sitting at her table since before the sun came up. The air was cool, soft mist was rising from the lake, and nothing broke the stillness but the frog sounds and the little pops the fish made when they broke the surface of the water.

It had been a long night, full of busy dreams and noises from Pauline who talked out loud and ground her teeth when she was sleeping. Yesterday they'd spent the afternoon out sunning on the dock, and once you got adjusted to the fact that Pauline had no mind at all, she wasn't bad to be with. She'd been full of talk about some stripper named Babette and how she'd gotten married just a month ago. Pauline was sure her turn would come.

Good luck, Annie thought. The sun was coming up now as she bent to read the letter she'd just finished. "Dear Aunt Maria and Uncle Emil: In case you wonder where I am, I've found a job. A good job with a future, so don't worry, but it means I've got to travel. Thanks for everything you've done. I've left most of my things behind, and once I'm settled, I'd appreciate it if you'd send them on to me. Stay well. Love, Annie."

Not a masterpiece, she knew that, but it did the job, and she'd be sure to send them money for the postage when she asked them for her things; they wouldn't send them otherwise. As soon as she was settled, once she knew where she was living.

"Hi, good morning."

Annie spun around. She hadn't heard the screen door open. Talker closed it softly.

"You're up early."

"I've got things to do today." He took a step or two, looked back. "You want to come along?"

She bounced up from the table, letter in her hand. "I need to find an envelope."

"I'll buy you one."

They took the van. He didn't feel like talking, that was clear, so Annie sat there watching him. He had fresh jeans on and a clean shirt, and his hair was still damp from the shower. She felt a sudden wish to know about him. Anything about him, big or small, it didn't have to be important. Would it be O.K. to speak? A question popped into her head. "How old are you?" she asked.

He looked surprised. "I'm thirty-two."

She'd figured he was even older, thirty-five or more. "Where do you come from?"

"Providence."

"Rhode Island?"

"That's the one."

"It's not the only one. They've got a Providence in Maryland and one in Utah and another one—"

"How do you know all that?"

She started telling him about her travel folders and how anytime that she got curious about a place, she'd check it out at school in the *Britannica*. And that reminded her about her *Almanac*. She told him how she memorized whole pages of it and how good it felt to know things.

He listened to her babble on. How she had graduated seventh in a class of ninety, English was her favorite subject, seven was her lucky number. And about her father, what he did before he died, Custodian at Something High in Harrisburg. All Talker's girls were screwed up, one way or another. Annie, too; she had to be. He wasn't sure as yet which of her screws were loose. He wasn't sure he cared.

He braked down for the Fallsburg Road, turned north toward Fulton, and switched on the radio.

The phone rang, sounding like a fire alarm. For just a second, Marcie thought her home was burning. Then her eyes came open and she lay there on her pillow, glaring at the phone. Her throat was dry, her head ached, and her memories of the night before were scattered. She remembered skinny-dipping, splashing in the pool with Dee, but how and when she got to bed, God knew. The bedside clock said seven-thirty. Van was nowhere to be seen. Out of the house already.

Marcie picked the phone up. "Hello, Mother."

"I've been waiting for your call, dear."

Every morning, rain or shine, they spoke. It was a ritual. "My watch stopped, I forgot to wind it."

"You're not still in bed, I hope."

"God no."

"I thought you might be, you were up so late."

It was the limit. "How would you know, have you hired a detective?"

"Eleanor MacFarlane called this morning. It was after two when Dee came home. You girls should really be more thoughtful, you know what these visits mean to Ellie."

A variety of answers flashed through Marcie's mind, but all she said was, "Yes, I know."

"Of course you do, I taught you to." The cool voice paused. "I've got to go. I'm overdue at the Pavilion."

Marcie nodded. "If I can, I'll see you there this afternoon."

"You couldn't come now, could you?"

"Now?" She had her day all planned. "I've got a million things to do."

"I wouldn't ask you if I didn't need you. Martha's back is out, and Lily called to say she . . ."

Marcie lowered the receiver. What would happen if she said she couldn't make it? Would the world end? Clearly not.

"I tell you what. I'll give you Betsy. She can fill in till I get there."

"Thank you, dear."

"I may be late," she added, in a rare display of independence, but by then the line was dead.

* * *

The Fulton County Fairgrounds were extensive. The eighty acres purchased by the founding fathers had provided more than room to grow; they gave the Fair an open, spacious look. Large fields of meadow grass and wildflowers, wilted from the lack of rain and freshly mowed in any case, lay between the main exhibit areas. Each principal activity was separate, by itself. The Midway occupied a corner of the Fairgrounds, not its usual location at the center. It had taken Talker quite some time to find it.

Annie, all eyes now, sat silent as they drove along the dirt road, past a scattering of rides and food stands. There were booths, stuffed toys and duck shoots, and some people from a church group were putting up a Bingo tent. On all sides, vans and trucks were pulling in, and by tonight there wouldn't be an inch to spare. His lot—they all had numbers—was a long way down the road, right up against the boundary fence, a million miles of cornstalks for a backdrop.

For whatever reason, he had no luck finding roughies, so he ended up hiring farm kids. Four of them, five bucks an hour. Big boys, they were strong enough and willing, but their skills were limited. Annie, it turned out, was good with tools and faster than the boys all put together.

They worked in silence for the most part. It was after ten before they had the bally stage in place and it was time to put the painted flats up. Talker climbed into the van, untied the flats and handed out the first one. That was when the talking started.

"Jesus, will you look at this." The boys stood by the painting, grinning at it.

"God damn. It's a strip show."

One of them looked at Talker. "Oh shit, mister, you must get to fuck your dick off."

"Stuff it," Talker snapped out. "There's a lady present."

When he'd handed out all the flats, he moved off with Annie to the far end of the stage and went to work. The boys, there was no stopping them, were full of whispered questions as they struggled with the flats. You think the girls strip all the way? Could you see beaver? Were their tits big? Words like pussy juice and poontang drifted softly in the morning air. To listen to them, getting screwed was all they ever thought about.

They were no different than the kids he came across back East. A little dumber, possibly, but that was all. Was it conceivable he'd ever been that sex-crazed back when he was seventeen?

It took him back. How had it felt to wake up with a hard-on every morning? Did he ever really jack off once a day and twice on Sundays? Had he, in the showers after gym class, checked out every dick in sight, comparing them to his? And measuring himself; how did you truly know how long it was, where did you put the ruler? When a fraction of an inch made all the difference, where exactly did your prick start? Back against your balls, or where? Was there a scientific way to do it?

And the girls. Forever looking up their skirts. At what age had he seen his first twat? Who did it belong to? Not Irene. She happened later. She had even let him touch it. All that hair, it felt like new wool, soft and matted.

Annie, reaching for a hammer, brushed against him. Talker all but jumped.

"I'm sorry. What's the matter?"

"Nothing." They were sweating, both of them, and he could see her through her T-shirt. What the hell, he'd seen her with it off. The only thing was, Amy would be fourteen soon, not Annie's age, not yet, but—

"You up there."

He turned. The local law was walking toward him. The approach was coming. He'd been wondering when. He'd paid a hundred bucks a night for Pat and Mike, the cops in Beaver Falls. The tariff would be steeper here, but he had come prepared for that, the bills were rolled up in his pocket.

"Right back," he said to Annie, jumped down from the bally stage. The local law looked fifty, tall and thin, with deep lines on his face and clear gray eyes. Light gray, almost no color to them.

Talker smiled. "Hi."

"I'm Sheriff Weller."

Talker held out his hand. "Hot enough for you?"

"I can't complain." The Sheriff's hand felt strong and dry, its knuckles slightly thickened from arthritis. "Maybe you can help me."

"Sure."

He pointed toward the Moulin Rouge. "I'm looking for the fellow who's in charge of that."

"You found him."

"You're McBride?"

"That's me." So far, so good. It meant the man had seen his application, put it all together, and come out to pick his money up. "What can I do for you?"

"Well, that depends. I'm not a man for jumping to conclusions, everyone's entitled to his day in court and all that shit, but I'm no bumpkin, son, and what I figure is, your business is purveying filth."

"I like a man who says things straight."

"I'm glad to hear that. Coming from the East the way you do, you've got no way of knowing how things are around here, so I'll tell you. This is Christian country, son. You understand me, what I'm saying?"

Talker nodded. "Sheriff, you may not believe this, but I'm sympathetic to your problem. More than that, it's one I deal with all the time."

"Don't b.s. me, son."

Talker looked straight at him; eye contact was important. "I'm no bumpkin, either. I've been doing this since I was twenty. Six months every year, from Maine to Pennsylvania, and one thing I've learned is, towns are different. No two places are the same. You think we do the same show every fair we play at? We're not crazy."

Talker moved a half-step closer, pressing in; a little crowding couldn't hurt. "I run a strip show. Ethnic dancing? That's a load of crap, you saw that right away. Some towns will go for anything. I'm talking pussy, Sheriff, by the footlights, in your teeth. You call that filth, you're right. But here's the thing. We've also worked at uptight places, towns as straight as Fulton, maybe even straighter. We can play it clean or dirty, any way you want it. You tell me. You want no pussy? Pussy's out. No pubic hair? We'll keep it covered. Nipples? Tits? Some fairs, you can't show navels. Hell, my girls will dance in burlap bags. Just tell me what my orders are. O.K.?"

"O.K. I don't want anything my kids can't see on television."

"It's a deal. You've got it."

"I'll be watching you, McBride."

"You wouldn't be a good cop if you didn't. What you really ought to do is come tonight and catch the show. Or send an officer. We're used to having them around. In fact, why don't you have some men on duty all the time? If they don't like us, they can close us down."

"Son, you can count on that."

The Sheriff turned to go—and Talker almost let him. It was tricky; what he had to say could work or boomerang. "Before you leave—can I be honest with you, Sheriff?"

"Shoot."

"Lots of times, the cops who watch want money for it. If that's how you run things here, I'll cough it up. But what I won't do—sometimes what they want is tricks. My girls aren't whores, and if some asshole on your force tries moving in, I'll tear his fucking throat out."

"You won't have to, son. I'll do it for you."

Talker watched him walk away. Not bad. In fact, he'd never done it better.

Annie had been watching. When he moved back up on stage, she popped the question.

"How'd it go?"

He grinned. "I should of been in pictures."

The Pavilion was a landmark. There was nothing on the grounds remotely like it. Built in 1912 to celebrate the Fair's first fifty years and lovingly restored to mark the hundredth, it was staggering. A triumph of Victorian invention, purest gingerbread, a two-tiered wedding cake of turrets, gables, bays and spikes, octagonal in shape and topped off with a cupola, it stood apart from all the other buildings on a stretch of well-kept lawn, approached by gravel pathways flanked with beds of roses. Though everybody called it the Pavilion, it was listed in the records as The Fulton County Women's Exhibition Hall for the Domestic Arts.

Marcie found a space up front, beside her mother's car, of all things, pulled in and turned off the ignition.

"Well." She turned and smiled at Betsy. "Here we are." They had said very little on the way. In fact, since she'd wakened Betsy up, there hadn't been much conversation—and there wasn't now. They both got out and started up a pathway.

Betsy looked angelic—pigtails, faded jeans, an ancient

shirt of Van's, much too big for her—and Marcie felt a sudden ache. A sharper one than usual. So near and yet so far, that's how she thought of Betsy.

Marcie touched her shoulder. "Thanks for coming to the rescue."

Betsy shrugged. "It's nothing, Mom."

"I mean it. You had better things to do, you must have, and I didn't even ask, I volunteered you. . . ."

"It's O.K., Mom. I don't mind."

"It's only that I've got the shop to open up, I can't dump all of that on Pam, and after that—" She broke off; the list was endless. "I just wanted to say thank you. I'll come back and set you free as soon as possible and—" Pause. "You know I love you."

Betsy nodded. It was true enough. Mom really cared. The only trouble was there were so many troubles. Not now, they could keep. She let her mother take her hand.

The interior of the Pavilion was open, spacious, and, in contrast to its outside face, surprisingly austere: bare dark oak floor and bare white walls that soared unornamented to the ceiling high above.

The scene, as they came in, was total chaos. There were women, women everywhere, perhaps a hundred of them. They were milling all around the rows of trestle tables, busily unpacking boxes filled with baking, knitting, canning, fruits and vegetables and patchwork, not to mention the collections of rag dolls and postcards, bottle caps and stamps and beer cans.

Here and there were faces Marcie knew, her mother's friends and people from the Club or shops in town. But mainly, they were rurals, farmers' wives and farmers' daughters. Marcie edged her way among them, past displays of table settings, lamp shades, sunshine cakes and baby bonnets. There were something like five hundred categories, fifteen hundred ribbons for the winners. It was burdensome to organize, a massive undertaking, and she sometimes wondered why her mother did it. Actually, she knew the answer: Mother loved it.

They were passing by the Junior Hobby section, tables filled with God knows what, when Marcie stopped dead. Betsy looked up at her mother's face. "Are you O.K.?"

"Fine, fine." The memory hit her without warning, hadn't

crossed her mind in years. She smiled. "Did I ever tell you I collected buttons once?"

"You did?"

"It started back when I was five or six." And for no reason she could name, she started telling Betsy all about it. "It began by accident." One afternoon, she'd been with Lenny Gifford in his attic, treasure hunting. She was going through a sewing box when something shiny at the bottom caught her eye. The button was a big one made of yellow metal, which she thought was gold, and bits of glass she took for diamonds. Lenny told her she could keep it.

"After that, I started seeing buttons everywhere. It wasn't hard to find them, all you had to do was look." It was the truth. They turned up in the strangest places: on the sidewalk, in the schoolyard, under people's sofas. Even at the start, she was particular about which ones she saved; no ordinary buttons, only pretty ones. She kept them in her bedroom in a Whitman's Sampler box.

It never crossed her mind that she was building a collection. Older kids and grown-ups were collectors; she was merely saving buttons. Ella had to tell her. Ella came in every day to do the cleaning. She was Marcie's friend, and one day she had marched upstairs to Marcie's bedroom with a book. A button book, with color photographs of buttons made of gold and silver, rimmed with pearls and precious gems; of buttons cut from ivory, jade, and stones with names like lapis lazuli and malachite; of buttons that were carved with unicorns and griffins, faces, birds, and flowers. It was love.

Marcie shook her head. "I thought they were so beautiful. Can you imagine?"

She started saving money: here a nickel, there a dime. She went to tag sales, rummage sales, garage sales; sometimes she would take her bike and ride for miles to get there. Then, the summer she turned nine—when Dee was off in Europe with her folks and there was nothing to do all day—it came to her: she would exhibit her collection at the Fair.

The mounting of it took weeks. Her heart was set on winning, and appearances counted a lot. She got some large sheets of cardboard from the print shop. Then she decorated them with things she drew and tiny pictures traced from magazines. And after that, she spread the whole collection out across her bedroom carpet; which to choose? And having chosen, she had sewn them into place with Ella's darning needle.

It was worth it. They looked wonderful. No question, she would win a ribbon. Maybe not a blue one; kids as old as seventeen could enter things in Junior Hobbies. Even so, the ride to the Pavilion was a tense one. Marcie sat in back, her buttons on the seat beside her. Mom had things to do when they arrived, so Marcie got in line alone and paid her entrance fee with money she had saved up: fifty cents.

The Junior Hobbies section was a big one. There were arrowhead collections, money banks and napkins, matchbooks, postcards, salts and peppers. Marcie found a place, arranged her things, and then, heart pounding, checked the competition. There were buttons everywhere, but none of them compared to hers.

That wasn't just a personal opinion: everybody said so. All the people who came by would stop and look and say nice things. And next day, when the judges came, they thought so, too.

"Go on, Mom," Betsy said. "What happened? Did you win?"

Marcie paused. Why had she gotten into this? The truth was, her collection hadn't won. Not anything. Tears streaming down her face, she had run off to find her mother.

"Mommy?"

"Yes, dear? Why, what's the matter?"

"I didn't win a ribbon."

"No, of course not. Oh, my dear, you didn't think you would?"

"Why wouldn't I?"

"How would it look, dear? What would people think?"

"They'd think my buttons were the best."

"No, I'm afraid they'd think you won because you were my daughter."

"Oh, you didn't, Mom, you didn't tell the judges not to, I mean not to . . ."

"I'm sorry, dear. I should have told you, shouldn't I? I thought you understood."

Marcie had gone home with her buttons, put them in a box, and never opened it again.

She smiled at Betsy. "Yes, what do you think? Of course I won. A bright red ribbon. Second place. There's Gram."

She saw her mother in the distance moving swiftly toward them, carrying a clipboard, every silver hair in place. Ladies kept bombarding her with questions. Did she pause or falter? Not a chance. A quick word here, a gesture there, and on she came. The Nazis could have used her, Marcie thought.

"How wonderful," said Harriet, as Marcie kissed her cheek. "I've got you both."

"I told you, Mother. I can't—"

"Nonsense, dear. You're here. No reason in the world you can't help out. You see how much I need you."

Like a fifth wheel. "I'll be back before you know it."

"Now, now." Marcie felt her mother take her hand. "You see the mob at Registration? Come along."

She actually took a step before she pulled her hand away. "I can't leave Pam to run the shop alone."

"Of course not, dear. You're right to feel that way. It's good for you to have a hobby."

Marcie felt herself begin to shake. "It's not a hobby. Buttons are a hobby. It's a business."

"Aren't you in a mood this morning."

Marcie saw red, saw the color. Things she'd longed to say for years—'You don't know who I am. Or care. Why should you, you're the center of the universe, you're all you ever think about. I've had it, Mother. You can fry in hell.' The words were on her lips. She bit them back. "I'll see you later, Mother."

Harriet's eyes were very bright. "I ask so little of you, dear. I never make demands. I give and give, that's all I do. You'd think that once a year—just look around you. I'm responsible for all this, and I'd think you'd want to help. What daughter wouldn't?"

Marcie couldn't win with words. She turned to go.

"You can't leave. What will people think, how is it going to look?"

"I'm sorry," Marcie said; and what was worse, a part of her still meant it.

"Mom?"

She looked down. It was Betsy; Marcie had forgotten she was there. She bent and kissed her cheek. "Be good," she said.

"You, too."

"You come along with Gram now." Marcie watched her mother put a hand on Betsy's shoulder, start off through the crowd. She felt a pang, a sharp one. Fourteen years; Marcie had known her all that time, had nursed her, changed her diapers, driven her to dancing school. A million things—and Betsy was a stranger. There was no one in the family like her. God might know what made her tick, but Marcie didn't. Didn't know her, understand her . . .

Marcie turned and fled.

She sat for several minutes in the car before she felt like driving. Then she backed out carefully and turned. She meant, she really meant, to go straight to the shop and work with Pam. Instead, she headed toward the Midway for a look at Paul McBride.

Nine-thirty, and already things were warming up. Van didn't mind the heat; it was the perspiration that disturbed him. Pausing by the office door, he glanced around the area at vast displays of farm machinery, gardening equipment, tractor–lawn mowers, things like that. Van's shed at home, a place he rarely visited, was full of it.

Then came the cars: Ford, GM, Steuben Motors— Chrysler Sales & Service. Van was proud of how it looked. And rightly so. They used to build a new stand every summer for the Fair. One day, it struck Van they were burning money; so he went to Ed to sell him on a permanent display. It meant a large cash outlay, but he had the figures down on paper, they could amortize it, there were tax advantages. Ed went for it.

The end result was handsome, well designed; he'd had a hand in that. It came apart like Lego blocks: they stored it through the year, and every summer all they had to do was truck it out and bolt it up again.

It needed painting, patching, little changes, things to keep it up-to-date. Van had been there since seven, checking details, making notes. If something could go wrong, it would. He couldn't forestall acts of God, but he had laundry lists of things to tell the painters, electricians, carpenters, not to mention all the calls he had to make and things to think about. Like Marcie with the farm boy, Marcie in the pool with Dee. And then, of course, the future of the Agency.

He moved into the office, where the air conditioner was humming. There were things to check here, too. The stacks of pamphlets, order forms, loan applications. And the bar. Ed liked to make his clients comfortable, and there was always ice and everything on earth to drink.

He sat down at the desk. More notes. The Board of Governors was set to meet at ten. They ran the Fair, Ed had been President for two years running. Van was looking forward to his turn. Not yet, but soon.

Just half an hour to fill. He checked his schedule. *Salesmen: noon.* Phil, Zack, and all the rest of them. Ed always gave the pep talk, he was good at that. *Cars: one o'clock.* That's when the boys from Service would be driving the new models down. They handled the entire Chrysler line. How many cars should he expect? He knew exactly, he just couldn't quite remember—

"Hi, son. How's it going?"

Van looked up. Ed had been playing golf. He had on yellow slacks and a bright blue sports shirt. Ed liked winning but he was a hacker, so they rarely played together.

"No disasters so far." All in all, the way he operated with the old man was amazing. In no way on earth were they the least alike. Aside from loving Marcie, they had zero things in common. Yet not only did they coexist, they got along. It took no end of care and compromise, but Van knew it was worth it.

Ed opened up the fridge. "I thought I'd drive you to the meeting. Want a Coke?"

"No, thanks." Van had the feeling it was now or never. "Can we talk a minute, Dad?"

"Sure thing." Ed sat and opened up the Coke.

"The truth is, I'm worried sick."

Ed straightened. "What's the matter? Are you all right?"

"I'm fine."

"There's something wrong at home?"

"No, nothing like that." Van paused. "I'm just scared about the business."

"It's a rotten year, that's all. Nobody's selling cars."

"Dad, Chrysler is the weakest of the Big Three. I don't like the way the future looks."

"You went to college. Business goes in cycles, son. We'll be O.K."

Van started rattling numbers off: production figures, deficits, a shrinking market share.

Ed shrugged. "I've been a Chrysler man since '44 when I got out of the war. They've been good to me, they made me rich. I'm loyal, but I'm not insane." He smiled. "I'm a natural salesman. Son, I could unload a casket to a corpse. The market's full of cars, the Japanese are everywhere. It doesn't matter what we sell. Relax."

Van couldn't. Ever since his marriage, he'd been counting on the Agency. He was a partner, strictly junior, but the day would come when Ed was gone and he'd be running it. He had no faith in imports, not in Fulton: Ed was living in a dream. Van thought about the costs he had to meet, the house, the style, Marcie's needs.

All Van could see was ruin.

Ed stood. "Come on, boy, let's see a smile. It's time to bullshit with the Board of Governors." He grinned and clapped Van on the back.

Marcie pulled up by the Bingo tent. No point in going closer, she could see enough. The painted flats with those outrageous dancing girls were no surprise. She'd seen through Paul McBride the moment she'd set eyes on him. She knew exactly what he was.

She watched him as he strained and struggled, working with some farm boys, putting up a tent. His clothes were soaked with sweat. She could imagine what lay underneath them.

Imagine was the right word. She had never met a man like Paul McBride. The closest she had come was years ago. At Denison. There was a girl she scarcely knew; Midge, Madge—Marge, that was it. She came from Shaker Heights, old money, archconservative, and, though she moused around in mousey clothes, not altogether bad to look at.

One day in spring, Marcie was working on the second chapter of her novel which, for reasons of its own, kept going off in all directions, when Dee came skipping in, a big grin on her face. "You'll never guess. I'll tell you. Mousey Marge is going with a trucker."

"With a what?"

"You know, a man who drives a truck. Can you believe it?"

"Frankly, no."

"It's true. You'll see."

And see she did. That evening, they were downstairs in the lounge when through the windows came the hiss of air brakes. They looked up and saw Marge racing down the stairs and out.

"Come on," Dee said. They followed her outside, ducked down behind some shrubs, and there he was, beside a trailer truck. He wore a T-shirt. He looked huge and dark, as if he hadn't shaved. Marge ran to him. He picked her up, right off the ground, and kissed her long and hard. Marge wrapped her legs around his waist. Incredible. Then, holding her with one hand, he opened up the cab door, tossed her in and drove away.

"Believe me now?" Dee whispered.

Marcie nodded, couldn't speak. She kept imagining what happened next. Where would they go? Some parking lot, no one around. Then what? Marcie saw his hands on Marge's blouse. He ripped it open, threw her down, her back against the seat, unzipped his blue jeans and exposed his instrument. The thing was like a nightstick; straight and just as long and hard. Marge whimpered as he pulled her knees apart and jammed it in. The whole thing, all the way. Marge cried out; then she started groaning, writhing. In and out the thing went. How could Marge stand the pain? Then, Marge was whispering, "Don't stop, don't ever stop."

For weeks, when Marcie tried to sleep, the fantasy would play. It turned itself on, there was nothing she could do but watch. That was almost twenty years ago, and even now—not often—it still played. And made her wet. It always did.

She rubbed her eyes to clear them, looked ahead. McBride was leaving, walking off. Good riddance. Time to throw the car into reverse and drive to town. She slipped the gear stick into first and started slowly up the road. She didn't mean to honk the horn, but somehow it just happened.

Talker stopped and turned. The car pulled up beside him.

Marcie flicked down her window. "Good morning, Mr. McBride." For just a flash, he looked surprised. No doubt about it, she'd surprised him.

"Oh," he said. And then, "Good morning."

"It's a busy day for you, I guess."

He nodded. "Yes, and then some."

He was squinting, it was hard to tell the color of his eyes. Gray-blue? She hadn't looked for details yesterday. She pointed toward the flats. "That's your show, isn't it?"

"That's me."

"It looks terrific."

"Thanks."

"I'm sorry the location isn't better. It's the best one we had left."

"We'll do all right."

"I'm sure you will. Good luck."

"The same to you, M'am."

Marcie smiled, touched the gas and started down the road. Her eyes stayed on him in the rearview mirror. He stood watching her drive off, hands on hips. She smiled. No harm done. Besides, with all the stress these days—and more to come, no doubt, no doubt—she was entitled to a moment's pleasure.

Talker turned. He figured she was watching in the rearview mirror. He'd been sure—not positive, but fairly certain—that he'd seen the last of her. You never knew.

"No thanks," he said. Not that he didn't want her. She was something special, but he'd learned his lesson long ago, his first year on the road. The show was playing tank towns in New Hampshire. He was twenty, horny all the time and into anything that moved. One day, this girl turned up, blue eyes and cornsilk hair and busting out all over. She was ready, he was ready. Bang, bang, bang.

As luck would have it, she turned out to be the banker's daughter. Like a good girl, she went home and told. The cops came out and found him. Beat him with lead pipes, they did. They nearly killed him; he was three months in the hospital.

The moral? Never touch a local princess.

Where was Annie? "Hey!" he shouted. "Move your tail, kid. We've got things to do."

7

DEE WAS DOING penance. Out till two, not up till ten; a poor beginning for a visit home, and Dee was sipping coffee in the breakfast room with Eleanor and paying for it.

"Yes, dear," Eleanor was saying. "But you'd scarcely set foot in the house when you ran off to be with Marcie. She's a lovely girl, I know how much you miss her. Being gone all day, I understand. But half the night?"

"I'm sorry, Eleanor."

"I sat here waiting for you. All alone. I make plans, too, you know. I thought we might—"

"I said I'm sorry. It was my fault. It was wrong of me."

Pause. Dee wondered what was coming next. Her mother had a menu, like a restaurant. Sometimes she saved dessert for last; you never knew. Dee visualized her finger moving down the page. It stopped beside "Career."

"The leading role? You played the lead?"

Dee nodded. "Yes."

"I feel so proud, you can't imagine. Were you good?"

The *Post* had said so, not the *Times*. "Yes, I came out of it all right."

Dee put her cup down. Minton. Eleanor had always liked "good" things, the big old house was overflowing with her vision of refinement. Dee had never known another home. They'd moved to Blanchard Street when she was three, and there were many things she loved about the place: the late nineteenth-century plaster work, the paneling, the spaciousness, the landing on the stairway with its bay and windowseat. That was her favorite spot, the best of all.

"So many people want to see you, dear."

Dee's heart sank. "Oh? They do?"

"There's Aunt Denise"—Dee had been named for her—"and Uncle George and Helen, and there's Ruth and Jane, I don't know where to stop."

Dee nearly told her, it was tempting. "Do I have to?"

"What a thing to say. They miss you and they care about you. Deeply." Eleanor's engagement book was on her lap. She opened it.

Dee loathed them all, and it was mutual. "I'd really rather not."

Her mother's eyes flashed. "Honestly. They love you and you know it. L-O-V-E, love. There's nothing on this earth more precious. It's my motto. Everything I do—"

"Can we postpone this?"

"What I thought was, lunch tomorrow—"

"Mother, please."

"All right. If you insist." She closed the book.

Dee knew she hadn't heard the last of it. There would be no way out, she'd end up seeing all of them—and being good about it. Aunt Denise had eyes like pebbles and a heart to match; and Uncle George had closed his mind in the Depression, when the banks did, never to reopen. She remembered how they used to treat her, all the ways . . . She felt the anger welling. Eleanor was talking; pay attention.

". . . how different things must seem to you."

Dee wasn't quite sure what the subject was. "Which things?"

"The town, your friends. So many changes in eight years."

The "eight years" was another menu item. Dee would hear a lot about how long she'd been away. The subject—dodging it was useless—would be dealt with head-on at some point.

Dee shrugged. "It's just the opposite. I feel as if I'd left here yesterday." And it was true enough. Her mother hadn't aged; she'd always been a handsome woman, and Dee hoped she'd be that wrinkle-free at sixty-five. As for the rest, the

town appeared untouched. Van seemed a little more remote—
Dee found him hard to read—and Marcie struck her as a bit
too thin. But otherwise? Dee smiled. "It's nice when nothing
changes."

"But they do, dear. Time exacts its toll, you know."

Dee knew what that meant. Eleanor, a quarter of a century ago, had cancer of the uterus. Though it was in total re-
mission, no trace of trouble since, the subject had a way of
coming up.

"You're looking wonderful," Dee said.

"I feel well, too, I'm glad to say, but I had you in mind."

"Oh?" Dee felt her stomach tighten. She looked nothing
like her age. Her agent still sent her out to read for parts of
twenty-five-year-olds, and no one ever questioned it. She
wasn't sure where Eleanor was heading now. "Go on," she
said.

The invitation wasn't necessary. "It's not good for you,
this living all alone."

That meant she wasn't married. "You get used to it, it's
not so bad."

"Do you go out at all?"

"Of course I do."

"What kind of men?"

"That's my affair."

"A mother has a right to ask."

"Oh, come on, Eleanor. You live alone in twenty rooms
here. You're no one to talk."

"I had a lasting marriage, I had you, a husband who
adored me. I still live on memories of Harold. There was
nothing that man wouldn't do for me."

Eleanor was off and running. Dee tuned out. She knew a
different version, she had grown up listening to it. Daddy had
been wonderful, that much was accurate. He'd owned the local Coca-Cola franchise, which in Fulton meant a lot. But not
enough for Eleanor. They lived as well as anyone in town, and
there was money in the bank. She wanted more. She pushed
him, drove him, yapping like a terrier: "You think too little of
yourself, you can be anyone you want to be, as big as
Murchison or Redding." Harold didn't want it; he liked his
hours, there was time for golf and cards and fishing trips. Besides which, did they lack for anything? So Eleanor would
back off, try again, attack with tears and screaming: "I don't

ask for much, it's not for me, it's all for your sake." And when sobbing didn't work, she'd move in with the cancer. "Do it now, while I'm still here. I live from day to day, who knows when I'll be gone."

Eventually, she drove him to it, made him sell the bottling plant. He'd bought land, built a shopping center, made more money—and the stress and pressure killed him. Take an easy-going man, a gentle, open, loving soul, and clamp him in a vise—it wasn't murder; but it was. Dee had stood at his open coffin dry-eyed, filled with hate for Eleanor. Dee wasn't twenty, it had been that long ago, and she still hated her. And still despised herself for all the bitterness and rage. The years of seeing shrinks had been no help, the feelings wouldn't go away.

That was her mother's crime. But Dee, too, was a criminal. She looked into her mother's eyes and read the accusation. She had gotten out of Fulton, broken free, and Eleanor would die before forgiving her.

"I ought to go and dress," Dee said.

"I wasn't finished."

"All I meant was, aren't we going out? I thought we'd spend the day together."

"Really?" Eleanor sat straight up. "Just the two of us?" She clapped her hands in sheer delight.

The girls were on their best behavior, out sunbathing on the dock. Though canoes, from time to time, passed by, and they could feel eyes staring at them, never once did they look up. Talker had laid the law down, no mistake. A word like "Christian" carried many meanings. What it meant out here was keep your knees together and your trap zipped up. No contact with the neighbors; verbal, physical, or any other kind.

As if they needed telling. They'd played towns where you could go to jail for thinking. So Pauline lay on her tummy, her transistor to her ear; and Skipper tried to doze, eyes covered by her sailor cap. Laurel sat a bit apart, legs crossed, head bent, as if contemplating her navel, lost in transcendental meditation.

Norma, at a picnic table in the shade, put down her ledger book and looked at them. Her girls. Although she wouldn't dream of laying down her life for them the way that Talker did, she liked them well enough, and mothered them from time to time. When necessary. Basically, like any impresario, she had a tendency to think of them as properties. They were her stock-in-trade, and it was up to her to keep them in good running order.

Not an easy thing to do. She'd never come across a girl like Laurel. Beauty, brains—she went to college in the East, a good school. Money, too. Her family lived outside of Philadelphia on the Main Line. What the hell sense did it make, with all that going for her? Self-destructive; had to be. One day, she'd self-destruct. As for Pauline, she could be as docile as a moo-cow when the stars were right, which wasn't often. Mostly, she was moony; Talker's word for it was "clinical depression." Skipper, on the other hand, was nearly always up or down, a barrelful of monkeys or a bushelful of grief. Talker had a word for that, too; he had words for everything.

That's how she'd come to notice him. Walter was still alive back then, and they were playing Maine, some tank town outside of Bangor. It was Walter's show, he owned it; like a good wife, she just tagged along and kept the books. He never fooled around, not that she knew of, so she wasn't jealous of the girls. He saw them as a business, just like she did.

It was midday, she had time to kill, and she was passing by a freak show when she heard that voice. "So if you're squeamish or your heart is weak, don't buy a ticket. We've got freaks you'll shudder at, deformities to give you nightmares." Rubes were buying tickets left and right, like crazy.

Norma walked away and had a think. Her Walter was a strictly so-so talker; dull, and that was being nice about it. So she waited till the freak show started, drifted back. She liked his looks—a little young, no more than twenty—but he had the right equipment.

"Got a minute?"

"Sure, I guess."

She introduced herself. He gave a name—Bob Johnson—but somehow she knew it wasn't his. To this day, she still didn't know his real one. Did he like his job? He shrugged; it paid the rent. How would he like to do the talking for a strip show?

"Girls?"

She saw his eyes light up, and when she named a salary, he was hers. And had been ever since. When Walter stroked out two years later, Talker took his place. Not in her bed, God no, but in most other ways. He never stole or cheated, he was always on the job, he kept the girls in order just right; friendly, gentle, sympathetic, and, when needed, really rough. He'd curse them out, slap them around. He had the knack.

And he looked after her as if he really cared. He'd fought her wars when they'd come up, he helped her keep the cash safe—there were times they traveled with a lot of it—and always saw her safely down to Lauderdale.

Where he went after that, or what he did, or how he spent his money, she had no idea. He never spoke about himself. Not even where he came from. With those license plates, he had to be connected to Rhode Island some way. There were times, a lot of them, when they would sit together boozing, often half the night. She'd tell him a lot of things, some of them pretty God damn intimate, but she got nothing in return. She used to wonder why. He was no criminal, he wasn't hiding from the cops or running; she was sure of that. And it would piss her off sometimes, the silence when his life came up.

Not anymore. Whatever troubled him was something really weird—it had to be—but he could keep his secrets. What the hell, it wasn't Norma's problem. She could love him like a son and still not give a damn.

She went back to the ledger book; the sight of money never failed to ease her mind. The way Talker was feeling, this was it; they'd play their week and fold the tent. She didn't really mind. She lived on half of what she made, and she felt ready to go South.

"So," Skipper said, "does anybody feel like screaming?" No one looked up. "Only me?" She never liked it when the season ended, and each year she liked it less. Off-season work was getting hard to find, and she'd be thirty in October. Where did Skippers go when time ran out? Fillies went to pasture, boxers went to seed.

She stood up. Someone had to talk to her, pay some attention. Anything to get a rise. "I think I'll go inside and masturbate. Who wants to watch?"

"You say it louder, I'll be selling tickets." Norma moved out on the dock. "We told you, none of that out here." She prodded Pauline with her shoe, tapped Laurel on the shoulder.

"Get some clothes on. Time to check in at the Fair."

                              *   *   *

The Fulton County Fair was operated by the Fulton
County Agricultural Society, and it was no small honor to be
on the Board of Governors. You had to stand for office; there
were annual elections, and the winners served a three-year
term. Each township in the county—there were twelve in all—
was represented. As a rule, the membership was evenly divided; twenty men from Fulton, twenty from the farms, plus
county officers and members ex-officio.

They were gathering inside the Commissary Tent, the
Fulton people on the left, the farm folk on the right, like
bride's and groom's sides at a wedding. It was done instinctively, and no one ever questioned it—not openly, in any case.

In actuality, the split seemed natural enough. Aside from
sitting on the Board, the farmers and the Fulton people went
their separate ways. Residents of Millerville or Fallsburg didn't
even shop in town. And except for all the vegetable stands on
country roads that sprouted in the summertime, no one in
Fulton had much contact with the world outside the city limits.

There were reasons for this, lots of them: like money, education, breeding—or inbreeding; that was touchy. Country
families, once they settled down, stayed put; and cousins married cousins all the time. Or so they said in Fulton, though it
wasn't altogether true.

In any case, the people did look different. Take away the
suits and coveralls and line them up naked against the wall,
they'd still look like a different species. It went deeper than
the farmers' tans opposed to getting bronzed in swimsuits.
Rural men looked bigger, thicker, heavier. Their speech was
different, too: a little slower, full of localisms. And their
women, though they worked hard, had a tendency to turn to
fat.

That's how Van saw them. And that business at the Club
on Saturday meant something. It was hostile, there was anger
in it, and Van always felt uncomfortable among the rurals. Not
Ed. He had a handshake and a smile for almost everyone. He
even knew their names. Van watched him circulate.

"Hey, Walt, how goes it? Good to see you, Willie. No hard
feelings, Barney?"

Barney Lovell shrugged. "Well, Mr. Steuben, truth is, I
was angry. Still am, I suppose. The Good Book says it's wrong

to harbor grudges and I'm working on it, but it's no joke coming up with all that money."

Ed knew he was lying. Lovell made a pretty penny from that camp of his. "I know," Ed told him. "But how would you like it if I came out, ripping up your woods?"

"Not much, I guess, but you're a rich man and I'm not."

The gavel sounded. Van sat down and saved a chair for Ed. Harvey Yaeger was the President this year. He owned the lumberyard. Van didn't like him very much.

The meeting came to order.

"Pam?"

"With you in a minute."

It had been a busy morning. They had sold a quilt, a set of ironstone, a silver Boston teapot—eighteenth century, though they couldn't swear to it; and a dealer down from Mansfield placed several pieces on hold. Marcie knew for certain he'd be back. There would be haggling on the prices, but she didn't mind a first-class haggle; she was good at it.

"What's up?"

She grinned at Pam. "You want to close for lunch?"

"You go, I'll stay."

"No deal. I feel like company."

Pam took a closer look at Marcie. She was glowing. "You look flushed."

"I do?"

"You have a fever?"

"Don't be silly."

Pam reached out and touched her forehead. It was cool. "What's with you?"

"Nothing."

"Sure? You want a glass of wine?"

"Why not?"

The two girls headed for the office. It was in the back and tiny, just room for the partner's desk and little else. Pam took the Chablis from the fridge. She had known Marcie since their freshman year at Fulton High, when she had moved to town. She'd liked her right away, instinctively, no special reason. But with Dee around, there hadn't been much room for her. So she had hovered in the background, always free if Marcie was. She'd been a plain girl, dates were few and far between, and how she'd envied Dee and Marcie, always so damned popular. And when they'd left for Denison, she went the other way, to Swarthmore—Pam had brains—and they'd lost track of one another.

Time, Pam thought as she poured out two glasses, had been generous to her. Her looks grew better as she aged, Dee left for fame and fortune in New York, and when Dr. Jerry Leggett, fresh from med school, hung his shingle out, her cup flowed over. And had kept flowing, ever since.

Pam loved the shop. She fit in perfectly with Marcie, who was great at selling; she was not Ed's daughter for no reason. Pam was happier with billings and accounts. And when they searched for inventory, driving through the state from town to town sometimes for days—flea markets, shops, on hands and knees in country attics—that was best of all.

Pam put the glass in Marcie's hand and smiled. "Happy days."

"The same to you." A toast that wasn't necessary. Pam and Jerry were the only happy people whom she knew. No, cancel happy. It was simple and misleading. Sadnesses and disappointments came their way, like everybody else's. But what they did have was contentment. Life could do its worst, no matter, they'd pull through. They were content.

It was amazing. Marcie wondered how it felt.

Talker took the left on Blanchard, driving slowly, taking in the look of things. He always scouted every town. The more you knew, the better. Knowledge wasn't power. What it did was make you safer. It helped cut down on surprises.

"Talker?"

"Now what?"

"Look at them." Eyes wide, Annie pointed out the window. "Have you ever seen such houses?"

"Sure. The world is full of them." They looked like something from a storybook. The outside might look good enough, but back behind the curtains, all the same crap went on.

He'd seen enough. Besides, he owed the girl one envelope. "Let's take a look downtown."

They parked on Main, beside the Post Office. He bought the envelope, she bought the stamp. Then out they went to case the place, a brisk walk down Commercial Street, then Cleveland Boulevard.

More of the same. It figured. People in those houses had to work and shop on streets like these. Where, oh where, he wondered, did the normal people go? The plumbers, gardeners, maids, the working stiffs who made this world go round? The Erie-Lackawanna—did it still have trains?—cut through the north of town. That's where they'd be, like always, on the wrong side of the tracks.

"Talker?"

"Um?"

"I'd love to live here. Wouldn't you?"

He shrugged. "It's nice enough." The light changed, and they crossed. He checked the street sign. LIBERTY, it said.

"Where do you live?" he heard her ask.

"Who, me?" Another shrug. "Around."

"Around? You mean it's not my business, right?"

"I mean around."

She looked at him. It didn't make a lot of sense. "Don't you live anywhere?"

He had to grin. "Come on, kid, everywhere is someplace."

Annie let it drop. She'd just been curious, that's all. And if he wanted to be secretive—or sensitive, it could be either one—he was entitled to. Besides, once Labor Day was over and the show broke up, she'd go her own way. So would he— and that would be the end of it.

They passed a shop, and something in the window caught her eye. She moved in for a closer look. Among the quilts and dishes, there were shiny bits of brass. All old. A few of them were household things, like the hot-water iron. Aunt Maria used to have one, and why someone would put it in a window made no sense: who'd want it?

Other bits were small, like dollhouse furniture. A rocking chair, a brass bed, tables. What had caught her was the bed. Back home—not Emil's place, her real home—she had fuzzy memories of a bed like that. Her bed; that's what it was.

Quick tears were forming, so she turned away and rubbed her eyes.

"What's wrong?" he asked her.

"Nothing. Just some dust, that's all." She rubbed some more.

"What's in the window?"

"Nothing. Don't you listen, don't you ever pay attention?"

"Show me."

"Why? You live around, why should I tell you anything?"

"Is it the sampler?"

"What's a sampler?"

"Maybe it's the brass dog."

Finally, he got it out of her. He glanced up, checked the shop's name.

Pam and Marcie, talking in the office, didn't see them looking.

8

HOME AT LAST. Van closed the front door, leaned against it, let the cool air wash around him. There were things to do at the exhibit; even now, at 6:00 P.M., the list went on till morning. And if that was how long it took, he didn't care. Let Zack and Mortie carry it, that's what subordinates were for.

"Hi, Dad."

"'Lo, Pumpkin." Bets was calling from the den. "Your mother home?"

"Not so far."

There was something in her voice. He shuffled to the door, looked in at her. "Are you O.K.?" She seemed all right.

"I'm fine." She smiled.

"I'm going up to shower. See you."

"I'll be here."

He turned the shower on, peeled off his clothes—they felt as if they were stuck to him—and dropped them in the hamper, where they could fester overnight. Then, opening the door, he stepped into the water, icy cold.

"OhGodohGodohGodohGod." He rarely swore, and anyway, it wasn't swearing; it was closer to a prayer of thanks. The business day was over, and he didn't have to see a car for thirteen hours, not until the Fair was open.

He liked cars, if the truth be known, and he was good at running things. The Agency worked like a Swiss watch, tick-tock. As a rule. Life's major turning points were hard to isolate: they simply seemed to happen, things evolved and there you were. Not so with Van. He'd seen his crossroad when he reached it, and he'd known what he was doing.

It was June, just after graduation. He and Marcie were engaged by then. He had proposed some weeks before, and she had wept and nodded, "Yes, oh yes," and they had climbed into the back of Marcie's car and fooled around. The next day, they had driven up to Fulton. Marcie absolutely couldn't wait to tell her parents. Harriet and Ed were not surprised. Van had, by then, spent several weekends in the house on Blanchard Street, and they had made him feel at home. They were delighted at the news, no doubt about it, glad to have him in the family.

And why not? Van's family had credentials, too. The first Van Buren came to Masillon in 1845, and it was generally believed he was related in some distant way to President Van Buren. No one knew for sure: there were some missing branches on the family tree, which made it difficult to prove. Or disprove. Van believed it, though he rarely said so; people didn't like it if you bragged. And who cared if his parents weren't included in the highest circles, like the Steubens were. They stood for something nonetheless.

The future in those days seemed filled with possibilities, and Van spent endless hours with Marcie, weighing them. His father ran his own insurance agency; not big, but big enough so that they never lacked for anything that mattered. And his uncle ran a chain of discount stores—if you could call two stores a chain—one in a shopping mall and one in Wooster. His uncle would have been glad to take him in, so would his dad; but there were other ways to go, like starting out and doing something on his own or taking off to California; lots of guys were doing that.

"You want to know what I think, Van?"

"No. What?"

The two of them were in their swimsuits, sitting on the boat dock at the Lodge. Dee's family owned it: fifty untouched wooded acres with a spring-fed private pond, not far from Fallsburg. It was totally secluded. Van liked it from the moment he had seen it: anything could happen there, and no one in the world would ever know.

That afternoon, Dee had called up to say that Dennis was

in town, so all of them had driven out together, stopping on the way to buy some beer. They had a few, and then—the Lodge had several bedrooms—they went in to change, but only Van and Marcie had come out.

"What I think is . . ." She paused. "It's nice here, isn't it?"

He nodded. She was wearing a bikini, which she couldn't at the Club. "It's beautiful."

"You know, these days, Dee makes no sense to me at all. New York is all she talks about. New York, New York." She shook her head. "I've always liked things here at home."

"I know."

"Van, have you ever thought of living here?"

"You mean in Fulton?"

"It could be terrific, if you wanted to. We wouldn't have to move to somewhere strange, we know so many people, everybody likes you. You could open up a business, Dad would help out at the start, I know he would. Or you could even join the Agency."

"You think he'd take me in?"

She grinned. "No harm in asking."

"Maybe not, but—" He broke off. "What are you doing?"

She was taking off her top. "Don't worry, we're alone, they won't be out for hours. Van?"

He liked small breasts. Hers were so firm and very white. "Uh-huh?"

"You've got to promise me you won't get mad, O.K.?"

"O.K."

"I went to Dad and asked him."

"What?" She had his full attention.

"You know what he said? He'd love to have you with him. He said you could try it for a year, and if you didn't like it, fine. And if you did—oh, Van—he told me you could be his partner."

"Me?"

Her eyes were shining in the sunlight. "Wouldn't that be something?"

They had sealed the bargain with a kiss, and to be fair, he had no right or reason to regret it. He had known what he was doing. Granted, he was only twenty-two, and all the different things he might have done—but madness lay in that direction, so he bent, reached for the soap, and lathered up.

As Marcie pulled into the drive, her mind was swimming.

She had twenty things to do—no, make it fifty—and the day
had sped away from her. She hurried to the front door, flung
it open, slammed it shut, and started off across the front hall.

"Hi, Mom." From the den.

She stopped dead. Betsy, for the love of God. She'd left
her trapped in the Pavilion, hadn't thought of her all day. Not
once. It wasn't hard to guess what lay ahead.

"Hi, Bets." She found a smile, put it on, moved through
the doorway. Bets was sitting on the sofa, legs crossed, dusty
sneakers on the fabric samples. Not by accident, but Marcie
didn't scold. "How are you?"

"Me, Mom? Really swell. I had a swell day."

Marcie picked up her cue, looked aghast. "Oh, Betsy. I
forgot."

"It's no big deal."

"I promised I'd be back. I'm sorry."

"You had better things to do, that's all."

"I didn't, honestly. I don't know what to say."

"Forget it. Who cares if I had a date with Denny? Being
stuck with Gram all day was great."

"I said I'm sorry."

"Really great. She's loads of fun, you know that, I don't
need to tell you."

Marcie's voice went up a notch. "It's all my fault, I'm to
blame, O.K.?"

"You know what's really great about your mother? On a
scale of ten—"

"Now, Betsy."

"She's a two, Mom, and that's being nice about it."

"That's enough, young lady."

"You know what she had me doing?"

"I won't hear another word."

Betsy stood up, cheeks bright red. "She had me—what's it
matter, but she could have thanked me for it."

"If she didn't—"

"I'm not deaf. She didn't, and she doesn't care."

"She loves you. If you don't know that—"

"You don't fool me. You think she's just as—"

Mrs. Beebe spoke. They hadn't seen her in the doorway.
"I don't mean to interrupt, but—"

Marcie spun around. "What is it, Mrs. Beebe?"

"Five's my quitting time you know, but you've been out all day . . ."

"I know that." There were times when Marcie felt she hated Mrs. Beebe. Something in those pale gray eyes was always judging her. That was ridiculous, of course, and most unfair. The woman had kept house and cooked their meals for years. She was a jewel, a treasure. Everybody said so.

"Supper's ready in the fridge, but there's a lot of things we need from market."

"Make a list."

"I've made one."

"Thank you. Where'd you leave it?"

"On the kitchen table, just like always. I've made coffee for your supper, but we're out of milk. It's on the list."

"I'll go to Peterson's tomorrow." Marcie didn't think she shouted, but she couldn't swear to it.

Talker looked around the tent. Not bad. Some things still needed doing, like he hadn't hung the stage lights and the speakers still kept shorting out. But no real problems. By the time they opened up for business, four tomorrow afternoon, he'd have the Moulin Rouge in running order. He had paid off his boys half an hour ago. They'd worked an honest day, and he had slipped them each an extra twenty.

He was beat and he was thirsty; sleep and beer, that's what he needed. With a grunt, he vaulted up on stage. The floor felt solid, but he walked around it anyway, just testing, then moved through the curtains to the van.

The girls were busy, taking costumes out of boxes, putting them on hangers, dumping makeup on the tables. Annie, sewing basket by her feet, mouth full of pins, was taking in a harem outfit, formerly Babette's. She knew what she was doing, she was used to hand-me-downs. No signs of jitters yet; but come show time tomorrow, he would have his hands full with her. All his girls had fits their first time on.

"So here's the thing." The girls looked up. He knew that Norma had been through it with them, but it needed emphasizing. "There's good money to be made here; lots of it for all of us. But what you've got to do is tone it down and keep it that way. Anyone works strong, they'll close us up that fast." He snapped his fingers.

"Gotcha," Skipper said.

"I'm serious. We don't expose our jollies here. The customers can yell for more, but they don't get it. Anyone throws money on the stage, you throw it back." He watched them nod. Then someone giggled. "I'm not kidding. They'll have cops at every show, and they're not on the take. They play it straight here."

Laurel looked up. "That'll be the first time."

"There's a first for everything."

He let it go at that and walked out on the bally stage. Their corner of the grounds was on a rise, and he could see it all from where he stood. Most lights were out. The only life was by the Swine and Cattle sheds. A lot of trucks, the farmers carting in their animals. The judging started early in the morning.

"It's a great life, don't you love it?" Norma said.

He hadn't heard her come. She had a beer for both of them. It wasn't cold. He didn't care. "Thanks."

"Me, I'm incurable. I'll never get enough, don't ask me why. When Walter found me, I was working in a dry goods store. I always thought I'd have a home and raise a family."

He'd heard her saga many times, he knew she wasn't rambling. She was asking questions: what about next summer, was he coming back again? She pulled this on him every year, the week before the season ended. Usually, he'd hem and haw, she'd offer him a bigger cut for one more year, and he'd say, "Maybe. It's a big decision, let me think it over." It was good for her to hang a day or two before he came around.

Another season? What the hell, why not? He grinned at her. "I'm hooked. You know that, Norma. It's a great life."

Sheriff Weller lit a cigarette and leaned against the side of his Command Post. That's what everybody called it, though, in point of fact, it was a camper fitted out with phones and radios. It stood, as always, near the ticket booths right on the entrance road, so he could keep an eye on everything that came and went.

He had a hard week coming up, the only rough one of the year. On heavy days, there could be fifteen, even twenty thousand people on the Fairgrounds. That was more than lived in Fulton altogether. They came in from all across the county and beyond. Although no liquor was on sale, a lot of beer went down, and there was always trouble. It was a lot more than his Force could handle, so the State Police came in to lend a hand. He always found them arrogant; they had a tendency to look down at the local law, and that was one thing Harry couldn't swallow. No one pushed his boys around.

It was a little after midnight, just a few more trucks to leave the grounds. He checked his list, he clocked them in and out. Just six, and he could lock up the gates and go home.

One of the six was coming now. He ticked it off, then signaled it to stop and ambled over.

"Evening, Sheriff."

"Had a long day?"

"Long?" Walt Greener scratched his head. "It's been a week since breakfast."

Greener was alone. "I don't see Marvin."

"Bet your butt you don't. He's back home mucking out the pigsties. Maybe that'll learn him."

"Listen, Walt. About the fine."

"I'm paying it." He sounded sharp. "And Marvin's going to pay me back, I don't care if it takes ten years."

"Cool down. I'm only saying—" Weller paused. He knew how much the money meant to Greener. He was only scraping by. The days of family farms were going, if not gone, and Marvin was Walt's only son who hadn't taken off to Cleveland, Youngstown, where the jobs were. Or, more like it, where they used to be.

"Look, Walt, there was no way I could help. Your boy was drunk, and using Longview for a highway was a damn fool thing to pull."

"You know what you can do with all them fat cats?"

"It's my duty to protect their property. The law's the law."

"I figure there's all kinds of laws. You know your Bible?"

"Sure I do."

"Well, you go home and check on Exodus. Chapter twenty-one, verse twenty-three. I'll see you." Greener nodded, shifted into first and moved off.

Weller didn't have to check. The verse went: "Eye for eye, tooth for tooth, burning for burning, wound for wound." Or something like that, more or less.

9

SUNRISE ON TUESDAY, August 31, occurred at 5:14 exactly. Fulton Radio—WRSF, 6.60 on your dial—went on the air at five. Those listening to the weatherman, and many people were, knew that the temperature was 81, the day was going to be clear, winds from the southwest would be running at 5 mph or less, and the barometer was steady. Highs of 95 or more were likely, and the THI was off the scale.

Among those who were listening were: Dee, who, having sworn off pills of any kind, had spent the night counting cracks on the ceiling; Ed and Harriet; both Greeners, Walt and Marvin; Sheriff Weller; Ticket-takers, Judges and Concessionaires; all cops, both State and Local; Pam and Jerry; Van, who had an earpiece in his ear, no sense in waking Marcie; Betsy, who was fully dressed and downstairs, on the phone to Denny, making plans.

And Talker. He was looking forward to the day. New Fair, new faces, lots to do. He switched off the weather, bounced up, and headed for the john. Quick shave and shower, any luck, he'd hit the Fair by seven, grab some breakfast, take a quick look at the livestock—for some arcane reason, he was nuts for cows and chickens—and get down to business.

Norma and the girls were sleeping late. They usually did,

on top of which, he never liked them on the grounds till two or three; they just got in the way. Or into trouble.

The parking lots along State 60 were enormous. If you counted the roped-off pastureland beyond them for the overflow, the place could take God knows how many cars. There were a lot of them already, early birds, when Talker zipped by, heading for the entrance gates. He had a Drive-On pass, a yellow card propped on the dashboard, and he flashed it to the cop on duty—and a smile; it never hurt to flash a smile as he drove on by.

The road was clogged up with delivery trucks; you name it, ice cream, doughnuts, franks and burgers, homemade fudge from factories, garbage food, all stuff he loved. Out on the field beside the stands, a lot of guys were tuning up their motors for the Tractor Pull at ten.

He pulled up near the Cattle Shed, though why they always called them sheds eluded him. This one was like a long, low, narrow Crystal Palace, freshly whitewashed, gleaming in the early sun. Some animals, both cows and bulls, stood quietly outside while farm kids groomed them, shining up their coats with metal combs and heavy brushes. Show animals were handsome, and he often thought they knew it. Body language, like the way they held their heads.

A boy and girl—she looked about fourteen—rode in on bikes. They stopped, got off. She had an air about her, something nice. She made him smile. "Hi," he said.

Though Betsy had been brought up not to talk to strangers, it was that kind of morning. "Hi," she answered, grabbed her bike, and hurried after Denny.

Talker moved into the shed. More grooming, smells and noises, farmers everywhere. He didn't envy them their lives, but it felt good to watch. He stayed until he had enough.

Marcie wakened with a jolt. Her head felt muzzy, and the clock said nine-fifteen. She stared at it. It couldn't be, she never overslept, and why her mother chose this morning not to call at seven . . .

She threw back the quilt, no time to shower, but she'd had one last night, cooling off from Betsy. So she threw some water on her face, combed out her hair, put on some makeup—there was always time for that—and headed for the

104 James Goldman

closets. What to wear? She had a date for lunch with Dee, that meant the Club. White slacks and sandals and a silk blouse. Blue? Why not?

She went racing down the stairs, grabbed Mrs. Beebe's sacred list, ran to the car and pointed it toward Peterson's. She could have phoned the order in, but these days who delivered?

She went up and down the aisles like a tornado, list in hand. If Mrs. Beebe named a brand, that's what she got. But when she didn't—if it just said starch or flour—Marcie knew the brands the old bag hated. She had ways of keeping score.

Back home, she dumped the goodies on the kitchen table; it took three trips back and forth from the car. Then it was die or have some coffee, so she made it, drank it down too quickly, burned her tongue. No question, it was not her day. She felt a craving for a cigarette—whatever made her give them up?—and by the time she reached the shop, it was eleven.

She parked in the lot, went through the back door, moved directly to the desk, and sat. She'd had a hard night, filled with dreams of running, missing trains and having phones stop ringing just before she picked them up. There was no earthly reason, none, for all of this anxiety.

She could hear Pam's voice faintly, up front, talking with some customer. No hurry, Pam could handle it. She needed time to pull herself together.

"Marcie?"

Maybe if she didn't answer, just kept mum. She pressed her lips together, closed her eyes.

"I could have sworn I heard the back door—there you are."

She forced her eyes to open. Pam was in the doorway, smiling. "Can I have you for a minute?"

"Now?"

"I'm with a gentleman who has a question."

"Is it hard?" She grinned, got up and headed for the doorway, when she heard the man speak.

"It's O.K.," he said. "Don't bother."

Marcie knew the voice. She'd heard it somewhere. Then she placed it. Paul McBride. One hand went out and clutched the door frame. She was not aware of it. A hard thing, like a fist, was pounding in her chest. It was ridiculous. A firm voice in her head said, 'Stop it.' So she did. She started forward, she was moving; and her voice, when it came out, was absolutely normal. "Yes? How can I help you?"

Talker all but jumped. What was she doing here?

She gave him high marks. That was Class A Number One surprise. He should have been an actor. He had tracked her down, that's what he'd done. Found out her name and what she did and where the shop was. He was looking for her, hoping that she'd be here.

"Oh." She stopped and smiled. "Mr. McBride. What brings you in?"

"It's this," he said.

The miniature brass bed, of all things. As if the man were interested in things antique. "Yes?"

"It's a present. Can you tell me anything about it?"

"Not a lot." She was amazed how easily the words came. She had picked it up for nothing, at a tag sale on a drive through Plains. "It's nineteenth century, mid- to late. It's made by hand, not from a mold. It's country work. Look here." She took it from his hand, brushing his fingers without meaning to, and turned it over. "See the joints? I'd say some local craftsman turned it out."

He had to hand it to her. She was cool. Just yesterday, he'd seen the interest in her eyes. Nothing showed just now, but it was there. "That's nice to know," he said. "And it's a hundred dollars?" It was crazy, spending that on Annie.

"Yes, but I suppose . . ." She paused. "It's not a rare piece, I can take off ten percent. It's yours for ninety." Let him wriggle out of it.

"The hundred's fine. I wasn't bargaining." He looked her in the eye and added, "Things are worth what things are worth."

She watched him, flummoxed, as he came up with a roll of bills and peeled two fifties off the top. He pressed them in her hand.

Her voice dried up. "You want it wrapped?"

"No, thanks." He grinned. "I'll eat it here."

"I'll give you a receipt."

She sat down at a little table, took a pad and pencil, started writing. Talker watched her. She was more than tempting, she was what he wanted, and he knew that he could have her. Knew it like his own name. He undressed her as she wrote, then blinked her clothes back on. He wasn't going near it.

She held out the receipt. He took it. "Thank you, M'am."

"Thank you, Mr. McBride."

He went without a backward glance. She watched him go. Her ears were ringing. She'd be seeing him again.

Pam couldn't wait. "You know him, Marcie? Where'd you meet him?"

"At the Fair." She shrugged. "I checked him in. I've got to make a call." She turned and headed for the office.

Talker settled on the front seat, stuck the brass bed in the glove compartment. Annie better fall down dead. He still had the receipt. What did he need it for? He opened it and took a look. Beneath the shop's name, street address, and phone, it read: "The Fallsburg Road outside the city limits. One o'clock. Be there. I'll find you."

Talker had to laugh. She'd spend a long time looking for him.

Dee picked up her phone. "Hello?"

"Dee?"

"Marcie?"

"Listen, something's come up and I've got to cancel lunch. O.K.?"

"O.K. What's come up?"

"Tell you later."

Marcie lowered the receiver. Would she tell or wouldn't she?

Annie had been sitting in the tall grass, gazing at the lake for hours. She'd had very little sleep; the dreams kept getting in the way. The worst was Skipper on that night in Beaver Falls when Annie had watched her through the curtain. And the faces of the men. Then, in the dream, it wasn't always Skipper; sometimes it was her. They kept on changing places as the men leaned closer.

It was awful. That was 4:00 A.M., and it was almost noon now and she couldn't shake the dream. Wide awake, the real world all around her, people fishing in the sunshine, it was just as awful.

There was no one she could talk to. Not the girls, who were still sleeping anyway. Or Norma, who was up and moving, having coffee by her cabin. As for Talker, even if he was around, he'd just be disappointed in her.

"Hi."

Annie turned. She saw a pretty girl about her age in jeans and work shirt carrying a mop and bucket. "Hi."

"I'm Lucy Lovell. My dad owns this place."

She made it sound important. Annie shrugged. "No kidding."

Lucy moved close, filled with curiosity. She had been bolted in her bedroom since her father dragged her home from jail on Sunday morning. He had cursed her, threatened her with purgatory, whipped her bottom with his belt, and locked the door. He came up twice a day, at least he fed her, but he hadn't said a word until this morning, when he handed her the mop and pail and told her to get the hell to work.

For two whole days, the only thing that kept her going was her bedroom window. Through it, she could see the cabins, see the girls—at night the ones in Kwitchergrowlin didn't pull their curtains. Lucy thought they might be hookers.

"Are you up here for camping?" Lucy asked.

"Nope."

"Fishing?"

"Nope."

"I guess you're just here on vacation."

"Not exactly."

"Well, aren't you the mystery girl."

"I strip." Annie said it to get rid of her.

"You do? You wouldn't pull my leg now?"

"I'm a stripper."

Lucy's eyes were bright with fascination. "What's it like?"

"Oh, nothing special. You just take your clothes off, that's all. You get used to it."

"Get used to it?"

"It takes a while. My first few times, sure, I was nervous. After that, it's just a job."

It felt terrific, talking like that. Lucy swallowed every word. Annie felt the bad dreams fading out. Five minutes more, and they were gone.

Talker checked his watch—twelve-thirty—looked down at the pie and coffee. Why in God's name had he ordered it? He got up, left a dollar by his plate—he'd liked the waitress—paid his check and left the diner.

It had been a struggle. These last ninety minutes, he'd swung back and forth a dozen times. Why not go out and meet her? What could happen? Chances were, she wouldn't show. It was a small town, anyone might see them, it was risky; think of all she had to lose. And if she did come, what he'd get was talk. That's what you got from ladies, earnest talk, hysterics, tears. It wasn't worth it. Nothing in the world was worth a beating like the one in New Hampshire. There was still a scar on his left shoulder from the pipes.

He got into the car and headed for the Fair.

Marcie had no memory of driving home. She told Pam she was off to lunch with Dee, went out the back, and here she was with Mrs. Beebe in the front hall.

"You're home early."

Damn; the woman promised to be late, and there she stood. "I've got some time to kill, I felt like working in the garden." Marcie smiled—quick thinking, that—and started up the stairs.

"You brought me Brillo. I use S.O.S."

"Oh, Mrs. Beebe, I'm so sorry."

Marcie showered quickly, brushed her teeth—she had forgotten in the morning rush—dried off, and powdered. No perfume. She wanted to feel natural. Then the mirror, just to check. She lingered longer than she meant to, looking at herself. For just a moment, she was back at Denison: the girl, the trucker, how he threw her in the cab. It was insane, what she was doing.

Panties first, then jeans; they fit like skin, she had to wrestle into them. No bra today. A navy T-shirt, sandals, and before she knew it, she was down the stairs and crossing the backyard. She knew that Mrs. Beebe would be watching, so she popped into the toolshed, found some pruning shears, and headed toward the back. Once there, she slipped behind the shrubbery, found the gate, undid the combination lock— her fingers trembled, it took time—and then stepped out into the field.

The stalks of corn, all yellow-brown and sere, stood soldier-straight above her head. She turned and started slowly through them toward the Fallsburg Road.

*   *   *

The shoulders here were broad and sandy. He pulled off the road, well off it, killed the motor, pocketed the keys, got out. The CITY LIMITS sign was legible from where he stood, a quarter-mile back or so.

He looked around. The road was lined with cornfields, both sides. It was one hell of a trysting place. The lady was crazy. So was he. He'd had the Fairgrounds in his sights before he turned the car around.

A little after one, but nothing ran on time these days. The road was fairly busy, people driving in to see the Fair. He figured she'd be driving out, he knew the car she drove. No sign of it. He hung somewhere between relief and disappointment. It was better if she didn't come. Anticipation was the best part, mental foreplay. He'd be free to dream, play mind games, fool around with images.

He nodded. All he had to do was take off—and he would have if he hadn't heard a whistle. Low and soft, behind him, from the cornfield. Talker turned. It wasn't easy spotting her. She stood, half-veiled by rows of corn. Not stupid; she was being careful. No way could it be the first time she had pulled a stunt like this.

He took his time, moved off the shoulder, down the little hill into the corn. He didn't speak or make a move. She dealt the cards, it was her hand to play. She looked at him, then turned and started moving through the stalks. He followed her. The sun was hot, and there were insects buzzing.

Marcie felt collected, cool, as if she knew what she was doing. Somewhere up ahead, if she remembered rightly—and she did—there was a space between the corn rows, like an alleyway that held a little melon patch surrounded by a bed of high, soft weeds.

He liked her in the jeans and T-shirt. He had seen her "lady" side, and it was real enough; but he knew there was more to her, a lot more—and he was about to get it. Time— the great thing was to take your time.

She stopped beside the melon patch and turned to him. She'd gotten this far, God alone knew how. She wondered what he'd do now: kiss her hand or jump her like some wild rabbit.

"Well . . ." He let it trail off. "Here we are."

She nodded.

"Funny thing." He grinned. "You know, I came that close to pitching the receipt. Life hangs by little threads, they say."

Another nod. She couldn't stand there like a dummy, not indefinitely. She had brought him here, she damn well knew the reason why, and she was acting like a virgin on her first date.

"Tell me something?"

Marcie almost nodded. Yet again. "Sure."

"What's your name?"

"You didn't read it on the sales slip?"

"I had better things to read."

"It's Marcie."

"Marcie. Short for what?"

No one had called her Marcia Jane since second grade; she'd seen to that. "I hate my name."

"I know the feeling. People call me Talker. I prefer it to McBride." He sat down on the grass beside the melons, squinted up at her. "I'm in no hurry, Marcie, but at some point we have got to face what all this is in aid of."

She was about to thank God that he'd brought it up when suddenly her knees felt weak, her throat went dry. She sat down on the grass beside him, more abruptly than she meant to.

Talker knew her problem cold. She was a princess with a secret itch. There was a lot of princess in this girl, and he had ways of cutting through that, but he wasn't going to use them. He leaned back, away from her.

"It all comes down to this," he said. "What do you want?"

She had to force the words out. "I don't know."

She meant it and she didn't. Talker knew that.

"Would you like me to get up and go? I don't mind, it's completely up to you."

She felt like crying, sighing, dying. God, what was she doing, making up rhymes like the lunatics? "Don't go."

"O.K. You want to sit and talk? I'm good at that, I do it for a living." He reached out and plucked a melon, took a jackknife from his pocket, cut a slice. He'd never understand how melons could lie in the sun all day and be so cool inside. "You want to talk about the weather?"

"I suppose you think that's funny."

"Nope. You want a slice?" He offered one.

That did it. Words came pouring out. "Look, Mr. Talker,

have yourself a good laugh, go tell the boys about it. How I got you out here and I couldn't do it. It was crazy, I was crazy, I don't know what I was thinking and I never fool around."

"Not ever?"

"Not one God damn time."

"You knew about this place."

·"I live just over there." She pointed toward her house. "Don't you believe me? You think I go after every jerk who comes through town?"

"No, I don't think that for a minute."

"I'm a decent, honest, married woman, and I've never been unfaithful."

Talker had her now. He grinned. "Not getting much at home, I guess."

"You rotten bastard. What a filthy thing to say."

"Come on, it happens in the best of families. No one's going to blame you if your man can't get it up."

Her face went white, her body shook. "You scum."

"I'm talking to you like a doctor. Take your best friend's husband, get a little on the side. Believe me—"

She pitched forward, threw herself right at him, clawing at his shirt and biting, anyplace, his hand, his neck, she didn't care. He grabbed her head and found her lips. Her mouth came open. He was home.

She didn't know what she was doing. They were rolling, she was tearing at his clothes. She heard strange noises; they were coming out of her. She had to have him. Somehow, she was naked. So was he.

She started coming when he entered and she didn't stop until he came.

10

IT HAD BEEN slow for an opening day; not that people hadn't
come to look around and pepper them with questions. But
there hadn't been one sale so far, and it was after three now.
Ed was outside on the platform, talking up a storm and slap-
ping backs. For all the good it did.

Van put down the phone, glanced at Betsy, shook his
head. "No luck so far."

"It's not important, Dad. Forget it."

"One more try."

She watched him dial. For once, why couldn't he say yes
or no, make a decision on his own? She loved him so much,
and she knew he could where business went. But when it came
to Mom . . .

"Hello?" He glanced up at her, nodded. Then, into the
phone: "What are you doing home?"

"I live here," Marcie told him.

"All I meant was, I've been hunting for you everywhere. I
tried the shop, Pam told me you were at the Club with Dee. I
called the Club, they couldn't find you, so I—"

"Come on, Van, what are you, a detective agency?"

"I only wondered . . ."

"For the record, lunch with Dee got cut short, I spilled
coffee on my blouse, came home to change." The lies came

out so naturally. It never crossed her mind that this was only the beginning. "So what is it?"

"Well, I'm here with Betsy."

"Oh? Is she all right."

"She's fine. She only wants to know—she ran into some boys and wants permission to go driving with them."

"Older boys, I take it."

"Sure, I guess." If they could drive, they'd have to be. He caught the tone in Marcie's voice, and he felt torn about it, too. His little girl was growing up. But all girls did, it had to happen, and besides, he trusted her.

"Who are these boys?"

"I'll ask." He did.

"For Pete's sake, Dad; they're seniors, they're from Fulton High. What does she think? I'm not a child."

"Take it easy." Then, to Marcie: "High-school kids."

"Where's Denny?"

"At the dentist. He'll be back at five, and so will Bets. Look, all she wants—"

"Well, I don't like it." Puppy love with Denny was enough to fret about; but boys of eighteen screwed around, as well she knew. "No, not one bit."

"She's not a child."

"I'll be the judge of that. We're having drinks with Dee at Longview. Six o'clock."

The line went dead.

"I'm sorry, kid," he told her; and he was. "No luck." He stood. "Give us a hug."

She could have kicked him, but she gave him one.

"See you at dinner?"

Betsy had her own ideas of Longview. They fell somewhat short of Chinese water torture, but not much. "I'm having junk food here with Denny, but we'll join you for the show." Loretta Lynn was playing in the stands tonight; and Betsy, who looked down her nose at country music when in public, loved the way she sang. So sad. It always made her cry.

She looked back at her father from the doorway. "Keep a secret, Dad?"

He nodded.

"You're the best."

She grinned and waved as she went out.

*   *   *

Talker was running late. Three-thirty, they were opening at four, the Midway roads were jammed with people, no way through. The T-bird crawled along.

He'd really lost it in the cornfield; lost himself, all track of time. They took a while to recover, had a smoke, a little talk. Then Marcie started fooling with the melons and the whole thing damn near started over when he caught sight of his watch.

He'd jumped up. "Holy shit," he said, and started scrambling for his clothes.

"What's wrong?"

"I'm late for work." His shoes and socks were hell to find; those weeds were deep. He got them on and turned to go. He almost left without a word, that's how churned up he was.

"Look, Marcie."

"Yes?"

He could have said a lot of things: I loved it, you were wonderful. Or made a move, like kissing her. Instead, he stood there like a jerk and said, "Will we be doing this again?" Instead of telling her, he asked.

She looked at him for a long time. Not from hesitation, there were no doubts in her mind. She found it difficult to speak, that was all. She nodded, whispered, "Yes."

He nodded right back. "Good." He didn't even think to ask the vital question. She did.

"When?"

By that time, he was starting through the cornstalks. "You know where to find me."

"So do you," he heard her say.

The crowd around the Bingo tent was really thick. He inched through, past the pizza stand, the ice-cream truck, the Whiz-Bang Midget Kar-Ride, gunned the motor, pulled onto the grass beside the bally stage and leaped out, then reached in for the brass bed. He felt odd about it now, uncomfortable. No reason why—he still wanted Annie to have it.

He expected chaos in the van; girls frantic, half-dressed, where was this, and that was broken. Questions, too. Like, "Jesus, Talker, where've you been?" He had an answer. Or: "What happened to your shirt, it's ripped to bits." He had an answer for that, too.

They scarcely noticed when he walked in. Annie looked

up from her sewing, grinned at him, went back to work. He thought she'd be hysterical. Pauline was dressed and ready, sitting eyes glued to the tube. The other girls were putting on their makeup, like the pros they sometimes were, and Norma sat with her beloved cash box, counting change.

You never knew with women. He went to the fridge, took out a beer. Thank God for something cold. The fans were on, the air was moving. It was like an oven, and his clothes were sticking to him, so he opened up his locker, changed to something fresh.

Five of. Just time to check the tent. It looked shipshape. The two cops Weller promised were on duty at the rear. "You boys O.K.?" They nodded. "Hot enough for you?" They grinned.

He went back through the curtain to the van. He usually gave a pep talk. "O.K., ladies, this is it. We're off and running. It's a big week; any luck, we'll all be rich. So let's show Fulton what we're made of." Then he grinned. "Not all of it. Remember that."

He took his hand mike, walked out on the bally stage and stopped dead. There were people lined up at the entrance booth. Already. Thirty of them, maybe more. And out in front, a crowd was gathering. He had a big sign posted: FIRST SHOW—4:00 P.M. Apparently, unlike a lot of towns he knew, the folks here could read.

"Hello, hello to one and all; and welcome to the Moulin Rouge. That means 'Red Mill' in French. There's nothing red here, but we've got some things for you that do go round and round."

The music started, right on cue, and Laurel moved out in her golden gown. A gasp went up, the crowd grew larger. Laurel, following instructions, didn't do a lot but stand there. In that dress, she didn't have to.

When his spiel was done, the crowd went surging toward the ticket booth. He moved to Norma.

"Will you look at this?" she said.

He nodded. Generally, the afternoons were slim. Around six, when the sun got low, things started picking up, but it was only after dark that business hummed. Not so in Fulton, evidently. Talker took the line in, made a guesstimate. The tent could take in 200 comfortably, 250 in a pinch. They wouldn't hit 200, but they wouldn't miss it by a lot.

His farm boys, all spiffed up today, moved to the booth. He grinned at them. "For you, it's free. Go on in and enjoy yourselves."

He knew that Annie went on third. He found her at a makeup table, costume on, hairbrush in hand. The harem costume looked like it was made for her. It had an open midriff and the pants were set just low enough, but not too low. Laurel was on now; music flowed in from the tent.

She saw him looking at her in the mirror.

"How's it look? Am I O.K.?"

She seemed so natural and relaxed. "You did a good job. You look great."

She smiled. "Thanks." She thought so, too. She'd practiced moving in it, and she liked the things it did for her.

"How are you, Annie?"

He was closer now. She turned and looked up. "Fine. I really am." She couldn't understand it. After all those dreams, where were the jitters and sweats? She wasn't outside barfing, she was in her makeup, cool as soda pop.

"You're on next."

"Yes, I know."

"It can be tough the first time."

"You don't have to tell me." He was worried for her. It was something; he could be the sweetest man.

"Anyway, the thing is . . ." Talker brought the bed out, held it in his hand. "I bought you something. Just for luck."

Her eyes went wide, filled instantly with tears. "Oh God, oh my God, Jesus God, you didn't have to."

"Take it."

Annie started shaking, she could scarcely hold it. It was perfect, it was beautiful, it was, beyond all things she'd ever had, most precious. Talker cared, he cared for her. Enough to love her? Did he, could he, would he ever?

On her feet, she flung her arms around him, held him hard and close as she knew how. She stood on tiptoe, pressed her face against his neck to kiss him. It was then she caught the scent. You couldn't miss it. Woman. He'd been with a woman. When? Just now, the scent was strong. What woman? Who and where and why?

She stepped away from him. Applause came from the tent.

"You're on," he said.

She didn't move.

He'd known it to happen. "Annie. Pull yourself together."

Nothing happened. She just stood there, looking through him. It was not a thing he liked to do, but it had never failed to work. He slapped her face.

She turned away and moved out through the curtain.

Dee was one martini up; or down, depending on one's *Weltanschauung;* she loved the word, it was the only thing she'd kept from three years married to a writer. She sat by a window in the Paddlewheel, where anyone who wanted to could stare at her. It was her first appearance at the Club since coming home, and, like Tandelayo in *White Cargo*—Dee had played her once—she was the subject of a lot of local curiosity.

She signaled to the waiter. Twenty: what a time of life. So sweet. Like lollipops. She looked up, met his gaze. The thought, apparently, was mutual. "I'll have another, please," she said.

"Right. You're the Bombay lady. Rocks and lemon twist."

She nodded, watched him move off. All she had to do was lift a finger, which she never did, not anymore. She let her gaze drift out the window, at the golfers as they shuffled through the heat. She'd had a nice day—any day when Eleanor was missing had a lot to recommend it—and she'd lolled around the house, not getting dressed till cocktail time.

Dee gave her mother credit—some, at least. The woman led a busy life. Lacking all sense of inner charity, she gave her time to every charity in town. There weren't a lot of them. A place like Fulton lacked for little. But God, out of His loving-kindness for her mother, had created a sufficiency of souls in need: the lame and halt, deaf, dumb, and blind. It kept her mother on the move.

"Dee?"

"Marcie."

"Am I late?" She knew she was.

Dee smiled. "You're here, that's all I care about. What are you drinking?"

"One of those," she answered, as Dee's drink arrived.

"Take mine. You look like you could use it."

"Oh? I do?" She'd dressed and put her makeup on so carefully: silk slacks, a long-sleeved, high-necked blouse. The waiter left to fetch another. Marcie shrugged. "I'm not surprised. I've had a crazy day, and I'm so sorry, breaking lunch."

"Don't be." Dee paused. "So tell me, what came up?"

"Well . . ." She launched into the same line she had fed to Pam. About some ancient bachelor who lived in a big, ramshackle country house out on the road to Oberlin. The place was jam-packed with antiques, some of them eighteenth century, and she hoped to get the man to part with them. It might take days, so if she failed to show up at the shop, that's where she'd be. But if Pam minded . . .

As she spun it out, her mind kept going to the cornfield. The two of them had lain there, side by side, exhausted, in the sunshine. They were drenched in perspiration, soaking wet. Wee rivulets of sweat ran down between her breasts; they tickled and she thought of brushing them away, but it was still too soon to move. She drifted.

Later, she heard Talker moving. He was sitting, lighting a cigarette.

"You want one?"

Marcie hesitated. It had been a struggle, going off them. On the other hand, why not? She was already on the road to ruin—one of Mother's favorite phrases—and the ride thus far had been incredible. She lit up and inhaled. It made her cough at first.

They smoked in silence. Then the talk began. No mention of what had just happened, not a word. He asked her idle, easy questions. Did she go to movies, was she good at sports, what were her favorite things to eat? Inconsequential, all of it, but very sensitive of him, she thought. Addressing what was going on or what might happen next, if anything—these things were burning coals, still far too hot to touch.

Then he had picked the melon up and cut thick slices for them both. It was delicious, cool and moist. She tried not looking at his body, really tried; but his eyes kept on ranging over hers. She knew they were, she felt it.

There was nothing in his looks that could account for what he did to her. He wasn't muscular or handsome; it was like the old song "Just My Bill." The things he said were interesting and funny. She relaxed; he made her laugh.

Then, on an impulse she could not explain, she took her slice of melon and began to rub its cool flesh over hers. Across her tummy, then her breasts. She saw things flicker in his eyes.

She felt it, too. They would have started up again, she felt it coming over her—and then he caught sight of his watch.

She'd had to creep back to the house, avoiding Mrs. Beebe; God forbid. Once safely in her bathroom, she had locked the door, then taken a quick look at herself. Her T-shirt was all ripped to shreds, and there were grass stains, dark ones, on her jeans. She'd have to throw the clothes away, some distant garbage can, just like a criminal disposing of the evidence. It made her smile.

She stripped and took another look. Good God. Never mind the grass stains on her knees and elbows or the streaks of dust and mud. One good scrub, they'd be gone. But what about the bruises, black-and-blue marks? Thumb and finger-prints, the things were visible already, wherever she looked. She felt a momentary thrill, then panic: how the hell could she explain them? No way. It meant slacks and long-sleeved blouses, and no swimming for a while. As for Van? She'd have to wear a nightshirt, which would call for some explaining, but she'd find a reason.

So she filled the tub, stepped in, leaned back . . .

"And that's what came up?" Dee said.

Marcie nodded. Pam had swallowed it.

Dee kept a straight face. "Business first, I always say."

"I hoped you'd understand."

"Of course I do. That's what old friends are for. What really happened?"

Marcie straightened. "Come again?"

Dee had to grin. "It's me you're talking to."

"I swear, Dee, I don't know what makes you think—"

"I'll tell you. One, I had a hunch the moment you sat down; I caught it in your eyes. And two." Dee reached out, touched the bruise on Marcie's forearm where her sleeve had slipped back. "Either that old bachelor is a grabber, or you've—"

"I give up." Marcie faced the truth. She'd wanted to con-fide in Dee from the beginning. Dee alone would understand. She wouldn't find it sordid.

"Listen," Marcie said, and spotted Van across the room. She squeezed Dee's hand and whispered, "Later."

11

THERE WERE NO private boxes in the grandstand, only count-less rows of well-worn bleacher seats. But for the Steubens, Reddings, Brinkers, Oberlanders, Clarkes, and other spines of the community, it was no different from the pews in Church. Each family had its place, sat where it always sat, and all the ushers knew it. Sometimes they had problems keeping all the front rows clear of interlopers. Even roping off the section didn't always do the trick.

Tonight, thus far, was trouble free, and as he moved the ropes, the usher had a smile for Marcie, Van, and Dee. They were the first to come. Van smiled back, then watched the girls move in and take their places. He'd been watching them all evening long. They'd sat through dinner like two kids in high school, little nudges, secret looks. And for the whole walk through the parking lot, they'd lagged behind him, heads to-gether. All he heard was muffled whispering and giggles.

Though he struggled hard against the thought, he felt the laughter was at him. All his life—he'd walk into a crowded room or he'd be standing in a shop—whenever someone laughed, he'd feel he was the butt of it. He'd tell himself it wasn't logical, it made no sense, but it still bothered him a lot. He'd even talked to Sandy Stone about it once. A touch of paranoia was the answer that he got; no one was altogether free of it. Sandy should know, he was an analyst. Van had no intellectual objection to the answer. It just didn't help him much.

Van wondered, more and more as time passed, why in hell he didn't have a better time of it. He was a good provider, worked hard, paid his dues. He tried to be as patient, generous, and kind as he knew how. He never stepped on other people, never argued or offended, and what did he get for it? What was the payoff?

"Stop it." Had he said it in his mind or spoken it out loud? Sometimes, these days, he wasn't sure. He moved in, sat beside his girls. They smiled at him.

Dee, to tell the truth, was stunned by Marcie's story. Not by what she'd done, but by the fact that she had done it. Marcie, of all people. Never once, in all these years, had Marcie shown her any sign of what was stirring deep inside her. Time wrought changes; maybe it was something new. For certain, it was there.

Dee knew these feelings all too well. She let it drop. At least the evening would be free of Eleanor. She'd called in at the Club, proclaiming that she had a headache. Dee believed her; too much fucking charity'll get you every time. She looked around. The stands were filling up, and Ed and Harriet were coming down the aisle.

Ed was in a great mood. He was looking at a sellout crowd. He'd had to fight to get Loretta Lynn. There was a Dolly Parton faction on the Board, a big one, but Ed got his way. It wasn't easy, but it rarely mattered to him how his victories were achieved. He drew some lines—he never stole, and if he stabbed you, it was always from the front—but winning was what counted.

At times like this, he even could enjoy what Harriet was saying, and he added little interjections as she took him through the triumphs of her day. The crowds at the Pavilion and the jam and jelly prizes; Mrs. Kemble won for lingonberry marmalade, as well she should have.

Bets and Denny were the last to come. Still eating. Marcie watched them; where in heaven did they put it? As they squeezed by, Marcie took her daughter's hand.

"Yes, Mom?"

"About those boys this afternoon . . ."

"I understand."

"It's for your own good."

"I know that."

"Sometimes I worry, I can't help it."

Betsy nodded. "Sure you do."

Bright spotlights hit the stage. The backup band came out and started doodling, tuning up. A hush fell. Then Miss Lynn appeared. Eight thousand heads turned, sixteen thousand hands began to clap.

Bets snuggled close to Denny, took his hand. Miss Lynn began to sing, and Betsy smiled, waiting for the tears to come.

Talker was in deep shit, and he didn't like the feeling. Annie hadn't spoken to him once, all evening long. The crowds had been terrific; they were more than ready, and a line or two was all it took to whip them up. Tonight, he figured they were drawing in at least 225 a show. Two bucks a head, three shows an hour, it was just eleven now. That came to $21 \times 225 \times 2$.

To hell with it, the numbers didn't cheer him up. He went inside the van to talk to Annie. She was sitting at a makeup table, looking at her face.

She saw him coming. What to say? She felt like she'd lived through a lifetime in a single day. Not old or wise. Just through it.

Out on stage the first time, she'd been blind. The tears, the lights, her face burned where he'd slapped her and she couldn't see the stage floor, let alone how far it went. She didn't want to fall off, so she stood while the music started.

There were people in the tent, a lot of them; she knew that, she could hear. She'd had no time to practice, but she had a sort of dance in mind. Choosing that harem costume was no accident. She'd danced in *The King and I* in high school, she remembered what the moves were like; the way her arms and fingers went in little airy gestures. Delicate. And how the teacher made her keep her back arched and her head held high and still.

She started moving, concentrating hard, no time to think of Talker. Then her vision cleared and she could see the faces out front. They were younger than the old goats she had glimpsed in Beaver Falls, less awful-looking. And so far as she could tell, no one was jacking off. A lot of them had hands in pockets, that was natural, men were always sticking hands in pockets; but those glassy eyes they got when meat was being beaten—that she couldn't see.

She moved a bit more freely, then she even risked a smile. Men smiled back. Imagine that. She had three minutes to get through before the record ended. Could she make it? Suddenly, the music stopped, and people started clapping. It was over. Off she ran.

Since then, she'd done it twenty times. Each time felt different, easier, a little better. She was learning. If you moved your hips like this or that, the men out front reacted. Or she'd move a hand across her midriff, toss her head a little. Every time, there was a difference in their faces or the way they stood. She even thought their breathing changed.

Annie liked the feeling. It was new to her, and hours went by before she named it. Power. It was power that she felt. Like in the movies, big shots at a conference table and the star would make a move—he'd yawn or take a note or scratch himself—and all the other guys reacted. They were scared of power or they envied it or wanted some. That's what the star had. Annie had it, too.

It was a dizzying experience. She'd spent her whole life saying yes to Aunt Maria and Uncle Emil, terrified of their displeasure. Anytime they wanted, they could throw her out. And if she belted Jan or Ignace now and then, it didn't come from strength so much as desperation.

As for the applause, she loved it. No one had ever clapped his hands for her alone before. They liked her, liked her dancing, and the only thing that killed the day was Talker and his Woman.

That was hard. It took her hours to get hold of it. He did care; otherwise no brass bed—and she would keep it till the day she died. The fault was hers. She was the dumb one, having daydreams that could never happen. Talker had his own life. Hell, for all she knew, he had a wife and kids or he'd been living with a woman, keeping her for years. What claim did she have on him? Zero. None at all.

"Hi, Annie. How's it going?"

"Pretty good." The man looked like a puppy with its tail between its legs. A lot of girls would let him stay that way a while, and she was tempted. She just couldn't do it, that was all.

She stood up, hugged him, kissed his cheek. "I love my present, and you're not so bad yourself," she told him. Then she turned away. "I'm on," she said.

Ed liked the Harem Girl. She couldn't dance for beans, she'd starve to death in Vegas, but there was something—Harriet would say an air—she had an air about her that got to him. Not to mention she was young. The young ones always reached him. Back when he was thirty, forty, fifty, girls of eighteen made him crazy. They still did. It wasn't cradle-snatching, nothing like it. Down deep where it mattered, Ed was twenty-three forever.

All the other girls looked nice enough; firm thighs, good tits—at least what you could see of them. But they weren't fresh, they'd been around, he found them shopworn, secondhand. He figured fifty dollars tops and you could have your pick. But not the Harem Girl.

He turned to Van, gave him a nudge. "What do you think?"

Van nearly answered, 'What about?' "She's nice," he said, and wondered how he'd let himself get dragged here.

"Only nice? What's wrong with you? Where are your gonads, boy? The kid's terrific."

"Not my type, but I can see what gets you, Ed." Van nudged him back. "She's got a pretty pair of boobs."

"And then some." Van was O.K., decent as the day was long, but did he have to be the biggest stiff in town? Ed turned and gave his full attention to the stage.

Word of the Moulin Rouge had taken very little time to reach him. It was after five, Van had just left, the evening shift was late, and he was manning the exhibit all alone. When Zack and Phil appeared, he was about to ream them out when they confessed what held them up. Ed really ought to see the show, there was some good stuff on display.

Ed hadn't seen a girlie show in years, and by the time he picked up Harriet at the Pavilion, he was going. Come what may. The only trick was slipping off without the ladies. It turned out to be no trick at all. For once the grandstand show was over, Harriet went home to bed, Bets and Denny wandered off, and Dee and Marcie went for ice cream and a gossip. So he grabbed Van by the arm and went.

The Harem Girl was finished, to be followed by a tootsie

in a sailor cap and middy blouse and not much else. This one could move, she knew her way around. Ed wished the girls would take it all off, let him have a good look, but the Fair Rules didn't stand for that. He knew; he'd helped to write them.

On the way out, he was thinking, maybe Mansfield. Fulton didn't have a cat house, all the good ones were in Akron, but when you got desperate, Mansfield was the nearest place. It was a long drive there and back; he didn't want to go alone. He turned to Van.

"You want to go get laid?"

Van stopped dead. "What?"

"I thought we might drive down to Mansfield."

"Are you crazy?"

"Hell, I know it's late, but we'll be home by three."

Van stared at him. He knew Ed did this kind of thing. Not straight from Ed—this was a first—but people gossiped. "Come on, Dad, it's me you're talking to."

If there'd been anybody else—but Van was it tonight. "Come on, son, it'll do you good."

"I've got to tell you—" Van broke off, then gave it to him straight. "For godsake, Ed, I'm married to your daughter."

"So?"

The man said, "So?" Van heard him say it. "Jesus, Ed—"

"You have a problem?"

"Don't you?" Marriage vows meant something. ". . . and cleave only unto her." Some things in life were sacred. Not that they were great in number, but . . .

Ed bit the bullet. They'd never had a man-to-man. It looked as if it was now or never. "Listen, Van, don't get me wrong. I love my wife, I'm faithful. I would no more—"

"Faithful? You just asked me to a cat house."

"Listen. Girls like Marcie, and the same thing goes for Harriet, they're brought up in a certain way. You understand me?"

"Not exactly."

"They know men have needs. It's only that—here's how I see it. Having an affair and getting serious about some woman, that's a sin. I've never done it, and I never will. But now and then, a fellow has to have his ashes hauled. It's only natural. So what's the answer? Whores."

Van looked at him with disbelief. "I don't care how you see it, Ed. That's cheating."

"You're not thinking. Who gets cheated? Not the girl, I pay her price. Not me, and that's for sure. And Harriet? She can't be hurt by what she doesn't know."

"You really mean it."

"Listen, I've seen marriages go on the rocks because the man denies himself. That's no good. Things build up inside. Take me. I'm married forty years. We're happy. Last thing on this earth I'd do is get you to betray my daughter. You'll feel better. So will she." He couldn't make it any clearer. "So—you want to have a go at it?"

"Some other time."

"You mean like never?"

"Dad, I'm sorry, but I can't."

Ed shrugged. "O.K. You think about what I've been saying. When it makes sense, let me know."

They walked together to the parking lot and said good night.

Ed couldn't shake it. All the way home, he kept seeing girls in various positions. Even when he got upstairs and looked at Harriet, the feelings wouldn't go away.

He found her sitting up in bed preparing for tomorrow, sheets of paper spread all over, making notes.

"Still up?"

"You're late."

"I had some drinks with Van. You work too hard."

She smiled. "It's my pleasure."

Ed began undressing while she cleared her notes away. He'd always liked her looks. At twenty, she was slim and pale and elegant. No beauty; handsome—and she still was. Harriet was God damn handsome; that was that. He glanced down at his shorts. Old Jolly Roger stood at half-mast, neither up nor down. He wondered which way it would go.

"Harriet?"

"What is it, dear?"

He turned to face her.

"Oh," she said. "I see." Invisibly, she made a face; inaudibly, she sighed. She never, ever, let it show. It was a woman's role to understand these matters. And submit. She had been taught submission long ago; her mother knew, she was a master.

"Come here." She smiled, drew back the quilt, reached for the Vaseline. She used it on her hands at night, and, when Ed wanted her, which happened all too often, she was always dry.

He took his shorts off. Standing tall, he waited by the bed till she was ready. Slowly, carefully, he settled down; he knew she didn't like his full weight. Then he put himself inside—she never helped—and closed his eyes and thought about the Harem Girl.

"Hi, honey."

Marcie glanced up from the magazine as Van moved in and closed the bedroom door. He looked exhausted. "Where'd you go with Dad?"

"We had a drink or two." He felt a twinge of anger. Why the nightgown? That was easy. Messages: it was her way of telling him he kept the house too cold. He paid the bills, he had some rights, and if he wanted it at sixty-five . . .

"You have a good time?"

"You know Ed." Van dredged a smile from somewhere, took off his jacket. Seersucker: old and blue and wouldn't it feel good to scissor it to shreds.

Marcie watched him place it on a hanger. With such care, like a raw-silk dinner jacket. Little things—it was the little ones that drove you up the wall. But they had big things, too, and Marcie knew they had to talk. Not chit-chat, which they managed well enough. They hadn't been alone since driving to the Club for the Buffet. That felt like months ago.

Van had his trousers off, the hanger in his hand. In seconds he'd be safely in the bathroom, not to reappear for hours. God knew what he did in there. Read magazines, most likely. That's what she did.

"Van?"

"Uh-huh?"

She sat up straight, reached out to pat a corner of the bed. They had to start in somehow. "Got a minute?"

What was coming? "Sure." He hung up the trousers.

"Tell me about your day."

He almost laughed. The Chrysler talk with Ed, his fears

of doom, the girlie show, the healthy role that hookers played in wedlock. "Well, there's not a lot." He sat down on the bed. "What would you like to know?"

She bit back the irritation. Would she be asking if she knew? "Whatever. Anything at all."

He shrugged. Sometimes he wished that they could tell each other things, the way Pam and Jerry did. Not every detail; there were secrets Jerry kept, and marriage wasn't a confessional. Besides, the way he felt that moment, he'd have rather seen the dentist. They had sold one car that afternoon, he told her that. And all about the boredom at the Board of Governors. And what he had for lunch, he threw that in. "That's pretty much what it was like."

Pure chit-chat, and she hadn't waited up for this. She'd meant, she'd truly meant to have a real talk. There was so much she had just found out about herself. She couldn't tell him, but she needed something from him. Reassurance that he loved her? Probably. She felt so guilty.

And what was she doing? Looking at him in his shorts, comparing him to Talker. Van was kinder, gentler, all the things she'd always known she wanted in a man. And handsomer. It wasn't even close. A man like Talker, you could pass him on the street and never notice him. That song again. She felt a little crazy. Where in God's name was her self-control?

She saw herself lean forward, as if Marcie were across the room and watching. "Van?" she whispered, then reached out and took his hand and pulled him toward her.

Van's heart sank. Not now, he couldn't; but he let himself be drawn. He stretched out close beside her. How long had it been since last time? Much too long, he knew that, and if she were feeling—

"Kiss me."

So he did. He moved his tongue across her lips, he cupped her breast, he felt her hand start creeping down.

She wanted him. He always did it with the lights out and his eyes closed. Little chance he'd see the bruises. If he did, she'd think of something. "More," she whispered.

He knew her hand was on his thing. The trouble was, he couldn't feel it. Nothing. No sensations. It just lay there like the worm it was. It had to stand up, he could will it. Voices in his head were shouting, "Do it, you can do it, what's the matter with you?"

Her hand was moving up and down. It wouldn't help, he knew it; he felt so ashamed. He couldn't bear it.

"Marcie?"

"Yes?"

"I don't know what's the matter."

"Take your time. Relax. If you start worrying—"

"It isn't going to work. I'm beat, that's all it is. I really want to, I just can't."

"It happens, these things happen." Was she actually saying that? She sounded understanding, sympathetic. "Honestly. It doesn't matter."

He was sitting up now. "Yes, it does; I know it does. I'm sorry. Maybe in the morning."

"Sure."

"I mean it."

"It's a date," she said. She even smiled.

He headed for the bathroom; she leaned back, turned out her light. The thing to do was make her mind go blank. No thoughts, no images. She was a strong-willed girl, no reason to see Talker lying in the sunshine. No excuse.

Van took less time than usual. She lay there on her side, her face away from him as he slipped into bed. She heard him whispering good night. She whispered back and tried to wait until he slept. She couldn't.

Moving quietly, she stepped into the bathroom, closed the door, switched on the light. The gown came off over her head. The bruises hurt a little when she raised her arms; she didn't really mind.

She turned and faced the mirror, let her eyes move up and down, all over, every thumbprint and fingerprint. She even saw his hands.

She raised a finger to her lips to lick it, but there was no need to. She was wet already. Watching closely, she began ever so gently to abuse herself.

It took no time at all.

12

TALKER WOKE UP yet again. Another sunny morning, six o'clock. He'd had enough dreams in one night to last a month. The air was cool, it drifted in through open windows, and he lay there with a film of sweat all over him. This Marcie business needed calming down. High time he put it in perspective, saw the thing for what it was. He tried the numbers game. It went like this: How many women had he had? It started back when he was thirteen, Sally Willis in an alleyway. It was her first time, too; he liked it more than she did. After that?

Time was, he kept a record; names and dates and places, like a Mobil Travel Guide. It made him feel important then. How many women? He'd been in the saddle almost twenty years, twelve months a year, an average of—no reason to inflate the number—give or take five different girls a month. Which came to what? It didn't matter. Maybe once or twice, in all this sea of half-remembered females, had there ever been a Marcie.

Clearly, this was going nowhere, so he got up, put on some trunks and went out to take a swim. The water popped his eyes wide open. It was cold, just what he needed. Not a ripple on the lake. The mist enveloped him. A few deep breaths, and then he floated on his back and took stock of his circumstances.

Being logical was not a snap at times like this, but he had

read enough to know the cardinal rule: begin at the beginning. Question one: was he fucking crazy? Judging by the turmoil in his genitalia, his local-princess rules were up in smoke. So he was crazy. Question two: how crazy? There was more to life than fornication. He had known that for a year or more. No revelation; just a growing sense that time was passing, he was missing out on things. What things? He couldn't name them, but he did know that his body had a mind; like day and night, you can't have one without the other. Question three: was Marcie just another piece of tail or something more?

That's when he started swimming. All across the lake and back. Swim hard enough, it occupies the mind. You think of breathing, kicking, stroking. Stroking took him back to in and out. He gave it up, sat on the dock to catch his wind, and when he headed for his cabin, there was Annie at a picnic table with two mugs of coffee.

"Here." She shoved a mug across the table.

Talker sat down. "Where'd you get it?"

There were hot plates in the cabins. "I can cook."

He took a sip. The stuff was good. "Not bad for a beginner."

"Thanks." She would have loved to make him breakfast, but the grocery wasn't open. From the way he looked, he could have used it. "Trouble sleeping?" Annie asked.

"Not me." He took another sip.

"Me neither." He was lying, but that only made them even. When they talked, his mind kept drifting; she could see it go. Whoever he had found, she had to be some woman. It had kept her up all night, and gazing at him now, she hoped he'd choke. Confused was what she felt. She knew she hadn't lost him yet; you can't lose what you never had. And was it up to her at all?

"So what's on for the morning?" Annie asked him. "Any plans?"

"Could be. I haven't made my mind up."

That could mean he didn't know or he had private plans or he was waiting— Annie stopped herself. When Uncle Emil's cronies came for poker, there was a phrase they used: "You play it as it lays." That's what she had to learn to do. "Just let me know. I'm bored to death out here."

"O.K.," he said, and went inside to dress.

*   *   *

Van was up at six, too. He was looking forward to the day, at least the second half of it. He loved his Wednesday afternoons. Marcie was sleeping soundly, so he broke their morning date, shaved, showered, tiptoed from the bedroom, down the stairway. He found Betsy in the kitchen.

"Hi." She smiled at him, a Twinkie in one hand, a glass of orange juice in the other.

"That's your breakfast?"

"Yum," she said.

He poured himself a glass of milk. It soothed the dull ache in his stomach, made it go away. He'd gone to Dr. Christiansen about it, and the old man told him not to worry. Great advice but hard to follow.

Betsy polished off the Twinkie, stuffed another in her pocket. "Going to the Fair?" she asked him.

"Could be."

"Can I hitch a ride?" She loved to get there early. Watching people set up was like being backstage. It felt good to be behind the scenes. You saw what made the wheels go round, you learned what ordinary people didn't know.

She had a secret, and the whole way out she longed to tell him. Only, would Dad take it right or wouldn't he? Like pulling daisy petals off: she tells him now, she tells him not.

"Dad?"

"That's what they call me." Lord, how he adored her.

"How'd you like the show?"

"I think Loretta Lynn's terrific."

"Not that show."

He looked at her. "I don't know what you mean."

"The Moulin Rouge."

"What makes you think—"

She should have kept her trap shut. He was frowning. Too late now. "I saw you there. I didn't mean to. I'd been on the Whiz-Bang thing with Denny, we went off to get some pizza and we saw you going in. With Gramps."

He shrugged and grinned; what else was there to do? "It's what I get for letting you stay out late."

Dad was funny with his grins. Sometimes he meant them, sometimes not. She risked it. "What's it like inside?"

"It's not for little girls."

"Or little boys, I know all that, but what's it like? What do they do, Dad?"

Not yet seven in the morning and he had this on his hands. "They dance around, that's all."

"That's all? I heard it was a strip show, that's what everybody's saying. Don't they take their clothes off?"

It was a real grin this time. "Not in Fulton, no they don't. And what's it to you, anyway?"

She shrugged. "Just curiosity, I guess."

"You know what happened to the cat."

"I'll bet the girls are pretty."

"Subject closed, O.K.?"

"O.K."

She looked sincere. He hoped he'd heard the last of it.

Marcie sat up when she heard Van pulling from the driveway. She felt rested and alert. Alert was good. What happened next was up to Talker. She had made the first move, which was unbelievable enough. But it took two to play. For all she really knew, she might have seen the last of him.

Still, on the other hand, she had to be prepared. The whole thing was so risky. In a place like Fulton, walls had eyes and doors had ears. Which meant that meeting him again was like a Malay tiger trap. She had to be a clever girl. One false step and the town would skewer her.

She got up, moved to take the gown off, left it on. The bruises were distracting and she had to think. As clearly as she knew how.

Marcie started making plans.

Nine o'clock found Talker standing in the hut they called the Grocery Store. That's where the pay phone was. He pushed another quarter in. It dropped; he got the dial tone.

He hesitated, wiped his forehead. He was dealing with a Rubicon. You cross it and there's no boat back. Who was he kidding? No way was he stopping now. He had the number right in front of him. He dialed. Three rings. Four.

"Good morning. Johnny Appleseed."

Her voice was music. He'd thought nine o'clock would never come. "You're there," he said.

Her breath caught in her throat. "Uh-huh."

He thought she didn't sound the least surprised. She'd known he'd call. What did it mean? Was she in as deep as he was? Maybe not. He made it casual. "So I was wondering, maybe if you've got some time—"

She cut him off. Her voice was calm and even, God alone knew how. "You understand, we have to be extremely cautious. If we use our heads, there shouldn't be a problem. Are you listening?"

"Yup."

"It's very simple. This is all you've got to do."

She told him, hung up, sat there shaking. Done is done, she told herself, picked up the phone, called Dee and asked if she would leave the Lodge key underneath the doormat. Dee was merciful; she didn't ask why.

The next thing was a note to Pam. There was a tremor in Marcie's hand; she had to write it twice. "Dear Pam, I told you this might happen and I'm sorry, but my bachelor with the antiques called in early and I've got to go. I just might wrap it up today, so wish me luck. I'll get back when I can. Love, M."

She put it carefully on Pam's side of the desk, got up, went out the back, and locked the door.

When Marcie finished, Talker took off like a bullet from his cabin, scrawled a note for Norma—he had things to do in town, he'd see her at the Fair by three—shoved it underneath her door, and headed for his car.

He let Annie come along, why not? Depending on the time he made, he'd either drive her to the Fair or drop her off where she could get a ride. She prattled all the way to town. He didn't listen, but he found her chatter vaguely pleasant and she didn't seem to care.

She damn well knew what he was up to. She had seen a porno movie once, and she could read his thoughts like headlines. It was no fun sitting there and playing chatterbox, but it beat screaming. "Play it as it lays" was only half the battle. What remained was independent action, doing something on her own. Like what? Who knew?

Just past the Country Club, she asked him to pull over. Lots of traffic going in, no problem thumbing. She got out and closed the door. She had to have one parting shot. "Have fun," she told him.

"Thanks." He grinned and whizzed away. He didn't even notice how she'd said it.

Talker knew where he was going, more or less. The Woolworth's was on Third Street, with an all-day parking lot behind it. When he found it, he pulled in, got out, and locked the car. Then, following instructions, he turned left and made for Third and Chestnut. There, as she had promised, was a bus-stop sign. His orders were to stand there, as if waiting for a bus.

Marcie drove to Blanchard Street and got the key. Then—no hurry, it would take him forty minutes easily from Carthage Lake—she headed for the Agency. Dad rarely came in early, and she knew Van wouldn't be there. Better still, it didn't matter if he was; the tale she had to tell was bulletproof.

Almost every time she passed by Steuben Motors, Marcie felt a touch of pride. When Dad put up the Agency, he did it right. It was a handsome building, made to last. The showroom ran for half a block on Pleasant Avenue, with a huge service area around the side.

She turned the corner into Service. Nate and Al—she made a point of knowing names—were busy doing whatever mechanics did. They greeted her with big hellos; what could they do for her?

"I think the motor needs some tuning; it keeps stalling out on me."

"Could be the points," Al said. "Or maybe a new set of plugs. If that's not it . . ." He shrugged. "It's going to take a while."

"Oh Lord." She shook her head. "I've got no time."

"Why don't you take a loaner for the day?"

"Oh." Marcie smiled. "I never thought of that."

Nate pointed toward a group of cars. "They're all yours, Mrs. V. Just take your pick."

She chose a coupe, dull gray, innocuous, and thanking them profusely, made her way to Third and Chestnut. There he was. She pulled up, jabbed the window switch. "Get in," she said, "and keep low till we're out of town."

Betsy strolled outside the grandstand, passing time, just waiting. Denny wasn't late yet; it was only ten-fifteen and cycling in from his place was no joke. Another year and they would both have learner's permits. Betsy planned to throw her bike away; or better, immolate the thing and—

"Hey."

She turned and saw him pedaling toward her. He was grinning, winded, and his shirt was dark with sweat. He skidded to a stop, jumped off.

"Been waiting long?" he asked.

"Just got here. Look at you." She brushed the damp hair from his forehead. "You're all sticky."

"Thanks a lot."

"Come on." She took his hand. "Let's go."

The first stop was the bike racks, lots of spaces; then they headed for the entrance to the stands. The judging had begun at ten, there weren't a lot of people yet, no ticket line to speak of.

In they went. The field was filled with farmers, animals, and judges. Lots of things were going on at once. At one side, they were judging Baby Beef. And next to that, the Holstein Show and, at the far end, Betsy's favorite, they were shearing sheep.

The best thing about being early was, they let you wander on the field. You could catch the smells and see the faces. When they reached the sheep, they moved in close. The farm boys worked in pairs. One held the sheep down while the other used the shears. When they were good, it looked like magic, wool just seemed to fly away in sheets, as if the stuff were zippered on. When Betsy'd had enough, they wandered to the Holstein Show.

This competition took all day, there were so many animals. They were divided into classes: Junior Heifers, Intermediates and Seniors, Junior Yearlings Not in Milk . . . The list went on forever; there were ribbons for each class.

They got there for the Junior finals. Six calves under nine months old; born after January 1, those were the rules. They looked adorable. They all had ropes around their necks, with farm girls holding on to them.

"You get to pick first," Denny said. "Who's going to win?"

"The big one at the end," she answered.

"Never happen," someone said. They turned. A girl was standing next to them. "The one with white socks, in the middle. That one there." She sounded sure.

She was a pretty girl, no doubt about it; really pretty, grown up, maybe twenty, dressed in jeans and T-shirt. No bra, Betsy noticed. Denny noticed, too.

"What makes you think so?" he asked.

"The lines, the bones. It's in the bones."

They watched the judge move up and down. He stopped at Betsy's calf and ran his hand along its shoulders.

Betsy gave the girl a nudge. "You want to bet?"

"How much?"

"A dollar?"

"Shake."

A minute later, Betsy forked over the money. "How'd you know?"

"It's easy, I was brought up on a farm."

"Around here?" Denny asked.

"In Pennsylvania," Annie said. The boy was cute, or would be when he grew up, and the girl was something else. They looked about fourteen to her. Maybe they knew their way around. "You kids from Fulton?"

Denny nodded. "Born and bred."

"Where can I get a lunch that's not a sandwich?"

"In the Commissary," Betsy said.

"How do I find it?"

Betsy figured she could miss the Baby Beef Show. "Follow me."

They talked some on the way, exchanged their first names, things like that. They were a pair of nice kids, Annie thought, but still so young. The girl reminded her of Susie in some way she couldn't name. She envied them a little, living in a town like this. She was about to say so when they stopped and Denny pointed.

"There it is."

She thanked them, turned to go. "Nice meeting you."

"Same here."

Then Annie asked the fatal question. "You come here often?"

"Every day."

"Who knows, could be we'll meet again."

"You work here?" Denny asked.

"I'm with the Moulin Rouge." She watched their eyes go round like saucers. Annie grinned. "You've heard of it?"

The three of them had lunch together.

*   *   *

Dee was feeling really miffed. It wasn't just the Lodge key; Marcie had been welcome to it, and it wasn't hard to picture what was going on out there. No siree. Marcie in the bedroom, on the kitchen floor, the dock, wherever, getting boffed until her teeth shook loose. Dee didn't mind that; if she wanted boffing, she could get it anytime.

No, what Dee really minded was, she'd counted so on Marcie. Marcie always got her through these trips to home. She was her lifeline, sole companion, boon, and comfort, and if things went on the way they were, Dee might just up and die.

Where was she? At the Women's Garden Club, for Jesus' sake, with Eleanor and Harriet and all of Harriet's Committee women. Having lunch. The one thing that she mustn't do was have too much to drink.

She signaled for the waiter, tapped her empty glass; another margarita. He was moderately cute, and five would get you ten—she mustn't do that, either. So she put her hands down on her lap and dug her nails into her palms and listened to her mother talk to Marcie's.

Such good friends, they deserved each other. Years ago, in high school, she and Marcie used to hold 'whose-mother-was-the-most-horrendous' contests. It was good fun, and they'd laugh until they cried or cry until they laughed. It worked both ways, it didn't matter. Sometimes Marcie won, like when the Great White Harriet—she smiled like a shark; not easy when you only had one row of teeth—

"Is something wrong, dear?"

Dee looked up at Eleanor. "Oh heavens no." And then: "Excuse me."

As was usually the case, the ladies' room was near the bar. Her waiter stood there, and she briefly contemplated goosing him as she passed by; the place could use some livening up.

The lavatory was as spotless as an operating room, and smelled of artificial lilac spray. Perfection. She moved into an empty stall, made sure to lock the door, and sat down on the toilet lid. Self-pity was revolting, and she never, under any circumstances, let herself sink into that. Besides, what was the trouble, anyway? She'd always been the girl with everything: looks, money, status, even talent.

She had actually come home with half a mind of settling

there. Or trying it. It was absurd of her, of course. "The self-same world beneath your feet . . ." etc., etc. She wanted so much to belong to someone, something, somewhere. And she didn't. It was all her fault, needless to say. She made a mental list of all her blessings. When she got to twelve, she stopped. It didn't help. No guts, that's what her trouble was. *Coraggio, cara mia*. Dee spoke no Italian; it was from some opera.

When she got back to the table, both the moms were talking softly, heads together. Dee crept in behind and eavesdropped.

Eleanor was saying ". . . and I try denying it, but Dee is such a disappointment."

"Marcie, too," sighed Harriet. "I don't know why. God knows, we tried."

Dee sat down, picked up her napkin, smiled sweetly at them. "Fuck you both," she said.

It was getting on to lunchtime, and the two of them were lying in the sun again and dripping wet. Like yesterday, except it was a dock this time and not a melon patch. He glanced at her and watched her breathing ease off, quiet down. She was as spent as he was; they both needed some recovery time. He closed his eyes and listened to the quiet rippling of the water.

When he got in at the bus stop, he had done as he was told and hunched down on the floor. He started talking, but she shook her head, so he just sat there looking at her legs. He wondered how she'd take it if he raised her skirt a little. When he did, her hand began to move as if to pull it down, then stopped and went back to the wheel. He hadn't looked up skirts since high school. It was hot stuff then. He had to smile; it wasn't half bad now.

When they were safely out of town, he got up on the seat, leaned back. They hadn't said a word so far. His legs felt stiff. He stretched them, glancing out the window. They were whizzing down the Fallsburg Road, cornfields on all sides. They passed the spot where he had parked just yesterday.

"Where are we going?"

Marcie shrugged. "A place I know."

"How far?"

"Another twenty minutes." Pause. "You want some music?"

"Why?"

"It helps to pass the time."

"That's not a problem." He began to run his fingertips along her thigh. She stiffened for an instant, then relaxed. He pulled her skirt back further, fingertips still light and easy. When her breathing changed, he drew the skirt back all the way; he liked to see what he was doing. Yesterday he hadn't had the time to notice, but she kept herself well trimmed, clean edges. Talker liked that. When he touched her, she was more than ready.

"Watch the road," he said.

"I am, I am."

It happened sooner than he thought. One sharp intake of breath and then she stiffened, rigid, threw her head back. They went weaving off the road. He grabbed the wheel and jammed his foot down on the brake. They'd damn near gone into a ditch.

"You should have warned me," Talker said.

"I didn't know."

He let her catch her breath. "I'm not like this, I'm really not," he heard her say. He let it pass.

"Why don't I do the driving?"

Marcie nodded. Talker helped her move across him. He was rock-hard and he wanted her to know it. Then he slipped behind the wheel and got them on the road again.

"I just keep going?" Talker asked her.

"There's a turn. I'll let you know."

She watched him drive, hands steady on the wheel. She knew his problem, she had felt it. When she looked down at the bulge, her impulse was to let him suffer, do him good, and she was half-surprised to see her hand move toward his zipper. Not a steady hand; it fumbled as it pulled the zipper down. He popped right out.

She looked at it, then started bending. She had never in her life done this before. She'd tried with Van; she coaxed and teased him, she was gentle, but it never happened.

The way it felt between her lips was quite surprising; velvety, both hard and soft. Her head moved up and down, she ran her tongue along it, just like in the porno movies she had watched with Dee. The passion always looked so phony. Suddenly, it started twitching, more and more convulsively, and there was warm stuff in her mouth, and what in God's name happened now? She swallowed it, the stuff went down. She couldn't say a lot for the consistency, but it was slightly salty, and she liked the taste.

When she sat up, they'd almost missed the turn.

13

VAN HAD A natural fade. His long balls always drifted slightly, right to left. Like Lee Trevino, only less severe. The fourth hole was a dogleg, made to order for him. Carefully—you let your concentration waver and you might as well go home—he took the club head slowly back. He paused, then started down. He pressed his left heel hard against the turf, shifting his weight, bringing his hips into the shot. His hands were in position, leading slightly. His wrists snapped as the club head met the ball.

Tha-wacko. Off it sailed. He kept his head down, raising it in time to see the ball go soaring straight and true. He had his rhythm right today, his swing was grooved. He rarely knocked a drive three hundred yards, but this one wouldn't miss by much.

He picked his tee up, turned, and bowed. He got a "Fuck yourself" from Jerry Leggett and an "Atta go" from Sandy Stone. Bob Houseman simply sighed and turned away.

They were a fixture. Every Wednesday afternoon, the four of them assembled in the Men's Grill for a light lunch, and then went out and hit the course. They played in rain, they played in snow unless the stuff was deep. And even then, they'd meet for lunch.

Doctors, as the whole world knows, are serious about their golf, and Jerry, Bob, and Sandy were the best at Longview. All of them were scratch, or nearly. Jerry was in general practice, Bob did neurosurgery, and Sandy was the only analyst this side of Akron with credentials. They were friends, of course—not close, except for Jerry. It was the game that knit the four of them together.

They switched partners every week. This Wednesday, Van was paired with Sandy. Now and then, it crossed Van's mind to have a lengthy talk with Sandy, maybe in his office. Nothing serious or formal, just a talk. And here they were, their caddies at a distance, strolling down the fairway side by side and trading jokes. Van picked up his from Ed. He never got the laughs Ed did, he didn't tell them half as well, and why in hell was it so hard to say, 'Look, Sandy, can I come around and see you?'

Sandy, short for Sanford, was the Club Jew. There was no, repeat no, prejudice in Fulton, none whatever if you didn't count the coloreds, and the Governors of Longview had been pleased and proud to let Sandy in when he applied. It proved a point.

Exactly what it proved to Sandy was a lot less clear. He never practiced his religion, save for driving up to Akron with his wife and kids each year for the High Holidays. He knew he was a Jew, he wasn't hiding, and what landed him in Fulton, where he was the one and only, was a complicated story.

"... and the salesman said, 'I'll ask my wife.'" Van looked at him. Apparently, it was the punch line, so he laughed. He had a tendency to do what was expected.

"Tell me something, Van?"

"Sure thing."

"What's on your mind?"

Van thought he felt sweat break out on his neck, but he was sweating anyway. It was an opening, the chance he had been waiting for. "What makes you ask?"

"No reason." Sandy shrugged and signaled for his caddy, turned to Van. "What do you make it to the green?"

"About one-eighty."

Sandy nodded, took a five—what did they used to call them, mashies, niblicks?; he had learned golf from his father—took a practice swing, addressed the ball, and let it fly. It bounded past the sand trap, stopping in the frog hair just short of the green.

He looked at Van and shrugged. He knew Van's problem, knew exactly what was eating him. His brother, Lee, had suffered from it. Yes, and suffering it was. He liked Van, he'd have liked to help him, but the patient had to want it first. And even if Van asked for help, he had his doubts. There were some things in all of us too painful to be touched.

Van stood beside his ball. He'd knocked the thing a mile. He took a seven, lined it up straight for the flag stick—his short irons had no fade. The ball came in above the hole, exactly where he'd meant it to, and spun back down.

Van turned and grinned at Sandy. "Well, at least I'm good at something."

Sandy broke a rule, he could have kicked himself. "You want to drop by sometime?"

"Where?"

"My office."

"Why? What for?"

"A talk. That's what we do there."

"I don't know . . ."

"I've got an hour free. How's ten tomorrow morning?"

"Ten?" Van frowned. "That's really hard for me."

"Forget it." Sandy smiled. "I don't know why I asked."

Van took the deepest breath he'd ever taken. "I'll be there."

Norma floated on the water, belly up. She used to fret about her figure, but she didn't anymore. In fact, she kind of liked the way things had been spreading these last years. It made her comfortable.

What didn't make her comfortable was Talker. He was making it with local tail. The way he showed up yesterday for work, you couldn't miss it. And that note this morning. Things to do in Fulton? He had found the town pump, that's what he was doing. Pumping.

Every two-three years, it happened. Some young trick would catch his eye and off he'd go. She'd heard his lead-pipe story, and she knew he played it safe. What bugged her was he'd go around ass dragging, half-dead on the bally stage all week. Some fairs they played were hopeless: Gabriel could blow his horn, it wouldn't bring a customer. But Fulton was a live one, and she wanted Talker on his toes. She'd damn well have some words with him.

The day was getting on. She'd have to get the girls up soon. The curtains on their cabin were still drawn. She sighed, rolled off her back, and sidestroked toward the shore.

Inside the cabin, Skipper lay on Laurel's bed, just holding on. That's how it usually started; Skipper needing comfort, Laurel giving it. She always took her time; she knew that Skipper liked it that way. Lying still, just being held. They never spoke at times like this.

She was a funny girl, this Skipper. Tough as leather, fearless, brave. Laurel had seen her knock men down. Big men. Fists flying, knees high, groining them. She'd come to Laurel's rescue more than once.

Laurel began to stroke her hair. When Skipper snuggled closer, Laurel ran her fingernails ever so lightly up and down her back. Then Skipper sighed and arched her neck so Laurel could begin to kiss it.

Sometimes, though not often, it would work the other way around, with Skipper taking charge. She had a thing for Laurel's breasts. She'd hold them, fondle them, caress them, lick them, kiss the nipples. At the very end, she'd suck them. That's when Laurel generally would come to life.

It all seemed natural to both of them. They liked men, they preferred them. Only now and then, it had to be a woman. It was gentler, intimate, more sensitive; but they were neither of them queer. They talked about it openly, and there was nothing wrong with them.

They were kissing on the lips now. Skipper shifted, stretched out on her back, and spread her legs apart. As Laurel's hand began to travel, they heard Norma's knocking at the door.

"Get up, you two. Let's move it."

Laurel moved it, placed her lips for just a moment right where Skipper wanted them. A lick and a promise, that was all. Then both of them got up.

Lucy Lovell had been peeping through the curtains at the back the whole time. No one noticed her.

Ed was sitting in Jack Morgan's office, legs crossed, in a leather armchair. He'd been doing business with First Federal since he'd opened up his Agency, back when Jack's father ran the bank. Ed hadn't had a pot to piss in, and he needed fifty thou for start-up costs—and got it.

It was the only bank Ed ever used. They valued him, he valued them. When Jack took over, nothing changed. He was a friend, a crony; they were poker buddies. It added a dimension to their conversation.

"Damn." Jack guffawed, slapped his desk. "Where do you get them from?"

"It's not the stories, it's the way I tell 'em."

"You're a threat to human decency." Still grinning, Jack leaned back. "O.K., you old fart, you're too late to buy me lunch. What are you here to do me for?"

"A half a million dollars."

"Oh?" Jack straightened. "In some circles, that's a sum of money."

"It's a dewdrop for a bank like yours."

"I wish it were. What do you want it for, if that's not prying?"

"Just between us?" Ed leaned forward.

"Shoot."

"I'm thinking of expanding."

"Into what?"

"I've been a car man all my life, it's what I know. There's not a Honda or a Toyota agency in fifty miles."

"So?"

"I've got deals set with both of them."

"You're crazy."

"Like a fox. I need the cash to close the deals and build a showroom."

"You've already got a showroom, and if I were you, I'd sell it. That's if you can find a fool who's big enough."

Ed grinned. "That's why I'm rich and you're a bank employee."

"Come on, Ed, you read the papers. No one's buying cars right now."

"You know me, I'm a believer."

"So was Martin Luther, and they nailed him to a church door."

Ed let it pass. Jack's knowledge of a lot of things was narrow, but he did know how to run a bank. "Jack, it's a license to print money. If you want in, I'll make room for you."

Jack looked at him with puzzlement. "You're sixty-eight, you never have to earn another dime. What do you need it for?"

"It keeps me going." Ed stood up. "I'll bring the figures by. You look them over. If they strike you right, we'll talk some more. And if they don't—" Ed paused. "I hate to say this, Jack, I've never used another bank; but if you don't like what you see, I'll walk across the street."

"You wouldn't do that."

"Not if you don't make me."

They were sitting in the kitchen, naked as two jaybirds, smoking cigarettes and drinking beer. His eyes were on her body, moving here and there; and Marcie felt it, even when she looked away. It seemed incredible. She was exposed completely to a total stranger, and it filled her with the strangest joy. She loved it.

Talker could not fathom why her body made him crazy. It was nice, damn nice, in fact; but put her on a pedestal and she would not bring traffic to a standstill. There were other things about her, qualities she had; that had to be the reason. Like she was the only girl he'd been with in a long time who did not drink beer from bottles.

Marcie used a beer glass. It was conical and had a college seal on one side. Talker couldn't read the name.

"I like it here," he said. "It's nice."

"I like it, too." Dee's father had built the Lodge a zillion years ago. It stood on fifty wooded acres by a private lake, and every inch of it was filled with memories.

"You come here often?" Talker asked.

"Not anymore."

"Why don't you?"

"It's not my place." Why Eleanor still kept it up made little sense, she never used it; but there were other things on Marcie's mind. She burned with curiosity; there were so many things she longed to know about him.

"Tell me something?"

"Sure," he said.

She rose to get another beer. Her question took her by surprise. "How old are you?"

"You first."

She lopped off three years without thinking. "Thirty-five."

He added three. "Same here."

She brought out two beers, put them down. "You like it,

working with a strip show?" All those girls around, it had to be a field day for him.

"It's a living."

Marcie grinned. "That's all?"

"That's all."

He didn't want to talk about himself. She didn't care. "I know it's not my business. Even if we're having"—was she blushing?—"I mean, even if we're here like this, I've got no right to pry."

He had to tell her something. "Look. It really is a living. You know what I make a year?" She shook her head. He always kept it private, but he told her. Actually gave the numbers. Was he crazy?

It was more than Van made. "That's a lot."

"What's more, it's all in cash. I pay my taxes, but it's up to me what I declare." What was he saying to this woman?

"How did you get started?"

"Do you have a week?"

She did. He was the one who didn't; he'd be gone by Monday. "Sure, if that's how long it takes."

"You asked for it." The thing to do was cut it short. Besides, she didn't really want to know. A few well-chosen lies and they'd be off the subject. Beneath the table, Marcie raised her foot, began to run its bottom lightly up his leg. He looked into her eyes and lost his cool.

"My people didn't have much. Ever since I can remember, they were always running short. So I was taking odd jobs before I learned to read. Delivering papers, shoveling snow, all kinds of kid stuff."

Marcie pictured him in short pants in some dreadful neighborhood, drunks sprawling in the gutters while toughs roamed the garbage-littered streets. She got it all from movies; she had never seen real poverty.

She looked like she was listening, so he risked a little more. "When I got older, I found out I had a knack for fixing things. Bring me a broken bike or anything that had a motor, I could make it go." He grinned. "And no one ever taught me. I just understood the way things worked, don't ask me how." He still felt proud of it.

Marcie nodded, eyes on every feeling as they moved across his face. "And after that?"

He hesitated. Everything, his whole life changed the day

the talking started. He had lifted something from a store, his one-and-only crime. The cops had caught him dead to rights, red-handed, and he had talked them out of it. It was a revelation. Words. Words could do anything if you knew how to use them. You could get your own way, snow your teachers, catch the girls and make them follow you around.

He boiled it down for her. "I made a great discovery. I could talk."

She frowned; she didn't follow. "Could you spell that out a little?"

"Rhetoric," he said.

She blinked. What was he doing with a word like that?

He caught her thought and grinned. "Surprise you?"

God, she thought, I've done it now, and started to deny it. Something told her not to. "Yes," she said.

He liked her answer. "Talking, using words right, opens doors. When I was twelve or so, I found out I could sell. It almost didn't matter what, old pots and pans, used clothes, whatever I could lay my hands on. After school I'd set up shop on corners. Some of what I sold was hot, but what the hell, I didn't steal it." Later, he worked door-to-door, sold vacuum cleaners, housewares, encyclopedias, and, for the one year he was married, cars. He left that part out.

Van could sell, too, Marcie thought, but not like this. It was an effort for him, never easy. Talker, it occurred to her, had things in common with her dad.

"One time," he said, there was no stopping now, "I even had a shot at radio. No big deal, it was just a small-town station. They were glad to have me, and I wasn't half-bad."

Marcie nodded, she believed it. "Yes, I'll bet you weren't." He could have made it a career. Why hadn't he? She asked him.

"I got bored."

It was the first false note she'd heard. "What really happened?"

Talker shrugged. "Why would I lie?" The truth was, it meant having roots, not being free to move. For certain, he'd have met a girl, they'd have had some kids, and that wrote *Finis* to it. Life was over.

"Did you ever go to college?"

"Nope."

He had the mind for it, she knew. He wasn't what he

seemed to be; the inside didn't match the surface. What was wrong with Talker? Had he thrown himself away? "Why didn't you?" she asked.

In point of fact, he had applied and been accepted. At Rhode Island Polytech. He'd still had crazy dreams back then, the summer he was eighteen and the roof fell in on him. He shrugged again. "Who had the time?"

"You're lying."

"Maybe. What gives you the right to know it all?"

"I'm sorry," Marcie said. She meant it.

It was time to wrap things up. She'd come too close already, and he had himself to blame. "When school was over, I took off, just bummed around and saw the country. I'd take a job when I was broke, and one of them was at a carnival. The rest, as people say, is history. What's your story?"

Nothing to compare to his. Her life was paved with creature comforts. Marcie grinned. "Tune in tomorrow." Then she got up and moved closer. It was happening again. She couldn't understand it, and she didn't want to try. She bent, began to kiss his neck. He drew her down and sat her on his lap.

"What is it, don't you ever have enough?"

She kissed him till she felt him rising, pressing up against her bottom.

"Talker?"

"Ummm?"

"I've got a great idea."

He checked his watch. He had time for a quick one. "Tell me."

Marcie stood up, got down on the kitchen floor, on all fours, bottom sticking in the air. She pointed with a finger. "Do it there."

He got up. "Are you sure?"

"Just do it, Talker. Do it. Please."

The lady had said please. How could a gentleman refuse?

14

THUS FAR, IT had been a gray day for the Greeners. Starting with the Baby Beef Show. They were showing a Late-Summer Bull Calf. Walter knew his bulls from *A* to *Z*. This one had everything, including breeding. Came from champion stock, and there was no way it could lose.

The judges had them down to five, and Walter sent a wink to Marvin, who knew how to show a bull; he kept the rope taut and its head held high. The judges walked right by, like three blind mice. No ribbon, nothing.

Walter's stomach knotted up. What was the fucking point? It wasn't just the cash that went with winning, it was all the breeding money. With a first, he could have had that bull out knocking cows up all across the county.

It was only the beginning. They were judging swine early that afternoon, and Walter had a Senior Sow, a genuine Mae West of pigs, a beauty. When they passed her by, he stood there speechless, gray with rage.

"I don't believe it," he heard Marvin saying. "Jesus Christ."

He didn't need his kid right now. "I gotta see a man about a horse," he said, and stormed out to his panel truck. He got in, slammed the door, and opened up the glove compartment. There, where he had left it, was a bottle. It was good stuff. He should know; he'd made it.

*   *   *

Lunch in the Commissary went like lightning for all three
of them. For Bets and Denny, it was like peeping through a
window at a world they'd never known, and never would. Annie loved the endless questions. She felt wise beyond her
years, a woman of the world. There wasn't anything they
didn't want to hear about: the costumes and the dances, just
how far they went, the other girls, the barker—that's what
they called Talker—and her life, how long she had been doing
this and did she like it and the men out front who came to
look. It was a torrent.

They were both such kids, but she could still remember
being young and curious. A lot of what she said was true—or
half-true. And when things were asked she didn't know, she
made up the answers. And now and then, an outright lie; like
had she ever had a man? Of course she had, what did they
think?

Before she knew it, it was three and time to go to work.
They left the Commissary tent and started toward the Midway, when this man came up to them.

"Hey, there."

They stopped. He winked at Annie. "I know you."

She'd never seen the man before and told him so.

He grinned. "I saw your show last night." He took her by
the arm. "You doing anything right now?"

The man was steady and his speech was clear, but Annie
caught it in his eyes; the way Uncle Emil's got sometimes. The
guy was roaring drunk. She shook free. "Listen, mister—"

"Twenty bucks. I got it on me. Here, you see?" He took
some money out.

"Let's just keep moving," Denny said.

"Come on, you little tramp. My money isn't good
enough?" He grabbed her by the shoulder.

"Let me go."

"You heard her." Denny stepped in. "Get your hands off."

Betsy came to life. "I'll call a cop."

She didn't have to. "O.K., everybody, what's the story?"

They looked up and saw a state policeman wearing corporal's stripes.

"You want to know, I'll tell you." Denny pointed at the
man. "This guy just came up to my friend and propositioned
her."

"The hell I did. You going to listen to some kid or take my word for it? It was the other way around."

"Now hold on," Betsy said.

The corporal looked at her. "I want to hear from you, I'll ask." Then, to the man: "Let's get this straight. You say she propositioned you?"

"Damn right she did. The girl's a slut, works at the strip show. You ask anybody here, they all know me, would Walter Greener pick up a slut?"

Annie's voice shook. "You're a liar."

"Am I? Listen, Officer, I'm a God-fearing, honest—"

"Bullshit." Annie's face was chalk white. "You're a fucking drunken slob."

That's when the officer grabbed Annie's arm, and Betsy turned and ran. She took off like the wind for the Command Post. It was just around the corner. In she flew and slammed the door.

Sheriff Weller spilled his coffee. "What the hell?"

Words started pouring out of Betsy. It was hard to follow. Weller thought he recognized her. "Look, young lady, just calm down." He placed her: the Van Buren girl, Big Ed's granddaughter. "What's the problem?"

Betsy told him; partly there in the Command Post, partly on the way. By then, both of them were running. When they turned the corner, Denny was in trouble, too. The corporal had him by one arm and Annie by the other.

Weller blew a gasket. State cops, they weren't worth the powder. Was he pulling in the Redding boy, for godsake? "Hey, you bonehead!" Weller shouted.

"What?" The corporal looked up. "Who you calling bonehead?"

"Twenty questions," Weller told him. "Let the boy go. And the girl."

"Come off it, Sheriff. You don't know what happened."

"Yes, I do." He turned to Greener. "Go on home, Walt. Sleep it off. And get your kid to do the driving, or I'll put your butt in jail."

"Look, all I did was—"

"I won't say it twice." He turned to Annie. "These things happen."

"It's O.K., no harm done."

Weller nodded, took the corporal by the arm. "This ain't

Columbus, fella. This is my town. Come along, I've got some things to teach you."

It was over. Annie looked at Denny, then at Betsy. How to thank them, what to say? "I won't forget. Not ever." Then she turned and ran.

Marcie turned right onto Sunset Crescent. She'd dropped Talker off in town—they'd fixed a time to meet tomorrow, needless, needless, needless to say—picked up her car from Service. What she needed right now was a little time alone.

She pulled into the drive, braked, left the motor running and the air conditioner on, leaned back and closed her eyes. At least the loathsome Mrs. B. was out today; her varicose veins were acting up again. Marcie's head was spinning. Much too much was going on. She had to show up at the shop or give a call to Pam, and either way, it meant another lie. And they were going to the Fair tonight, the whole famdamily, and for the last half hour—even though she'd cleaned herself— something had been trickling down between her legs.

She killed the motor, got out, checked her slacks. Was there a spot? A small one, but you couldn't miss it. Thanking God she was alone, she hurried to the house, and she was racing to the stairs when someone said, "Is that you, Marcie?"

Marcie felt like screaming. "No," she said. "It's just us chickens. Hello, Mother."

Harriet was standing in the doorway to the living room. She smiled. "I just dropped by to have a chat."

No way out; Marcie knew that smile. She crossed the hallway, smiling back. "I didn't see your car out front."

"I got a ride from Eleanor."

"Oh, that's right. Did you have a nice lunch?"

"It was lovely, dear. Dee joined us, and I gave a little speech to my committee. Thanking them. They've worked so hard, you know."

They moved into the living room. "You want a drink?"

"This time of day, dear? Surely not."

"Well, I do and I'm having one." The shades were drawn against the sun, pray God the dribble didn't show. She opened up the bar and took the vodka from the fridge.

"Yes, lunch was quite a grand occasion. We began with madrilene, you know the way they make it at the Garden Club, so clear and cool."

"Yes." Marcie nodded, poured herself a stiff one, scarcely listening as her mother took her through the menu. Sighing as the icy vodka trickled down her throat, she nearly missed the kicker at the end.

". . . and I'm so concerned that something may be wrong with Dee."

"Oh?" Marcie turned. "What's wrong?"

"I came here hoping you might know."

"What happened, Mother?"

"Nothing, really."

"Oh, come on. I know that look."

"It's not worth bothering about."

"Good. We can drop the subject." Marcie's glass was empty, so she filled it up again.

"It's only that, well, Dee went to the ladies' room and Eleanor and I were talking, chatting on the way we do, about—"

"If there's a point, I'd like to hear it."

"Patience, dear. I'm coming to it. Now you've made me lose the thread. Where was I?"

"Dee was in the john and you were gossiping."

"That's right and, dear, when Dee came back, I cannot tell you how disturbed she was. She's changed so much. This living in New York, it does strange things to people."

Marcie tried to calm herself. "It's sweet of you to be concerned. What makes you think she's changed?"

"Oh, Marcie, dear, she cursed at us."

"She didn't." Marcie fought back the giggles. "What did she say?"

"It's not a word that ladies use."

"Whatever could it be? The s-word or the f-word or—"

"I'll thank you not to make a joke of it." Her eyes were bright with anger. "What I came to say is this. I think you should see less of her."

"What?"

"It's for your sake, for your own good."

Marcie could have strangled her. "I've got some news for you. I'm thirty-eight, that's old enough to choose my own friends. Dee's the best I've ever had, and you say one more God damn word—"

The doorbell rang.

"I'll get it." Marcie pivoted, stormed out. "I'm coming."

Dee stood on the doorstep with a suitcase in each hand. She smiled. "I heard you had a guest room."

Marcie stared at her. "What happened?"

"I checked out of Blanchard Street. The service isn't what it was." She moved in, Marcie shut the door. Dee grinned and nodded toward her slacks. "I know what you've been doing."

"Oh, for Christsake," Marcie whispered. "Not now. Mother's here."

Dee put the suitcases down. "No shit."

"What happened over lunch?"

"She hasn't told you yet?"

"You swore at her."

"And Eleanor. I nailed them both. I don't suppose she told you why."

"I didn't ask."

"Where is the old bag?"

Marcie pointed to the living room. Dee took off like an arrow; Marcie hurried after her.

Dee moved into the room, all smiles. "Harriet." She clasped her hands. "So soon again."

"What are you doing here?"

"The same to you, dear lady."

Harriet stood up. "The less we say, the better. I'll be leaving now."

"I don't care, suit yourself. I'll tell what happened if you're here or not."

"You have changed. You were such a lovely girl."

"You wouldn't know one if you saw one."

"That will do."

Dee turned to Marcie. "So I told them both to fuck themselves."

"You didn't." This was serious, no time to burst out laughing. "Why?"

Dee turned to Harriet, eyes burning. "It's a funny thing with kids. Some of us want our parents to be proud. We really work at it. It means a lot. And if we're both such disappointments to you, you can fry in hell."

"How dare you?" Harriet stepped back and turned to Marcie. "Did you hear the creature? Never in my life—do you intend to let her speak to me like that?"

All Marcie thought was, this could not be happening. She couldn't take it in. Her mother asked her something. How in

God's name could she answer? Dee was right, the words came from the heart, and Mother had been dreadful, true, but still, she was her mother. Marcie wished she were invisible.

At which point, Van breezed in, fresh from his golf game. "Hello, everyone. What's new?"

When Talker pulled up at the show a little after three, the only thing he wanted was a long, cold bath. He didn't get one.

He felt drained. In every way. When he was eighteen, he could do it two, three times a day and walk off in a mood for more. Now look at him. He got out of the car. It wasn't age, it was the heat. The hot air wrapped around him like a barber's towel. On top of which, he'd spilled his guts out to a woman he scarcely knew. Except, he told himself, you couldn't really call it spilling, and it wasn't all his guts. There were a lot of things he'd never say.

He took out a cigarette and was heading for the van when Norma got him.

"How's it going, fancy pants?"

"Who, me? I can't complain."

"I'll bet you can't. So who's the lucky tramp this time?"

He didn't need this. "Norma, I do not know what you mean."

"You get a day's pay for a day's work."

"Who's not working? And I'm not some stiff you hired, I'm a partner."

Norma beat a small retreat. "I know that, honey, and I don't care who you're dicking. Keeps you young, I always say. I hope she's sweet and sassy."

"Thanks."

"Look, all I'm saying is, you look like dead meat."

Talker grinned. "I've never let you down, right? When that happens, it'll be the day." He slapped her on the bottom, vaulted to the bally stage, and moved into the van.

The air inside was something, like a secret weapon. Bottle it and you could sell it to the Russians. But what got his full attention was the atmosphere. He knew his girls and they were haywire, every one of them.

He took a few steps in and whistled. No one bothered to look up. Pauline lay on her cot, eyes on the ceiling. Skipper, in a corner of the van, sat naked on the floor, head in her hands. Laurel, legs apart, was clipping public hair, always a sure sign of emotional distress. And Annie, ramrod-straight, sat at a makeup mirror, looking through it. Angry? Smoke was coming out her ears.

He'd been neglecting them, and well he knew it. It was strange, the way they all depended on him. He had several explanations, some of which were partly true. The fact remained, he owed them; they were his to carry through the summer.

"So, how goes it, Annie?" Silence. He reached down and touched her shoulder. Nothing moved, her eyes included.

"Get lost," she said.

"That's instead of hello?"

"Do me a favor. Just butt out."

"Come on." He smiled. "What's the matter?"

"Nothing."

"I've seen nothing. That's not what it looks like."

"Look, go find yourself a kite and fly it."

"Fine. O.K. Don't tell me." Usually, that got an answer. Not this time around. "You win, kid. Have it your way."

He stayed put a moment more, then turned to go. He had to strain to hear her words.

"Where are you when I need you?"

Talker swallowed hard. He didn't have an answer, not for that one.

Outside, in the sun, the customers were gathering.

15

THERE WAS HEAVY silence after Harriet stormed out. No one knew what to say. The three of them stood in the living room, eyes almost meeting but not quite.

Van broke the silence, got as far as "Well . . ." when Harriet stormed in again. She had forgotten that she had no car.

"Take mine," Van said.

"Or mine," said Marcie, throwing her the keys.

"Oh, very well." No "Thank you." Just another angry look and out she went.

Van hated fights. How well he knew that Marcie had her difficulties with her mother. Now and then, there'd be an outburst. Like a summer storm—big wind, quick thunder, followed by blue sky. What the issue was this time he didn't know, but clearly it had been a corker. Both girls shook with anger, he could see them vibrate. They looked absolutely white.

"Christ," Dee said to Marcie. "How about your mother?"

"She's not easy."

"Easy? She's a killer, but she's milquetoast next to mine."

Marcie felt like flying off in all directions. There she stood, with Talker on her mind and Talker on her slacks and Mother driving home in tears—God knows what crap she'd lay on Dad—and Van just standing there like always, not one mote of understanding. She was furious with everyone. But most of all, with Dee.

"You know what really gets me, Dee?" Her voice was raw, it sounded hoarse. "The thousand times I've wanted to tell Mother to go fuck herself—and you, you got to do it. I could kill you."

Spinning on her heel, she stalked out of the room, grabbed both of Dee's bags and went steaming up the stairway to the guest room.

Betsy cycled home alone. The day had been too much for her to handle: meeting Annie, learning all about the show, the drunk, the ghastly things he said, the moron state policeman. Afterward, she talked with Denny, but that didn't help much. What she needed was a grown-up. Mom was out, she'd never understand; so Dad was it.

When she got home, they both were in the bedroom, getting dressed for dinner. Perfect: there was never anyone to turn to. Betsy galloped up the stairs; she had to change for dinner, too.

She slammed her bedroom door and threw herself down on the bed. Someday, she'd show them all. She'd be a famous writer and she'd put them in her books, tell all their secrets. They'd be sorry.

Ed was humming as he drove home. He was in a great mood. He'd be hearing from Jack Morgan in a day or two. Jack always liked to think things over, but he'd come up with the money. Plus he'd sold two Darts that afternoon. For cash, right on the barrelhead.

And when he pulled up, there was Marcie's car parked in the drive. Terrific. They had planned to meet at dinner and she couldn't wait; she'd come by early.

He parked, got out, still humming, took the front steps two at a time, moved in and slammed the door.

"Is that you, dear?" The voice was Harriet's. It issued from the parlor, sounding like the breath of doom.

He moved into the doorway. Harriet, eyes red from weeping, sat beside the TV in her favorite chair. The news was on. She wasn't watching it. "Where's Marcie?"

"Home, where she belongs."

He wondered what that meant. "I saw her car."

"I borrowed it."

Ed always played these scenes the same way, took his time. Whatever grief was eating her would come, like death, when it would come. Determined not to lose his mood, he ambled to the butler's tray and poured himself a stiff one. "Ask me how my day was."

Tonelessly, she spoke the words. "How was your day?"

"Terrific." Careful not to ask how hers had been, he took out a small cigar.

"Must you smoke?"

Ed recognized deep water. "Got a headache?"

"That's the least of my concerns."

He turned. "I think I'll go upstairs and change." Moves of this nature usually hurried things along."

"You go right ahead, dear. I'm not coming."

"Oh?"

"I know how much these family dinners mean to you, but we don't have a family anymore."

"I see." He braced himself. "Since when is that?"

"Since Marcie turned against me."

It was coming now. He took a chair. "What happened?"

"It's too terrible."

"I can't believe she'd turn on you."

"Dear Lord, if only that were true."

"She must have had a reason."

"None. No reason whatsoever. It was spite. She's always been a spiteful child."

Ed could feel the anger start to rise. "That's not the Marcie I know."

"You know nothing." Then the floodgates opened. Harriet poured out her version: how Dee, quite unprovoked, had lost her temper over lunch; how she, like any loving mother, had warned Marcie to beware of Dee; and then, how Dee had stalked in, hurling curses at her.

Ed just sat there listening, careful not to interrupt. When she sat back, clearly finished, Ed spoke up. "So that's what happened?"

"Ed, can you imagine?"

"Frankly, no. It's bullshit, Harriet."

Her eyes went wide. She gasped. "What are you saying?"

"Never kid a kidder. I'm a specialist in bullshit, it's my stock-in-trade. What really happened over lunch?"

"I told you."

"You left out the good parts. Something made Dee lose her temper."

"She's a bad seed."

"Harriet, we're not in court, I'm not about to cross-examine. If your story's full of holes . . ." He shrugged, stood up.

"It really wasn't anything."

"Then I don't need to hear it, do I?"

"Eleanor and I were talking, that's all. She said what a disappointment Dee was. I said so was Marcie, and Dee overheard us."

"What?" The top of Ed's head came detached, went flying off. "You said what? Jesus Christ, what's wrong with you? You can't have meant it."

"Yes, I did."

Ed threw his glass across the room. It shattered on her favorite lamp. He'd been a pitcher back in high school, and he hadn't lost his touch.

"Look what you've done," she cried.

"You are the fucking limit, Harriet. I love my daughter, I'm so God damn proud of her . . ." Words failed him, he was choked with rage. He turned and started for the door.

"Where are you going?"

Ed glared back. "Where do you fucking think I'm going? Fucking out to fucking dinner."

It was a little after six, the tent was full, the show was on, and Talker watched it from the back with Tom and Ozzie. They were good as cops went, on the level more or less, and he would chew the fat with them sometimes. Just idle talk.

Tonight it wasn't idle. They had no experience with strip shows, there were things they didn't know and needed to. So he was telling them.

"You know what's playing in the stands tonight?"

"Sure," Ozzie said. "The Demolition Derby."

Talker nodded. "It's like this. In my experience, those shows do funny things to people."

"Funny things?"

"They get stirred up. They watch cars bash and slam around, and when they come to catch our girls, they're apt to get a little crazy."

"Like?"

"You never know. They'll pick fights with each other, try to get on stage and mess the girls around."

"Don't worry," Tom said. "We'll be right here." Tom was big, no fat on him, and like most really strong men, he was quiet, slow to anger.

Talker smiled. "I'll worry anyway, but I just wanted you to know."

The 1856 House was, by far, the finest restaurant in town. Though new wings had been added through the years till no one knew which parts of it, if any, were original, the place retained its atmosphere. Pegged floors, rough beams, framed lithographs of pioneer days, flowered chintzes everywhere. The waitresses wore antebellum costumes, and each table had its bowl of daisies and its reproduction oil lamp.

Ed got there late. He spotted Marcie, Van, and Betsy at a table in the bay. They had Dee with them. Just as well. There were two empty chairs, for him and Harriet.

He stalked across the room, still plenty ticked off. "Look," he said before he sat, "let's all relax a little. Harriet's not coming."

"Oh Lord." Marcie shook her head. "She must be terribly upset."

"Yeah. You could say that." Ed sat, signaled for a waitress, ordered a bourbon on the rocks. "A double double with a twist."

Marcie couldn't read her dad. She knew there'd been a scene with Mother, it was on his face, she didn't need the double double to confirm it. She had not the slightest doubt what Mother told him, but the question was, had Daddy swallowed it? The one thing she was sure of was that she wasn't backing off from this one. Not one God damn inch.

Dee was her friend and Dee was staying. They had settled that one in the guest room. Dee was saying things like, "Look, I'm in the way here, I'm just making waves, I'll check in at the Fulton, get a room there." Marcie, in no uncertain terms, had told Dee she should shut the hell up. After which, they hugged and kissed, and that was that.

Van was sweating, making little stabs at small talk. Betsy watched him. What was worse than sad? Despair? How could he have helped her? She felt like James the snail—she loved her A. A. Milne: "James gave the huffle of a snail in danger and nobody heard him at all."

Ed's drink arrived. He took a long pull, put the glass down, looked at each of them in turn.

"O.K.," he said. "Let's put it on the table. First of all, I love my wife, I'm loyal to her, I don't like it when she's miserable. It hurts me."

Marcie's heart sank. He had bought it all.

"Marcie, I know how your mother works. She doesn't think so, but I do. And Dee, you know I loved your dad, but Eleanor is something else again. I know what really happened and I'm fucking mortified. The two of them should have their mouths cleaned out with Brillo, and I want you both to know, so far as I'm concerned—"

"Oh, Daddy." There were tears in Marcie's eyes.

"Don't interrupt. You're both terrific."

Marcie, by that time, was on her feet. She flung her arms around her dad. Dee, feeling a stab of longing for her own father, turned away—she couldn't bear to watch them—and buried her face in her napkin. Van was smiling with relief, and Betsy wanted hugging, too, but no one noticed.

"One more thing," Ed said. "I want this cleaned up. I don't care how you girls do it. Lie a little, lie a lot; just smooth it over."

Marcie nodded; she would find some way to bridge the gap with Mother. Dee nodded, too; she'd hand some guff to Harriet—but not to Eleanor. It was too late for that.

The stands were full, the whistle blew, and fifty cars burned rubber. Off they went, around the track. A cheer went up, and Lucy Lovell turned to Marvin Greener.

Lucy had permission from her dad to be there. It had taken tears, enough to fill the bucket she'd been working with all day. He even drove her in, then went off with some cronies. Marvin, on the other hand, had slipped away. His dad had gone on drinking, and by six o'clock his head lay on the kitchen table. Passed out cold, he'd sleep a week. So Marvin hauled him into bed, called Lucy on the phone, and took off in the truck.

They hadn't really been together since that wild night on Saturday, and they had both been going crazy. In the stands, with people everywhere, it wasn't easy making up for lost time. Kissing was O.K., a lot of kids were doing it. He'd managed to slip one hand underneath her blouse, and she had one hand on his thigh.

Whenever they heard fender-bending, they'd look up to watch the action, cars smashing into other cars or spinning off the track to slam against the wall. It was exciting. Gradually, the track began to fill up with abandoned cars while the survivors wove around them.

It made Lucy hot. Between the action on the field and Marvin, it was getting hard to breathe. She leaned close, whispered in his ear. "Guess what I saw today?"

"What?"

"Two girls necking."

"Bull."

"I did. Two strippers from the show. You know they're out at our place. I watched them through the curtain. They were in the same bed, naked."

"Doing what?"

"They kissed each other's tits."

"They did?" She had his interest now.

"And that's not all. You know where else they kissed? Down there," she said.

He shook his head. His eyes were bright. "You're kidding me."

"I thought it was disgusting," Lucy panted.

"Did they come?"

"How can you tell with girls?"

"Maybe they thrash around like we do. Did they?"

Lucy nodded. "Yeah. Like crazy."

"No shit."

She could see him bulging in his jeans. She moved her hand in that direction.

Marvin groaned. "Oh Jesus, Lucy, don't do that."

"O.K." She grinned and took her hand away. She knew her Marvin. When they did it later, he'd be crazy.

Cars were crashing, people screaming. It was heaven.

"I know, I know. It's terrible."

"It is. It breaks my heart," said Harriet, phone cradled to her ear. "Oh, Eleanor . . ."

"I'm sorry." Eleanor was weeping, and she paused to wipe her eyes. "She doesn't love me, and I don't know why. I tell you, I go over it and over it. I nursed her, changed her, I played endless games. She laughed so, she was such a happy child." Another pause. "You know, to this day, I still have her first tooth and an envelope with locks of hair."

"And when they met in nursery school. Remember that? Together every day. We'd have tea on the porch and watch them playing on the swings. And in the sandbox, how they got so dirty . . . oh my God. What happened?"

"All Dee ever had from me was love. With all my heart and soul. I covered her with love. And what thanks did I get for it? She left me, moved away."

"It doesn't matter where they are. I talk to Marcie every day, I see her all the time, I think of things to please her, make her happy. Eleanor, there's nothing she could ask of me I wouldn't do. I've never once denied her anything."

"The truth is . . ." Eleanor choked up. "I think Dee hates me. Oh dear Lord."

"She doesn't. Nonsense. You know better."

"Marcie cares for you, at least."

"I wish she did."

"Oh God, oh God. I can't go on."

The line went dead. "Hello, hello? Please, Eleanor . . ."

Harriet put the phone down. There was no one else on earth that she could share these things with, so she huddled in her chair and wept alone.

You couldn't miss the difference. Ever since the Derby ended, just like Talker said, there was a change. Annie stood peering through the curtain. She could see it in their faces, and their voices had a different sound as they stood waiting for the show to start. And here and there, they jostled, elbowed one another, pressing to get nearer to the stage.

Skipper moved in close beside her, took a look. "Don't ever let them throw you, kid. They give you shit, you give it back."

"Right." Annie wondered how you did that. All those men, and you were out on stage alone. She took another peep.

The tent was jammed. One guy—he looked to be about her age, well built and kind of handsome in a rural sort of way—was pushing hard to get up front. She hoped there wasn't trouble coming.

Marvin didn't mind the curses or the elbows in the ribs.

Lucy had told him what the two girls looked like, and he wasn't going to miss a chance to see them close. One of them sounded pretty, and it made no sense. A pretty queer? He'd always thought they got that way from being ugly. No men want you, what's a girl to do? He couldn't wait.

Outside, Norma signaled Talker: They were full up. "Next show starts in fifteen minutes, boys and girls." It got a laugh; there were no girls. "So have a beer or take a pee, but don't get lost."

He put his mike down, moved into the van. Skipper and Laurel looked O.K., but Annie had the jitters and Pauline was fretting with her costume, looking shaky.

"Attention, all hands," Talker said. "Remember, sticks and stones can break your bones, a little rowdiness can't hurt. We've got two good cops at the back, and I'll be right behind the curtain. Anyone starts making waves, you go about your business and, like Greyhound says, just leave the rest to us." He grinned. "O.K.?"

He turned and went to start the tape, then paused and sent a look at Annie. Where was he when she needed him? He didn't think she would tonight. But if she did, he'd be there.

"Here we go." He flicked the switch, the music started, Laurel glided through the curtains. Coarse vulgarities and whistling filled the air. He hurried to the curtain, opened it a slit, and eyed the house.

There was some shoving, nothing much. It didn't bother Laurel. Never did. She simply plied her trade like the professional she wasn't. Once, he'd asked her how she did it. "I obliterate them," she had said. "The men aren't there. I blot them out."

When Laurel came out, Marvin's eyes popped. She was gorgeous. What a waste. Her dress fit like a condom. Jesus. He looked up at her and spoke.

Talker saw it, couldn't hear him. Laurel kept on moving, and the kid kept on talking. Other voices joined him. "Take it off . . . let's see some twat."

Something that the kid said got to Laurel. She stopped dancing, headed for him. Tom and Ozzie at the back were wide awake; they caught it, they were on the move. They didn't get far. Scuffling broke out near them. Men were shoving, shouting at each other. Tom and Ozzie went to stop it.

Heads turned, then the scuffling started spreading, like a wave across the tent.

By this time, Laurel and the kid were shouting. He heard Laurel yell, "Go suck yourself, you fuckhead."

"Who's a fuckhead?"

Talker took off, bolted through the curtain as the kid began to heave himself on stage. Talker got his hands on Laurel, shoved her to one side. The kid was almost on the stage when Talker took one leg back, kicked him squarely on the chest. You kick too high, you catch the windpipe, you can kill them. As it was, the kid dropped like a stone.

16

DINNER STRETCHED FROM six to nine. For Marcie, it went like a shot. After the hugging and the tears, it felt so good to sit and talk; and by the time they reached the Fairgrounds, crowds were streaming from the grandstand. Just as well. She never liked the Demolition Derby, and they'd had their share of smashups; it was quite enough for one day.

Betsy picked up Denny by the ticket booths and, for a while, the six of them just strolled along. The sky was bright with moon and stars, a little breeze had come from somewhere, and the air, for the first time in days, felt fresh.

There were a lot of people, some of whom they knew—"Nice night, Ed; good to see you Marcie; hiya, Bets; some evening, isn't it?" They passed by couples sitting on the grass, and little family groups on benches. From some corner of the Midway, fireworks were going up. A modest show, the big one came on closing night, but they stood still, like children, fascinated by the little blips of colored light that rose, only to arch and fade away.

Marcie felt a surge of warmth. They were a family, after all. And Dee, too; she was part of it. She glanced at Dee.

"A penny for them," Marcie said.

Dee smiled. "They're nice." And it was true enough. There was a sweet sense of belonging. Pure illusion, wishful thinking, mixed with memories of how things used to be.

They stopped to get some ice cream as they wandered toward the Midway. Bets drew Denny to one side.

"I'm O.K. now," she said.

"You talk things over with your dad?"

She shook her head. Listening to the talk at dinner, all the compromises and the making do, had been an education. Most of the questions that had troubled her—how could a nice girl be a stripper, what made men get drunk and do such dreadful things—seemed much less puzzling. It was life, that's all. The way things were.

"I worked it out myself," she said. She saw her mother smiling at them.

Marcie knew she loved them all. Including Harriet. She'd deal with that tomorrow, she would find a way. She hadn't thought of Talker once all evening. He was separate, not just a secret, but apart from this. A family was what mattered. She took Van by one hand, Betsy in the other.

"Hi," was all she said to them.

The tent was being emptied out. Talker had just announced there would be no more shows tonight, and everyone was milling, grumbling. Lucy looked for Marvin everywhere. She found him finally, propped up against a tree trunk, leaning forward.

"Marv? What's wrong? Are you O.K.?"

He looked up. He'd been dragged out by some cop who'd reamed him good and left him there. At least he hadn't been arrested. "Sure," he said. "Don't I look great?"

"What happened?"

"Nothing much. Some big cocksucker came along and kicked me. Thinks he's heard the last of it? He's got another think. I'll tell my dad and we'll be back, we'll learn him."

"Marv?"

"Yeah?"

"Why'd he kick you?"

"For the hell of it."

She shook her head. "I know you, Marv."

He shrugged. "So there I am, just looking at this girl you saw. She's something, so I tell her so. She gives me lip. You think I'm going to take that? So I go for her."

"You went up on stage?"

"I started to. That's when the asshole kicked me."

"Jesus, Marv, sometimes you've got no brains at all."

It pissed him off. "You watch it, Lucy."

"No. You watch it. You got us arrested once already. I've been scrubbing floors, and you've been shoveling barns out. You just better hope your father don't get wind of this."

She had a point. "O.K., O.K. I'll watch it. Satisfied?"

She shrugged. "I guess."

He felt a little better. "Look, you gonna leave me sitting here all night?"

She bent and took his hands. He got a good look at her knockers as she helped him to his feet. They never failed to stir him up. "I'm really sorry, Lucy. I'll be good from now on."

"Promise?"

"Cross my heart." He crossed it, caught her eyes, and grinned. "You know what we should do?"

She recognized the look. "Uh-huh."

"You wanna do it?"

"Sure, O.K." She looked around.

"Not here," he said. He slipped an arm around her waist. They walked for a while, until he found a spot: a stretch of grass and shrubs behind the Bingo tent.

They settled on the grass. The fact that someone might just come along and see them only made it more exciting.

Talker was sitting on a corner of the bally stage, legs dangling. All the lights were out. The girls were dressing in the van, and he was watching Sheriff Weller talk with Tom and Ozzie over by the road. He wondered what was coming. Weller turned and started toward him.

"I hear you had a spot of trouble."

Talker stood. "That's fair to say."

"I don't much like it."

"I don't, either, but it happens sometimes Derby nights. I told your boys it might be coming."

Weller nodded. "So they tell me. Look, son, you know how I feel. I could have done without your show. This Fair is rough enough when things are normal."

It was Talker's turn to nod. He knew exactly what was coming. It was So long, Fulton County. Weller, sure as hell, was going to close them down.

"So here's the way I see it. Tom and Ozzie told me everything. What eats me . . ." Weller paused. "What really eats my guts is, you've been level with me. You played fair. We made a bargain, you've stuck to it. How can I back out of it?"

Amazing. Weller was an honest man. "So what's the verdict?"

"I'd give two weeks' pay to close you down. You don't belong here for a minute. I just wish to hell this thing tonight had been your fault, I'd love to lay it on you, son."

"I've got to tell you something, Sheriff."

"Don't. You thank me and I'll belt you one. I give my word and I can't break it. That's my problem." Weller turned to go. "Just don't take me for a sucker."

"Never in this world."

Talker held his hand out. Weller shook it.

Van was getting into bed. "Nice evening."

Marcie nodded, wishing there were more of them. "I loved it, too." She sat beside him in her nightgown.

Van leaned forward, gave her hand a squeeze. "I never thought, when we sat down to dinner . . ."

"Yes, I know." She smiled. "Dad can be amazing sometimes."

"He's the best." It wasn't easy, saying that. Van knew he came in second best, and it would always be that way. He looked at her. He had to ask it. "Tell me, are you ever sorry we got married?"

Marcie felt her heart thump. "What a question."

"That's no answer."

"Yes, it is." She bent and kissed his hand.

Van sighed. "I know things could be better—don't deny it—and a lot of it is my fault."

"My fault, too."

"I only wanted you to know . . ." He looked away. "It's just that sometimes, I don't give enough. I get too wrapped up in myself and I forget—"

"We all do. No one's perfect—even you."

It got a smile from Van. "I do keep trying, don't I?" Marcie rose and moved to her side of the bed as he went on. "It's stupid, but I hate to make mistakes. There's always something more I should be doing, or a better way to do it."

Marcie slipped between the sheets. "You ask too much."

"I know." At times like this, he marveled at her. She could

be so understanding. And compassionate. He shifted to his side and looked at her. "I love you, Marcie."

"I love you."

He kissed her on the lips; so gently. Like that first time, on the hillside; and how much she'd liked him for it. She remembered.

He edged closer. Then his hands were moving up and down, across her body. Marcie sighed and listened to his breathing deepen. When the time was right, she raised her gown and helped him find her.

It was vital to respond. She knew that, and she tried so hard.

Talker had waited till the Sheriff disappeared, then broke into a tap dance, scuffing up the dust. The show was still on. So was Marcie. He let out a whoop, a big one, vaulted to the stage, and headed for the van.

The scene inside was not good. All his girls were shaken up. Pauline was tube-glued. Skipper, just her panties on, was throwing spitballs at the walls, while Laurel, naked at her mirror, combed her hair as if she meant to pull the roots out. Annie—she was dressed, at least—looked as if the world had ended. As for Norma, there she sat, cash box in one hand, whiskey bottle in the other.

"Hey, hey, hey," he said. "What is all this?"

Only Norma looked up. "Can it, Talker. We've just been closed down, right? What the hell do you expect?"

"Closed down? Who says? What channel are you watching? We're in business."

All of them were listening now. He brought his hands together, one sharp clap. "Now, ladies, I'd appreciate it if you made a stab at looking decent. We have had enough shit for one day. We're going out to celebrate."

It sounded simple, but it wasn't easy. Fulton, by this time of night, would be a tomb. And even if he found a spot, the evening would be filled with looks of local disapproval, and he'd had enough of that. So he put Annie in his car, let Laurel take the rest of them, and headed for the Fallsburg Road.

There were plenty of joints in operation, life went on outside of town, but every parking lot was jammed with cars and pickups. That meant local yokels, and if one more bumpkin tried to move in on his girls tonight—he couldn't take them all on. What he wanted was a place where they'd be left alone.

It took half an hour to find it. There it stood, THE HAPPY HOUR BAR AND— Where the GRILL had gone, he didn't care. There was one dusty Harley parked in front; that's all. He pulled in and they piled out.

The place was just right—empty, clean, and seedy—and the bartender was glad to see them. "Call me Charley, take a table, any table."

They chose a big one in a corner, ordered boilermakers, fries, and burgers. Call-Me-Charley had a wife somewhere in back, and if they wanted steaks instead, she had some. Steaks it was.

It took a round or two for them to start unbending. He'd been right; they hadn't liked not seeing him, they needed him around. Nobody asked what he'd been doing, they just pretty much ignored him, talked among themselves.

It wasn't till the third round came that Skipper broke the ice. "Hey, Talker, you remember Crockett County?"

That had been four years ago, New Hampshire. Only Skipper had been with the show then. Talker spun the story out. The girls had been abducted, kidnapped by a bunch of drunken farmers. It took Talker and the Sheriff half the night to find them. When they did, the girls were in the kitchen, drinking beer. They found the farmers in the bedroom, bound and gagged. He told it well; he had them howling.

After that, it seemed like everybody had a story. Norma, Laurel, even Pauline had a tale to tell. By that time, they were drunk enough in Talker's judgment, so he called a halt and paid the bill.

The air outside cleared no one's head. He turned to Laurel.

"Can you drive?"

Her smile was slack. "I'm sober as a judge."

"Go slow, and don't get lost."

"Sure, sure."

He turned and looked for Annie. She stood by the door-jamb, holding on. The ground was tilting; she had never had so much to drink.

He took her arm. She leaned on him a little as they made it to his car. He turned to her and smiled. "Are you going to make it, kid?"

"Who, me?" She felt the ground begin to pitch. She reached up, grabbed his shoulder, and then, stretching tall, she kissed his lips.

"What's that for?" Talker asked as both her knees gave way. He caught her well before she hit the ground, opened the car door, got her in.

Out for the count was Annie. Not a move or murmur all the way back to the cabin. Talker parked, then moved around to her side.

"Annie?"

Silence. So he picked her up—the girl weighed nothing—carried her in both arms to the cabin door. He got it open, moved in, gently lowered her onto the bed. A slit of moonlight caught her face. She couldn't be as lovely as she looked. Who could?

He turned to go, then stopped. He couldn't leave her like that, she'd be miserable enough come morning. So he took her shoes off. Then her socks. He meant to stop there, but he didn't. Moving gently, he removed her jeans, her panties, T-shirt. There she was. He felt the same ache as when he'd seen her for the first time.

He bent down and moved her head so she'd be comfortable. She murmured something. She was out, no doubt about it, but her lips were moving. Then he heard. "I love you." Faint but clear. "I love you." And again. "I love you, love you."

Talker smiled. It had to be some boy back home. It wasn't him she meant. He moved across the room, went out, and softly closed the cabin door.

17

"OH, TO HELL with it."

Dee had been looking at the clock since four-fifteen. It said six-twenty now. Enough. She headed for the bathroom, washed and brushed, made monkey faces in the mirror, grabbed her robe, and went downstairs.

She heard the singing from the hall. At this ungodly hour, who could sing? Did Mrs. Beebe come this early? Had the woman lost her mind?

She stopped dead in the kitchen doorway. "Marcie?"

Marcie broke off in mid-melody, looked up, and smiled. "Hi."

Dee shook her head in disbelief. "You want to tell me what you're doing?"

"What's it look like? Making breakfast for the family."

Dee thought it looked like Armageddon. Yards of broken eggshells on the counter, batter of some kind dripped from a mixing bowl, and things that she assumed were sausages and bacon smoked in skillets on the stove. Dee had to smile. "I guess you do this all the time."

"Oh, I just felt like it today."

"I think the bacon's burning."

"That's the way Van likes it."

"Want some help?"

"No, thanks. I'm doing fine."

Dee beelined for the coffee, poured a mug. It was too hot. She hardly noticed as the life-restoring stuff went down. The singing started up again. Dee turned. "I hate to rain on your parade, but do we have to do that?"

Marcie looked blank for a moment. "You mean sing?"

"You got it."

Marcie smiled. "Oh my goodness. Are we grumpy? Did we wake up in a bad mood?"

"Tease me and I'll bite you."

"What's the matter, Dee?"

It was an invitation. She declined. "You making pancakes?"

"Yes—with berries in them. If there's anything that Betsy loves . . ." She shrugged. "I don't mean to go on burbling. I'm just happy, that's all."

Dee sat at the kitchen table. "I'd have never guessed it."

"This is going to sound a little soppy—I know you, Dee; it's what you'll think—but last night at the Fair, it hit me like a thunderbolt. I love my life, I love my family. I'm just so lucky."

Dee was grinning.

"See? I knew you'd find it funny."

"Nope. I'm only wondering, have you found another place or are you going to the Lodge again?"

"That's finished." Marcie turned off the bacon. "All done and over with. The chapter's closed."

"Uh-huh."

"I mean it, Dee." Marcie sat down next to her. "I can't explain what I've been doing. All I know is, it's been like a fever—and it broke."

"Have you discussed this with your stud horse?"

"That's no way to talk about him."

"Have you told him? Does he know?"

"I'm doing that this morning."

"Lotsa luck."

"He'll understand. Dee, you don't know him. He isn't what you think."

"Which is?"

"He's not a tramp. He's sensitive, intelligent— What are you smiling for?"

Dee would have told her if it hadn't been for Van. He walked in, looking fresh and snappy. And to top it off, the man was whistling. The two of them, they were a pair this morning.

"Hi, Dee; hello, honey. What have you been up to?"

"Guess."

He hugged her, kissed her on the lips. "I'm ravenous." He meant it. He felt wonderful. No burdens on his back, not since last night. And first thing he was going to do, come nine o'clock, was call up Sandy Stone and cancel the appointment. It had been an aberration to begin with.

Marcie smiled. "Is Betsy up?"

"She's on her way."

"Oh, good. I'll get your juice; Dee, bring the coffee. We'll be ready in a minute." Marcie looked up. "There you are, dear."

Betsy nodded from the doorway. When had Mom cooked breakfast last?

"Come here," said Marcie, arms outstretched. "We need a hug."

"Sure thing, Mom." Hers was not to reason why. She felt like she was playing in *The Waltons*.

Annie stumbled toward the bathroom. It was awful. She was going to barf again. This made how many times? She didn't know, she didn't care. She knelt and let her head rest on the porcelain. It helped to ease the throbbing. She retched, but nothing came. Small wonder. What was left to come?

She stayed there for a while, just in case. Her memories of the night before were few and far between. The kidnap story, steak, and all that whiskey. Instantly, her stomach tightened. She would never, ever drink that much again. And for passing out in public—she had done that, hadn't she?—it was humiliating. Only jerks like Emil, Jr., pulled that kind of stuff.

What else had she done last night? Well, she remembered leaving, clinging to the door, Talker had helped her to the car, and that was that. She hadn't kissed him, had she? No way. Wanting to was one thing, doing it was out.

Her stomach muscles eased. She stood and went back to the bedroom, past Pauline, who lay there on the other cot, still fully clothed. So bombed last night she couldn't even take her things off, she'd be out for hours. It was only then that Annie realized she was naked. Somehow, she had managed to undress herself; not bad, considering.

And then she saw her jeans and T-shirt, neatly folded. Talker. He'd put her to bed, he'd done it. It was too much. Annie sat down on her cot and blushed all over. Little did it matter that he'd seen her stripped before. They hadn't known each other then. She felt like such a child, so ashamed. Eighteen was old enough to take care of yourself—and look at her. How could she even dream of him?

She heard a rumbling sound. From where? Her stomach. It was going crazy. Food. She had to have some. She felt starved, and nothing in the cabin but some coffee. Annie checked her watch. Just eight, the grocery store was shut till nine. She couldn't wait, she'd fall down dead by then. There was a diner at the crossroads, and it meant an hour's walk—or she could thumb a ride.

She stood to get her clothes, felt dizzy, sat back down and tried to pull herself together.

Van chuckled as he made the turn on Blanchard Street. "For godsake, Marcie, you can't tell her that."

"I'm glad you think it's funny."

"Keep it simple. Just walk in and say you're sorry."

"I don't know." And Marcie didn't. Not a notion how to square things with her mother. She had played scene after scene out in her mind, and nothing bridged the gap. How angry Harriet had been when she'd walked out, the fury in those clear blue eyes. She couldn't shake the image. "Van, it isn't going to work. No matter what I say, she'll—"

"Never try outguessing what the other person's going to do."

"Thanks. That's a big help." Marcie saw the house ahead. Her car sat in the drive. "Oh Lord."

"She's not an enemy. She loves you, she's your mother."

"Have you ever met her? I must introduce you sometime."

Van pulled up in front and took her hand. "Calm down. It's going to work out. I have faith." He kissed her cheek. "That's just for luck, in case you need it."

Marcie took a deep breath, got out, faced her home. At least it used to be her home. It looked like Bluebeard's Castle. Slowly, every step took minutes, she moved up the front walk. Then the porch steps. Each riser seemed a mile high. She told herself this was ridiculous. She had a fourteen-year-old daughter; that was Betsy's age, not hers. And there she stood, as if the Principal had sent her home from high school with a note.

The door, as always, was unlocked. She opened it without a sound and tiptoed in. The house was quiet, hushed. They couldn't both still be in bed now, it was after eight. She edged into the hall and stopped. The air was filled with smells, aromas: fresh-baked bread, fruit pie, and muffins. What on earth was going on? Her mother hadn't baked for years. These were her favorite things. But not now, God forbid. Not after what she'd put away at home. Besides, it couldn't be for her.

Marcie cleared her throat. "Mom?" Not much sound came out. She tried again. "It's me, Mom. Are you up?"

"Oh, there you are, dear." Harriet moved through the kitchen door. She wore a pretty cotton dress and she looked perfect, every hair in place. "You're just in time." She beamed, took Marcie by the hand. "You come along with me."

They moved into the kitchen. It was spotless, not a mixing bowl or dirty dish in sight. The kitchen table was set for two. And on it, fresh as air, were all the goodies she had smelled.

"I made them just for you."

"For me? Oh, Mom." The woman must have started in the middle of the night."

"Now you be comfortable and let me serve. And there's some nice fresh milk to wash it down."

"I don't know what to say." She took her mother's hand. "Oh, Mom. I'm sorry, I'm so sorry."

Harriet looked at her, absolutely blank. "My dear, whatever for?"

Ed eased the kitchen door an inch, peered through the crack, and there they were, both at the kitchen table, chattering away. He grinned and deftly closed the door. It had to happen. There had never been the slightest doubt. The man was humming as he left for work.

Talker was sitting on a tree stump at the edge of CR 7, by the entrance drive to Carthage Lake. It turned out that the Lodge was not that far away. It meant a little detour for her, nothing much, and it was her idea to pick him up here. It was more than safe enough and she was due—he checked his watch: nine-thirty—any minute.

So he crossed his legs and went back to the Yellow Pages

in the County phone book. Phone books fascinated him, and every town they played, he made a point of thumbing through them. You could learn a lot. Like ethnic balance; were the listings mostly Irish, Polish, Waspish, what? You got a sense of what the crowd would be like. But the Yellow Pages were the best. How many churches, banks, bailbondsmen, doctors, lawyers, movie houses? And what businesses; where did the local money come from, were things rich or poor?

Today, however, he had other reasons. It had hit him in the middle of the night, and he'd gone sleepless ever since. The show was closing for the season Sunday. The takings here were rich, they didn't need another dollar; plus the girls were tired, wearing thin. And so was he.

Which left him free to go or stay, and what would happen if he hung around awhile? It meant not seeing Norma down to Lauderdale, but she was always telling him to buzz off, she had made the trip alone before. So there he was, no reason in the world he couldn't hold on for a week, a month, however long it took until this thing with Marcie ended.

It would end. It had to. There were limits to his self-deception; there was no way this could last for long. But while it did, he'd be a fool to give it up. He liked the way she made him feel; and what he did for her was damned exciting, too. She craved him. So, between the times when they could meet, it made good sense to get a job. Not for the money, he was flush; but just to pass the time and keep from going crazy.

According to the Yellow Pages, there were many things a man of his abilities could do in Fulton. Local radio, for one; he'd tuned in to the station, they could use him. Or repair work, he was good at that. Or even better, selling. Selling anything. It struck him he could even take a job at Steuben Motors. That was funny. He was chuckling when he heard the car.

He tossed the phone book in the weeds—it was too soon for her to know what he was thinking—stood and waved. He couldn't wait. It made him tighten just to see her coming.

"Right on time," he said as he got in. "Let's go."

She nodded, started driving slowly. Talker caught it instantly. No look, no smile, no kiss: It didn't take a genius. Something wasn't right, she had a problem. Let her bring it up. He sat back. "Gorgeous day."

He got another nod. So much for small talk. It occurred

to him he hadn't eaten. "There's a diner somewhere up ahead. You want to get some breakfast?"

"Jesus no."

She really was upset. In general, there were several things—not many, two or three—that had a tendency to crop up at this stage. He sat in silence, going through his checklist.

"Talker, this has got to stop."

He didn't blink. It topped his list, he'd dealt with it before. "I'm sorry. Come again?"

"It's not right and it can't go on." She'd meant to say it differently, more casually, blasé. But there he was, so close to her. She didn't feel blasé.

"I see." He nodded gravely. "Something's happened, hasn't it?"

"Not really."

"You don't have to tell me. I respect your feelings." Usually, that got things started, so he turned away, looked straight ahead, and waited. Not for long.

"I can't believe what I've been doing, I can't deal with it. I know it's wrong. And crazy, too. I have a family I love, a husband I adore, a daughter who's more precious to me—" She hadn't meant to choke up, but she did.

"I understand."

"I doubt you can. You have no way of knowing what I have at home."

He kept a straight face. "No? You think a man who leads my kind of life has no imagination? Just because my road is lonely doesn't mean—"

"I'm sorry. And I'm grateful—yes, that's true; I really am—for what you've given me. But, Talker, it comes down to this: I know where I belong."

"You think it's wicked, what we do?"

She nodded. "Isn't it?"

"God gave us our equipment and our feelings. If He hadn't meant for us to use them—"

"Not the way we've done it. No, not for a minute."

"You've enjoyed it, haven't you?"

"That's just the hell of it. I've had more joy with you in two days than I can remember. Ever, in my life." She turned and looked at him dead-on. "This is the hardest thing I've ever done. It's over, Talker. Finished. I won't ever hold you in my arms again."

Had she been listening to the soaps? It sounded like the kind of stuff Pauline was always glued to. Only, something in the way she said it caught his ear. She actually thought she meant it. Absolutely. Every word.

He let a moment pass. It had to look as if he recognized the depth of what she felt. A girl like Marcie needed careful handling. Talker knew exactly what to say.

Annie was trudging toward the crossroads when she heard a car approaching. She turned back to thumb a ride. The car was moving slowly. They were talking in the car; they never noticed her. But she saw them.

So that was Talker's Woman. Annie stared as they went by. What could he see in her, for godsake? She was ancient, skinny, worry lines and crow's feet. She had money; that you couldn't miss. But otherwise?

She had a chance. She felt her heart lift. There was hope. The two of them could bang away until they dropped; it wouldn't last. She turned and moved on toward her breakfast, all but skipping down the road.

The receptionist was smiling. "You go right on in. The doctor's waiting."

"Thanks." Van smiled back and wondered why he hadn't called to cancel. He had no reason now for coming. None. He felt at peace and so secure; he had his family. He had picked up the receiver, held it in his hand how many times since nine o'clock? Five, six—and here he was.

He paused outside the office door, imagining what lay ahead. A dim, grim room, shelves filled with rows of reference works, a flat, hard couch where he was meant to lie and pour his heart out. That's the way they worked, these analysts. He turned the knob.

"Come on in, Van. It's good to see you." Sandy got up from an armchair, smiling as he crossed the room. "How goes it?"

"Never better." It was good to make that clear from the beginning.

"Glad to hear it. Want some coffee, tea?"

Van grinned. "You run a restaurant?"

"I'm going to have some. Why not join me?"

"Coffee, black, no sugar."

"Coming up."

Van watched him open what he took to be a closet door. There was a little kitchen just beyond. The office was a shocker. Sunlight made its way through lightly curtained windows. There were comfortable upholstered armchairs done in a variety of brightly colored chintzes, no books anywhere, a sofa, coffee table, paintings on the walls, still lifes of fruits and flowers. Live and learn.

Sandy poured the coffee slowly. He had thought about Van's visit. He'd created it, in fact. He must have wanted it. And now that Van was here, his careful plays and ploys went out the window. Not to worry; he was good at winging it.

Sandy took the coffees, went back in. Van was examining the curtain fabric. "Here we go." Then, nodding at the curtain: "Are you into that?"

Van shrugged. "Not really. Marcie is, you know. The family room at home is full of samples."

"Is she good at decorating?"

"Not just good. She's fabulous. Who did your office?"

"Me." They sat down on the sofa. He had spent a lot of thought and money on the look of things. He knew what most of Fulton thought of him—of his profession, that was to say—and it was vital that they feel at ease. At home. And every object in the room announced, "No Quackery Allowed."

Van took a sip. The thing to do was turn the conversation onto Sandy. "Can I ask you something?"

Sandy nodded. "It's allowed."

"I've always wondered what it was that made you come to Fulton."

"That's an easy one. My mother's people came from Ashland. Fulton was as close as I could get." An outright lie, but no one ever questioned it. He glanced at Van and took a flyer. "Can I ask the same of you?"

"It's Marcie's home."

"That's everything?"

Van shrugged. "It seemed the thing to do. It doesn't matter anymore, it was decided years ago."

"By whom?"

Van stiffened. "What exactly do you mean?"

"Just asking."

"Don't you think I make my own decisions?"

"If you say so, sure I do."

"I've never once regretted it."

"You're lucky. It's not everyone who's happy with his life. You see much of your family?"

"Every day."

"I mean your parents. Are they still alive?"

"I see them now and then."

"I never hear you talk about them."

"There's not much to say. They're ordinary people."

"Any brothers, sisters?"

"No—can we call a halt to this?"

"I've got a brother. Want to hear about him?"

"Sandy, listen. I'm just taking up your time. I almost called to cancel, but I didn't want to hurt your feelings."

Sandy nodded. He had pushed too hard. "I'm always asking questions, it's an occupational disease." He smiled. "You want to talk about the weather?"

"What I'd rather do is go. I'm fine. There's nothing you can do for me."

"I'm glad to hear it." Sandy sat back on the sofa. "What's new since our golf game yesterday?"

"Is that a probing question?"

"Oh, come on, Van. It's a social inquiry. I didn't see you at the Club for dinner."

"I was at the '56 House with the family."

"Sounds nice. Were Ed and Harriet along?"

"Just Ed."

"How come?"

"None of your God damn business."

"Sorry. I'm all thumbs today. I keep upsetting you."

"I'm not upset. There was a family fight. It got patched up. You satisfied?"

"Van, you don't have to tell me anything."

"I didn't mean to shout."

"I'm used to it. Besides, it's good for you. You keep too much inside, you know."

"The hell I do."

"You know what Shakespeare wrote? 'The lady doth protest too much.'"

"You think you're so damn smart. You Jews are all alike."

"We're really not. My brother, Lee, is nothing like me. He got all the family brains. And talent, too. Am I the only Jew you know?"

"What difference does that make?"

"Not much. You ever yell at Marcie like this?"

"No!"

"Not ever?"

"Are you deaf, for Chrissake?"

"Don't you want to?"

"Shut up!"

"Is she perfect, Van? She must be if you never—"

"Stop it!"

Sandy stopped it. Van was bright red. Sudden tears were streaming down his cheeks. "Here." Sandy handed him a box of Kleenex, stood, and turned away, looked out the window. He was not, all things considered, bad at this. A subject on which Alice gave him very little peace. "You've thrown your life away, you're wasting it out here!" She was a good wife and loved him.

"Sandy?"

"Yup?" He turned.

Van's shoulders shook. He'd be a while, calming down. The man had so much pain to deal with. "Sorry. I don't ever cry, I just can't seem to stop."

"God gave us tear ducts, too, you know; not just the women. Would you like to come again tomorrow? I've got time."

Van choked up, then he got it out. "No. I'm not ever coming back."

Dee had no wheels. She needed transportation; Hertz or Avis or whatever, they were all the same. But when she brought it up at breakfast, Marcie took her head off. Rent a car while there were loaners at the Agency? Forget it and for shame.

So Dee had taxied down to Service, picked a car—the nearest one, what difference did it make?—and drove around. To nowhere in particular. In circles; perfect metaphor, it summed her up. There was a half-remembered song—some ancient comic, Berle, Durante; that was it, he sang it—which kept weaving through her thoughts. "Did you ever have the feeling that you wanted to go, and still have the feeling that you wanted to stay?"

The words were wrong, the thought was right. Unfinished business: that was what her shrink had called it. What was left to finish? Van and Marcie weren't a problem. Growing up? She'd done that years ago. What then? Was there a single reason why she didn't head for Akron-Canton, take the next plane to New York, get out of here for good and all? Why not? A single word kept coming up. Repress it as she might, it went on tolling like a bell. Eleanor.

How do you exorcise a parent? Death was no help; Dad was still around. And saying "Fuck you" was, she faced it, naughty. Nothing more. Like soaping windows on Halloween. She even used to soap the windows of her own home. Gratifying for the moment, but an empty gesture. Nothing changed.

Eventually, she gave it up, drove back to Sunset Crescent with a hot bath on her mind. She went up to the guest room, took her clothes off and, by accident, glanced out the window. There were Betsy and her boyfriend by the pool. Two strangers. Betsy had been six on Dee's last visit home. They dove in and began to swim.

They always used the house on Thursdays. It was Mrs. Beebe's day off, and Bets loved the freedom. Mom was at the shop, Dad was away at work. No grown-ups. Not that they did anything they shouldn't, though it did occur to her at times like this to take a risk or two.

She had been telling Denny all about the family breakfast. She was good at telling stories, better still at writing them. It was a total secret. No one knew, except for Denny. Both of them were laughing. It made swimming difficult; you kept on gulping water.

"And the best part"—Betsy stopped to cough—"the best was cleanup. Mom and Dad kept dropping things and saying how much fun it was and we should do it every day. Can you imagine?"

"No," he said, "I guess I can't." He stood up at the shallow end and looked at her. "You really shouldn't knock it all the time, you know."

"But, Denny, it's so phony. They don't mean a word of it."

"You know for sure?"

She nodded.

"How?"

She had a lot of answers, tried and true, but they kept sticking in her throat. She shrugged. "I know, that's all."

He shook his head. At least she had some parents. "Maybe it's the best that they can do."

She'd never thought. She felt quick tears. "Oh, Denny . . ."

"Yeah," he said. They put their arms around each other, that was all, and stood there for the longest time.

Dee hadn't meant to watch. She wiped her eyes and turned away. There was no getting out of it. She had to deal with Eleanor.

Talker came that close to losing his composure. Words had failed him. Let him down. It was his own damn fault. He'd been too sure, too confident. And what was worse, she hadn't cut him short. She'd let him babble to the bitter end, then turned the car around and dropped him off at Carthage Lake.

He started up the drive on foot. His first thought was, To hell with it, who needs her? Every Fulton had a girl like Marcie. Two or three, and maybe more. A dozen? It was possible. Across Ohio, Indiana, Illinois, and points west, girls like Marcie grew on trees, for all he knew.

He stalked on up the road, past old folks swinging in their hammocks, kids at play. A pox on all of them. He saw the truth now. Marcie had been playing with him, toying. Suckered him with all that "Oh, I'm not that kind of girl" crap. Never given head before? She'd done it like a pro—and he'd believed her. What a fool. He kicked a stone. The thing was bigger than it looked. He grabbed his foot, let out a howl, and stood there on one leg like a flamingo. Idiot.

He hobbled back to camp. No sign of Norma and the girls. They'd all been bombed last night, and it was still the middle of the morning, not eleven yet. They wouldn't stir for hours. So he got into his T-bird, slammed the door and went.

He took the drive at fifty. Let the brambles scratch his paint job, did he care? He skidded onto CR 7, came down on the gas, and let it fly. Speed always cooled him out. Go fast enough, whatever's bugging you gets left behind. He didn't know where he was going, and he didn't care.

Marcie was staring in the washroom mirror. On the outside, she looked fine, composed, at peace, herself again. Her insides were another matter. Not that she regretted what she'd done, not for a moment. But the truth was, it had not been easy. Talker had—no danger in admitting it, not anymore— the man had made a jumble of her. It was normal, only natural, that she needed time to settle down. Not much. A little while. Any moment now and she'd have all the equanimity a girl could ask for.

Good. She nodded at the mirror, smiled, and moved out to the office. Her side of the partner's desk was piled high with paperwork. Small wonder. She'd been gone since Monday, caught in all that stupid madness.

It felt good to be here, back where she belonged. When she'd pulled in, midmorning, Pam was glad to see her. No complaints, Pam was an angel; but it wasn't easy running things alone. Marcie had told her final lie—her country gentleman decided not to sell his treasures. Pam was disappointed, and so, Marcie said, was Marcie.

Since then, she'd been at her desk. The fabrics they had ordered from New York were late in coming, and she'd written off an urgent note. Polite enough, but urgent, just right. Then the billings. Mrs. Wankel, who was always late in paying, got a brisk reminder, and she was about to call the shippers up in Akron when she heard the front door open. Pam was there, she'd handle it. And then she heard his voice.

She froze. He had his God damn nerve. She'd handed him his walking papers. What more did it take? A fight, a screaming match? If that was what he needed, that was what he'd get.

She got up, moved into the office doorway.

"Marcie?"

"Yes, Pam?"

"It's the gentleman who bought the bed."

"Why, so it is. What does he want?"

"He says he owes us money."

"He owes *us*?" That was a first; she had to give him credit.

"Yes, M'am." Talker nodded. "Too much change, that's what you gave me, and I came to set things right."

"That's very decent of you." Marcie glared at him, not caring if Pam saw or not.

"He's brought back the receipt," Pam said, "and—"

"I'll take care of it. It's almost noon, Pam. Why don't you take off for lunch?"

"Oh, I'm all right."

"No, really. You've been stuck here two days running. You go on, I'll watch the store."

"You're positive?"

"Believe me."

Pam smiled. "I won't be long."

"Take all the time you need."

"O.K., if you insist. I'll just go and get my purse."

It took Pam half a month to get it and go out the door. He stood there waiting, nothing showing on his face. He wanted her to make the first move? Fine. She had one for him.

"Get the fuck out."

"In a minute."

"Do I have to call the cops?"

"I came to tell you something."

"I'm all ears."

"It's personal. Can we conduct this conversation in your office?"

"No."

"Why not?"

"Oh, what the hell." She turned and went back in. He followed, closed the door.

"You want to leave it open?"

"Fine. O.K. by me." He opened it.

"All right. Let's hear it."

Talker hesitated. He'd been sure he knew exactly how to handle this. There were a lot of things he meant to say. He'd been rehearsing for the last half hour. Some of them were touching, many of them true. But it had been so long since he had felt this way; and glaring at him now, the way she was . . .

"Marcie?"

"Yes?"

What was he going to say? He couldn't just stand there. "I'm sorry." It was miles from what he'd come to tell her.

"Oh?" The syllable dripped acid. "Why, what for? You walk into my shop, you compromise me, did you even stop to think?"

"I couldn't stop."

"Why not? You're horny, that's all. God, you're such a prick."

He winced. He didn't like that kind of language, not from her. "You mean a lot to me."

"Go find yourself a tramp and get it off with her."

"You think that's what I want from you?"

"O.K. Surprise me. What?"

He'd lose her if he told it all. "You're like no woman in my life. You're precious to me."

"You expect me to believe that?"

"Yes."

The man looked so sincere, but she knew better. "I know what you came here for. You think we'll shut the door and do it on the carpet."

"Will you stop it with that kind of talk, for Chrissake? It's demeaning."

"Coming from you, that's a laugh."

"I think about you, Marcie. I go crazy when you leave me."

"Can you die from lust? I hope so. Are you finished?"

"Touch me."

"Why? You think I can't? You're so magnetic?"

"Do it."

"Any place particular?"

"May I touch you?"

She stiffened. "Where?"

He brushed his fingertips across her cheek. She shivered. It could not be happening again. She had a will, and she could use it. "So long, Talker."

He would not say please. There were some limits, pride meant something. What he had to do was smile, turn, go out the door.

He never made it to the threshold. "Don't," he heard her say. "Don't go." He felt her arms, her lips were on his neck. He turned and held her.

"Oh dear God . . ." She didn't care what happened, nothing mattered. He was holding her so tight; she couldn't breathe, she thought she'd break.

He kissed her.

Marcie whispered, "Close the door."

He did. She leaned against the desk, she couldn't trust herself to stand, and watched him clear the papers off so they could use it.

18

KNOCKING. NORMA HEARD it, there was no mistake. The middle of the night and some damn fool was knocking on her cabin door. She groaned and checked her watch—twelve-thirty—and was about to drift off when it struck her. They'd been out till after two. It was the middle of the day, and Talker, bless his heart, had let her sleep it off.

There was more knocking. "Yeah, yeah, yeah," she mumbled as she got up and headed for the door. All things considered, she felt pretty good; she could still booze it with the best of them. Not bad for sixty-two.

"O.K.," she muttered as she fumbled with the knob. "I'm up. You satisfied?" She opened the door a crack.

"Good mornin', Mrs. Cusak."

It was what's-his-name, the creep who owned the place. She cleared her throat. "Uh-huh?"

"I'm sorry, but that Talker fellow took off hours ago, and I thought maybe you were oversleeping." Barney Lovell smiled. "Looks like I thought right."

"Thanks, Mr.—"

"Lovell. Barney Lovell."

"Nice of you," she told him, and began to shut the door.

"You have a minute?"

"Now?" She had a few, and better things to do with them. On the other hand, she'd been expecting static from the

Christian campers. Maybe this was it. "O.K.—but just hold on a minute. I'm not decent."

"M'am, you take your time."

She found her cotton wrapper, threw it on, moved to the john to brush her hair, decided it looked like a jungle, left it as it was and let him in.

He paused at the door. "I thought you might be thirsty, so I brought some soda pop." He had a can for each of them. "I heard you coming in last night. You sounded like you'd been carousing."

"Sorry if we woke you."

"I was up."

She led him to the little table. "Rest your bones here, Mr. Lovell."

"Thank you kindly." Barney fumbled with the flip-tops, got them open. "There you go."

They sat and drank. The stuff was icy cold, and Norma let it trickle down. "Well, Mr. Lovell?"

"Well . . ." He hesitated. "It's about you people being here. You know what I mean."

"Not exactly." It was coming now. They were about to be evicted.

"Folks here, they're not used to ladies who—well, you know, dance to make a living."

Norma nodded, took the bull by the horns. "You're saying they don't like it?"

"Yes and no. Some do, some don't. But just by being here, it changes things. No matter where I go, I get a buzzing. You're on everybody's mind. It's in the air."

"Have we done anything that's out of line?"

"No, M'am."

"You're sure of that? Last thing we want to do is be a problem."

"Well, you're not exactly what I'd call a problem. All the same . . . Take me, for instance."

"O.K., Mr. Lovell."

"Can I ask . . . I don't suppose you'd call me Barney?"

God almightly, Norma thought, the old goat wants me. "Sure," she said, "and you just call me Norma."

"It's a hard life, Norma."

Norma nodded. "Tell me."

"Ever since I lost my wife—that's ten years back. I lost her to a Lutheran; she always had an itch for Swedes. Just up and left me, and the truth is, Norma, things at Carthage Lake get pretty grim sometimes. The winters here go on forever, no one in the house but me and Lucy. It's enough to drive a sane man crazy."

"You should find yourself a nice plump widow, Barney, and go after her."

He leaned across the table. "Just what I was thinking. Norma—"

"Not me, Barney. You don't want me."

"Right this minute." He was on his feet now, circling toward her. "Norma, you don't know . . . I need you."

Norma stood. She didn't want to hurt him, but she knew he'd love it while it lasted, then he'd see her as a cheap old whore. The world was full of Barneys; they were like that, couldn't help themselves.

"You only think you need me."

"Norma, Norma." He had both hands on her breasts.

She took them firmly off. "Look, Barney, I'm just passing through, I'm gone come Labor Day. What you want is someone permanent."

"Don't tell me what I want."

"I know what loneliness is like. I live with it. But we're not bunny rabbits. Popping off a quick one isn't going to help."

"You want some money?"

"No."

"I know your kind. We set a price—"

"You're saying things you'll be ashamed of."

"Look at me." He pointed to his crotch. "I'm dying."

Norma had to smile. "You'll survive." She started to the door. "I've got to get my girls up, go to work."

His face was mottled, splotched with red. "A hundred bucks."

"Thanks for the soda pop." She drew the door back.

"Get this straight: no old whore turns me down."

She shrugged. "You live, you learn. I'll see you, Barney."

"Go to hell." He grabbed the door and slammed it hard as he went out.

Annie had eaten half the world for breakfast. Anything she wanted: brownies, apple pie, a tin-roof sundae, and a chocolate shake to wash it down. No doubt about it, things were going her way: Talker's Woman was a bag of bones.

She paid, she even left a big tip, then went out to thumb a ride. The very first car picked her up, a family from Mansfield going to the Fair. It really was her day. She sat back and relaxed. Today was Thursday. Sometime Sunday, Fulton would be history. So would Talker's Woman; left behind, forgotten. Then it struck her. Where would Annie be? Forgotten, too?

She needed time to think, to be alone. A quiet place. The Fair was out. So when they reached the Fulton line, she got out near the Country Club, thanked everyone politely, found herself a grassy slope, and sat. She had been careless with her Journal, not an entry now for days. She had it with her; and a pencil.

Back in high school, it had always helped her study if she wrote things down. It made her think. You broke the subject into sections, charted it, made columns using nice straight lines. Today's assignment was a tough one, even worse than Algebra. She found a fresh page, wrote the subject at the top. In capitals.

TALKER.

Now what? Break it down. She drew some columns. Wiggly lines, she had no ruler. Next step was to put in headings. *Talker's Past.* What did she know? Not much. His age, his hometown. Down they went. Then *Talker's Present.* That was easier. Her pencil flew. She put down everything he'd said and done since she had met him. It was just a week ago. She looked up, watched the cars go by, and let it sink in. Seven days. That's what the Lord took. Annie hadn't made her world, but there was nothing left of what had been before. It sort of qualified as a Creation.

Back to work. Next column. *Talker's Future.* Without thinking, she wrote one word: *Annie.* That was it, that's what it all came down to. How to make it happen?

Fresh page. *ANNIE.* What did Annie have to offer? Playing hard to get was pointless; he had seen her body, every inch. She had some skills: she cooked and sewed, knew how to run a home. But Talker didn't have one, not a place that counted—he was always on the move.

She had some money. Or she would have when the week was out. Two thousand dollars, Talker said, or thereabouts. It sounded like a fortune, but she knew it wasn't. Still, she wouldn't be a burden, she could pay her own way.

Sex. Did Talker want her? Kind of. Maybe. Annie wasn't sure. She caught him looking sometimes, but she couldn't read his mind. And even if she did it with him—Annie closed her eyes and saw them locked together, felt her nipples harden— would it make a difference? It would kill her just to be a one-night stand. She'd die.

And what was worse, she'd never done it. There he was, a man who'd had a million girls of every kind and shape and size. How could she please him? She'd be clumsy, make mistakes. She had a lot of instincts, God knows, but you couldn't just get in the saddle. First you had to learn to ride.

Or—it was a fresh thought, and it stopped her cold. Or was it an advantage? Did it make her special for him? Virgins were a rare commodity in Talker's life. And men liked virgins; they were always saying so.

The thing was, one way or another, Annie had to act. Do something. Make a move. She'd lose him if she didn't. Annie licked her pencil, wrote it down and underlined it: _What move?_

Then she closed her Journal. She felt satisfied. As always, it had made her think. She didn't have the answer, but at least she had the question.

Ed left the Fairgrounds, took the right, still whistling. Ever since he left the house, the world had had a rosy glow. No sales this morning, but he had two couples on the hook, and they'd be back. Van hadn't shown up, hadn't even called in. He was like that these days, moody and a little unpredictable, but everybody went through phases, and to tell the truth, Ed liked it better, now and then, not having him around.

Right at that moment, there was nothing on his mind but lunch. A gin and tonic in the Paddlewheel, a club steak in the Men's Grill, or perhaps the Special of the Day. Some Thursdays they had roast-beef hash, all burnt and crusty on the outside.

He pulled up at the Fallsburg Road, checked both ways, made the turn. About half a mile ahead, a girl was standing on the shoulder, thumbing into town. A pretty girl; you couldn't miss it, even at this distance.

If the hash was on the menu, he was going for it. "That's for me," he said aloud. The girl was closer now. He'd seen her someplace. He slowed down, no harm in looking. Then he placed her. There she was, in jeans that fit her like a rubber glove: his Harem Girl.

If there was one thing Ed could do like lightning, it was make decisions. But for the first time in how many years?—since he proposed to Harriet?—it took a little time. He weighed the pros and cons, then hit the brakes and pressed the window down.

"Miss? Can I offer you a ride?"

Van was driving slowly, aimlessly. To nowhere in particular. He felt like driving; that was why. Besides, he couldn't seem to think of any place to go. Correction: any place he cared to go. Not work. Not home. He still could not believe he'd wept in Sandy's office. Analysts were clever; that must be the reason. They got paid for playing with your feelings.

He turned a quiet corner, glanced down at the dashboard clock. It must be broken. Twelve-fifteen? Had he been driving for an hour? More? Just how long had he been in Sandy's office? Suddenly, the tears began again. He couldn't see to drive. The curb was vacant, lots of room to park. That was the thing to do.

He did it. What must Sandy think of him? How could he ever face the man, have lunch, make small talk, let alone play golf with him? He bit his lip and clenched his fists. Stress. That was all it was. A little too much pressure, all the worries over business. Stress did funny things to people, and the answer was relax, let go a little.

Fifteen minutes later, he was on the practice tee, kneeling by his golf bag. One by one, he took his clubs out and meticulously laid them on the grass. In perfect order. First, five woods; and then, nine irons. All the shafts were parallel. He nodded, finding it particularly satisfying. What next? He unzipped his bag, reached in, and found his tees, but not his golf glove. Not a matter of importance; he could do without it.

"Here you go, Mr. V."

Van looked up. Larry, the assistant pro, was moving toward him with four buckets filled with practice balls. They had red stripes around them. Crudely painted, sloppy stripes. Van made a mental note to take that up with someone.

"Thanks. Just put them down." Four buckets? Had he asked for four? Two hundred balls. It seemed a lot.

"Looks like you're really practicing today, I guess."

"I guess." The boy had no mind. What else did it look like?

"Nice day for it." Larry smiled. "Got a big game coming up?"

Van didn't feel like talking. "Yes," he said, picked up his driver and began to stretch. The stretching was important. You could hurt yourself if you weren't limber, and Van always took precautions not to hurt himself.

He teed a ball up, took his stance and blasted it, just let it fly. It didn't matter where it went, he didn't look. Another. Then another. He was feeling better every minute. What had Sandy asked him that was so upsetting? Something—but what was the subject? It was fading, gone already.

Sweat was pouring off of him. He had an iron now. A five. Three empty buckets. Where had all the balls gone? There was something on his left hand. Blisters. Big ones, but they didn't hurt. They should have, but there wasn't any pain at all. No reason not to keep on playing.

When all the balls were gone, he put the clubs back in the bag. The grips felt sticky, which was odd. He checked his left hand. Broken blisters, that was all. A little blood. He wrapped his handkerchief around his hand. No question, he felt wonderful.

Annie squinted at him through the window. She was always careful when it came to hitching rides with single men; but he was old, and that meant safe. Besides, he had a nice face, gruff but kind, like someone's grandpa.

"I'm just going into town," she said.

Ed smiled. "So am I." He reached across, opened the door, then sat back, watching as she got in. Poetry in motion. He had seen a lot of pretty girls, and had more than his share of them, but there was something different here. Just watching from the audience the other night, he'd caught it. But up close, she made his throat go dry. She had a quality—like what? The White Rock Girl, September Morn: all dewy innocence. He almost grinned; he must be getting old.

"Where can I drop you?"

"Anyplace, it doesn't matter." Annie closed the door. She figured she'd go window shopping, maybe buy a dress, something for Talker to admire, make him look twice.

"Well," Ed said, deciding to move carefully, "so what brings you to Fulton. Come to see the Fair?"

"I work there."

"Doing what?"

She wondered, would it shock him if he knew? She shrugged. "It's just a job."

He didn't press it. "You don't come from these parts, do you?"

"Wish I did. I've never seen a nicer place."

"Where are you from?" The moon, for all he cared. The point was just to get her talking.

"Well . . ." She felt like she could tell him things, and there'd been no one since she'd said good-bye to Susie that she could really talk to. Bets and Denny, they were kids, that's all. She looked at him. "You promise not to laugh?"

He nodded, crossed his heart. God, he could make the stones talk, he was good.

"The truth is, mister—"

"Call me Ed."

She couldn't; she'd been brought up to respect her elders. "The truth is, some of it is kind of funny. There's a strip show at the Fair. The Moulin Rouge."

He nodded. "Yes, I know."

She watched him carefully. "That's where I work."

Ed snapped his fingers. "Right. I knew I'd seen you. You're the girl—you wore the harem costume."

Was she blushing? Annie couldn't tell. "That's me."

"I liked the way you danced."

"You did? I don't know what I'm doing up there half the time."

"You'd never guess it. And I liked the costume, too."

She smiled. "You're not just kidding me?"

"Why would I? You're a very special girl."

"Oh, come on, mister. That's a line."

"You have a name?"

"It's Annie."

"Listen, Annie, when you get to be my age, you don't have time for lines. I call 'em as I see 'em. If I say you're special, just believe it."

Annie wanted to. "I wish I could."

"What kind of life have you been leading? Don't the boys chase after you?"

"Not so's you'd notice."

Something didn't add up. "Did they raise you in a convent?"

"Don't be silly."

"You must beat the boys off with a stick."

She felt like giggling. "Maybe."

"That's no way to treat us boys. Now, you don't have to answer this, but have you ever—"

"Listen, mister. I don't even know you. You can't ask me things like that."

Ed smiled. "I guess you haven't."

Annie stiffened. "What's it to you?"

"Don't you want to?"

Annie turned, looked out the window.

"Take your time," she heard Ed say. "Make it an honest answer."

There was moisture on her forehead. Annie wiped it. There was something in her Journal, but she couldn't seem to think. What was it? She had underlined it. *Make a move. What move?* Not this one. God no.

"I'm still waiting."

Annie turned on him. "What do you want to hear me say?"

"The truth, that's all."

"O.K., then dammit, yes, I want to."

"One more question."

"I'm in this deep, what the hell."

"Why haven't you?"

"I'm scared. How's that? You satisfied?"

"What are you scared of?"

"I don't know."

"It's time you found out, don't you think?"

She thought of Talker. It was time, and then some. "Yes," she told him. "Yes."

"When do you have to be at work?"

"I'm free till three or so." What was she saying?

"Good."

He reached out for her hand and held it, took a turn, and headed for the open country.

Talker sat in Marcie's desk chair, watching her. Somehow, they hadn't bothered taking all their clothes off. She was sitting on the desktop, facing him, dressed from the waist up. They had come so close to splitting—seconds, just another step or two—and she was looking at him in a way he didn't recognize. It crossed his mind to wonder what she really felt for him. He sensed a change. What was it?

"Feel like talking?"

Marcie nodded.

"It would help me if you put your legs together."

Marcie crossed them. She felt dizzy, and the room was swaying, so she grasped the desk's edge with both hands. It didn't help.

"That's better," Talker told her.

"Is that all you think about?"

He shook his head. "You'd be surprised by what I think." He reached down for his shorts and blue jeans. Maybe it was time to tell her he was going to stay in town awhile.

She cleared her throat. "What happened just now . . ."

"Yes?"

"I know it looks . . . I mean to say . . ." What did she mean?

"Go on."

The shop door had a chime that went off when it opened. Talker jumped up, got his shorts on, jammed his legs into the blue jeans.

Marcie said, "Oh Jesus."

Dee's voice floated from the front. "Hello? Is anybody in?"

Talker pulled his jeans up, shook her by the shoulders. "Get your clothes on."

Marcie stood up. He was right, that was what she had to do.

"Look, Marcie, we have got to talk."

"I know."

Dee's voice again. "Is anybody back there? Marcie?"

"In a minute, Dee."

"Tonight. When I'm through with work. O.K.?"

"God, I don't know."

"I'll meet you at the Lodge." He started to the back door. "Be there."

Marcie nodded, grabbed her skirt and panties, headed for the washroom.

"Marce?"

He went out, she flew in. Dee moved into the empty office, looked around. "Where are you?"

"Freshening up. Won't be a minute."

"Take your time." Dee went to work. She took some Kleenex from her purse and wiped the moisture from the desktop, picked up Marcie's shoes and put them on a chair. The blotters next; and then the papers. Was that all? What other damage had they done?

Marcie came out, calm and smiling. "Hi."

"The same to you."

"You free for lunch? When Pam comes back, the two of us could—"

"Tuck your blouse in. Jesus, Marcie, are you fucking crazy?"

"What?"

"Your shoes are on the chair."

"Oh." Marcie headed for them. All the dizziness came back. She sat.

"Just tell me, have you lost your mind?"

"I don't know."

"Pull yourself together, put the God damn shoes on."

Marcie nodded, fumbled with them. "Don't be angry with me, Dee."

"Why not? The shop was open, anyone could walk in. If I'd come a little sooner, I'd have found the two of you—"

"I know, I know."

"Stop crying."

Marcie had one shoe on. "Am I crying?"

"Oh, for godsake. Give me that." Dee grabbed the other shoe from Marcie's hand and jammed it on her foot. "Stand up. I can't have people seeing you like this. We're getting out of here."

Dee typed a note for Pam—some lame excuse—locked up the shop, got Marcie out the back, and headed for her car.

"Where are we going, Dee?"

Dee yanked the car door open. "Just get in."

Dee drove.

They were judging Junior Poultry in the Poultry Tent. Walt Greener, whose chickens were for eating, not for show, stood waiting outside in the shade. His thoughts were miles away. On Marvin. Always getting into trouble. First, the Country Club; and where the money for the fine was coming from, God maybe knew but Walter didn't. And as if that weren't enough, the fracas at the strip show last night. He had pulled the story out of Marvin when the boy came home. He knew his kid; something was up.

Marvin's version, he had learned from long experience, was sure to be a mix of truth and bull. Not that Marvin wasn't honest. He just saw things his way, and when trouble came along, somehow the other fellow always started it. But Walt had seen the bruises on his son's chest; they were real for sure. No matter how you cut it, that fast-talking bastard at the show had kicked his kid, and Walter wasn't going to take that lying down.

"Hey there, Walt. Sorry I'm late."

He looked up to see Barney Lovell moving toward him. He was hoping to hit Barney up for cash to pay the fine, so he put on a big smile. "Hiya, Barn. How are you?"

"Pissed. I stopped on the way in and had a few."

"This time of day? How come?"

"You know the old bag at the girlie show?"

Walt frowned and shook his head.

"She sits outside and takes the tickets. You remember."

"Oh yeah. Sure."

"You want to know the truth about her?"

Walt grinned and nodded. "Is it good?"

Ed found the spot. It took a while. Landmarks, even big ones like limestone boulders at the turning and the little hill-side on the right, were gone. Not there. He kept on driving, keeping calm. He hadn't been to Pussy Point—that's what they'd called it—since his high-school days. A lot can change in fifty years; if they can build a rocket to the moon, they can remove a hillside.

"Mister?"

"Yup?"

"Where are we going?"

"Just sit back, leave everything to me."

A minute passed, the cow path took a turn he recognized—and there it was, just the way it used to be. The weeping willows and the winding stream, and not a living soul for miles. He stopped the car and turned to her.

"Is this it?" Annie asked. She'd had some second thoughts

along the way, enough to fill a bushel basket, but she wasn't going to back down. Come what may, no matter what.

Ed nodded, smiled. This was it, all right; and he was going to have his Harem Girl. He got out, opened up the trunk, reached for the plastic bag. It held a car robe. Harriet was always cold in winter, it was her wool blanket, and the use he was about to put it to was curiously pleasing to him.

When he turned, he saw her standing by the willows, looking at the stream. Her back was to him. Everything about her—every line and curve, the way she stood, hands in her pockets, slits of sunlight glinting on her hair—it shook him up. And took him back. He'd lost it, done it for the first time, on this very spot. A girl named Alice something. They had both been scared to death.

He closed the trunk and moved across the tall grass. "It's a favorite place of mine, out here. You like it?"

Annie looked at him. "Sure. It'll do."

He bent and spread out the blanket. The grass was soft beneath it. When he looked up, Annie had her T-shirt off. He blinked. "What are you doing?"

Annie shrugged. "Just getting down to business, mister."

Did she have to call him mister? "There's no hurry. Take your time."

"What for? It's why we came here, isn't it?"

Her hand was on her zipper. Ed reached out and held it. "There's a lot you need to learn."

"I don't need you to tell me that."

"You're angry?"

"I just want to get it over with."

Ed smiled and shook his head. "The first rule—"

"Listen, mister—"

"No. You listen. First rule: getting there is half the fun." He sat, patted the blanket, waited.

"Oh, all right." She sat beside him. "Now what?"

"Well . . ." He paused. It wasn't easy, looking at the flatness of her stomach and those breasts. "Sometimes, it's nice to talk."

She couldn't understand him. "Come on, let's get going."

"Hold my hand."

"What's wrong with you? You think we're on a date or something?"

"Dammit, yes." He felt a flash of anger. "Listen, kid, you

want to go get raped, I'll drive you back to town, there's lots of guys who'll do that for you. Take my hand."

She took it. "Now what?"

"Kiss it."

"O.K., sure, if that'll make you happy." Annie raised it to her lips.

"Not that way. Here." Ed took her hand, caressed it gently, raised it, always looking in her eyes, then touched it with his lips. "You see?"

She did see, but she wasn't going to tell him. "So?" She watched him turn her hand and kiss the palm. It tingled faintly; it was nice. Then he leaned close and kissed her shoulder.

"Oh," she said. His eyes were on her breasts now, but he didn't make a move. It was the weirdest thing. The man was only looking, and she felt her nipples harden. She glanced down and checked them. It was true.

Ed caught the glance. He hadn't lost his touch. He thought about the next half hour. It would be that long, at least, before it happened. Sex without romance was nothing.

"Mister?"

"Yes?"

"I came out here to lose it, not to have a good time."

"Why not both?"

"Because . . ." She watched his hand move, felt his finger-tips along her neck.

Ed smiled. "It's possible, you know."

His fingers touched her shoulder now. She liked the way it felt. What was it she had meant to tell him?

"Just relax," she heard him say. "If something happens, let it happen."

"Oh, all right." He took his hand away. She wished he hadn't. "I suppose you want to kiss me now."

"Is that what you want?"

Annie nodded. "Yes."

He brushed her lips with his, just barely touching them, no more than that. "Now, Annie, have you ever seen a man?"

"You mean his thing? Sure, lots of times."

"Erect?"

She hesitated. "Standing up?" She shook her head.

He leaned back on his elbows. "Listen carefully. And do exactly what I say."

She looked at him and nodded.

"Undo my belt. That's right. And now the button." Annie's fingers fumbled with it, they were less than steady. "Good. Now, very slowly, pull the zipper down." He watched her. "All the way."

"Now what?" Her eyes were on his shorts. The bulge there looked enormous to her.

"That's a good girl. Now, this is tricky. Draw my shorts apart. I'm going to pop out when you do that—but you mustn't touch it. Got that?"

Annie nodded. Out it came. Her eyes grew wide. She licked her lips.

"No, no," he said. "Not yet. It's my turn now. I'm going to look at you." Her hands went to her jeans. He stopped them. "You lie back. I'll do it."

Annie stretched out on the blanket. Up above, the willow leaves were moving. She heard the rustling of the stream. She felt her jeans slip down. She raised her hips a little. Off they came. She spread her legs, just slightly, waiting for his touch, but nothing happened. Annie raised her head and saw him looking, just as she had looked at him.

"You're beautiful," she heard him say.

She found it difficult to speak. "When is it going to happen?"

"When?" Ed smiled and lightly ran one finger up her thigh. "When we can't stand it anymore."

19

ELEANOR PLUNGED STRAIGHT into the day. Enough tears had
been shed for Dee; more than enough. And if her precious,
only child was determined to go to hell in a handbasket, she
had only herself to blame. Not all the mother-love on earth
would change her now. Was it Emerson who wrote, "The moving finger writes; and having writ, moves on"? Whoever wrote
it knew what he was saying.

So she showered, put on something very smart, skipped
breakfast, went directly to her desk, wrote out her correspon-
dence, paid a bill or two. The cemetery was after her again
for Harold's perpetual care. She sometimes wondered why
she kept it up. Would Harold know? Would anyone? She
shrugged and wrote the check, then dashed off to her office at
the UCF.

It was a modest room. She'd chosen it with care. A life
devoted to good work required some show of humility. So
long as everyone in town knew, and they did, that the United
Charities of Fulton would be lost without her, all display of
pride or power seemed in highly doubtful taste. Though she
gave generously enough, you'd never find her name above the
new wing to the hospital. Not like the Reddings or the Brinkers. God approved of anonymity. Reverend Larkin said so
every time she brought it up.

Her desk was piled with papers, messages, reports, and

pleas for aid. The staff was well intentioned, but unless she told them what to do and how to do it, they were hopeless. Everybody wanted money, help, assistance. Ah, but only Eleanor could read those begging letters filled with grief and pain and see the truth behind them. Need and greed: it took real sensibility to tell the difference. So she read and phoned and issued orders, and by noon her desk was clear.

She felt dissatisfied; she hadn't done enough. Perhaps a personal appearance at the Children's Home for the Handicapped. The despair of others rarely failed to serve as a reminder of her own good fortune. Even though the sight of any disability—let alone deaf, blind, and spastic youngsters staggering around—was horribly upsetting, off she went.

Which made her very late for lunch with Harriet. A good soul, Harriet; not flawless, but she meant well. She was certain to be full of commonplace advice about Dee. Eleanor would cut that short. She didn't need it anymore.

She moved into the dining room at Longview and looked around. Although the luncheon buffet still remained in place, the staff was hovering behind it, obviously desperate to clear it all away. There were some couples still at lunch—new members, people of no consequence—and Harriet.

Harriet, by that time on her second vodka gimlet, looked across the room and waved. She rarely drank till cocktail time, but she knew what was coming—tears and, worst of all, self-pity—and she found herself in short supply of sympathy today. She had her Marcie back, and she had spent the morning doing happy things. Like pasting photographs in family albums, writing loving notes to distant relatives. Her best friend's litany of disappointment—that was something she could do without.

She put a smile on as Eleanor came rushing to the table, brimming with apologies. "My dear, I'm sorry I'm so late."

"Why so you are. I hadn't noticed." Harriet half rose and kissed her cheek.

"I've just been to the Children's Home, and things ran on and on."

"Oh, Eleanor, you know how that upsets you."

"Duty calls." She sat, took her napkin. "It's an obligation."

"Isn't that just like you? Troubles of your own and you put others first."

"What troubles?"

"You have Dee to deal with. Isn't that enough?"

"I see no need to bring her up."

"But, surely, Eleanor, you want to talk about her."

"No, I don't. I need a drink and I'll be fine."

"I'm one ahead of you." Why had she mentioned Dee at all? It was the gimlet speaking.

Waiters came and went. They smiled and chattered aimlessly through Eleanor's first Manhattan. And her second. The annual Club party on Labor Day weekend was the biggest of the year, and both of them were on the Dance Committee. They had hired Ben Burbidge once again, but he was getting on, and maybe next year . . .

In the middle of their third round, Eleanor let out a gasp and stood up suddenly.

"What is it, dear?"

"I can't stay here a moment more."

"Why not?"

"I'm going to cry."

They made it to the parking lot.

"Oh God, oh God . . ."

"What is it, Eleanor?"

She needed no encouragement. Tears started down her cheeks. "I've lost my little girl. She's gone."

"They have a way of coming back." Harriet nearly smiled, she felt so smug.

"Not Dee. I've showered her with love, I've never once denied her anything, I give and give . . ." She choked up, couldn't speak.

"Now, now; I've known Dee all her life, too. Don't forget that. She's a handful. Always was, but—"

"Little do you know. She's filled with poison."

Harriet was shocked. "That's not true."

Eleanor leaned back against the fender of her Cadillac. "It's Harold's fault."

"What is?" Things always had a way of being Harold's fault: the house on Blanchard Street, the neighborhood, the business that had killed him—and the poor man had been dead for twenty years.

"He had to go and leave her all that money. When they read his will, I could have died."

"But it was his to leave, you know."

"He ruined everything. If Dee were penniless, she'd need me."

"You don't mean that, Eleanor."

"The hell I don't. It set her free."

"You can't buy love with money."

"You're no one to talk. Who paid for Marcie's house? Who bought it?"

"That was different."

"How?"

"I love my daughter."

"And I don't?" Her eyes were bright with anger.

So were Harriet's. She'd been in such a good mood, and she wasn't going to lose it—not on Eleanor's account. "That wasn't what I meant."

"What did you mean?"

"I don't remember, never mind."

"You think I like it, having Dee at Marcie's house? How does that make me look?"

"I don't much like it, either. If I had my way—" She stopped herself.

"Oh, fess up, Harriet. You can't control your daughter any more than I can."

"Is that so? You don't see Marcie living in New York. She's here at home, where she belongs."

"She had no choice. You tied her here."

"I never did."

"At least I had the decency to let Dee go. I wish I hadn't, but I did it. God, you don't know the life she leads."

"Do you?" The thought of Dee and Eleanor exchanging secrets, being close the way she was with Marcie—never, not a chance of it.

"I know enough. I hate the acting. It's so cheap. No decent girl would dream of it. But what I hate most—I can't say it."

Harriet was fed up. "Fine. Don't say it. There's no need to tell me."

"It's the promiscuity."

"The what?"

"The boys, the men. Since high school. Oh, she thought I never knew. She still does, but she can't fool me. I watched. I listened. Didn't you?"

"What? Spy on Marcie? Never in this world."

"You should have. What do you think they were doing up at Denison? If Dee did things with men—"

"Not Marcie. She's a good girl."

"You don't know that."

"Yes, I do. I know my child. I brought her up right."

"Are you telling me I didn't?"

"If the shoe fits, wear it. Marcie has a husband and a family. I get what I want from her."

"Well, aren't you clever."

Harriet was furious. "She didn't run away from me."

"So I'm what Dee was running from?"

"I didn't say it, you did. I give Marcie love. True love. The real thing. And it pays off. When we fight, we make up. Just this morning—"

"I don't want to hear it."

"Eleanor, you should have seen the way she hugged and kissed me."

"You don't think that's going to last?"

"Forever."

"You're a fool."

"You think so?" Harriet was shaking now. "The truth is, you can't stand it. I've got everything you want."

"Ha. That's a laugh. I'm laughing, Harriet."

"If you'd like my advice—"

"The day I need advice from you—" She turned and got the car door open.

Harriet had waited years for this. "You're always spouting off about forgiveness. Every other word from you is—"

"Oh, shut up."

"Forgiveness is your middle name. You wouldn't know it if it kicked you in the teeth."

Eleanor got in, looked up at Harriet. "You're some best friend."

"I try to be."

"You know the truth about you?"

"What?"

To her eternal credit, Eleanor just smiled and slammed the door.

They drove off in separate cars.

The girls were sitting in the top row of the bleachers at the Fulton High Athletic Field. It had been Dee's idea. They needed quiet, and she thought they'd be alone. But far below them, high-school boys in shorts were scrimmaging and working out. School opened after Labor Day, another football season. Long ago, that meant so much. Young voices floated in the air.

They had said very little on the way out. It was time to start. "Look, Marcie." Dee paused. "Are you listening?"

"Sure."

"Stop looking at the field."

"We had some good times way back then."

"That's not the issue at the moment."

"O.K." Marcie turned to her. "What is?"

Dee felt like shaking her again. "Have you the faintest notion what you're doing?"

"Having sex, I think it's called."

"You're screwing with a tramp."

"He's not a tramp."

"All right; a bum, a pimp, a lowlife."

"He's not any of those things."

"Just how besotted are you?"

"I don't know—and who are you to scold me? You were always after me to do it. 'Come on, Marce, let's go to Pussy Point.' They named a grove of trees for you out there."

"They never did."

"Ask Charlie Black; he told me so." She hadn't thought of Charlie Black in twenty years. Where was he now? What did it matter?

"That's just boy talk." Dee felt so embarrassed. "If I fooled around a little . . ."

What's a little? Marcie wondered. Twice a week? "I've even seen you doing it," she blurted out.

"Like when?"

"On my first date with Van. How's that? I saw you in the bushes with that creep director, what's his name?"

"What were you doing? Peeping?"

"I was drunk. I didn't mean to see it."

"Swell, terrific. How'd you like it?"

"Not a lot."

"At least I didn't tease the boys to death."

"I never did that."

"You? Miss Cocktease of Ohio? What about that time with Bob Drake?"

"I told you?"

"Every detail. You stripped naked, all the way, but could he touch you? Oh no."

"That's not teasing. I was saving it."

"So now you're giving it away."

A cheer rose from the field. They turned to look. One of the boys was being hoisted to the shoulders of his teammates. Both girls sat in silence, watching. Echoes of forgotten games rang faintly in their ears.

"Lord," Marcie said, "they look so young."

"I was Homecoming Queen once. You remember?"

Marcie nodded. "I remember." She felt quick tears. "I'm sorry, Dee. You're right. I don't know what I'm doing."

"Sure you do. We both do. It's exciting. When you're with him . . . I know all about it." Images of men flashed through her mind. She looked at Marcie, felt a twinge of envy.

"Listen, Marcie. There are two rules you must never break. Don't put yourself at risk. You've got a life here, you can't fool around on desktops. It's not worth it. And the other rule—don't get emotionally involved."

"I'm not."

"It's me you're talking to."

"Do you know what it's like with Van?"

"I can imagine."

"It's not right, complaining. He's the nicest man I know. It's only that . . ." She couldn't finish it. The thought was too big. It went way beyond their life in bed; it stretched as far as she could see.

"You chose him, Marcie."

"And I loved him, too."

Talker had gone tearing out the back in total disarray. Not very dignified, as exits go. He looked around. The little parking lot was clear. No witnesses. God only knows what story he'd have told them.

He leaned back against the wall, zipped up, tucked in his shirt, then wondered what was going on inside the shop. He knew who Dee was: Marcie's best friend in the world, she'd told him that. And more. If Dee was in the office now, she had to know what happened. Couldn't miss it. Even so, he wasn't worried. Best friends didn't tell tales out of school, and chances were Dee knew about him anyway. So why the panic just now? What was that about? It wasn't all from Marcie; he had felt it, too. He'd grabbed his pants and run. Just like he'd run from Sandra, run from everyone and everything. It was ridiculous. He had to stop it, he was sick of running.

He checked his watch. One-thirty, time to kill. He ambled to the street. He couldn't keep his thoughts from Marcie: what was going on inside her, what would happen at the Lodge tonight? More sex, of course. But after that? He'd have to level with her, wouldn't he? Not just his plans to stay in town. About himself, his past, the whole damn catalog of things he'd done and hadn't done. Face it, he was the subject of the evening. It was Talker up on the examination table. That was not a place he'd been before.

He waited at a corner for the light to change. There was a Post Office across the street, and, for no reason, Talker thought of sending out the money order early. Every Saturday, like clockwork, he sent money home. He never checked in, never wrote. How long since he had made a phone call, spoken to them? Four, five years. No point to talking, nothing ever changed. But sending money was a duty, so he crossed the street and walked in. There were long lines at the windows. It could keep.

Half an hour later, he was on the Fairgrounds, looking at the car displays. The area was busy, filled with farmers, townies, kids in strollers. Families. Talker moved along. No question, when he took a job in town, cars were for him. Some place would take him on, he was too good. He'd do repair work or he'd sell, he didn't care. GM or Ford.

They both had dull exhibits, nothing to write home about. Steuben Motors was a palace by comparison. It took him by surprise. He knew that Marcie came from money, but he'd never realized how much. Did it matter, make a difference? Not a lot.

There were salesmen busy hustling on the platform. Three of them. Could one of them be Van? Was that the purpose of this visit? Had he come to check him out? Could be—and if the guy was up there, which one was he? One of them was damned good-looking, with a bandage on his left hand. Too good-looking; there was something wrong about him, something funny. Talker ruled him out instinctively.

It was between the other two. A tough call. Talker was about to make it when somebody called Van's name. The fellow with the bandage turned, and Talker shook his head. He stood there watching Van a long time. What the hell, he thought; why not?

He took the stairs and wandered on the platform, waiting for an opening. It came.

"Nice-looking cars," he said.

Van nodded. "Thanks. We like to think so."

"This one here." He turned and pointed.

"The New Yorker," Van told him. "It's a winner, top of the line. She lists at—"

"I don't care about the price. I'm interested in the performance. You know, pickup, speed, what can she do?"

Talker sized him up, half listening to the spiel, which wasn't much, in any case. Close to, Van was taller, in good shape, good manners, pleasant, not a bad guy. What was wrong? And then he got it, loud and clear. Van had no balls. There was no heat in the man; those clear blue eyes were empty. What was Marcie doing with him? Going crazy? Was that why she was so hot to trot? Was Talker just for fun and games? Impossible. She'd tell him so tonight. She'd hold him, whisper all the things she felt; he meant so much, she needed him, she couldn't do without him.

"She gets eighteen miles to the gallon."

Talker blinked, came out of it. "Not bad."

"There's nothing like her on the market."

Talker kept a straight face, nodded. "You don't know how right you are." He thanked Van, said he'd think about it, left the platform, moved off in the crowd. He had fresh things to think about. Like breaking up a marriage. What if Marcie left her husband? Did he want that? No, thanks. That was more than he could handle. Talker shrugged. Why borrow trouble?

Still, it shook him up a little. Things were happening so fast. You wander aimlessly for years, and suddenly—he stopped dead. Staying on in Fulton meant a permanent address. Well, semi-permanent. And that meant more than magazine subscriptions. He knew what he had to do. He bought himself a Pepsi, got a pocketful of change, and headed for a phone booth.

It was doorless, hot as hell inside. There was no seat, so Talker stood, put in a quarter, dialed "O," and waited.

"Operator."

"How much is a call to Providence?"

"Rhode Island?"

Annie had played that game with him. How many had she said there were? "Yeah. That's the one. Station-to-station."

"One moment, please."

He thanked her when she told him, hung up, checked his change. More than enough. He put some quarters in, began to dial, got three digits out, went blank. What was the number? How could he forget? He hung up, got his wallet out. He used to carry it, he had it on a card, a slip of paper, something. There it was, tucked behind his driver's license. In ink, thank God. It hadn't blurred or faded.

He put more quarters in the slot. His hands were moist, the coins were slippery. He dropped one, picked it up, went on, began to dial. Would Sandra go along with him? Why not, why wouldn't she? The call was going through. It started ringing. One, two, three. Was no one home? He should have thought of that. Five, six.

"Hello?"

The voice was a young woman's. Talker didn't recognize it. Had he dialed the number wrong? "Is this five-five-five, six-eight, seven-one?"

"That's right."

"Is Sandra there?"

"Who's calling, please?"

"Tell her it's John."

He heard a gasp. "Is that you, Daddy?"

Talker's heart sank. Amy was a child. What was she doing with a grown-up voice? "Hi, honey. Yes, it's me. How are you?"

"I'm O.K."

"That's great." What next? He had so much to say to her. "I miss you, baby."

"Do you really?"

"All the time. You know I do."

"How come you never call?"

The sweat was trickling down his forehead, stinging in his eyes. "I'm always meaning to."

"Oh, sure."

"I love you, Amy."

"That's why you're around here all the time."

"Oh, honey, look—"

"I wouldn't know you if I saw you."

Talker knew the feeling. "We can try to fix that. Is your mom around?"

"I'll take it, give it here."

No problem recognizing Sandra's voice; a little older, deeper—she'd been nineteen when he left her. "Hi," he said. "It's me."

"I know it's you."

Not very friendly, but he had to win her over. "So, how's everything?"

"Are you in trouble, Johnny?"

"No."

"Then what's the great occasion?"

"I just felt like checking in."

"Makes sense to me. A phone call every four, five years, why not?"

"Are you O.K.?"

"We're getting by, thanks."

"Are you married?"

"What's it to you?"

"I'm concerned about your happiness, all right? It's not a crime. A girl like you should have a husband."

"One was plenty."

"Look, I tried. I did my best."

"You ran out. You're a classic, Johnny. Off to work one morning and you never came back home."

He felt the anger starting. Hell, she'd never understand. She was a pretty piece back then, and she'd come on to him. Fresh out of high school, both of them. They'd had some good times, but they'd never been in love. And when he knocked her up, he did the decent thing, he married her. Destroyed his life, that's all he did. The dreams went down the drain: no college, future, none of that. Nineteen, stuck with a wife and baby, but he tried. He got that job, he brought that paycheck home. He'd hacked it for a year. For Jesus' sake, he'd even done the midnight feedings. "Sandra, look. I did my best."

"That's nice to know."

"I never meant to, but the day came when I had to go. It was get out or die."

"You know what that makes you?"

She'd tell him anyway. "What?"

"One selfish bastard."

"Would it help to say I'm sorry?"

"That makes three of us."

This wasn't going in the right direction. "Do you get the money?"

"Yes. We get it."

"Every week?"

"Yes. Every week."

"Is it enough?"

"Yes. It's enough."

"What's Amy like?"

"What do you care?"

"Come on, give me a break."

"She's beautiful."

"Go on. How tall is she? What color is her hair?"

"It's green."

"For Chrissake, Sandra. What's it cost you? Tell me."

"Golden brown."

"You have a photo you could send?"

"You have an address?"

"No, not yet."

"I didn't think so."

"Listen, Sandra. Things are changing." It was now or never. "Actually, that's why I'm calling. I'm about to get a place, and I was wondering, maybe Amy'd like to come and visit."

"What?!"

"No big deal, just a few days."

"You'll see hell freeze over first."

"Come on. I am her father."

"Johnny, you could lie there dying—"

"Ask her. Ask the kid. Go on."

"What for?"

"Are you afraid to?"

Sandra laughed. "Scared shitless. Amy, guess what? Johnny's asking if you want to visit him."

He strained for Amy's answer, heard a door slam.

"So? What did she say?"

The operator cut in. "Fifty cents for three more minutes."

"Oh for Chrissake." Talker jammed the quarters in. "Hello, hello?"

"She isn't coming, Johnny."

"Give her time to think about it."

"That's a deal. Next time you call, ten years from now, we'll talk about it."

"I could come home, get to know her."

"Are you deaf or stupid? No one wants to see you. Ever."

Sandra hated him. She always would. "Things change, you never know. I'll call more often."

"Spare yourself. You think this is a kick for us?"

"It's not a ball on this end, either."

"Have a great life, Johnny."

"Don't hang up!"

"You're screaming."

"No, I'm not."

"So long."

The way she said it split him open. "What the hell, at least send me her picture. Would it kill you?"

"Can you hear me laughing, Johnny?"

"Jesus Christ, you fucking bitch—" The line went dead. "Hello, hello?" He made a fist and hit the phone. It hurt. He stood there sweating, the receiver in his other hand. Someone was speaking to him. Talker turned. A kid was standing there.

"Mister? You finished with the phone?"

He nodded, hung up, left the booth. He felt the least bit dizzy, and the glare seemed very bright. He headed for the nearest tent, went to the back and knelt down on the grass to vomit. Nothing came.

Norma looked around the van. Some days weren't worth the paper they were printed on—and it was just midafternoon. The girls were lying on their cots like half-dead fish, gills flapping, still hung over.

Getting them this far had not been easy. It was after one when she had finished with the sex-crazed Lovell, then she'd had to drag them from their beds and dump them in the shower. And as if that weren't enough for one day, it was getting on to show time and no Talker and no Annie. Not a sign of either of them.

Norma sighed, went out onto the bally stage and looked around. She had some words for Talker. Choice ones. He had found town pumps before, but he had always done his humping on his own time. They were partners, they had always been a team, but she was doing all the pulling these days, and it wasn't fun. Somehow, the zip and zest were going out of things.

The heat was getting to her, so she clambered off the stage and settled on the tree stump in the shade. A few more nights and they would fold their tent and steal away. Another summer ended. Talker would take off and go wherever, like he always did. As for the girls, they'd make it through the winter one way or another. Then she frowned. Would Annie? Norma liked her; she was bright, worth worrying about. But what she knew about life you could scribble on a pinhead. Still a virgin. Come next week, she'd be out on her own. She'd have her wages, maybe something extra, but when that was gone, what would she do? Wait tables, drift around?

Enough. She wasn't Annie's mother, she was no one's mother, and she had herself to deal with. She was sixty-two and rich enough to live forever. Was it time to quit? Not yet. She closed her eyes and thought about her condo in Fort Lauderdale, her terrace on the ocean, all her blue-haired lady friends. It was a wonder she fit in, but fit in she did. The winter months sped by and—

"Hi."

She looked up. There was Annie, grinning like a cat in cream. Norma told her so.

"Who, me?" She had been so afraid of doing it, and when it happened, it was bliss.

"You're late."

"I know. I'm sorry."

"What have you been up to?"

"Nothing much."

"You want to tell me?"

Annie shrugged. She couldn't wipe the smile away. "Just wandering around."

"Come closer." Norma knew the signs; the way her eyes looked and the light flush on her cheeks. "Been with a man," she said.

"What makes you think—"

"Well? Haven't you?"

It showed. Could everybody see it? "No, not me. And even if I had—"

"Why do a thing like that? What did you go and lose it for?" No answer. She pressed on, she had to ask. "Tell me you didn't turn a trick."

"You mean for money?" Annie shook her head.

"Then why?"

"Because I wanted to."

"Who with?"

"Some man I met."

"Oh, honey . . ." Norma took her hand. "Are you O.K.?"

"I'm fine, I really am."

"You're sure?"

"Oh, Norma . . ." Annie sat down on the ground and started talking, couldn't stop. How gentle he had been with her, how long he'd made her wait, and how exciting it had been. She left some parts out. Like the moment he had let her kiss his thing and lick it everywhere, all over. It was dizzying, her head felt light. After that, she'd lain back, spread her legs for him. And then what? Had she really whimpered, begged for him to do it? When he did, it hadn't hurt. And when she came, the world went white, and that was all she remembered till he woke her up.

She'd bled a little, but he'd taken out his handkerchief and wiped it all away. Then they had driven back to where he'd picked her up. She knew she'd pleased him, and he didn't have to say so, but she loved it when he did. And then he took her hand and kissed it. That was all. He never said good-bye. She'd watched him drive away and didn't even know his last name.

". . . and I'm glad it happened."

Norma smiled. "You're lucky. It's not always like that."

Annie nodded, put her head on Norma's lap. "You won't tell anybody, will you, Norma?"

"No, not me."

"You promise?"

Norma ran her hand through Annie's hair. The poor dumb kid. "In love with Talker, aren't you?"

"No."

"Don't worry," Norma murmured. "I won't tell him." She glanced up, and there was Talker trudging toward the bally stage. He looked like he'd been whipped, and Norma never kicked a man when he was down. She'd kick him later.

"Come on, kid," she said. "Let's go to work."

20

THURSDAY NIGHT WAS poker night. Van was the youngest regular. The rest were Ed's friends. Adam Brinker, Jack Morgan from the bank, Harvey Yaeger from the lumberyard, George Clarke who owned and operated Fulton Oil & Gas. Dee's dad had been the seventh member; but at Ed's insistence, he had never been replaced. Instead, they had a pool of floaters they could draw on. Almost anyone in town was glad to be included. It was Willy Oberlander's turn tonight. His people owned the granary.

Wives were invited, and they usually came along. Separate but equal, they would spend the evening gossiping or knitting or whatever women did when left alone. The one rule was, they stayed out of the way. No matter where the game was played, that room was sacrosanct: no ladies were allowed.

The game rotated every week. It went from George's house to Ed's to Harvey's; and the order never varied. Score one for the wives. They had to come up with the dinner and the snacks for fourteen people, let alone deal with the mess next day. Once every seven weeks was quite enough.

Tonight was Van and Marcie's turn to host the gathering. It had completely slipped her mind, and she was still at the Athletic Field with Dee when she remembered.

"Holy shit," was what she said.

Dee almost jumped. "What's wrong?"

Marcie bolted to her feet and started moving. "Tell you on the way."

They raced to town, stopped near the shop so Dee could pick up her car, then tore toward Sunset Crescent. Marcie hadn't ordered anything: no greens, no vegetables, no steaks for Van to grill—pray God they had some in the freezer—no dessert, no Cheetos, Fritos, all the after-dinner garbage for the men to nibble on.

Was she hysterical? Worse come to worst, she'd think up some excuse, and they could dine on peanut-butter sandwiches for all she really cared. The world was coming down on her, that's what it was. She had this man, she couldn't keep her hands off him, it had to stop, she couldn't stop, and she had to meet him at the Lodge tonight. How was she going to handle that? And how in God's name was she going to get there? Sneak out of the house in front of everybody?

Sunset Crescent just ahead. For one mad moment, Marcie thought of whizzing right on by and never going home. Like Peter Pan: straight on till sunrise.

"Fuck it." Marcie jammed on the brakes, took the turn, went skidding down the street and up the driveway. Dee was right behind her.

"I like the way you drive," Dee said as they went running up the front walk.

"Thanks a bunch."

She hurled the front door open, raced across the hall. She heard Dee slam it shut as she went rushing to the kitchen. Twice in one day: breakfast and now this. She reached the doorway.

"Hello, Mrs. V."

"Hi, Mom."

"Oh." Marcie sagged against the door frame. There was Mrs. Beebe at the kitchen table, trimming steaks. On the counter, there were heads of lettuce, red and yellow peppers, onions, bags of junk food. Bets and Denny sat beside a bushel basket, husking corn.

"Oh," Marcie said again, then turned away and did the one thing she was capable of doing: bursting into tears.

Dee helped her to the den and made the first of several drinks.

*   *   *

Ed was looking forward to the game. In fact, he couldn't think of much he wasn't looking forward to. He'd been magnificent that afternoon. Stupendous. Gable in his prime, Don Juan, Jack Kennedy: he stood beside the studs of history. But it was even more than that. He felt as if the sum of his experience, his fantasies, and all the women he had ever known had been expended on his Harem Girl. If, God forbid, he never got it up again, it was enough. Tomorrow or the next day, he'd feel differently; but on this Thursday afternoon he understood what Moslems got from Mecca. He had visited the Shrine.

Not even Harriet, whose nose was seriously bent out of joint, had any notable effect on him. He heard her bustling in the parlor as he slipped into the house. There were some grass stains on his knees and elbows that he wanted to take care of.

"Is that you, dear?"

How, he wondered, could she make a simple greeting so sepulchral? "Yup."

"Home early, aren't you?"

Ed paused in the doorway. "Well, it's hotter than a devil's dick out, so I cut the day short."

"Did you have a nice one?"

"So-so."

"I had lunch with Eleanor."

Whatever that meant, there was no sense going near it. "Harriet, what can I tell you? You're a saint." He turned to go. "You plan to change for dinner?"

"No," she said, "I hadn't thought so. Why?"

"No reason. If you like the way you look, that's swell with me."

He took the stairs two at a time.

Van stepped into the front hall, closed the door. His clothes were sticking to him, and the cool felt glorious. He didn't feel too bad himself. He'd sold two cars that afternoon, the couples Ed had softened up. But he had closed the deals, that was what counted.

He was loosening his tie when Dee appeared, a tall and frosty glass in hand. He grinned and nodded at the drink. "What's that?"

"A gin and tonic."

"It looks wonderful."

"It's yours." She put it in his hand.

"Where's Marcie?"

"Upstairs in the bedroom."

"Right." He started for the stairs. "It's poker night tonight, you know."

Dee had to grin. "We know. Believe me."

Van moved on. He could have done without these Thursdays. Not that he was bad at poker. He could hold his own: he'd learned, he'd had to. And he understood the value of these get-togethers. Half the power of the town in one room; useful things were said, alliances were formed, and deals got made. And it was flattering to be a part of it; Ed didn't have to bring him in. But even so . . .

He walked into the bedroom. "Marcie?"

"Here I am."

She sounded odd. He turned. She was reclining in an armchair, feet up on the hassock, wearing nothing but her panties. "Hi. How are you?"

"Just the least bit buzzed, but otherwise . . ." She shrugged and let her head rest on the chair.

He put down his drink, took off his jacket. "How was your day?"

She paused to find the right word. "Unforgettable."

"Are you O.K.?"

She grinned. "I'm going to make it. How was yours?"

He sat to take his shoes off. "It got better as it went along."

"What happened to your hand?"

"I scraped it." Why lie? He could hit a million golf balls if he chose; he was entitled to. His shoes were off. He stood. "Is Betsy home?"

"She's gone to spend the night at Denny's place."

"How come?"

"She asked me and I said O.K."

He frowned. Just yesterday, she'd made a whole scene over Betsy going for a ride. "You think that's wise?"

"For godsake, Van, what's going to happen?"

"Nothing, I suppose."

"They're children. Don't you trust her?"

"Sure, of course I do." His pants were off now. "Look, about the steaks tonight . . ." He hesitated.

"What about them?"

"It's a furnace in the backyard. Could we do them in the kitchen?" .

She sat up. "For Jesus' sake, you live here, you've got rights, it's your house. You don't have to ask permission."

"All I meant was—"

"Drop it. Yes, we'll do them in the kitchen." She leaned back again. "What's wrong with you?"

"I try to be considerate. Is that a crime?" He turned and got a hanger, hung up his trousers. He couldn't seem to get the creases right, they kept wrinkling on him.

Marcie watched him struggle, felt like screaming. What would happen if she did? It might be interesting. Or would it? "Van, do me a favor?"

"Sure."

"Describe our lives."

"I don't know what you mean."

"You have trouble with the verb? Describe: to furnish a description."

Wouldn't it be something, just for once, to lay it all out. "It's a good life."

"That's a start. Go on."

He swallowed hard. "I think I'm very fortunate. We're privileged. We have Betsy, friends and family, you get pleasure from the shop."

She had to grin. "I did today. Go on."

He'd never struck her. What would it be like? "Look, Marcie, we've got company in forty minutes. Shouldn't you be getting dressed?"

"You've got a point." She stood and slipped her panties off. "I think I'll go like this."

He started toward her. "Are you drunk?"

"Not nearly, nothing like it."

"Put some clothes on."

"Screw the poker. You play host, I'll stay up here."

"You can't do that."

"Why can't I? Say I've got a headache. People get them."

"You're the hostess."

"I don't want to be a hostess." Tears were burning in her eyes. She blinked them back. "I'm young, for Christsake. I'm still young. You want a hostess, get yourself some blue-haired biddy."

"You're my wife."

"For what that's worth."

He didn't recognize his own voice. "Do you want to have a fight?"

"Why not?"

"I've had a shit day."

"So have I."

"You want to hear about it?" Was he crazy?

"It's a deal. You tell me your grief, and I'll tell you mine."

He felt consumed with rage. The words were on his lips when Marcie's eyes grew wide. What was she doing? Pointing to his crotch. He looked down. He was rigid. Jesus, at a time like this.

She reached for him. She held it. "That's what rage'll do for you."

Incredible. He'd read about it, but he'd never half believed it. "Suck it."

"Now?"

"You heard me."

Marcie blinked. Was this her Van? He'd never let her do it. Ever. Wordlessly, she went down to her knees. Her mouth was open when the doorbell rang.

"Shit," Van said. "Someone's early."

"It'll be my fucking mother."

Van was past all caring. "Let Dee talk to her, for Chrissake."

Marcie nodded.

Smoke was rising from the chickens. Hundreds of them, split and peppered, sputtered on the open grill. Huge stewpots filled with fresh-picked corn sent clouds of steam into the air. Behind the line of butane stoves, men melted home-churned butter, worked on sauces, hot and sweet. You had a choice. The Fulton County Firemen's Annual Barbecue was an event. Three-fifty bought you everything from soup to nuts, all you could eat, and people came from everywhere in Fulton County.

Folks had been lining up since five, and when the dinner bell rang out, there was a cheer as people beelined for the food. You picked up metal trays and started down the tables.

Firemen's wives—they did the baking; corn bread and those giant brownies—heaped your tray full as you moved along.

There was a whole contingent in from Carthage Lake, and Barney Lovell led them toward the trestle tables lined with wooden benches that stretched out from here to there. Lucy was with him, dressed in something proper and demure for once; he'd seen to that. The bunch of them sat down, held back just long enough for Barney to say grace, then plunged in.

Barney's mind was on the fine. He'd had a long go-round with Walt about it. He was sympathetic to a point. These were hard times for men like Walt. Real hard if coming up with half the fine, $250, was more than Walt could handle. God knows why he'd given in. He'd told Walt yes, he'd lend the money. Didn't even ask for interest. It would trickle back in time, he knew that, but the question was, how much time? What he made in summer had to last him through the year. Nobody lived in tents or rented cabins in December. There were taxes, bills, repairs; he had himself to think about.

It was all Lucy's fault. Walt was no friend of his. They knew each other, nodded and made small talk at the grocery or the hardware store. Their main connection was those kids of theirs, and God forbid the two of them got married; he'd end up supporting them, he knew it.

"Dad?"

He looked at her. Too pretty for her own damn good. "What is it now?"

"You have to take my head off?"

"Eat your supper."

"I'm not hungry."

"Eat it anyway. I'm paying for it."

Lucy bit her lip. She couldn't wait to finish high school. One more year and she'd make tracks. Clear out, just like her mother did. If she could wait that long. She turned and looked around for Marvin. Was she serious about him? Yes and no. He was attractive, fun to be with, and he sure knew how to press her buttons, but he had no future. He'd be sweeping out the henhouse all his life.

She spotted him and waved. They'd get together later, and she knew what that meant.

So did Marvin. "Dad?"

Walt's mouth was full. He hadn't missed the Barbecue in forty years. "Uh-huh?"

"I don't guess you'd have an extra five."

"Five what?"

"Oh, come on, Dad."

"You plan to spend it on the Lovell girl?"

"Would I do that?"

The kid was crazy if he didn't. She was hot. Sometimes Walt had half a mind to slice a piece off for himself. And if she hadn't been Marvin's, chances were he might have tried. It wasn't easy being widowed at his age, and what he needed was a young wife, something cute and juicy. What he also needed was the money to afford her. He was stretched just feeding Marvin, and he'd have to buy her clothes and take her places, keep her happy. No way it could happen, but he dreamed about it, even if his fool tool stiffened every time he did. He felt it stirring, and it wasn't right. No man his age should have to jack off all the time.

The truth was, he was jealous of his kid. Not just because of Lucy. Marv was young, the doors were open, he still had a chance. Walt didn't, and damn well knew it. He was trapped. He couldn't sell the farm. These days, who'd buy it? And what would he do without it? What else did he know?

He reached into his pocket, found some singles. "Here you go, kid. Blow it on her. Every dime."

"You mean it, Dad?"

"Hell, yes. And while you're at it, plow her once for me." He grinned and took a bite of corn bread: "You know, do one for the Gipper."

Walt clapped him on the shoulder. Life was difficult, but not impossible. He had his health, his land, and all the chicken he could eat. He'd even gotten Barney to lend him his half of the fine. It took some doing, but they had a date. At noon tomorrow, they'd go pay off Sheriff Weller. Barney was a weasel, but he wasn't going to weasel out of this one. No, sir.

Walt picked up a chicken breast and dipped it in the sweet sauce.

"Dee, dear."

Harriet stood in the open doorway, smiling.

"Oh," Dee said, "it's you."

"I know I'm early. Aren't you going to ask me in?"

Dee nodded. "Please." She had one mother: Eleanor was plenty, thanks; she didn't need to deal with Marcie's.

"Where's my angel?"

"Still upstairs." What was this angel stuff? And what the hell was keeping Marcie? "I'll go get her."

"In a minute, there's no hurry. Where's my kiss?"

Dee nearly said, 'Your what?' She watched, deprived of speech, as Harriet took both her hands and kissed her cheek.

"Oh, Dee," she sighed, "we used to be so very close."

What was the woman up to? "I remember."

Harriet stepped back. "I had lunch with your mother."

"Did you really?" It was coming now.

"She doesn't understand you, Dee. Not like I do. She misses you, but she has no compassion, not a glimmer of it. Children grow and change. We have to let them go. You need to lead your own life. Just like Marcie."

Dee had to smile. She should only know. "You want a drink of anything?"

"I'll have some iced tea later, dear. I'm very proud of Marcie."

Dee threw caution to the winds. "It wouldn't hurt to tell her so."

"She knows it. I'm so proud of both of you." She put an arm around Dee's waist and looked about. "It's such a lovely home. I don't know of a nicer one. Do you?"

Dee thought about her garden duplex in the Village. West Eleventh Street. She missed it. She belonged there. "No, I don't."

"You know what makes it beautiful? It's not the trappings, it's the atmosphere. It's filled with happiness and love." She took Dee's hand and started toward the dining room. "I want to show you something."

What was coming now? Dee wondered.

Harriet stopped in the doorway. Everything was set for dinner, and poker evenings were supposed to be informal. "We're not eating on the terrace?"

"We decided it's too hot out."

"Very sensible." She moved in. "Everything you see here has a story."

Dee was starting to enjoy herself. "I didn't know that. Tell me."

"Well . . . the table and the chairs were gifts from Ed and me. The Jensen silver, too. The corn plates come from Geraldine, Van's mother. And the glassware . . ." As the list went on, she moved around the table, rearranging forks and spoons, adjusting doilies.

Dee watched, fascinated. What a woman. Eleanor, at least, was up front. By comparison, at any rate.

"The pictures on the walls came from my mother's home, and—"

Mrs. Beebe entered from the kitchen with some flowers for the sideboard. "Something wrong about the table, Missus Steuben?"

"Did you set it?"

"Just like I've been doing it for years."

Marcie heard their voices from the stairs. They sounded tinny, and she couldn't place them for a moment. Strangers? Not on poker night. She stopped and held tight to the banister. She felt a little short of breath, but that was easily explained. She'd raced into the bathroom, splashed some water on her face, thrown on a cotton dress and sandals, dragged her hairbrush through her hair. And where was Van? He'd thanked her, actually said, "Thank you," and gone off to take a shower.

There was moisture on her forehead, and the place was like an ice house. What was happening to Marcie? Funny way to put it, but she felt outside herself. There was more to life than penises. That didn't sound right. Peni? Did it have a Latin plural? Instantly, she thought of Talker. They would do it at the Lodge, she knew they would, she wanted it.

"Oh Jesus," Marcie said aloud. The sound of her own voice helped make things real. "Jesus, Jesus, Jesus." That was better. She released the banister and went downstairs.

"Oh, there you are, dear."

"Hello, Mother."

"Don't you look nice."

Mother kissed her. Dee, across the room, was smiling. That beat fighting. She thanked God for little favors. She heard Mother talking. Good girls listened to their mothers.

". . . and I've just been telling Dee who gave you all these lovely presents."

Marcie looked around the room. She didn't see a single thing that she could call her own.

21

TALKER LEANED AGAINST the boundary fence behind the tent. The girls were dancing, he could hear the music. He had fifteen minutes to himself. He needed them.

The sun had just gone down, leaving an afterglow that turned the endless rows of yellowed cornstalks to a color that he couldn't name. It was a time of day he didn't like. Between the dark and the daylight; that rang bells. The Children's Hour.

Why in hell had he called home? Why do a crazy thing like that? He never really thought about them. Even when he sent the money, did he wonder what their lives were like? He shook his head. He didn't miss them. Down was down, no turning back, not even if he'd wanted to. And yet he'd stood there dying in that phone booth, asking could he visit Amy. What was that about? And begging for her picture. Screams and curses. Amy was in diapers when he'd left.

He wiped his forehead. What he had to do was think, and what he needed was some aspirin. Things inside his head were throbbing. How was Marcie? What had she been doing since he scrambled out the back? Was she in better shape than he was?

"Want a beer?"

He turned. Annie stood there in her harem pants and bra.

"It's icy cold." She held the can out.

"Thanks." The last thing he needed now was company.

"You look a little down," she said.

"It's just the heat." He shrugged and turned back to the cornfield.

"Yeah. It's awful." Annie leaned against the fence and watched him. She'd been watching him since he came shuffling up the road. Poor Talker, he'd been cut off at the knees by something. Plain as day, you couldn't miss it. Norma saw it, too. When Annie asked her what she thought, she answered, "Just a mood. He's moody sometimes."

Annie didn't think so, but she kept it to herself. She had a hunch that kept on growing. She felt sure now. He had lost his Woman, she'd walked out on him. It had to be. A moron could have seen it coming. Chase a local rich bitch, this is what you got.

And she felt sorry for him, too; at least a little. Talker wasn't used to losing women. He was much too special; and when things broke up, she figured he did all the walking out. No wonder he was cut to pieces. But the main thing Annie felt was hope. Not huge amounts, just some. The road was clear, the way was open for her. Sure, it was a narrow one and filled with tiger traps, but it was there.

"You feel like talking?" Annie asked him.

It was darker now. Faint moonlight touched her shoulder, cast a shadow in between her breasts. Enough of that. He turned away. "What's on your mind?"

She longed to tell him, wrap herself around him, but that had to wait. "Oh, nothing much. I missed you all day long. Where were you?"

"Here and there." He sipped his beer. She liked him; that he knew. She'd kissed him last night, plastered though she was. And it was mutual; he liked her, too. She made him smile. He slipped an arm around her waist. "And what have you been doing?"

"Me?" She'd never tell him. "Guess."

"You slept late."

"Wrong."

"You fooled around at the Fair."

"Uh-uh."

"You went to town and window-shopped."

She shook her head, pressed closer to him.

"I give up."

"You lose. That means you've got to kiss me."

"That's a new one."

She was stretching up on tiptoe, like the night before. He bent and kissed her cheek.

"You like me, don't you, Talker?"

"Sure I do."

"How much?"

"In pounds and ounces?"

"Oh, come on, be serious."

He caught it in her eyes. All those "I love you"'s last night when he left her. It was him. What was he going to do with her?

"You want me, Talker? Would you like to have me?" She had told herself to wait, the time was wrong.

"Who wouldn't? You're a lovely girl."

To hell with waiting, watching out for those tiger traps. "I want you."

It was tempting. Last week—hell, four days ago, when there had been no Marcie, he'd have taken her. And maybe even kept her for a while.

"I want you now," she whispered.

Talker stepped away and shook his head.

"Why not?" Her hands went to her bra. She took it off. "Why don't we?"

What in God's name could he say? What wouldn't hurt her? "I don't want to be the first."

"You're not." She gasped; she'd said it, it was out.

"What do you mean, I'm not?"

"I lost it."

"When?"

"This afternoon."

"How fucking could you?"

He looked crazed. It frightened her. "To please you, learn to please you."

Talker slapped her face, he shook her. "Jesus Christ." He slapped her face again. "You fool!" He could have killed her. "Jesus, Amy." Talker raised his hand again.

"You're hurting me."

He stopped dead. Amy. He'd just called her Amy. There were red marks where he'd struck her. "Oh my God." His head was throbbing, he slipped to his knees. "I'm sorry, I'm so sorry."

Annie stared at him. The man was weeping. Who was Amy? Some girl. How he must have loved her. What was she to do? She moved close, put her arms around him. "It's all right."

He shook his head.

"It's all right, Talker. I forgive you."

Van was smiling; couldn't stop it. Grinning like an idiot. The more he thought about the scene upstairs, the more he felt like crowing. True, one swallow didn't make a summer— get him; he was making puns—but it could be a sign of things to come.

He glanced around the table. Dinner, served by Mrs. Beebe and her cousin Lillian, was drawing to a close. How time flies when you're feeling cocky. More puns. He was on a roll tonight.

"Right, Van?"

Ed was speaking to him. "Absolutely." That was how to deal with Ed, agree with him. Ed and his cronies had been talking business all through dinner. Adam Brinker carried on about the tax laws; old ones, new ones, all they ever did was soak the rich. Jack Morgan was depressed about the Federal Reserve, there hadn't been a decent man in charge since Eisenhower. And George Clarke was grousing about oil prices and the God damn Arabs, how the only good one was a dead one.

Who cared? They were always grousing over something. Anything, you name it: rainfall, crops, the ERA, the GNP, inflation. It was up or down or in or out, and that was always wrong or bad or worse. The thing they didn't like was change. To Van, the thought came as a revelation. Nothing ever changed in Fulton, from the streetlights to the city dump. Was that a blessing or a curse?

He left it to the oracles and glanced at Marcie. It was time to leave the table, and the hostess usually gave the signal. He'd been glancing at her all through dinner, but he never caught her eye. He didn't now.

Van put his napkin down and stood. "Well, shall we?"

All the men got up on cue. The ladies nodded, wished

them luck, and went on chattering as Van led the procession to the den. It was his job to set things up for poker night. Each detail had to be just so; the boys—that's what they called themselves—were very finicky. The folding table with its plywood poker top—he'd wheeled it in from the garage—sat at the center of the room. Its green baize cloth was neatly draped, no creases, and the bridge chairs stood around it.

Van took in the room, going through his checklist—coasters, ice, booze, mixers, ashtrays and cigars; had he forgotten anything? As always, once they hit the den, Ed played host, he took charge. Not at Jack Morgan's place or Harvey Yaeger's: just at Van's. Six times a year times sixteen years. Did Ed know he was doing it, was he aware? Van wasn't sure. In any case, it rarely failed to tick him off. But not tonight. It didn't matter, water off a duck's back. Let him.

Van moved to the desk and took out two fresh decks of cards. The poker chips were on the table, in the leather box his dad had given him. Jack Morgan did the banking, and why not—he was a banker, wasn't he? The box had a large V on top, embossed in gold. Tonight, Van thought, it stood for Victory.

"You fellows know the one about the rabbit and the cat house?"

It was Harvey Yaeger talking. Conversation always changed at game time. No more business, it was jibes and dirty jokes from now on. Boy talk, like the locker room at Longview. Van, who usually found Harvey hard to take, said, "Tell me." With a smile.

If anybody asked them, they'd have said they played a friendly game. The stakes were low, and with the worst luck in the world, you had to strain to lose a hundred dollars. Underneath, as Van well knew, the stakes came close to life and death. The money didn't count. They played to win.

They sat, Ed cracked the decks, took one, and shuffled. Everybody laughed at Harvey's joke. They cut for deal. Ed won.

"Straight poker. Five-card stud."

"What's wild?" Adam Brinker asked.

Ed grinned. "Just me."

The first few hands were nothing much to talk about. And then, a big one came. Van had a full house, Ed drew to an inside straight and got it. Up and up the pot went. Van kept raising Ed; he couldn't lose tonight. Jack Morgan, who was clearly bluffing, stayed in with them.

It was Ed's turn. Silence as he huffed and puffed; he smoked cigars on poker night. He picked up some chips, tossed them in. "O.K., wise guys. I call you." He spread out his cards. "Beat that."

Jack Morgan grinned at him. "Would four queens do it?"

"Every time, but you don't got 'em."

One by one, Jack put the queens down.

"Fuck it."

Jack was raking in the chips. "I love sore losers."

"I'm not sore."

"I'll tell you what, Ed. Just so you don't sulk all night—you've got the loan."

Ed sat back in his chair. He hadn't brought up the loan since the visit to Jack's office. Never press things; eagerness looks weak. "The whole half-million?"

"Every dime."

Ed grinned. "I figured you'd come through for me." He raised his glass and drained it dry.

Van didn't choke or speak, turn red or white or anything. His stomach was in knots, the blood was pounding in his ears, but these things didn't show. What loan? What half-million? What the fuck was going on? Van felt like screaming, taking Ed by the throat. He couldn't. Not in front of all these people. Later, when he got the old prick by himself, he'd give it to him, lay him out. But God forbid, not now.

He threw in his hand, took the fresh deck, started dealing. Not a tremor in those hands. Did he have self-control? Incredible. He should have been a diplomat.

"What are we playing?" someone asked.

"I'm sorry," Van said. "I forgot." What were they playing? Poker, that was it. "Seven-card stud. Red eights and one-eyed jacks are wild."

"That's all?" Ed asked.

Van knew Ed hated wild cards, so he threw in split-whiskered kings.

"We're out of ice."

Van looked up. It was Adam Brinker, getting juiced again. He hadn't spent a sober night in thirty years.

"I'll get some more." Van sounded calm and casual. He stood up, got the empty bucket. "Be right back."

He made it to the kitchen, opened up the freezer. Mrs. Beebe and some other woman, Lillian, her cousin, that was it, were busy with the dishes.

"Can I help you, Mr. V.?"

Van spun around. "Don't talk to me!"

"You've got no call to raise your voice."

"It's *my* house, isn't it?"

That shut her up. The ice felt hot, which didn't make a lot of sense. He filled the bucket. It was crystal; heavy. He had given it to Marcie for some anniversary. Or had she given it to him? He closed the freezer. It was good he'd left the den. A smart move. It restored his equilibrium.

The boys were waiting when he got back, telling jokes. "Be with you in a sec," he said. And then, to Adam: "Scotch, rocks. Right?"

He got a nod and made the drink, then started to the table. To his own surprise, he stopped and, in the calmest way, said, "Tell me, Ed, about the loan . . ."

"Terrific, isn't it?"

"I'm sure it's great, but what's it for? We're solvent, there's no problem."

"We're expanding."

"Oh." Still calm and cool. "I didn't know."

Ed shrugged. "I didn't want to get your hopes up."

"Nice of you. If it's all right to ask, just what are we expanding into?"

"Jap cars."

"Gee, Ed, how'd you ever think of that?"

"I'm smart. We're going to make big money, son."

"I'm not your son, Ed. I'm your partner. I've worked side by side with you for sixteen years. A long time, and you know what I've found out?" Van leaned close, whispered in his ear. "You suck shit."

"*What?*"

Van tossed the scotch in Ed's face. "And you know what else? I'm out, I'm gone. You can take Steuben Motors, Dad, and shove it up your ass."

That made things clear. He'd summed it up. Had he forgotten anything? One small detail. He took the empty glass and hurled it through a windowpane, then turned and said, "Excuse me, gentlemen."

The ladies had all settled in the living room. For Marcie, it was torture. Harriet was still exuding love in all directions, Dee looked ready to decapitate her, it was ten o'clock already, and the poker could go on for hours. Talker would be waiting at the Lodge soon, and if Captain Kirk could beam her out there . . .

When the glass went through the windowpane, the crash went through the house. The ladies straightened.

"What was that?"

God, what next? Marcie thought. "I've no idea."

The front door slammed.

"I'll go and see."

She got up, hurried to the hall. Dee followed her. By that time, Ed was moving from the den, a handkerchief in hand. Scotch in the eyeballs hurt like hell.

"What's happened, Daddy?"

Ed was furious. "Your dickhead of a husband doused me."

"Van did *what*?"

"He blew his frigging top, the jerk."

"Where is he?"

From outside, they heard a motor revving. Marcie hurried to the front door, pulled it open. "Van?"

His car was spinning gravel, backing down the drive. Then, tires screeching, off it went. She started out.

Dee followed, grabbing her arm. "Where are you going?"

"After him."

"Why bother?" Ed was outside, too, now. "He's not going anywhere. He'll just come crawling back to me."

It was her way out, she was free and clear; but something in that last remark turned her around. "What did you do to him?"

Ed shrugged. "You wouldn't understand. It's business."

"Great. Thanks for the compliment. I run a business, too, you know."

Ed couldn't stop himself. "You run a hobby shop."

Things were getting out of hand. She'd settle with him later. Go to hell would do for now. She said it and went racing for her car.

Dee took off after her. "Wait, Marcie. Listen."

"Not now." She could deal with one thing at a time, but when they came in twos and threes—Van, Talker, and her father—it was too damn much. It wasn't fair.

"Calm down."

"I'm calm, I'm perfectly all right."

"You're off the wall. Where are you going to look for Van? It makes no sense, you don't know where he's going."

"I can't stand here doing nothing." God, what was she doing, telling lies to Dee?

"Ed's right. He'll drive around and come back home. He won't get into trouble."

Marcie felt a sudden ache for Van. What was he going through? Poor bastard. First the bedroom, and now this. What lousy, rotten thing had her own father pulled on him? And was she any better? No.

"Oh, Dee, I'm such a wreck."

"I know. Come on, let's take a walk or something."

Marcie couldn't look her in the eye. "I'm not going after Van."

"Then where on earth—" Dee broke off. "Jesus, Marcie, not tonight."

"I've got to see him."

Dee felt like shaking her again. "The sky is falling, Chicken Little. Look around you."

"He's expecting me."

"Big fucking deal. You got screwed once today. What's happened to you?"

"That's not why I'm going."

"Sure. You're going to talk about the weather. Think the rain'll hurt the rhubarb?"

"Let me go."

Dee hadn't realized she was holding her. She stepped back. "Have a ball."

"Oh, please, Dee, don't be angry. You're the only friend I've got."

"Too bad I'm not enough." Dee turned away. "God help you."

The Redding place had fifteen bedrooms. Seven, if you didn't count the quarters for the staff. Whenever Betsy spent the night, she always got the pink one. She had liked it, back in grammar school, but these days it looked cutesy to her. All those frills on everything. Pink was for babies, little girls.

They stood outside the bedroom door now. It wasn't all that late, but they were getting up at dawn and it was time to

say good night. They didn't want to, either of them. It had
been some evening. Betsy said so. Denny nodded.

They'd had dinner in the sun room. It had been Brigette's idea. She'd cooked three courses, set the table, and
served them, just like grown-ups. Even gave them wine. Just
half a glass, with water in it. She was French. She understood.

After that, they slipped outside and necked a little, took a
swim, and necked a little more. Their hair was still damp from
the pool.

"I like to come here," Betsy said.

"I like it when you do."

She looked at him and grinned. "Well, it's that time again,
I guess."

"I guess."

She held out her cheek to be kissed.

He bent and whispered in her ear. "Can I come in?"

"You know you can't. The Dungeon Master's watching."
That was Mrs. Yorke. She had been Denny's governess, and
when his parents were away, she ruled the roost. In general,
during daylight hours, they were left alone. But once the sun
went down, forget it. If it wasn't Mrs. Yorke, then it was Jean,
the parlor maid, and sometimes even Mark, the butler. Talk
about surveillance; it was like the Pentagon.

Sometimes it struck them funny, and they'd make a game
of it. But more and more, they liked it less and less. They both
knew right from wrong, they'd never go too far. And what the
Mrs. Yorkes of this world never understood was, if they
wanted to, it was a snap. With all the fields and woods around,
they were as free as air.

"She isn't watching."

"How do you know?" Mrs. Yorke could see through walls.

"She's in Mark's room, watching television."

Betsy giggled, turned the knob, and slipped in, Denny
right behind her. Starlight seeped in through the windows.

"Should I turn the light on?" Denny asked.

Somehow, that summed up why she loved him. "I don't
know, why bother?"

Denny edged in closer to her. "Now what?"

"I don't know." She kept a straight face. "We could always
sit and talk."

"That's just what I was thinking." Denny kissed her.

"Ummm," she said.

It went on for a while. When she began to feel him through his trousers, Betsy stepped away. If Mother ever knew, she'd die. Correction: she would kill Betsy first, and then die.

"That's enough," she told him.

"Are you sure?" She nodded, but he knew she wasn't. "Maybe I should lock the door."

"You think so?"

Denny's ears were ringing as he fumbled with the lock. It took forever, but he got it. They had never been alone like this before. He turned and looked at her. She was, beyond all dreams and movie stars, most beautiful.

What now, what was his next move? Denny couldn't seem to think. He took her in his arms. "Oh, Bets . . ."

"I know," she whispered; and she did know.

Denny kissed her, felt her tremble. "You O.K.?"

She wasn't. "Sort of."

"What are we going to do?"

She knew the answer, there was only one. She said it. "Wait."

"What if we can't?"

"We've got to."

"We'll go crazy."

"No, we won't. It only feels that way." She ached for him. What if she gave in? Did she want to? Yes. And no. She couldn't think straight. What would happen? She'd regret it, he'd regret it, they'd regret it.

"Denny, listen."

"What?"

"We can't." She stepped away.

"Why can't we? Half the kids in high school do it."

"They're all older—and that doesn't make it right. When girls get married—"

"You're not going to wait till then?"

"I want to try."

"We'll never make it."

"Don't come closer."

Denny stopped. What stopped him? All he had to do was touch her. He could see it. All the light was on her face.

She tried to take a deep breath, but she couldn't. Everything was pounding. He looked terrible. She had to give him something.

"Denny?"

"Uh-huh?"

"Would you like it if I took my clothes off?"

"All your clothes?"

She hesitated. Why not? "All of them; so you could look at me. You'd like that, wouldn't you?"

He cleared his throat. Who wouldn't like it? "Sure."

"But that's all. Understand?"

He didn't. "Are you saying . . . I don't get to touch you? I'm supposed to stand here while you're—"

"Denny, please. You've got to promise."

"That's a lot to ask."

"I mean it."

He believed her. Better half a loaf than nothing. "O.K., Bets."

He'd keep his word, she knew he would. "Here goes."

She bent and took off her sandals. And then her blue jeans: first the button, then the zipper. It kept getting stuck. She got it down, slipped off the jeans, and stood there in her shirt and panties.

"You're not stopping, are you?"

She was tempted, but she didn't. There were just four buttons on her shirt. It took forever. Done. She left it hanging and looked up at him. His mouth was slightly open, and his eyes were huge. She took her shirt off.

"Oh God, Bets . . ." Her breasts were milk white, pure, like snow. The rest of her was tan.

She glanced at him again. His eyes were soft now, and he looked about eleven, like a kid at Christmas. She was pleasing him. So far, so good. Now came the hardest part. She looked down at herself. Why was it such a big deal? Every woman had one, there were billions of them in the world. What made it wrong? Her hands were shaking, she could feel the cotton, the elastic. Nothing made it wrong. She did it. There the panties were, around her ankles on the floor. She couldn't look at him, not yet.

Except for centerfolds, which didn't count for all that much, he'd never seen a naked woman. There it was. In shadow, and he couldn't see it all that well. The room was silent, he could hear the humming of the air-conditioning.

"Is something wrong?" she whispered.

Denny shook his head. "Is it all right . . ." He cleared his throat. "Can I just walk around you?"

Betsy raised her eyes and saw his face. What power did her body have? It always looked O.K. to her, but nothing to write home about. How could it make men feel that way? Amazing. "Sure," she said.

He walked around her slowly, once. Then once again. He'd never get enough of looking at her. Not for hours, not for years. "Are you scared?" he heard her ask.

"A little."

"So am I. You think it's time for you to go?"

He saw her eyes. She'd never looked like that before. What was it? Did she want him, too? There was an easy way to find out; all he had to do was touch her. "Yeah," he said. "I guess it is."

"I love you, Denny."

He was moving to the door. "I love you, too."

She watched him go, then turned and faced the full-length mirror. She moved closer to it, let her eyes go up and down.

"Well, look at me," she whispered. She was smiling.

Ed moved back into the hall. He needed time to simmer down. The sons-in-law of this world, you could fold them three ways. And his Princess, what about that? "Go to hell." Was that a way to treat a father? Marcie needed straightening out, a good old-fashioned talking to. Don't think she wouldn't get it. Come tomorrow morning . . .

He heard footsteps. Dee was coming in. He turned. She looked as if smoke was coming out her ears. He didn't care. "So? What did Marcie have to say?"

"Don't talk to me."

She swept past him. She could hear the women buzzing in the living room. She moved in. They were standing in a cluster near the doorway. Natter, natter; tongues like asps. The room went quiet when they saw her.

"O.K., ladies, any questions?"

Everybody spoke at once. Dee raised her voice, cut through it. "Quiet down, one at a time."

"What's happened? Tell us everything."

That came from Helen Yaeger, Biddy of the Year in '66 and still proud holder of the title.

"Nothing much. A poker argument. Boys will be boys, you know."

"Where's Marcie?" Harriet looked so concerned.

"She went out for a drive."

"She didn't. In the middle of a party?"

Dee tried to summon all her self-control. There wasn't any. "Harriet, you take the fucking cake."

"I like that," Harriet shot back.

"You're not the only one. You're all a bunch of winners."

"Listen here, young lady—"

"Keep it to yourself. If Marcie had a brain cell working, she'd be in New York with me. I don't know how she stands it here. I can't, and that's for damn sure."

She felt like crying suddenly. Not here, she'd die first, not in front of them. She turned and, careful not to rush, moved to the stairs.

Ed saw her going up. There'd been a scene. He didn't care, he'd get it all from Harriet; her version, anyway. She'd be up yakking half the night. He'd had a bellyful of women.

Ed moved back into the den. The boys were waiting for him. Adam had a fresh drink, and Van's hand was cleared away, his cards were gone. But otherwise, you'd never know a thing had happened. They were friends, real friends, the best.

"Well, boys," he said, "what can I tell you?"

"It's the same old story," Willy Oberlander said.

Jack Morgan nodded. "Run a family business, these things happen."

"Don't they just." Ed headed for the bar to make himself a drink. A double; he could use it. All of them had family businesses, inherited or they had founded them. And all of them had sons or sons-in-law.

"Comes with the territory," Adam said. "You think Van's a pain? You're lucky. You know Phil?" They did; his daughter Nancy's husband. "Phil the fuckhead. You know what he pulled on me?"

They all had stories. Spoiled, disappointing sons; or daughters who got fooled by fortune hunters. Ed sat down and listened to the grief. What was it with the younger generation? They were soft or lazy. They had no respect. The greatest shortage these days wasn't law and order. It was character.

"O.K.," Jack said. "Who opens?"

Harvey Yaeger threw three blue chips to the center of the table.

Ed picked up his cards. A pair of jacks and three threes. Life was what you made it, but from time to time, a little good luck didn't hurt. Ed kept a poker face. "I'll see you and I'll raise you five."

No one mentioned Van again.

22

"LAST SHOW FOR tonight, boys. You don't want to blow it."
Talker paused and checked his watch. Eleven. He'd been on a
roller coaster. Hitting Annie, breaking down; rock bottom. He
was on the rise now. Five, ten minutes, he'd be in his T-bird,
flying down the road, stairway to paradise.

He looked out at the upturned faces. "Boys, when God
created women, why do you suppose He made them so beautiful? I'll tell you why. To drive men crazy." Laurel came out
through the curtain. "Seeing is believing." Laurel set her hips
in motion. Talker raised the mike and whispered, "Round and
round she goes. Last chance tonight."

That got them moving to the ticket booth. He switched
the mike off, turned and followed Laurel through the curtain.
All the girls were in their costumes, dressed and ready, eager
to get out, go home, or do whatever.

Annie sprang up when she saw him. Talker knew he
owed her; more than he could pay right now. She'd lost her
cherry just for him, she'd held him when he went to pieces,
and she hadn't asked a single question. She was smiling, and
her eyes were shining. She was coming to collect the debt.

She moved in close, looked up. "How are you?"

"Fine." That seemed abrupt, a little short. "I'm feeling
good."

He did look better. "Good enough to celebrate?" She grinned. "I thought we might go out tonight."

He shook his head. "I can't."

"How come?"

"Oh, come on, can't a fella keep a secret? You don't tell me everything."

There wasn't much he didn't know. "That isn't true."

"I'm busy, Annie. Things come up, I'm sorry. Honestly, I wish I could."

The man was lying in his teeth. "Oh sure."

He smiled. "Take a raincheck? How about tomorrow night?"

She saw right through him. "All you'll do is break it. You're still seeing her."

"Still seeing who?"

"Oh, come on. I saw you in her car this morning. She's a dog."

He didn't want to hurt her. "Annie, listen—"

"Why? You'll only lie to me." She felt like such a fool. She'd built a house of cards, that's what she'd done. Applause came from the tent; the crowd was getting restless. "Start the music."

He felt rotten. She deserved the best he had to offer. He reached out to take her hand.

"Don't touch me, Talker. Never. Not until you mean it." She stepped back. "And that'll be the day."

What could he do? He turned the tape on. She was moving toward the curtain. Out she went. He left the van and went to Norma in the ticket booth to say he'd see her in the morning.

Norma started talking, but he cut her short and moved off down the road. There was a small lot for Concessionaires just past the Ferris wheel. He'd left the T-bird there. He tried to think of Marcie, of all the things he had to tell her, but the day kept crowding in on him. He'd lost his woman, won her back, met Van, called Sandra, gone to pieces, and stabbed Annie in the heart. It was enough to last a month.

He moved into the lot, got out his key. He loved that car, and he had been neglecting it. No question, it could use a good wash and a wax job. When? As soon as he had time. He was just a few yards off before he saw it. Scratches. Some damn fool who shouldn't have his license had scratched the door. He swore and moved in closer. How bad was it?

"What the hell?" No car had done this. It was writing, there were words. All over. On the door, the hood, the fenders. Scratched in with a key or something sharp. Words like *filthy bastard, prick, get out of town, cocksucker, pimp.*

Too much. Too God damn much. What kind of crazy motherfucker did it take to pull a thing like this? Who hated him? Rage flooded through him, filled him up. He ran his hand across the finish. True, it wasn't ruined, he could have it buffed out, get a paint job. But the guy who did it—

What was that? He pivoted. Was someone in those bushes? Watching, laughing? Filthy bastard. Talker took off, flew across the ground, and dived in. There were branches, brambles, nothing else. He crouched there, panting. He had scratches on his hands and face.

He stood up and made it to his car. His hand was shaking, he used both to fit his key into the lock. He got in and sat still for a minute. Not a chance to even up the score; that's what he had to face. He'd go see Sheriff Weller in the morning, show the damage to him, sure. But what the hell could Weller do? No more than he could.

There was more to Fulton than he'd thought. It only looked liked paradise. It had its dark side and its crazies. Then it struck him. What if there was more to come? He wasn't leaving town, for damn sure. It took more than this to scare him off.

He got the engine started, let the brake go, turned the wheel. The thing to do was go around with both eyes open. He was good with trouble. He could take it. He could dish it out.

Sometimes Marvin wished his father kept his trap shut. Handing him the money didn't happen very often; that was O.K., even generous. But saying "Go slice off a piece for me" was something else. Embarrassing. It didn't sit right. No kid likes to think about his father humping, dipping it in honey. Marvin saw the way he looked at Lucy. If the man was hungry for a woman, let him get one on his own. He'd been a widower for ten years, what was wrong with him?

Marvin missed his mother. He'd been only seven when

she died, and she had been a long time doing it. Still, he had memories of Mom when he was little. They would go do things together like—

He cut the memories and thought about the money in his pocket. There was just so much four bucks could do for you, but he'd gone far with less. He finished his barbecue, picked up his brownie, started off to Lucy, and then changed his mind. Her dad was yakking at her; no sense getting caught in that. That man was Big Religious, a Bible walloper from way back. Not that Marvin didn't go to Church, but Jesus, there were limits. So he wandered off and leaned against a tree and waited.

She came walking toward him slowly. From the way she looked, her old man must have given her some beating; fire and brimstone, all that God stuff. It would wear off in a while. It always did.

"You goin' my way?"

Lucy looked at him and shrugged.

"What do you feel like doing?"

"Dying."

"Right." He grinned and slipped an arm around her waist. "I know a great place where the two of us can kill each other. Let's get going."

"Very funny."

Lucy moved his arm away. He didn't mind, she'd come around. "Let's try the Midway, play some duckpins." It could run a buck or two, but what the hell.

"Let's not."

"Look, Lucy, I can guess the way you're feeling—"

"No, you can't." He had no way of knowing now. But later, when she told him, if she told him . . .

"Want to see the giant pumpkin?"

"What?"

"In the Pavilion. Thing must weigh three hundred pounds."

"Oh, come on, Marvin. Grow up."

"Any day now." Marvin took her hand, she let him—good sign—and they started walking down a path to nowhere in particular when Donny Moore came trotting up.

"Hey, Marv, what's doing, where you goin'?"

"To the moon, what do you think?"

"Same here. Why don't we join up?"

Donny was O.K. And so were Jackie Bowles and Bob Vermillion. They hung out together, and they all had girls they'd picked up. Nothing great, but willing, from the look of them.

They all expected Marvin to take charge. He'd become a kind of hero since he'd torn the Country Club apart and spent a night in jail. He hadn't bragged about it. People knew, that's all; word got around. He didn't mind; it made him feel like someone special.

So he led them off to see the Tractor Pull. It wasn't much to watch, but it was free. When it got close to eight, they headed for the grandstand. None of them had tickets. At three bucks a throw, forget it. They just stood around and watched the crowd go in. Who cared about the Tournament of Thrills? At least the sun was down, and it was dark enough to neck now. Marv was ready. Lucy wasn't.

What she needed was a change of scene. His dad had kept the truck, so he moved off to Donny Moore and pried his Jeep loose for the night. They left the grounds, stopped long enough for him to drop two dollars on a pint of rye, and he was bouncing toward the Fallsburg Road now, Lucy at his side and nothing on his mind but getting laid.

The top was off. Lucy was leaning back, eyes on the stars. She was a Capricorn, and paid attention to her horoscope. She only half believed the stuff, but it was something to hang on to. Every month she read the ones in *Modern Screen* and *New Romances,* but the one in this week's *County Journal* was a winner. Lucy knew she had to get away, leave home for good, and what the entry said was, "You are going take a trip with fame and fortune at the end of it."

"Hey, Lucy."

"Not now. Can't you see I'm thinking?" What could she be famous for? No problem. With her face and figure, maybe she could be a model, pictures in the magazines. It paid a fortune, she'd get rich, and when that day came, she was coming back to town with jewels on that would choke a horse and rub their faces in it.

"Hey, come on. What do you feel like doing?"

Marvin's hand was on her thigh. He had a one-track mind. And most nights, so did she. She loved the way he made her feel when they were doing it. The whole world fell away, and for however long it took them, she was wrapped up, warm and safe. She couldn't even hear her father's voice.

She moved his hand. What did she feel like doing? Talking. At some point, they had to talk. "Oh, I don't know."

"I've got it. Let's go skinny-dipping."

Lucy shook her head. "No way."

The Fallsburg Road was coming close. He pulled to one side, stopped, unscrewed the bottle cap. What Lucy needed was some juicing up.

"You want some rye?"

"The stuff is warm."

"Warm, cold, it does the trick."

She took a swallow, made a face. It tasted sweet and oily, and it burned.

He took the bottle, had some, screwed it shut, and headed for the intersection. He was going to take a right, toward home and all the lakes and ponds. The night was hot, he'd get her stripped and in the water, not a chance he wouldn't score.

"Go left," she said.

"To town? What for?"

"Just do it."

Marvin did it. She really was in a mood tonight. They hardly ever went to Fulton. There was nothing there worth doing.

"Go slow," Lucy told him. They were passing by the Country Club. The columns out in front were lit up like a palace. She had been inside the Clubhouse. Last June, she had gone to get a job. They took on kids for extra help in summer, and what Lucy wanted was to be a waitress with a pretty uniform. Maybe she'd meet some nice guy from the right side of the tracks. You never knew where that could lead.

They sent her to some prissy woman in an office. Forms and questions: name, address, what school, what work experience. The woman heard her out, then spoke.

"We have an opening in the kitchen."

"Thanks, but, see, I want to be a waitress."

"Sorry, but those jobs are taken."

"What if something opens up?"

"We'll see."

So Lucy put in three weeks in the kitchen, slaving over pots and pans. And then it happened. Two kids left, a waiter and a waitress. Lucy went to see the woman.

"Here I am. You got two openings. Which one's mine?"

"I'm sorry, dear. They're filled already."

"No, they're not." She knew it for a fact. "The jobs are there. Why can't I have one?"

"There's no point in arguing, Miss Lovell."

"I'm not arguing, I want a reason."

"Very well, if you insist. You're not the type of girl we want."

Things blew sky-high after that.

"Marv?"

"Yeah?"

She nodded toward the Club. She had her answer, but she wanted his. "Last Saturday, you want to tell me why you plowed it up?"

"Hell, I don't know. Just drunk, I guess. Besides, you egged me on." He grinned. "We showed 'em, didn't we?"

She pressed him. "Who'd we show?"

"I don't know what you mean." He knew, all right. If you didn't count the jerks who came to Fallsburg pussy-hunting— and he'd knocked around his share of them—he didn't know a soul from Fulton. Not to speak to. They went to different schools, they didn't even meet in sports. The Fulton kids played in a different league.

There was no "who." When he'd torn up their golf course, he was showing "them." They had it easy, had it all. Their fancy cars and fancy clothes and fancy colleges and jobs ahead of them. Sometimes it ate him up alive. "Who cares about their fucking Club? They had it coming."

Lucy nodded. "Take the left," she said.

"Where?"

"Where I'm pointing."

Marvin took the turn on Sunset Crescent, braked, and had some rye. A long pull. He was feeling churned up.

Lucy had some, too. It tasted better this time, less disgusting. "Take it slow. I want to see the houses."

"Why?"

"Because they're fucking beautiful. You satisfied?"

She looked out at the houses as they crept along. She knew about them, there were pictures in the *Fulton News*. She kept on thinking, Someday, someday.

"Marv? You ever think about the future much?"

He rarely did. Why should he? He was only seventeen. "Sure, all the time."

"How do you see it? Five, ten years from now, what's up the road?"

"You, me, and kids."

She saw the same thing, all too clearly. "Where would we be living?"

"I don't know."

His hand was on her thigh again. "Don't do that, Marv. I'm talking."

"And I'm listening. You go right ahead." He kept his hand in place.

She looked at him with angry eyes. "I've got to think and make plans. All you think about is getting laid. What kind of future have we got here? I'll work at the five-and-dime, and you'll sweep barns out?"

Marvin jammed the brakes on. "Listen. I'm no brain, but don't you take me for a dummy. I got eyes. I see my dad. He's broke, he's going to stay broke, all he'll ever be is broke. I figure either I get off my butt or thirty years from now, that's me. For Jesus' fucking sake, you think I want that for a life? I read the magazines, I watch the tube. I know what's out there, and I'm getting me a piece of it."

"How?"

"How in hell do I know how? I'm big, I'm strong, there's plenty I can do. Don't you think for a minute there's no place for me."

She knew exactly where it was—down near the bottom. "Marv, I'm late."

"You're late for what?"

"My period, you jackass. Six days late."

He stared at her. "You're telling me I've knocked you up?"

"I don't know, it's too soon to tell."

"Fuck." Marvin ran a hand across his forehead, looked away.

She knew what he was feeling. Buried. If she went away and had the child, she was buried. And if Marv stuck to her, came along, it buried both of them.

"Look, Lucy, lots of girls are late."

"I know that."

"Sometimes, two–three weeks."

"You think I'm stupid? Marv, what if it's there?" She touched her stomach. "What if something's really in there?"

"You could lose it."

She'd been mulling that one over. Dad would tell her it was murder. Maybe he was right. "I don't think I can do that, Marv."

"You're sure about that?"

Lucy nodded.

"Well, that doesn't leave a guy much choice. If you're knocked up, I think I'd better marry you."

"That's swell, Marv. Thanks a lot."

"I mean it, Lucy."

"Why? Why do an asshole thing like marry me?"

"Because I love you."

"Oh, come on."

"You know I do." He put his arms around her tight. "You know it like you know your name."

His lips were on her neck now, he was kissing her. "Oh, Marvin, don't . . ." She sounded funny. Was she crying?

"I'll take care of you. You'll see."

She felt his hand inside her blouse. "I won't live in some damn fool farmhouse, doing chores."

"You won't. I promise you."

He couldn't. He could mean it till the cows came home, it didn't matter. She'd leave him behind, she'd have to.

She was trying not to sob when Marvin kissed her. She could feel it happening, the way it always did. She fought against it.

"Lucy . . . Lucy . . ."

"Find a place to park," she said.

"What's that?" He looked at her.

She looked at him. He might just be the sweetest man on earth. She kissed him on the mouth, then drew away. "We can't stay here. We'll get arrested."

Van felt as free as air. It was a dizzying experience. He could do anything he wanted. Drive to Akron, catch a plane to anywhere or have a few drinks at the Club or go to Mansfield and get laid. He was his own man, out from under.

Someone ought to hear the news. Whom could he tell? He thought of Pam and Jerry, other friends; but it was late, they'd be asleep. He took a turn and found himself in front of Sandy Stone's house. Lights were on downstairs; they hadn't gone to bed yet.

Van was reaching to turn off the motor when he stopped. What was he doing here? The last thing he had told the man was, "I'm not ever coming back." But he had things to say now, answers to those questions Sandy kept on throwing at him. Why was he in Fulton, did he make his own decisions, was he angry with his wife?

Damn right he made his own decisions; he had turned a corner, found himself. And damn right, he wasn't angry, not at Marcie. She had done him in the bedroom, and let Sandy suck on that. If he was sore at anybody, it was Sandy. Smug and oh-so-wise, he thought he had the answers, knew it all. It would feel great to lay him out. 'I blew Ed away, what have you got to say to that?'

Van knew exactly what he'd say. He'd have more questions. Why was Van so sore at him? Was he an enemy? Did Van have many enemies? To hell with this. Van put the car in gear and came down on the gas. He was a man with things to do. Important things.

He parked on Pleasant Avenue, got out, unlocked the showroom door, stepped in, and closed it. Should he turn on the lights? Why the hell not? Come tomorrow morning, half the town would know what happened. There was nothing to keep secret, and if anyone was watching, let 'em.

There were models on the floor. This year's or last year's? Did he care? Not anymore. Besides, they looked alike to him. When he was growing up, each line of cars had family traits, you knew a Plymouth when you saw one. And they had real names, not made-up crap like Darts and Furies. Take DeSoto. Didn't even make them anymore. He'd had one, back at college. When you closed the doors, they sounded, they were solid. Everything was tin today, he'd spent his best years selling junk.

He crossed the floor and moved into the service area. It had a skylight, he could see. There were some tools and rags left on the floor. And an oil slick. What was it with those clowns? You use a tool, you put it back; you make a mess, you clean it up. If he had told Zack once, he'd told him—habits: they were hard to break. He'd never have to deal with Zack again, not ever. What a feeling. On a workbench just ahead, he saw what he was looking for: two clean, large cardboard boxes.

He was whistling as he moved into his office, flicked the

lights on, looked around in wonder. Could this really be the place where he'd pissed sixteen precious years away? Had he picked out those paneled walls—why pickled pine?—and chosen all that leather furniture? He must have liked it at the time.

He had to clear some space to put both boxes on his desk. He sat and then methodically, beginning at the bottom, started emptying the drawers. He found the most amazing things. Old letters, maps for trips they'd never taken. Why? He liked to drive, he'd wanted to see Yellowstone, Mount Rushmore, Mammoth Cave. And there were crayon drawings Betsy had made—birds, flowers, a stick figure of a man with scrawly letters at the top: "to daddy, happy father's day." How long ago was that? She was his little Princess then. She still was, always would be. Daddy's girl.

He left the contracts and the loan forms where they were. Whoever sat here next, poor fool, would need them. Whom would Ed replace him with? Phil West from Ford? If he could steal him, absolutely. Ed was always raving on, comparing him to Van. Well, Ed could have him and good luck.

One box was nearly full. He put his calendar and Rolodex on top, and all the pictures in their frames. What was he doing? Shots of him with Bets and Marcie, those he'd keep. But Ed and Harriet? He slipped their photos out and tore them into little pieces, tossed them high into the air, and watched them flutter down.

What next? What else was there he gave a damn about? He stared around. His trophies. They were precious, and he'd almost overlooked them. There were easily a dozen, maybe more; golf tournaments he'd won. From high school, college, at the Club. He kept them here. There never seemed to be a place for them at home. Marcie kept moving them, she couldn't find a room where they belonged. To hell with that. He'd keep them in the bedroom if he wanted to.

He wrapped them carefully in paper towels and packed them, lugged the boxes to his car. He put them in the trunk, then turned and gazed at Steuben Motors. Ed had built a business, and you had to give him credit. But you didn't have to love him for it and you didn't have to eat his shit.

Van went back to his office for a final look. He thought of calling home and telling Marcie not to worry, he was fine and dandy. It was better face-to-face. There was so much to talk

about: his future, all those plans to make; they'd be up half
the night.

He turned to go, then stopped. Just one more thing he
had to do. He found a magic marker and approached the wall
behind his desk. He wrote it out in large block letters: VANNIE
DOESN'T LIVE HERE ANYMORE.

Ed was backing out of the driveway. Harriet, who hadn't
said a word—not yet—was smoldering with questions, like a
signal fire. Let her. Several winning hands had come his way,
along with several drinks, and all he wanted was some resting
space. He'd had two family rows tonight. He didn't need a
third one.

"So?"

Her *s* was sibilant when she was angry, and she sounded
like a snake. It always irritated him. He put on what he took to
be a puzzled frown and handed it right back to her. "So?"

"What went on?"

"When?"

"Ed Steuben, don't play dumb with me."

"You mean the poker game? I came out twenty bucks
ahead."

"Watch what you're doing, there's a stop sign."

"I can read." The Fallsburg Road was clear. He turned
and waited for the ax to drop.

"What did you do to Van?"

"What did *I* do?"

"He left the house, that's all I know, and Marcie's looking
for him right this minute."

"I know that."

"Who broke the window?"

"Van did."

"Why?"

"Beats me, you'd have to ask him. I mean, what's the
sense of breaking windows?"

"Ed." She took a deep breath. "What are you ashamed
of?"

"Nothing. All that really happened was, Van tendered me
his resignation."

"He did what?"

"He up and quit."

"Dear Lord." It took some doing, but she had him started.

How to get the rest of it? She took his hand and patted it. "You poor man, after all you've done for him."

What was she pulling now? He nodded. "Yeah, I know, I know."

"It won't be easy, making do without him."

"I'll get by."

She felt him stiffen. Good. "You're no spring chicken anymore. Van did so much, he worked so hard."

"The boy did fuck-all."

"Really, Ed."

"Fuck-all, Harriet, and it's my business. I don't want to talk about it."

"But we have to—"

"Drop it!"

"Anything you say, dear." She sat back. The more she thought, the more she simmered. She'd known Van almost half his life. He never lost his temper, he was always kind and gentle. What in God's name had Ed done to him? What awful thing?

"Ed?"

"What is it now?"

She tried to make herself sound calm. "Just wondering. Sometimes, you know, you can be such a bastard."

"*Me?*"

"You must have cut Van's heart out."

Ed saw bright red. "I borrowed half a million bucks from Jack, and Van went crazy when I told him."

"When you told him?"

"Called me names and—"

"Just hold on. You never talked it over with him? You just went and did it?"

"It's my business."

"He's your partner."

"Junior partner. If it weren't for me—"

"Shut up. He's Marcie's husband, Betsy's father. He's a good provider, and he's faithful. That's a damn sight more than you are."

"Who are you accusing—"

"Stow it, Ed. The whole town knows. Now, listen close. You're going to Van tomorrow, and you're going to patch it up."

"If you think for one God damn minute I'm about to kiss his rosy red—"

"I don't care what you kiss. I put this family back together once today. It's your turn. Do it, or I swear to God, I'll have your ass."

She never swore. He'd seen her lose her temper—hell, she did that all the time—but this was something else. "Oh, come on, Harriet."

"You do it, or I'll take my sewing scissors to your private parts."

She didn't really mean it, he knew that. "What am I going to say to Van? I've got my pride."

"You won't go far on that without your oysters."

"Jesus, Harriet." He couldn't recognize her, there was so much anger in her.

"Nothing tears my family apart. You hear me, Ed?"

He heard her.

23

THERE WERE LEARNED journals, files, and reports on Sandy's desk. He liked to do his reading in his study, after dinner and the kids were put to bed. The room was comfortable and quiet, reassuring; all those framed diplomas on the walls. He'd damn well earned them, every one; how many years of study at Mount Sinai in New York?

"Who counts?" This was addressed to Mort, his Irish setter, who was looking up at him, tail thumping on the floor. "Forget it," Sandy told him, opening a file. Eleanor MacFarlane. She'd appeared that afternoon, first visit, just to talk about her daughter, Dee. He knew who Dee was, he had met her once or twice: a gorgeous girl though not a happy one— but Mamma had the problems. Little did she know it. And she never would. Sometimes the people here . . .

He put the folder down. He couldn't concentrate, his thoughts kept wandering to Van. He'd muffed it somehow, scared him off. The man was so repressed; it was a miracle he'd come at all. Mort's tail kept thumping. "Oh, all right."

He found the leash and they went out into the dark. It was a pleasant quiet neighborhood: nice houses—not like Sunset Crescent, but it suited him. They strolled along. He always let Mort run the show; the beast had likes and dislikes. In particular, he had a deep attachment for some bushes on the corner, which was where they were when Van drove by them. Sandy knew the car. He watched it pull up by his house.

"Well, how about that?" Van had come to see him. Just to talk, or was there something new he couldn't handle? Sandy didn't care. The point was, Van was there, still sitting in his car. "Come on, you mutt." He tugged the leash and started down the sidewalk when he heard the motor rev. The car sped off.

"Aw, fuck it." Would Van ever come again? If not, should he pursue it? After seven years in Fulton, did he really know these people? From the outside, absolutely. They had rules and regulations, patterns that they never broke. There were restrictive covenants on half the properties in town. It was a gilded cage; they paid a price for living here. So many things were either never done or never mentioned. Suicides went down on the death certificates as heart attacks. Regardless of the drinking, Fulton had no alcoholics. They refused to see it. As for sex? They did it, there were children in the schools to prove it, but the guilt and the contortions they went through were monstrous.

Things were just as rigid out beyond the city limits. The specifics changed, that was all. Some farm folk fucked liked bunnies; others went to Church and prayed for the destruction of the fornicators. It was something. More than he could deal with, even if he wanted to. He had his wife and kids, his home and garden, golf and free time, just enough of it.

He moved into the front hall, closed the door and locked it, let Mort off his leash, and moved into his study. He had left the light on. He found Alice waiting for him. Barefoot and a little rounder than she used to be. He liked her that way.

"Well." He grinned. "How long have you been waiting here?"

"Since yesterday. I've come to see the doctor, and I'm never late for my appointment."

He moved closer. "What's your problem?"

"What's yours?"

Sandy shrugged. "I think I've let a patient get away. Or I never had him to begin with."

"Patients come and go. You know that. What makes this one special?"

"I don't know. I like him, he's a nice guy. He reminds me of my brother. Tell me something. Are you ever homesick?"

"This is home."

He shook his head. "You know what I mean. Do you miss New York?"

"Sure. Now and then."

"I dragged you out here. I could always take you back."

She smiled wryly. "It's the only Bible quote I know. 'Whither thou goest, I will go; and where thou lodgest, I will lodge.'"

"But would you like to go back?"

"Only when you're ready."

Sandy looked at her a long time. Was there any place where he belonged? Did all Jews wander? By no means. He turned away. "Let's go to bed."

Somehow, Marcie made it to the Lodge. On automatic pi-lot, flying blind. She had no memories of the drive, how long it took, if she had wandered, lost her way. But there she was. She cut the engine and the lights, then let her head slump forward on the wheel.

Her day went running through her mind, at high speed, like fast forward on a tape. From playing Jolly Mom at break-fast to her mother's hugs and kisses, caving in to Talker on the desk—and there was more, but all the images were blurring and their voices squeaky—high, like Donald Duck's.

"Stop it." Marcie straightened, looked around. Who said that? She did. And a good idea it was. She turned off the tape, left the car. The sky was filled with stars. The air was full of bugs: gnats, flies, mosquitoes, moths.

She hurried to the Lodge. Where had she left the key? She found it, stepped inside, flicked on the lights, and slammed the door. Then opened it again, just wide enough to push the buttons and unlock the lock so he could get in when he came. She checked the time. He wouldn't be there for a while.

What to do? The TV set? She couldn't sit still, couldn't watch. She fluffed some cushions, looked around for ciga-rettes—she would have killed for one—then went and opened up the fridge to check her beer supply. There was enough.

The house was hot. She found the thermostat and set the thing for 65. Van's temperature. What was she doing? What was he doing? Did he need her? Did she care? Don't answer that. She felt like crying, but she didn't. She had Talker on her hands.

She headed for the bathroom, started taking off her clothes. A shower; that would clear her head. She turned the knobs as hard as they would go. No hot; the water heater wasn't on. So much better.

She stepped in, closed the curtain and let out a gasp. The water took her breath away. Like icy needles, stabbing at her. Good: she needed punishment. She'd broken every rule she lived by. What would Reverend Larkin say? Aside from coveting thy neighbor's wife, was there one Commandment she had left unbroken? "Thou shalt not commit adultery." "Honor thy father and thy mother." "Thou shalt not—"

She saw a shadow. On the curtain. Someone in the bathroom. *Psycho*. Tony Perkins. She went rigid, and the air was filled with screaming. She was screaming.

"Jesus, Marcie." Talker whipped the curtain back. She went on screaming. "Hey, it's me." Her eyes were bulging. "What's the matter? Stop it." He reached out, she edged away. He stepped into the shower, getting soaked, to hell with that, and wrapped his arms around her. She was shaking. "Come on, baby; that's a good girl."

"Talker?" It was just a whisper.

"That's more like it."

He turned off the water, got her out, and wrapped her in a towel. She clung to him. He helped her to the living room and sat her in a chair. "You feeling any better?"

"You're all wet."

He grinned. "I'll live."

"You've scratched your face."

"I ran into some bushes. You want coffee, tea, a drink?"

She shook her head.

"I'll be right back. Don't go away."

He moved into the bathroom, stripped, hung up his wet clothes on the curtain bar. It was some way to start the evening. He had heard the shower running, he'd just wanted to surprise her, and instead, he got the screaming meemies. She'd been terrified. He'd been in better shape himself. He'd have to watch his step, be careful how he handled her. Things had to go the way he wanted. If they didn't—none of that. Think positive. He took a bath towel, knotted it around his waist, and went back in.

She hadn't moved an inch.

There was a chair close by her. Talker took it, looked her over. "Well?"

"You have a cigarette?"

"They're drying out. You need one, I can put them in the stove."

"Don't bother."

"It's no bother." He was half up.

"Don't. Just don't. O.K.?"

"You want to tell me what's the trouble?"

"There's no trouble."

Talker had to get it out of her. He couldn't play his cards right if he didn't know the game. "You look like you've been through the wringer."

Marcie shrugged.

"You can't fool me. My girls are messed up half the time. I know it when I see it, I'm an expert."

"Do you screw them all?"

"Oh, come on, Marcie."

"Do you?"

"No." He had to level with her. If you want to get, you have to give. "It happens sometimes. I can't lie to you. It doesn't mean much. They get lonely, I get lonely. You know what that feels like, don't you?"

"Maybe."

"Having someone . . ." Talker shrugged. "It can mean anything. A little or a lot. Five minutes' pleasure or the world. That's what you are to me, you know."

She half believed him. "That's a line."

"We've all got lines. What's yours?"

"I don't know what you mean."

"What's hurting?"

"Nothing."

Talker took her hand. "Then how do you account for all the messages you're sending?"

"You don't want to hear about it."

"Have it your way."

That was all it took. Her day came pouring out. She couldn't seem to stop herself. There was no order to it: telling Dad to go to hell; the burnt-up breakfast bacon; Mother with her mix of love and crap; what Dee had said; the football boys; her stupid tears; the God damn poker game. He'd asked for it; he got it. Everything, the kitchen sink. Except for Van's erection; that was his, it wasn't hers to tell. The more she said, the worse it got. And funnier. You pile grief on grief, it turns into a joke. She even laughed out loud at one point; Dad was calling Van a dickhead. "Jesus, Talker," she was saying, "who'd believe it? And Dee had to put my shoes on. Am I going crazy?"

"Nope."

And going out to look for Van. The lie to Dee, she was ashamed of that. She told him so. And at the end, she thought she knew how strippers felt. The word was naked.

"That's the works?" he asked.

"That's it, I guess."

"How does it feel?"

"To have it off my chest, you mean?" She thought about it. "Better."

"Good." Not altogether honest, but he said it anyway. She'd left him out. He'd heard about the fucking pancakes, Mrs. Beebe, notes for Pam—who were these people, anyhow?—but not one word about himself. He'd figured in her day, he'd been there.

Her towel had slipped a little. She adjusted it. She felt a need for reassurance. "Talker?"

"Yes?"

"What do you think of me?"

"You're kidding."

"I mean, after all the things I've done."

"We've done" was what she meant. He *had* been on her mind. The whole time. "If you want to know, I'll tell you." It was now or never. "In my own way."

"Sure."

"You ever hear about the Princes of Serendip?" He was showing off; he had to. What she thought of him made all the difference. "It's a boring story. They were always finding precious things by accident. They'd get lost in the woods and stumble onto buried treasure. Serendipity."

"Uh-huh." How did he know those things? She didn't.

"I never meant to come to Fulton. How I ended up here . . . wandering, that's what it is. I've spent my whole life wandering. It feels like freedom, but it's not. You go from state to state, you stay in one place long enough to start to make some friends, and buzzers go off in your head. Alarm bells. Time to move again. It's bumming, from the verb 'to bum.' You bum around."

He took a breath. "I called my home this afternoon. Well, not my home exactly. Where my wife and daughter live."

"You're married?"

"Used to be. I left them, Marcie. I ran out. I pay their bills, I have the money, but it doesn't seem to count for much. The truth is, Marcie, coast to coast, I've never been responsible to anyone for anything. I own a car, the clothes I wear, and nothing else. That feels like freedom, too."

He got up, started pacing. "People tell you life's a rat race. That's not true. It's not a race unless you run, and, Marcie, I'm so sick of running. I can't do it anymore. I'm going to stay in Fulton."

"What?"

"I'll get a job, that's easy. But it's not the town that I can't leave. It's you."

"But—"

"Let me finish." He moved closer to her. "I know what the problems are. I'd cut my wrists before I did you any harm, but I can't leave here. I'm in love with you."

"You're not."

He took her hand. "It's easier for me to say it. You'll get used to it in time." He bent to kiss her.

"Don't." She ducked away, her towel slipped off. "Don't start all that."

"You know you like it."

"I can't help myself."

She stood. He caught her, put his arms around her. "You should also know—"

"Let go."

"I lied about my age. I'm really thirty-two." He felt her shaking.

"Talker, please . . ."

"I've got a real name, too. It's Johnny."

Did he love her? Was it true? Did Van? Did she love anyone? Now he was kissing her. "Oh God . . ." She couldn't stay here. Not tonight, with Van the way he was. She never should have come.

"I want you, Marcie."

Christ, what else was new? "I want you, too. It's killing me." She wrenched away. "I've got to go. Van needs me."

"So do I."

She tried to speak, then turned and bolted from the room to get her clothes. He let her go. He knew what guilt could drive you to. At least she knew he loved her; and he thought she loved him, too. She was as caught as he was. She'd be back.

Annie couldn't sleep. It was impossible. The air inside the van had sewer breath, and even with the fan on full, she turned and twisted. She felt moist and sticky, and her cot was like a rocky road.

She'd stayed behind when Laurel and the others left to have a drink or two. She couldn't go, she had to be alone. She had a lot of tears saved up, she couldn't keep them in, and she did not want anybody watching, asking questions. She'd been such a fool, pinned all her hopes on thin air, nothing. She had no one in the world to blame except herself, and no one in the world to tell about it.

Sobbing hadn't helped. The only thing that happened was she got her pillow wet. She sat up, threw the thing across the van. That didn't help much, either; she was so damned angry. Uncle Emil had a saying. "Kid," he'd say. "Fuck all but six, and save them for pallbearers." Annie didn't have six.

"Fuck 'em all," she said, got up, put on a cotton shift. She found a fresh sheet and a pillow, left the van, slipped through the boundary fence, and moved out on the cornfield. She liked sleeping out-of-doors. Back home, when the walls closed in, she'd sneak out of the house and spend the night among the barley and the soybeans.

It was shadowy between the rows of corn; they rose above her head, and she felt curtained off and safe. She found an open spot she liked, spread out the sheet, lay down, and put the pillow underneath her head. She heard the crickets, but she couldn't see them.

Stars were random, patternless—she knew all that from school—but you could play around with them. Stare long enough and they turned into shapes of all kinds: faces, houses, animals, most anything you wanted.

You could count them, too, like sheep. She was exhausted, and she knew it. Nothing left inside, that's how she felt. She started counting, got to ten and thought of Talker. He was with his Woman, doing it, that very minute. Damn. She wasn't concentrating. Counting only worked if it was all you thought about.

She got to fifty-six and fell asleep.

Dee was prowling through the empty house. From room to room, upstairs and down; she couldn't sit still, come to rest. She cleared away the mess left from the poker game and straightened up the living room. She'd even placed a call to Akron-Canton Airport, tried to make a morning reservation home. She got a tape recording. Once you crossed the Hudson, everything closed early.

It was just as well. Marcie had made her promise she would stay till Sunday. "You don't want to miss the big dance, do you?" It had been important once. She'd had some wild times, including visits to the shrubs behind the caddy shack. Incredible. She'd really done those things.

She didn't do them anymore. Not frequently, at any rate. The men she knew were nice enough, but interchangeable. She always made the moans and groans she knew they liked to hear. Sometimes she'd even come. But passing thirty made a difference, God alone knew why, and somehow all the fizz and kick had left the bottle. Life was going flat. She wished to hell she had a man to love. Where was he?

She went back to the living room and made a virgin scotch and soda. She had sobered hours ago. She thought of calling Marcie at the Lodge and screaming at her. It would feel good, she'd enjoy it, but there wasn't any point. You can't lead other people's lives. She couldn't even lead her own.

But there was one thing that she could do. Had to do. Wait up for Van. He couldn't come home to an empty house, not after what had happened. Someone had to be here for him, and if Marcie didn't give a damn, Dee did. Not that she cared for Van that much. What made his wheels go round eluded her. Somehow, the man was like a cat; he came and went and left no signs behind. As if he'd never been there.

"Hi."

Dee's heart skipped. Van was standing in the doorway, and she hadn't heard his car pull in. "You startled me."

"I'm sorry."

"You O.K.?" She had a robe on, nothing else. It had come slightly open, so she closed it.

"I'm terrific."

"Glad to hear it." He was smiling, he had eyes like Krazy Kat's.

"Where's Marcie? Up in bed?"

"She's out."

"This time of night? Out doing what?"

She'd never tell him; it would kill him if he knew the truth. "She's looking for you. She got worried."

"Really?"

"You've been gone so long."

"I thought of calling from the office. I've been cleaning out my desk."

"You're really going through with it?"

"Do dogs have fleas?"

The man was flying high now, like a toy balloon. But he'd come down. She felt a surge of feeling for him, real compassion. "Can I get you anything?"

"I've had enough to drink, thanks."

"Are you hungry?"

"Me?" He looked surprised. "Yes, come to think of it, I am."

"What would you like?"

"Surprise me."

Dee turned on the kitchen lights. She knew exactly what to make him.

Van sat at the kitchen table, watching her. He couldn't help remembering how she had looked stripped naked, swimming in the pool. He used to wonder, back at Denison, what might have happened if he made a move. He wondered now, envisioning the beauty underneath the robe. He'd never do it, take the risk, but it was nice to think about it.

"So," Dee said, not looking at him, busy at the counter, "you're at liberty."

"At liberty?"

"That's what we actors call it. Unemployed."

"Oh, that." He hadn't thought about it. "I'll be fine." He would be. He was young, still in his thirties—even if the big four-oh was coming in November. He was bright, experienced, hard-working, skilled at management. He really ran the business; everybody knew it. All Ed did was glad-hand, talk a good game, make connections. Half the businesses in town would grab him, make him offers. They'd be lined up to the corner.

"That's the way to feel," Dee told him. "Standing on your own two feet, there's nothing like it. I should know."

He nodded. He admired her for that. She could have stayed at home, the way Marcie had. But it was right for Marcie, she belonged in Fulton. Yes, but how would she take his decision? Would she stand behind him, back him up? There would be hell to pay, he knew that. Family ties and family business. Come the morning, there'd be phone calls. Bright and early. Harriet would put the screws on Marcie. So would Ed, for all he knew. But Marcie wouldn't give an inch, she'd never let him down.

"Well, here you go."

"Just what I wanted." Dee had made a chicken sandwich, white bread with the crust cut off and lots of mayonnaise. A glass of milk. And chocolate brownies. Everything a boy could ask for.

Dee sat down beside him and watched him take a bite. He chewed but couldn't seem to swallow. It was coming any minute now. She handed him the glass of milk.

He took it, swallowed, got it down. "You know the truth, Dee?"

"I could guess."

"I'm in deep shit."

"I know, but you can handle it. You'll be all right."

"I want to be my own man."

"Sure. Of course you do."

"I'll never make it."

"Who says?"

"Dee . . ." He choked up. "Strange to say, I haven't got a lot of friends. I don't know why."

"You've got me."

"God, I wish you lived here."

"Wouldn't help, it wouldn't do you any good. And as for me . . ."

"I don't know where to turn."

"Come here." She edged her chair up close beside him, took his head, and gently moved it to her breasts.

"Oh, Dee . . ."

"I know, I know." She pulled her robe back, just a little. "There. That's better, isn't it?" He nodded. Tears began to trickle, she could feel them on her skin. She put one arm around him. "There, there."

Marcie watched it from the doorway. "Hi," she said. "I'm home."

24

HARRY WELLER'S DAY began a little after 5:00 A.M., with stabbing pains from his bursitis. Left side, elbow, shoulder. Nothing chronic, it just came and went; but when it came, it was blue murder. Harry swore under his breath. He hadn't hit the sheets till one. The mess-ups at the Fair were endless; fist fights, drunks, car accidents, and he had no one to complain to. Martha suffered from insomnia, and if he woke her up at dawn for sympathy, she'd kill him. So he padded to the bathroom, shaved and showered, dressed and headed for the kitchen.

Coffee, he was dead without a cup or two, but Mr. Coffee wouldn't work. The fool contraption sat there with its lights on, doing nothing. Harry made a quick search for the coffeepot. To hell with these machines, give him a good old-fashioned percolator any day. He couldn't find it, so he left a note for Martha, drove off to Diana's Diner for a jolt of java and some Danish. They were yesterday's; today's weren't in yet.

"Sorry, Sheriff."

"So am I."

He choked the pastry down and headed for his office. At the Fair all day and half the night, it was his only time for checking in. God only knew what lay ahead. Last night, some damn fool greenhorn on the Force arrested Adam Brinker. Drunken driving. God almighty. There were certain people in this town you had to treat with kid gloves. Pie-eyed, falling down, no matter; what you did was drive them home. So he'd gone down to Brinker's cell, awakened him, profusely kissed the ground he stood on, promised to ream out the idiot who brought him in, and drove him to his residence.

What would it be this morning? What fresh, stupid new disaster—Harry stopped himself. The Fair was over Saturday, just two more days to go. The tunnel wasn't endless; there was daylight, he could see it. And he used to like the Fair. He was its lord and master, he'd enjoyed it.

He pulled into his parking place and trudged into the station house. Night staff was still on duty, looking bleary, waiting for relief, the lucky bastards. Harry sat down at his desk and checked the blotter. No important names today. Thank God for little favors. Toward the bottom, something caught him.

Harry sent for the arrest reports. Four women. Charge: Soliciting. Name, age, address, occupation. There it was: exotic dancer. Talker's girls. He'd known it had to happen; he'd been waiting for it. Give a stripper time enough, she'd put it up for sale. The one mistake he'd made was letting them set up here in the first place. Talker was no pimp, and the old woman was no madam, but he'd let himself get sold a bill of goods. There were no hookers, not in Harry Weller's town.

He got up, went to check them out. They each had separate cells; he ran a class act. Sound asleep. They looked so young. What got them into lives like this? He stopped dead at the fourth cell. They'd pulled in the old broad. She was sitting up and staring at him. No way was she selling it, not at her age. He had to ask.

"What are you doing here?"

"You're some dumb cop if you can't figure that out."

Harry liked her spirit. His grandmother was a killer. Still alive at ninety-three, she smoked a pipe and opened soft-drink bottles with her teeth. "You want to talk?"

"To you?"

"Come on." He opened up her cell and took her to his office.

"Have a chair."

She sat.

No 'Thank you, sir.' He glanced at her arrest report. "Now, Norma—"

"Tell you what. You call me Mrs. Cusak, and I'll call you Sheriff."

"Fair enough." He felt at home. "What happened?"

"Ask the jerk who pulled us in."

"I'm asking you."

"We're innocent, but you're not going to swallow that."

"I might. Mind if I smoke?"

"I'll take one, too."

He lit it for her. She sat back without a word. He had to grin. "You're welcome, Mrs. Cusak."

"So, you want to hear it?"

"Any time."

Talker said the guy was a straight shooter. Norma took a flyer, told the truth. "You know a place called Randy's Roaring Twenties?"

"It's a roadhouse."

"It's a dump."

He shrugged. She wasn't wrong about it.

"You know who goes there?" Norma asked.

The place was popular. "A lot of people."

"Wrong. A lot of assholes. Farmers, townies, I don't know; all assholes look a lot alike."

He kept a straight face. "Want some coffee?"

"Is it free?"

He picked the phone up, sent for some.

So far, so good. She pressed her luck a little further. "Tell me, Sheriff, you know what it's like to have a label?"

"Sure." He had one, didn't he?

"My girls have labels. Not their fault. Some people earn them. Some don't. They stick to you, either way. We didn't do a damn thing, Sheriff. We just sat there having drinks and telling off the assholes."

"Someone called the cops," he said.

"It wasn't necessary."

"No?"

"By then the fight was over."

"Oh? What fight was that?"

"It's like this, Sheriff. No one paws my girls around. They kept on coming over, one clown in particular. He weighed two-fifty, maybe more, and he was six foot three, at least. I asked him nicely, Go away. The next time, I was less polite.

He told me where to stick it, and I lost my temper. I admit it. I got up and laid him out."

"You laid him out?"

"I broke a bottle on his head."

"Uh-huh." He kept a straight face. He believed her; he could see the whole scene: Norma on her feet and—he glanced at the arresting officer's report—Walt Greener on the floor. It would be Walt; you poured enough beer into him, and off he went. "Just tell me one thing, Mrs. Cusak."

"Yeah."

"The charge here says 'soliciting.'"

"Aw, grow up, Sheriff. We were marks. What are those assholes going to tell a cop? 'It's our fault, Officer. We're acting like a bunch of rectal orifices'?"

Weller laughed. What was he going to do with her? "You want to call me Harry, Norma?"

Marcie lay in bed and listened to the water running. It was six, the sun was up, and Van was showering. She'd had no sleep at all, there was so much to deal with, and she felt— Van's golf expression—as if her wheels were falling off.

It had been twoish when she'd walked into the kitchen and seen Van's face amid Dee's boobs. She had expected many things—she'd spent the whole drive home preparing, like an actress playing scenes—but she had not expected this. She could have killed them both.

"O.K., just what the hell is going on?"

They separated slowly, not a sign of guilt. Dee had the gall to look at her and smile.

"It's good you're home."

"I've gotta give you credit, Dee. You get an 'A' for acting. Close the robe, for Jesus' sake."

"Calm down, there's nothing going on."

"You could have fooled me. What the hell, you two go right ahead, don't let me interrupt."

Van sounded weary. "Stop it, Marcie."

"Sure, why not, why should I mind? A little infidelity is what we need around here. Do you know where I've been half the night?"

"Dee told me—"

"I've been scouring the streets for you. You have a fight with Dad, you throw a drink at him, go storming off. I tell you, I've been going crazy, worried sick. Hell, I've seen streets I didn't know existed. I've been everywhere. No sign of you. No fucking wonder. You've been here the whole time, making out."

"I just got home."

"Oh, tell me more."

"It's true," Dee said, eyes blazing. She was furious with Marcie: all stops out, what a performance.

"O.K." Marcie turned to Van. "I'm gullible. I'll bite. Where were you?"

"At the showroom."

"That's a good one. At this time of night?"

Van nodded. "I've been cleaning out my office."

"With a Hoover? Aw, give me a break."

"I packed up all my things. They're in the trunk."

"I'm sorry." Marcie shook her head. "There's something I'm not getting."

Van looked puzzled. "Don't you know?"

Dear Lord, what now? She moved in closer. "Van, what's happened?"

"I've resigned."

"You've what?"

"From Steuben Motors."

It was patently impossible. Her ears were ringing. She sat down. "You're serious?"

"I quit my job."

There was a multitude of things she nearly said. Like: have you lost your so-called mind, or it's impossible, you can't, you want to ruin everything? Instead—and how she sounded calm, she'd never know—she said, "That's all I need."

Van nodded. "It's been some night."

"Hasn't it? You packed, came home, Dee made a sandwich for you, took you in her arms. They ought to put us on the soaps."

Van sighed. "You mind if we postpone this? I'm not sure—I don't think I can handle all of it right now."

She felt her anger rising. "Oh, come on; give it a try."

Dee put her oar in. "He's exhausted, Marcie."

"He can talk."

Dee sent a look at her. "And you're exhausted, too, I'm sure. If I were you, I'd let it wait till morning."

Van stood up. "A good night's sleep. We all could use one. Thanks, Dee."

"Any time."

He turned to Marcie, kissed her cheek. "You look the way I feel." He smiled. "Don't stay up too long."

The two girls watched him leave the room. They waited, eyes averted, till they heard him on the stairs.

Dee broke the silence. "Jesus, Marcie, what a show."

"The same to you. You always had the greatest tits."

"Yours aren't so bad. Whose mouth have they been in tonight?"

"I've done a lot of things, but coming on to my best friend's husband—"

"Never."

"Someone had to start it, and it wasn't Van. The day he makes a move—"

Dee slapped her face. "You've got that coming, and a whole lot more. How selfish are you, Marcie? You're just like your mother. All you sing is me, me, me."

"You slapped me," Marcie gasped.

Dee rode right over it. "Oh, I can understand that 'I'm so worried' crap you laid on Van. I'm even for it, you can't tell him you've been climbing someone's pole. God, I'm so angry. But what really steams me—you expect me, Dee MacFarlane, to believe you give a damn where Van's been putting it? Accusing me. Hell, he could stick his thing in the disposal—"

"That's not fair."

"Don't hand me fair. Did you, did I hear you—did it occur to you to ask him why he quit? What drove him to it? How he feels? Did you express the least confuckingcern about the man? Or did I miss your sweet compassion?"

"I was going to ask him."

"When?" Dee stood. "Come next Saint Swithin's Day? I give up."

"Dee—don't go."

"Why not? I've said my piece, you've got the gist of it."

"I should have asked. I didn't think."

"You didn't care." Dee started off.

That tore it. Marcie jumped up, hurried after her. "I do care. He's been on my mind all night."

"While you've been on your back."

"Give me a break."

"Give me a reason why."

"I need one."

Dee turned back and looked at her. "I guess you do."

They talked a long time. It was after four when Marcie dragged her aching body up the stairs and dropped it into bed. Van was asleep by then. She nearly woke him, thought the better of it, turned and faced the wall.

She heard the shower stop. He'd come out any second. Marcie knew they had to talk. There was, God knows, enough to talk about. But it was so important, and she had to be so smart about it, so alert. She didn't have it in her now, she couldn't bring it off.

She closed her eyes, rolled on her side, and practiced making sleep sounds, breathing deeply. She heard the door come open, heard his bare feet on the floor.

"Marcie, are you awake?" she heard him whisper.

Marcie didn't stir.

Talker was jogging. Carthage Lake had hiking trails that ran along the shore, and he was out among the pinecones and the brambles, being careful where he put his feet and thinking. Jogging cleared the head, the same way swimming did.

He may have slept, he wasn't sure, but soon as there was light enough, he'd dressed and hit the trail. One thing he knew: no matter what today might bring, it couldn't rival yesterday. Thursday had been a blivet, two pounds of shit in a one-pound bag. He'd always kept his feelings tucked away, and last night, like a broken faucet, everything came pouring out. With what result? She'd gone home to her husband.

What he had to do was get inside her mind and feel her feelings. Marcie had a home and family, a husband; but she didn't love Van. Couldn't. There was nothing in the man. That wasn't fair, but there was not enough for Marcie. Talker was the man for her; she loved him, it was carved in marble. She just had some trouble dealing with it, that was all.

He ducked a low branch, stumbled, kept on going. What he had to do was get her off the dime. He had some crazy thoughts, like marching straight through her front door and taking her away, kicking and screaming, did he care? But he knew better. Marcie called for patience, careful handling.

By the time his cabin came in sight, he knew exactly what

to do. His mind was crystal-clear, and he was smiling. It might take a while, but what the hell, he wasn't going anywhere.

He went back to his cabin, showered, shaved, and dressed. Which slacks to wear, what shirt; he felt like looking nice today. The first thing on his docket was the car. And after that? He made a mental list and went back out. No sign of Norma and the girls. They loved their sack time, they'd all be asleep for hours. Laurel's car was nowhere to be seen, but she liked parking it behind her cabin.

"Morning, mister."

Talker turned. Old Barney what's-his-name was standing by his T-bird. "Nice day."

Talker nodded.

"I've been looking at your car. Somebody scratched it up some."

"Yeah."

"You plan to drive the thing around with words on it like this?"

"No."

"Glad to hear that. I was going to have you move it, keep it somewhere else."

"How come?"

"It's offensive. You don't mind me saying so?"

"A little." Talker bristled.

"I've got children staying here. You want them reading filth like that?"

"If they don't know the words by this time, they're retarded."

"Listen, mister. When you came, I told you this was Christian country. We don't like you and your kind."

"You came to see the show. I saw you going in. And half the people staying here, I've seen them in the crowd. You tell me, where the hell are all the Christians?"

"Watch your tongue, boy."

"Watch your own. You think I did this to my car? One of your God damn Christians did it."

Barney's face was turning red. "You Godless bastard."

Talker felt like nailing him. "That's shocking language. Filthy talk. You know the words, all right."

"Damn right I do."

"I don't suppose you scratched them in."

"What?"

"Were you at the Fair last night?"

"Are you accusing me—?"

"Just asking."

"Listen, Mister Pimp."

That did it. "No, you listen. I can quote the Bible, too. You name a verse, I'll give it to you. Only I don't wear it like a flag." He yanked the car door open, got in. "So take a message, tell your friends. If I find out who pulled this shit, I'll break his teeth and hand them to him on a plate."

He got the motor going. Did he mean it? Bet your ass. He took off in a cloud of dust.

Betsy was doing breakfast things. She knew her way around the kitchen, and Brigette, who drew the line at getting up at dawn, had given her permission. Juice and English muffins, butter, marmalade for Denny, jelly for herself. Grape, raspberry and currant, even mint; she didn't care.

She paused to check the kitchen table. Rushing; she had spilled the juice and singed the muffins, scraped the burnt part off on the counter, left it there. "Oh, come on, Bets." Now she was talking to herself.

Why be hysterical, what was the point? "Be realistic." She knew how. What had she actually done? Not all that much. She'd let him look at her. Big deal. She let him see her in that swimming suit. What was the difference? All the world. And last night, was it his idea? Oh no. She had suggested it; she made it happen. Good old Bets had let him see it all—and once you took your clothes off, could you ever really put them on again? When Denny looked at her from now on, what exactly would he see?

"The milk." She hurried to the fridge to get it. Worse and worse. What Denny saw meant nothing, not compared to what he thought of her. Did she seem easy now? And cheap? "Oh Lord," she said aloud, remembering the moment at the mirror, smiling at herself. What kind of girl had she become? She had the milk out when the worst came thudding home. She closed the door and leaned against it, closed her eyes. The worst was, what did he expect? What did he think was coming next?

"G'morning, hi, how are you?"

Betsy mumbled something, kept her eyes down on the floor; she couldn't look at him.

"I didn't get that."

"I'm O.K."

"Me, too. I'm sorry if I'm late. I didn't hear the dumb alarm." The fact was, he'd been up since four, four-thirty; and the truth was, he'd avoided coming down. He'd felt a little shaky, cold lumps in the stomach. Had they gotten in too deep? What was he going to say to her?

"I burned the muffins."

"I don't mind." He sat down at the table, put his napkin in his lap. His hands felt clammy. What about last night? Pretend it hadn't happened? Just go on like always? Maybe. It was easier, pretending. He watched Betsy drink her juice. He cleared his throat. "Look, Bets . . ." It hung there in the air.

"What is it?"

"Nothing. Only . . . do you think, you want to talk about last night?"

Eyes down, she shook her head. She didn't even dare to look at him; she'd see what he was thinking.

"Fine, O.K. by me." He felt relieved. He'd had to bring it up, it was the only thing to do, but what he would have said was far from sure. So much of it depended on what she said. "How'd you sleep?"

"Oh, I don't know; a little restless."

"I know what you mean." Two wet dreams in a single night. He'd only started having them six months ago. The first one shook him up. He had no parents in the house to tell him things; was it abnormal, was he freaky? In the end, he found the answers in a book.

He got his juice down, took a muffin. He was reaching for the butter when he brushed against her hand. They both jumped back. For Denny, it was touching fire.

"Sorry."

"Sorry."

Did she feel what he did? Did he even want to know? What if she did, what if she didn't? Questions, questions. "Bets?" he said.

"Uh-huh?"

"Why won't you look at me? You haven't once, this whole time."

"I don't know." She shrugged. "You'll look the same as yesterday."

He nodded. "Sure, why wouldn't I?"

She raised her eyes and gazed at his. They were in trouble and she knew it. So did he.

Ed was banging things around the kitchen. Harriet could hear him from the stairs. Once in his life, the man could make a breakfast for himself, it wouldn't do him any harm. She hadn't spoken to him since the ride home in the car. And why not? She had nothing left to say. For his part, he had done some muttering and mumbling, even said good night. She'd let it pass in silence. Let him stew. Until he worked things out with Van, he had no voting rights around her house.

She was moving toward the kitchen door when Ed came barging out. "I made the coffee."

What did he expect? Applause? She shrugged.

"You're welcome and don't mention it."

"Where are you going?" He was moving to the front door.

"What's it look like? Out."

"Out where?"

"The showroom. Satisfied?"

"It's early, it's not nine yet."

"You may not believe this, Harriet, but I not only own a wristwatch, I can read it."

"Wait."

He turned back in the open doorway. "Yes, my dearest?"

"Don't you bother coming home unless you've—"

"Let me guess. Unless I've fucking talked with fucking Van."

He slammed the door. She smiled. She knew her Ed; he'd do it. And he'd do it well. He could deny it till the moon went blue, but family meant as much to him as family meant to her.

She hurried to the kitchen, poured herself some coffee, knowing it was poisonous—Ed couldn't boil water—pulled a chair up to the wall phone, dialed, and sat. Three rings, four, five. She frowned. At eight, she stood. It never went past ten. Eleven.

"Hello, Mother."

"Oh, my dear, I didn't wake you, did I?"

Marcie, who had finally, at last, incredibly found sleep, said, "Yes."

"It's nearly nine o'clock, you know."

"That's news to me."

"Don't hang up."

Was she Clark Kent's mother, too? Did she have X-ray vision? "O.K., Mom, what's on your mind?"

"My family is in ruins, that's what's on my mind. Where's Van?"

"I haven't got a clue."

"You don't know where your husband is?"

"He's almost forty, Mother. He'll be careful crossing streets."

"I fail to see what's funny."

"I've been up all night." Her voice was rising. "I don't feel good."

"I should hope not."

Marcie sat bolt upright. "What?"

"I trust you set Van straight last night."

"We didn't talk." She thought she heard the phone drop. "Mother?"

"Didn't talk? The earth is crumbling. Don't you care? Do you know what your husband did to Ed? Have you the least idea—?"

"You've got that backwards."

"I do not."

"Dad acted like a shit." Her mother gasped. "Go on, gasp all you like. He treats Van like a lackey. Van's a partner in that business."

"Did he earn it, child? He did not. Your father made him one. Out of the goodness of his heart. And what thanks does he get? I ask you—?"

"Harriet—" Her voice was shaking, she was holding the receiver with both hands. "You've lost your mind."

"You listen to me, Marcie. You get up and find your man and shake some sense into his head. You tell him he should go to Ed on bended knees and beg him for his job back."

"Mother, I salute you. You're the best." She blew a kiss into the phone and hung it up.

"Hello, hello?" The line was dead. It didn't matter. Harriet sat back and smiled. Just a housewife she might be, but she knew how to close a deal: you play both ends against the middle. Either Marcie got to Van or Ed would. "Harriet," she said aloud, "you're a good woman."

She got up, put the receiver on its hook, and had another sip of coffee. It was cooling off and tasting better.

*   *   *

"You know what you can do with Fulton?" Skipper said. She raised her bottom from the dock, leaned forward just enough, and farted.

"Can't you see I'm eating?" Pauline asked.

"You're always eating." Laurel grinned. "You want another blast? She farts at will, you know."

The girls sat close together, feet dangling in the water, bags of junk food all around them. They had made a quick stop on the way and bought the store. How Norma had gotten them out of jail, they'd never know. They were in deep shit— and for doing nothing; that's what rankled—when Norma woke them up and said, "Let's move it, girls; we're out of here." When Laurel asked her how she'd done it, Norma answered, "Charm. I've got more charm on me than dogs have fleas."

"She's something," Laurel said, glancing at Norma, who was sitting at a picnic table drinking coffee.

"I don't see what's so great about her." Pauline stared glumly at her candy bar. "I've never been in jail before. I've got a record now."

"And it'll dog you till the day you die."

"Oh, Laurel . . ." She burst into tears.

"For Jesus' sake, Pauline." Laurel got to her feet. "I'm going swimming."

"With your clothes on?"

Skipper leaped up. "Wait for me."

Norma watched them jump in. They could use some cooling off. Before the trouble in the bar, they had been bitching at her, why close down after Saturday? They always worked past Labor Day; and sure it was a blow if Talker left them high and dry, but they could find some stiff to take his place. Not fill his shoes, who could? But just to stand in for a week or two.

And where was Talker now? Past nine o'clock and he was gone again, if he'd been back last night at all. His place was with them in the bar; he should have been there, he owed it to them. When the cock got hard, the brain went soft, and his was mush. She shook her head; maybe the girls were right. Another week or two, why not? She'd had it with Ohio. West Virginia wasn't far.

Lucy, at the kitchen sink, watched through the window. It
had been a long night after Marvin dropped her off. He loved
her, he would do his best. Some best. The two of them and a
baby living in his father's house. Or starving in some city
where he couldn't hold a job worth having. It was no life. Not
for Lucy. Not for anyone.

The breakfast eggs were sticking to the plates. At least the
house was empty; Dad had gone to town, and she was free to
cry without him preaching at her. Two things were for certain: she could not stay on at home, and she would never set
foot in a church again. She'd had enough of that.

She took a plate and cracked it on the sink. It split in two.
Not bad. She cracked the other one. "Hot damn." She felt a
quick, short spurt of joy, then scurried to the garbage can and
hid the pieces. Mamma got out, Mamma ran away. Wherever
Mamma was, no matter what the poverty or shabbiness, it beat
this shit hole.

Lucy went back to the window. Maybe Mrs. Cusak was the
answer. She'd been thinking of it since the third day she was
late. Today, tomorrow, that was all the time she had. She
glanced down at her body, ran her wet hands down her hips,
across her breasts. It was as nice a body as those other girls'.
She nodded. It was plenty good enough.

Ed stomped into the showroom, glared around, and
headed for his office. All he'd thought about on the way down
was what a banner day this should have been. He had his cool
half-million from Jack Morgan, he was set and ready, deals to
close and moves to make, calls, contracts, lawyers, builders—
all the stuff that dreams were made of.

And instead? The steady flow of crap from Harriet was
heavier than usual. Accustomed to it as he was, he had to
think back years to find a time when there had been this much
of it. And playing kissy-kissy with his damn fool son-in-law was
worse. Not that he had it in for Van. What Harriet had said
was true enough. He worked hard, he was capable, a decent
husband and God knows the guy was faithful, wouldn't even
go to Mansfield to have his ashes hauled. What burned Ed was
apologizing. He'd done nothing wrong, and Van was raining
on his day.

He was halfway across the showroom floor when Zack and
Mort came swooping down on him.

"Hey, Ed."

"Not now."

"There's something that you ought to see."

"This minute? I've got things to do."

"It won't take long."

"It better not." He snapped it out; he didn't like the way they looked, both serious and smirking. They were heading for Van's office. Was he in? Ed tried to calm himself. The office door was open.

"After you," Phil said.

Ed paused. He didn't like the sound of it. "You boys have things to do?"

"Well, sure, but—"

"Go and do them."

"Right."

Ed watched them move away, walked in and read the writing on the wall. Big, bright red letters: VANNIE DOESN'T LIVE HERE ANYMORE. Ed dropped his teeth. "For Jesus' fucking sake." If Van had been there, he'd have killed him. Last night had been bad enough. He'd had a drink thrown in his face, but, bottom line, it wasn't out in public. Jack and Harv and all the others, they were friends, old friends and equals. Sure, they'd talk about it to each other; certain people at the Club were sure to know. But only certain people. Ed could handle that.

Had Van gone crazy? Washing dirty linen where the world could see it? People here at work, employees. It would be all over town. No wonder Zack and Mort were smirking. Every joker on the street, bus drivers, postmen, shopgirls— Christ, who wouldn't know about it? Van had made a fool of him. Embarrassing? It was exfuckingcruciating.

Ed stormed over to the wall. He couldn't leave it there. He rubbed. It got him nothing. "Shit." Ed made a fist and hit the wall, felt better even if it hurt. No problem here. He'd wash it off; and if that failed, he'd take a crowbar, knock the wall down. He left the office, closed the door, and started off toward Service.

The boys were busy out in Service. Did they know? He couldn't tell. He sent them all another smile. "Good morning, how's it going?"

"Fine . . . you bet . . . nice day . . . how are you, Mr. Steuben?"

Not a smirk in sight. So far, so good. "I've got some clean-ing up to do. I'll handle it." He filled a bucket, squirted in some liquid soap, and took some clean rags and a sponge.

The stuff came off. It was a little tricky. If you got the ink too wet, it ran. The paneling had cracks, and where the stuff had gotten into them, it took a lot of rubbing. Ed removed his jacket, loosened up his tie. He'd worked hard when he was a kid, he didn't mind a little sweat. In fact, when he was done, he didn't feel half bad about it. He could still put in a day's work with the best of them. He even smiled; he had a lot to say to Vannie when he found him.

He left the bucket in the middle of the office. With a note. "I cleaned your mess up. Ed." Van would be coming back. The day he had the balls to quit would be the day. True, Ed still had to talk to him and make nice, among other things; he'd promised to, and if he didn't, it meant death by Harriet.

He took his jacket, went out, closed the door, and started toward his office. Zack and Mort were watching him. If it turned out they'd blabbed, he'd can them. But for now, he shrugged it off. "It's just a joke. A family joke." He grinned. "You know how families are."

They'd either swallow that or not; he'd have to see. He took his key, unlocked his office door—he kept a lot of papers that were no one's business—and moved in.

Ed liked his desk. He'd had it made to order; nothing in the catalogs looked big enough. No morning mail yet. Nothing on his calendar, no dates except for dinner, but he had a lot to do. He picked the phone up. Jane, his secretary for the last ten years, was late again. She usually was, but she had other attributes, like she would die for him. Besides, he liked to dial his own calls.

There were several possibilities. Call Jack, go over to the bank and sign the loan. Or buzz his lawyer, Marty Switt, and fill him in. He even thought of talking to Toyota in New York, but that was wrong, a big mistake. You take your time, play hard to get. He'd cut himself a killer deal.

So in the end, he dialed Harvey Yaeger and made a date for lunch. No reason, just to chew the fat. He never thought of Marcie once.

25

TALKER COULDN'T SHAKE it. Doing ninety on the way to town did nothing for him. He had won his fight with Lovell, scored more shots than he had taken. No relief. The world was full of hypocrites, he knew damn well they grew on trees, but they got to him every time. Some prick like that had scratched his car, it had to be.

He pulled into the Fairgrounds. It was after ten, the place was filling up. He checked the faces; were they pointing at him, staring at his T-bird? Some: not many, but enough. School buses, a whole line of them, were crawling up the road. He braked and swore, then shook his head. He had to cool down. Weller was his first stop of the day. The man was going to see his car, read every word of it. What happened next was up for grabs.

He spotted Weller and some cops by the Command Post. "Here we go." He pulled up, got out, slammed the door. It got a look from Weller.

"In a minute, fella."

Harry knew what Talker wanted. He was there to bitch about his girls. He had some bitching of his own to do. He turned back to his men. "These last two days are always murder, and the heat's no help. Just do your damndest, and come Sunday, we can sleep a week. Get going and good luck."

He nodded to them, turned, and moved to Talker.

"O.K., let's hear it."

Talker pointed to his car. "Go take a look." He watched while Weller moved around it slowly. He showed nothing, not a muscle moving on his face. Full circle. Talker looked him in the eye. "I'm waiting."

"Well, I'd say you need a paint job."

"No shit."

"You want my advice, try Steuben's, they're the best in town."

"That's all you've got to say?"

"What do you want from me? A manhunt?"

Talker felt the steam build up. He kept it in. "Things like this happen all the time, I guess."

"No, sir, they don't. First time I've ever seen a job like someone's done on you."

"I want to know who did it."

"Hire a detective."

"You're a cop."

"Now listen, boy—"

"Don't call me boy. We're not in Mississippi."

"Right you are. You're in my jurisdiction, and I've had enough of you. And all your women, too. If you're pissed off because they spent the night in jail—"

"They *what*?"

"Got picked up for soliciting."

"Now just a God damn minute."

"Shout at me, I'll book you."

"On what charge?"

"I'll make one up." He paused. "Now listen, Mr. Talker." Harry sounded calmer, even if he wasn't. "Turns out they were innocent. I let them go. But here's the thing. You people don't mean trouble—see? I'm ready to believe that. But you make it. Just by being here. Those girls of yours attract it, like lightning goes to lightning rods."

"Have they once stepped out of line?"

"That's not the point. You see those buses?"

Talker nodded. "Sure."

"Today is friggin' Sousa Day. I've got four hundred horny high-school kids here playing marches. When that's over, they go crazy, they'll be in the cornfields laid out end-to-end."

"What's that to me?"

"I'll level with you, son. From here till closing Saturday,

it's more than I can handle. Every year, things boil over; drunks and troublemakers. It's a mess, and you're the frosting on the cake. I don't need you on top of it. You're closed."

"When?"

"As of now."

"Oh, come on, you don't mean it."

"It's been no fun knowing you."

"Hold on." The man was turning, starting off. "We've kept to our part of the bargain. Tell me one complaint you've had."

"Just from the ministers who run the Bingo tent. Said you were poisoning the atmosphere."

"They're losing business to us, you know that."

"It's what I told them."

Talker nodded. "That confirms my first impression. You're a fair man, Sheriff. You see both sides."

"Make that three sides. Right now, I'm just seeing mine. You're out."

"I'll tell you what. Let's split the difference. Close us up tomorrow. Friday's big. It means a lot." The words were coming now. "I'm thinking of the girls. They don't have much, and every dollar makes a difference. Just between us, they're not long on useful skills, they don't hook, and the summer money has to go a long way."

"Not my problem."

"No. It's mine. They trust me to look after them. You add them all together, you won't get one normal brain. They need me, and I'm asking you to help me help them."

"Nothing in it for yourself?"

"No." This came from the heart now, it was easier. "I'm flush, I'm tired of this life, I'm finished with it. Closing us suits me just fine. I'd like it, you'd be doing me a favor."

"Well . . ." The fellow had a way about him. Harry half believed him.

Talker let the silence stretch. Sometimes it scored more points than words. He took out his cigarettes, offered one to Weller.

Harry took it. "Fuck it, you can have your Friday."

Annie woke up in the van. The sun had gotten her at dawn, and she had shuffled back inside; she wasn't ready for the day. She checked her watch: ten-thirty. It was here, ready or not. Her mouth felt full of fuzzballs, and her eyes felt puffy, she was sticky everywhere and dirty. One day older, but no wiser. What do girls in love do when their men are into someone else? She saw the writing in her Journal: *Make a move.* She'd made one, and where had it taken her? Not very far.

She got up, wiped her body with the cotton shift. It only smudged the dust and moved the film of sweat around. Terrific; and the only clothes she had to wear were yesterday's. She'd had to be alone last night, all by herself; for all the good it did her. She put on the clothes, went to a makeup table, checked things out. She looked like Pigpen. Never mind. The thing to do was hitch a ride to Carthage Lake and shower for an hour or two. She put some cold cream on her face, wiped it away with Kleenex, brushed her hair and went outside.

The sun was bright. It hurt her eyes. It never used to. Was she really growing old? The area was full of kids and Mommies, squeals and shouting. Annie winced, moved quickly off, stopped long enough to buy sunglasses and a cola. It was then she heard the music.

Sousa marches. Annie loved them. Back in school, she'd dreamed of being a drum majorette. She'd even tried out once or twice. She had the figure, but she couldn't catch the damn baton. The cola stung as it went down, but it was icy cold, it cleared her throat. She turned and headed toward the music.

The sound came from a grassy field, like a parade ground. It was big. A lot of people—old folks, kids—were lined around the edges. Annie found an open space, edged into it and gasped.

There were a dozen bands, at least. From township after township. She could make the names out on the banners: Dwaynesville, Fallsburg, Miller's Crossing. They marched one band at a time; the others waited in formation. Every school had different uniforms, bright colors, blue and gold or red and white. With big brass buttons, lots of braid. The air was stirring just enough to flutter all the flags.

The band from Thompsontown was on the field. Sun shimmered on the brass, the snares and bass drums cracked and boomed, the majorette was something. Annie watched the baton spin and arch up through the air. March blended into march. She knew them all: "Semper Fidelis," "Stars and Stripes," "King Cotton," even "Hands Across the Sea." She felt tears in her eyes, but they were happy ones for once; she didn't bother rubbing them away.

Betsy was on tiptoe, peering through the crowd. She wanted company, distraction, anyone to ease the tension, break the mood. Things had been difficult with Denny ever since that look across the table. It had meant so much, and both of them were scared to deal with it. They either babbled mindlessly or sat in silences that stretched forever.

"Denny, look. That's Annie, isn't it?"

"Where?"

"Over there."

He turned and nodded.

"Let's go talk to her."

"What for?"

"Come on." She started off, not waiting for him. Annie was a godsend. Betsy had so many questions, things to ask and learn about, and no one on this earth to talk to. All her friends were useless; they were her age, and she'd choke before she told them, anyway. But Annie had the answers. She knew everything.

She waved and called out, "Annie, hi!"

Annie thought she heard her name. She turned, saw Betsy and her boyfriend moving toward her. Betsy was all right, considering how young she was. Besides, she'd brought the Sheriff, saved her from that drunk the other day. She waved back, started for them.

Betsy looked at her. "Are you O.K.?"

The tears were running. Annie grinned and wiped them. "It's the music."

Betsy nodded. "We've been here since ten, before it even started. What have you been doing since we saw you?"

What a question. Passed out drunk and lost her treasure to a total stranger, held the man she loved while he had gone to pieces . . . "Nothing much. Just working."

Betsy gestured toward the field. "You had enough of this?"

"I guess so."

"Great. Let's go do something."

"Not right now. I never made it home last night. I've got to shower off or die."

Light bulbs flashed in Betsy's head. "I've got a great idea. We'll go to my house."

"Your house?"

"It's not far, just twenty minutes on a bike."

"I haven't got one."

"I do. Denny, you stay here awhile, come by for lunch."

"But—"

"See you later. Come on." She took Annie by the hand. "I'll ride you on the handlebars."

Dee knew exactly what to do with days like this: sleep through them. Shrinks call it a symptom of depression. Little did they know. She'd wakened every hour on the hour, groaned, turned over and gone back to sleep. Not this time. There was knocking on her bedroom door. She pulled the pillow from her face. "Is that you, Marcie?"

"She's gone out. It's Mrs. Beebe."

Swell. "What time is it?"

"Eleven."

"What's your problem? Do you want to clean the room?"

"Your mother's downstairs. Says she wants to see you."

"Tell her she can—" No, that wasn't right. The woman wanted something from her, and what greater pleasure was there than withholding it? "Tell her I'll be down in a minute."

It was more like ten. "Good morning, Mother. What's up?" Eleanor looked lovely. Bernard Shaw was wrong when he said, "Women over forty have the faces they deserve."

"Well, dear, I was driving to the country. You remember Thelma's Vegetable Stand?"

She used to go there all the time with Dad. She nodded.

"I was thinking, why not buy some fresh things and go home and make a salad? Just the two of us." She beamed. "Now wouldn't that be nice?"

The only time her mother ever hit the kitchen was to lacerate the cook. "You're going to make the salad?"

"But of course, dear."

That she had to see. "I'm yours."

The Cadillac was spinning down the county road toward Dwaynesville. Eleanor had Dr. Stone to thank for this. She had been pouring out her heart about Dee's dreadful life, especially the shame and scorn she had for acting, when the man had interrupted, cut her short. "That isn't going to change, you know. It's her profession, and when you attack it, you're attacking her."

She told him that was arrant nonsense, but the more she thought about it, the more logical it seemed. And if she wanted Dee at home, it might be wise to show some interest. So she'd driven to the library, found half a dozen books on theater, and stayed up reading half the night.

"Well, dear, I've so many questions. Do you mind?"

Dee braced herself. "I'm ready."

"Tell me, how is Stanislavsky?"

"Dead."

"I know, dear. What I meant to say was, do you use his Method?"

What was this? A change of tactics? Some new game? Dee played along. "It's useful sometimes. Not so much in Shakespeare, but you can't do Shepard without it."

"Shepard." Eleanor looked blank. "Of course. Did you know there's a theater in Mansfield now?"

Dee nodded. "It's non-Equity."

"What's that?"

"They don't use union actors."

"Well, you'd never know it. They're so good. I've started going all the time."

"What have you seen?"

She hadn't been there once. "Oh, comedies and tragedies. Do you know Howard Prince?"

"It's Harold Prince."

What did she want, perfection? "Do you know him?"

"No."

"Well, I'm surprised at that, I must say."

"He's important, Mother."

"So are you, dear."

"No, I'm not. I work, I'm busy, I get decent parts sometimes, but—"

"That's no way to talk about yourself."

"Look, Mother, what's this all about?"

"I don't know what you mean."

"You hate, loathe, and despise my work."

"I'm trying not to. Oh my God, is that a crime?"

Dee knew the tears were coming now; they always did. "No, it's no crime. It's just a lie, that's all."

"I don't know what you want from me."

Dee turned away. The only things she wanted were the things she'd never hear: I love you and I'm proud of you.

That's all. It wasn't much. She bit her lip: self-pity, how she hated it. Outside, she saw a flyblown wooden shack, walls all but falling down. She recognized it. Thelma's had been closed for years.

"We've just gone past it."

"Past what?"

"Thelma's. Anyway, it's closed."

"I can't believe it." Eleanor looked back. The car veered slightly, caught the shoulder, started skidding.

"Mother!"

"What now?" Eleanor turned front and panicked, jammed on the brakes, jerked the wheel. It threw them off the shoulder toward a phone pole just ahead.

"Watch out!" Too late. The car was skidding into it. Dee ducked her head and turned as she flew forward, took the impact on her shoulder. Not too bad. She heard the motor running, and they hadn't knocked the pole down.

"Mother?" No response. "Are you all right?"

"I don't know."

She looked O.K. No blood. Dee's heart was pounding. "What's the matter, where's it hurt?"

"It's funny." Eleanor was frowning. "I can't seem to move my head."

Whiplash, or something worse? Keep calm, don't think about it. "Listen. Here's what's going to happen. You sit very still, don't try to move. I'm going to get out, go to your side, shift you just enough so I can drive. You understand me?— And don't nod, for Jesus' sake."

"I understand." She watched Dee move around the car. Dee cared, she really cared. Through all her fear and pain, she wondered, had she won her daughter back? It was a costly way to do it. If it worked.

Marcie jumped into the golf cart, switched it on, and came down on the pedal. Little wheels spun on the grass. "Hey, watch it!" she heard someone shout. She didn't bother looking back. By that time, she was fifty yards and climbing, down the center of the fairway. First hole. Only seventeen to go. She planned to take them one by one, in order. Van was out here somewhere, they had said so when she called the pro shop.

In this heat, the course was empty; just a foursome here

and there. She drove around them, drove right through them. If they didn't like it, they could go bitch to the Greens Committee. Van was Chairman this year, he could deal with it.

She cut some corners, whizzed through sand traps, leaving tracks a mile wide. She knew it was against the rules; and for a minute, she knew how those kids felt when they tore the course up. They were letting steam off. On the seventh hole—she checked in all directions, not a soul in sight—she drove the cart across the green. "Take that, you bastards!"

It felt great to let it out, but who the bastards were, she didn't know. Not Dad, not Van, not Talker. All they did was love her, but they put her in this squeeze play. If she stood by Van, her family would kill her. If she let him down, got him to go back, it meant trampling on his dignity and cutting off his balls. Where did that leave her? In a vise. Which only tightened when it came to Van and Talker. Van was good. Did that make Talker evil? How? She cared for Talker. Cared? She craved him. Sometimes it felt out of all control. She squeezed her eyes tight, tried to make his image go away, and ran into some bushes.

"Jesus, Marcie, you should have your head examined." Maybe Sandy Stone could help. Dee went to shrinks for years, and she was more screwed up than ever. Marcie didn't have years. Van was just ahead now, drinking from the water fountain on the thirteenth tee. Thirteen: some lucky number.

Marcie couldn't find the brake. Van saw her coming, stepped away. She ran into the fountain, just the way the kids did. Thump.

She looked at Van. "I didn't mean to do that."

"I believe you. Something wrong?"

"You're kidding."

"I mean something in the last two hours."

"Nope."

"Look, you come winging in here driving like a banshee, there's a reason."

"You and I have got to talk."

"I'm playing golf now."

"You can't do two things at once? I chased you half the night, and I'm still chasing you." She heard her mother's voice, like a commander, snapping orders. "What should I do, make an appointment, call the office? You don't have an office anymore."

"I've got six holes left to play. I'm playing them."

He sounded as if he meant it. She could use a little time, her mind was scrambled eggs. She nodded at the cart. "Does this thing have reverse?"

Van nodded, leaned in, pulled a lever. Marcie edged back from the fountain. Van moved in, inspected it.

"No harm done."

"Gee, that's a relief."

"Can I, for forty minutes, have a little peace?"

"I'm sorry. You go right ahead. Don't let me make you nervous."

Fat chance. Thirteen was a long par three, an elevated green, trapped on all sides. He teed up his ball, took a five iron. Normally, it carried, it was all he needed, but his hand was killing him. He wasn't playing very well. He glanced at Marcie. She was watching like a hawk. He took a practice swing, approached the ball and set himself. For all he cared, his hand could fall off; he was going to nail it.

Marcie watched the ball sail up, then lost it in the sun. He really had a pretty swing, like a professional. She hadn't watched him play in years. The ball came down. It hit the green, spun backward, stopping six feet from the cup.

Van offered up a prayer of thanks, then turned to get his golf bag.

"Put it in the cart," she said. "Why walk when you can ride?"

They rode in silence to the green, both looking straight ahead. Van pointed. "Pull up over there."

They both got out. Van took his putter, strode out to the green, turned back. "You want to hold the flag stick?"

"Sure." She took it, watched him move around the green, surveying every rise and dip. He bent and moved a leaf, took something from his pocket, diddled with a tiny pockmark on the grass. He took forever.

Six feet wasn't far, but it was downhill, fast and tricky, broke a little to his left. He lined up the putt, calmed himself. Just touch it delicately. It went five feet past the hole.

He could have kicked himself. In front of Marcie, fluffing it. He should have had a birdie. Careful not to look at her, he lined it up again. At least it was uphill this time, a firmer stroke. It lipped the cup, kept rolling downhill. He was farther off than where he'd started. In the end, he took a five.

He felt like slitting both his wrists. Was Marcie smiling? "Something's funny?"

"No."

He threw the putter in the cart. "All right, let's have it."

"Now?"

"Don't tell me, let me guess. How dare I tell your old man where to stick it? Don't I know he gave me everything I've got? O.K., so far? Am I on-line?"

She shook her head. "No, not exactly."

"What does 'not exactly' mean?"

"Dee told me what your reasons were."

"You think they're shit?"

"I haven't said that."

"You don't have to. I know where you stand. I'm ruining your family, tearing it apart. That's what you got from Harriet this morning, right? The old bag wouldn't miss her morning call, she really gave it to you on the phone."

"O.K., you're right, she gave it to me."

"I've got something you can give to her." He raised his middle finger, stuck it high into the air. "And save some for your old man."

"Van—" She'd never seen him like this, wouldn't have believed it.

"I'm not finished. I am sick to God damn death of working for him. I'm not ever going back. And as for you—" He stopped himself. He wasn't deaf or dumb or blind; the way she'd acted all week long, the bruises everywhere. He hadn't brought it up, he wouldn't now. He didn't want to think about it, didn't want to know. "What you can do is climb back in your wagon and go tell the old folks what I said."

She didn't move.

"Go on, what's wrong with you?" He turned to get his golf bag from the cart.

"I haven't said my piece yet."

"I forgot." He turned and smiled. "You want to slice me up? Go right ahead, I'm used to it."

She let him have it. "That's a stinking thing to say. How rotten do you think I am?"

"Be careful, Marcie."

"Why?"

"It's not some game we're playing. It's important."

"Jesus, Van, give me a little credit." Marcie choked her

anger down. "Last night, I'm in the dining room and Mother's cackling on about how we got this from her and that from Dad. Was there one single damn thing that was yours or mine? Not anywhere."

"I thought you liked it that way."

"So did I." She shook her head. "I got you into all of this. I set it up, I talked to Dad. 'Just try it for a year,' I told you. God, I thought I was so smart." She stepped away. "You want to hate me for it, you're entitled."

"I don't hate you. Jesus, Marcie—"

"Shut up. Van, I'm out of this; I've had it, being in the middle. What you do is your decision. Sell insurance, drive a bus. For one time in your life, you stand up on your own two fucking feet."

She wheeled around, ran to the cart, jumped in, and gunned it.

"Marcie?" It was too late, she was zooming off. He watched her go. She left him with a lot to think about.

Betsy knew the shortcuts, took them all. Up Meadow Lane, down Linden Road, the pathway through the vacant lots, then onto Elm. They talked a little on the way, just chatter: were the summers all this hot, was there a decent burger place in Fulton?

Annie hadn't ridden on the handlebars for years, not since she was a kid. She liked it, but it wasn't fair. Betsy was doing all the work.

"Why don't you ride and let me pedal for a while?"

"I'm fine, and anyway, we're nearly there."

"We are?" She looked out at the houses. They were palaces. And what was Betsy doing, riding up to one of them? "You live here?"

"This is it." She braked. They both hopped off. "Come on." They started up the front walk.

Annie looked around. It hadn't dawned on her before. She turned to Betsy, blurted it. "You're rich."

"Not really." Betsy rarely thought about it. "Denny's rich. We're comfortable." She shrugged and moved into the front hall. "Anybody home?"

"Just me," said Mrs. Beebe, calling from the back somewhere.

"I've brought a friend. We're going up to my room."

"You want lunch?"

"We'll make it, you don't have to bother."

Annie's mouth hung slightly open. She'd seen homes like this in magazines, and here she was inside one. "Who was that?"

"Just Mrs. Beebe. She's the cook."

"Your mother doesn't do the cooking?"

Betsy giggled. "Thank the Lord. Come on."

They started up the stairs. All Annie wanted was to look around, but Betsy seemed in such a hurry. She began to wonder if there was a reason why she'd been invited. Stranger things had happened, but what could a girl like Betsy want from her?

They started down the hallway, carpet thick as autumn leaves and crystal doodads on the walls. She knew the word; she found it: sconces.

Betsy stopped outside a door. It had signs taped all over it: KEEP OUT, NO ADMITTANCE, BETSY'S PLACE, ABANDON HOPE, ALL YE WHO ENTER HERE.

"Your mother lets you get away with that?"

"She hates it." Betsy grinned and moved in.

Annie stopped dead on the threshold. It was twice the size of Uncle Emil's parlor: comfy chairs, a desk, a sofa, tons of books, and best of all, what Annie always dreamed of having: a four-poster bed.

"You like it?"

Annie nodded.

"So do I. It's all mine and it's private, you can lock it from the inside. Annie?"

"Uh-huh?"

Betsy burned with questions, couldn't wait. But something Grandpa Ed was fond of saying stopped her: 'Always give before you get.' 'The bathroom's this way.' Betsy crossed, opened a door. "You take your time—and if there's anything you need, just holler."

"Thanks. You're sure it's O.K.?"

"Don't be stupid."

Annie moved in, died and went to heaven. How did people live like this, where did the money come from? Everything was beautiful. The space, the tiles had flowers painted on them, carpet underneath her feet, a bathtub and, as if that weren't enough, a shower with a glass door.

Annie stripped, turned on the water—there were nozzles everywhere, all over. Streams of water, velvet needles, played on every part of her: head, breasts, thighs, bottom. Ecstasy, that's what it was. It filled her head with dreams; not just of Talker, it was more than love or sex. Possession: having something like this of her own. There had to be a way.

"Don't be ridiculous." She found the soap. If wishes were horses, beggars would ride. There was a brush, too. Annie used it, scrubbing hard to drive the dreams away. It helped a little.

Betsy flopped down in a chair, got up at once and went on pacing. Up and down. Much more of this, she'd wear a pathway in the carpet. What was going on in there? The longest shower in human history? Maybe she should write the *Guinness Book of Records*. Was it stupid, telling everything to Annie? She kept trying different versions in her head. No matter how she phrased it, it came out the same way: juvenile. She started nibbling at her nails again.

The shower stopped. She felt so young. Well, why not? What did they expect of you at fourteen? Wisdom? Mom was almost forty, and the wisdom she had wouldn't fill a thimble. Betsy sat. The thing to do was look composed. And feel composed. And be composed.

The door came open. Annie moved in, hair still damp, all wrapped up in a bath sheet. "Feeling better?"

Annie grinned. "And then some. That was great. And really nice of you. I mean—"

"Shut up. Sit down. O.K.?"

"O.K." She sat down carefully; she didn't want the fabric to get wet.

"I've got to talk to you."

"Uh-huh?" She'd known it; nothing in this life was free.

"It's like this."

Annie waited. Betsy's fingers clasped and unclasped, tied themselves in knots. "Oh, come on, Betsy. How bad can it be?"

"The worst."

"I'll bet." A girl like Betsy had no way of knowing what the worst was.

"Just because you think I'm privileged . . . you don't know."

"I never will, at this rate."

Betsy looked at the carpet, felt her cheeks burn. "Here's what happened."

Annie listened. Some of it was jumbled, but the gist of it was clear: alone with Denny in the bedroom, all that moonlight, heavy breathing, stripping all the way.

". . . and then he walked around me twice and looked at everything."

"Did he attack you?"

"No."

"He copped a feel or two?"

"He never touched me. He just went away, we never even kissed good night."

"That's all that happened?"

Betsy looked up for the first time. "Yes."

It sounded like a fairy story, innocent and sweet. And what a good kid Denny was. She envied Betsy. There she sat, all twisted in her chair, and she had everything. A pretty face and figure—she'd be something when she grew up—money, parents, brains, a Taj Mahal to live in. What could possibly be missing?

"O.K., Betsy, I'll bite. What's your problem?"

"What's my problem? Are you dense? We've gone so far. What happens now?"

"Zip happens now."

"But Denny wants me."

"Let him suffer. Do him good."

"I want him, too."

"You want to fuck him?" Annie stood up. "Are you crazy? How old are you?"

"I'm fifteen next June."

"You're fourteen for the next nine months, and you've got shit for brains. Sweet Mother Mary, do you want to foul your life up?"

"No . . ."

"You want to be a teenage mother?"

"That's ridiculous."

"No. You're ridiculous. It's fucking puppy love. There's nothing wrong with that, but you don't go and screw your brains out." Annie stopped for breath. She felt so angry she was shaking. "Listen. God gave you a cherry. Oh, excuse me, what you people call a maidenhead, O.K.?"

"O.K."

"He did that for a reason. You know why?"

Betsy sat looking at her, eyes like saucers. "You're so angry."

"It's your life, what do I care?" She turned away, then turned right back. "For Chrissake, Betsy, save it. I did, and God knows I'm not a saint."

"You think I'm being stupid?"

"On a scale of ten, you're out of sight. Forget about it."

Betsy loved her for her anger, but she didn't understand it. Why, where was it coming from? She stood. "What difference does it make to you?"

"What difference?" Annie hadn't thought. When it came to her, she said it. "I'd give anything to have your life."

"You wouldn't want it." Betsy burst out sobbing, threw her arms around her.

"Take it easy," Annie whispered.

"Same to you."

They both needed holding, so they held each other for a while.

Annie was the first to speak. "It's funny, isn't it?"

"What's funny?"

"I don't know. You have some Kleenex in this place?"

"Right over there." She started toward her vanity. "Besides, your hair's a mess. Here—use my brush. I'll be right back." She turned and hurried from the room.

Annie sat down, wiped her eyes, then blew her nose. It was a crazy outburst, all that yelling, but it cleared her head. She checked the mirror; she was looking better, too. She picked the brush up. There were little silver frames all over. Family photos. Betsy as a kid and Betsy older, Betsy with her mom and dad.

Annie drew the brush once through her hair. It took that long before it hit her. "Holy shit . . . oh holy shit." It couldn't be. She looked again, picked up a photo: Betsy and her parents hugging. "Oh my God." No doubt about it. Betsy's Mom was Talker's Woman. She kept staring at the picture. Betsy's Mom. The world was bigger than a bread box, but not much. She put the frame back down.

What had she blundered into? "Jesus." Annie put her elbows on the table, then leaned forward, head in hands. She felt a little dizzy. "Take it easy. Just calm down and—" Annie blinked: another frame, another photo. Annie's mouth fell open. It was too much. She leaned closer. No way around it. There they stood, with smiling faces: Betsy, Talker's Woman, and the man she'd lost it to. She'd thought he looked like someone's grandpa. He was Betsy's.

"Oh my God . . ."

26

FOR MUCH OF Fulton, Friday was a busy afternoon. Some shops and offices closed early for the three-day weekend. There were salesmen, clerks, and secretaries rushing off in all directions: to the Fair, north to Lake Erie with the wife and kids, or to the back porch with a six-pack and a radio. Other businesses were gearing up for Labor Day: last chance to turn a profit from the crowds before the summer ended. Cooks and waitresses in restaurants and diners, men and boys at filling stations; all of them were moving fast.

In fact, except for Van, who was relaxing in the Longview locker room, not many folks were sitting still. Talker was burning up the road to Carthage Lake to break the news to Norma and the girls. Marcie, feeling she was on a roll, was barreling toward Pleasant Avenue to have things out with Ed. Eleanor was in Emergency while Jerry Leggett checked her over. Dee, between the phone calls—where was Marcie when she needed her?—paced up and down the corridors. Marvin, in a frenzy of uncertainty, was in his bedroom staring at an open suitcase: was he running off with Lucy, yes or no? Lucy, in her bedroom, too, was fretting at her closet: what to wear and how to act when she went out to talk to Norma; it was now, this afternoon or never. Annie—God alone knew how— was acting normal, finishing her lunch with Bets and Denny in the kitchen. Harriet was out at the Pavilion giving orders;

every single thing had to be cleared away at closing time tomorrow.

Only Ed was feeling relatively placid as he tooled his way to Longview and a two-martini lunch. He'd deal with Van whenever, either coddle him or slice him up like barbecue; there were a lot of ways to win, and Ed knew most of them. It wasn't till he reached the Club gates that he thought of Marcie.

There was Sunset Crescent just ahead, and had she even crossed his mind? "Oh Jesus, Ed." She was his Princess, treasure, baby, with the whole world on her back, and what had he been doing for her? Nothing. "Christ, how selfish can you be?" He knew the answer, checked his watch. He had the time. Drop by the house and hold her hand and say how much he loved her. It was true.

He turned into the Crescent, looked ahead, and jammed his brakes on. "God almighty." Betsy and his Harem Girl were standing in the driveway, talking. Betsy gave the Girl a hug and handed her a bike. Her bike, the Schwinn he'd given her. What was this? And to top it off, the Girl was pedaling straight toward him. Ed began to sweat. What if she spotted him and stopped to talk and Betsy saw it? How—oh please, Lord, tell me how—could he explain it?

Annie saw him, all right, but she didn't blink or turn her head. She pedaled right on by.

Ed offered up a prayer of thanks and pulled into the driveway, wiped his forehead and got out. Betsy was heading for him, arms outstretched for a hug. She always wanted one from him. She got it.

"Hi, Gramps."

"Hello, honey. How's it going?"

Betsy grinned. "Not bad today."

Ed turned and pointed to the corner just as Annie turned it. "Who was that?"

"That's Annie."

"Oh?" Ed could have told her that much.

"She's a friend of mine."

He didn't like the sound of that. "A friend of yours?"

"I met her at the Fair."

"What was she doing here?"

"I asked her by for lunch."

"She took your bike."

"I loaned it to her." Betsy smiled. "I'll get it back."

Ed wondered how to press it further; what in hell had they been saying? Had he come up in the conversation?

"Want to come in for a sandwich?"

"Not right now." He'd find a way to press it later. "Is your mom in?"

"She was gone when I got home."

"You know where I could find her?"

"No, but maybe Mrs. Beebe knows." She turned to go.

"Don't bother." Marcie wouldn't give the time of day to Mrs. Beebe. "When you see your mom, just tell her . . . tell her I dropped by."

"I'm going out, I'll leave a note."

"You do that, honey. Thanks." He bent and kissed the top of her head. "I love you, Bets."

"I know that."

All through lunch, Ed couldn't shake it. The martinis didn't help. He laughed at Harvey's jokes, made all the right responses; but what had his Harem Girl found out? A little or a lot or nothing? Could she name him, point a finger at him? Hell, for all he knew, the girl was jailbait, underage. Ed was a man of action; doing nothing drove him nuts. But what else could he do but wait and see?

Talker pulled up in a cloud of dust. To date, the day had been for shit. He'd had no time for Marcie or his car, and he did not look forward to the next ten minutes. All the girls were either dead or on the moon or in the cabins. He was angry, hungry, thirsty, weary; in that order, more or less. He whipped into the grocery, bought a Coke and candy bar— some life—and made for Norma's cabin door. He knocked.

"I'm decent. Come on in." Norma had heard his car drive up, and she was sitting in a wicker rocker, ready for him.

"Norma—"

"Gee, it's great to see you, Talker. Have a chair and take a load off."

"Anything you say." He knew her moods, he didn't want to make this any worse than necessary.

"So, what's new since we last met? Been getting any nookie?"

"Nothing but the best." He braced himself for what was coming. "Nice of you to ask."

"It's not my business where you put your dick. You know that, honey." Norma smiled. "But what does concern me— and don't take offense, it's just a question—where the fuck were you last night?"

"Look, Norma."

"If you wonder why I ask, it's not because of idle curiosity. Far from it. I'm hysterical. You damn well know we need to wind down when the show is over. And you damn well know what things are like here. And you good and damn well should have been with us last night."

"O.K., I should have been there."

"Do you fucking know what happened?"

"Since you ask me, yes, I fucking do."

She rode right over him. "I, Norma Cusak of Galt Ocean Drive, Fort Lauderdale, I spent the God damn night in jail."

"I know that."

"Like some lousy hooker, picked up for soliciting."

"I know that, too."

She heard him now. "How'd you find out, who told you?"

"Sheriff Weller."

"From the horse's mouth. What have you got to say?"

"I let you down. I'm sorry. I apologize."

"Too easy. First, you kiss my ass. Then, you apologize."

"Look, Norma." Talker's throat dried up. "You don't mind if I sip my Coke?"

"Please. Be my guest." She'd badgered him enough. He looked like dog doo, and she started wondering what was troubling him. "Are you O.K.?"

"I have been better, thanks."

"Don't tell me the town pump dried up?"

"Give it a rest, for Chrissake."

Norma started rocking. "Honey, Norma is your friend. You just tell Norma all about it."

Talker nearly grinned. "Is there one reason why I like you?"

"Don't ask me."

He took another swallow. "It all started with my car last night. Some pissant scratched obscenities all over it."

"You're kidding me. Like what?"

"You want to know, go out and look. So, bright and early, I drive in to show the thing to Weller. Maybe he'll do something."

"Did he?"

Talker nodded.

"What?"

"Look, Norma, just don't shoot the messenger, O.K.? He closed us down."

"He what?"

"He says we're trouble—and he isn't wrong."

"I thought the old fart liked me."

"That's got zip to do with anything. I got him to hold off a day. We work tonight, but that's it." Talker watched her carefully. He'd seen her blow sky-high on less.

She stopped the rocking. "You know something? I can live with that. It's only one night's takings, and I've had it with this town."

He heaved a sigh. "We never should have played this place."

"Spilt milk."

He blinked. "You mean it?"

"I can't wait. The only question is, where do we go from here?"

He frowned. "I thought we had that settled, Norma."

"Oh, come on. This is no way to end a season. What's another two, three weeks?"

He looked away. He owed her so damned much, no end to it. "I'm sorry, I can't do it, I can't cut it anymore."

"Aw, sure you can. You feeling down? Who wouldn't? Fulton is enough to—"

"That's not it." What could he say? He didn't want to tell it all.

"I'm waiting."

"Well . . ." He squirmed a little. "I'm in love."

"I don't believe it. Have you fallen for the pump?"

"Can you for Chrissake call her something else?"

"Oh, you poor baby." Norma took his hand and squeezed it. "Lost your bearings."

"No, I haven't."

"I can see it all. A cute white house, a picket fence, a sand-box for the wee ones."

"Cut it out." He pulled his hand away, got to his feet.

"I know you, Talker. Better than you know yourself. There's nothing in it."

"That's for me to find out."

Norma knew when she was right. She also knew when she was beaten. "All you'll do is hurt yourself."

"It's worth the risk."

"You stay around this town, you'll end up in the boneyard."

"No, I won't." He turned to go. "I'll see you later."

Norma longed to stop him, throw her arms around him. "Talker?"

"Yeah."

"Show starts at four. You're late again, I'll shave your tail."

"I'll be there."

Norma watched him drive off from the cabin doorway. Poor damn fool. She couldn't run his life for him; she had her hands full with her own. What hurt was losing him; not from the show, that didn't really matter. From her life. She didn't want to give him up. "Oh, what the hell."

She turned and found a road map, took it outside where the air was, spread it on a picnic table. South: that was the way to go. No problem. There were other talkers, she could run the show alone, she'd done it after Walter died. Tomorrow she'd pick up some roughies, pack the van, and find another fair to play. The girls would be in heaven, it was what they wanted. She leaned closer to the map. Pick up the Interstate and—

"Mrs. Cusak?"

Norma turned. The Lovell girl. All dressed up and no place to go. "Not now."

"I've got to talk to you. I really do."

"I'm busy. Can't you see?"

"The truth is, Mrs. . . ." Lucy bit her lip. "I'm desperate."

Norma took a closer look. The girl was in a state, you couldn't miss it. "O.K., honey, what's your name?"

"It's Lucy."

Norma pushed the map aside and leaned back. "All right, Lucy, lay it on me."

They had taken Eleanor to X Ray. Jerry had appeared just long enough to tell Dee not to worry. Things so far looked reassuring, but he couldn't know what they were dealing with until he'd seen some pictures.

Great. Dee shifted on the bench, put down her plastic

cup. The coffee tasted thin and bitter, and how good a man was Jerry? As a human being, no complaints. But as a doctor, was he good enough? The hotshot doctors in New York were monsters; you could have a seizure in the waiting room and no one with a medical degree would pick you up off the floor. She'd seen it happen more than once. But when they did come, they were tops.

The door to X Ray opened. "Dee?"

"Right here." She got up, hurried over. "Well?"

He smiled. "Relax. She'll live to fight another day."

"There's nothing wrong?"

"Well, not quite nothing. There's a hairline fracture on one vertebra. Up here." He pointed to his neck. "It takes a little while to mend. I'd put most patients in a neck brace, but your mother . . . I don't trust her. You can take a brace off and, for all I know, she wouldn't wear it half the time."

"That's Eleanor."

"She isn't going to like it, but I want to use a cast. Unless she runs into another pole, there's no way she can hurt herself."

"When can I see her?"

"Give me half an hour."

Eleanor lay on her back, eyes on the ceiling. She was fuming. They had put her in the wrong room; it was tacky, all the suites were on the corners. And the nurse had hairy lips, and Jerry Leggett wasn't fit to doctor dogs. He'd put this thing around her neck, and never mind she couldn't turn her head; the thing was ugly. For the next God knows how many weeks, what was she going to wear? She'd have to go around like Katharine Hepburn, scarves from shoulders to her chin. Her neck was beautiful, one of her finest features, not a wrinkle. She had had it tucked in Akron. No one knew.

She sighed. She didn't mind the pain; a little pain was good for you, and anyway there wasn't much of it. The thing to do was count her blessings. There were two that came to mind: she wasn't dead, and maybe Dee would have some feelings for her. Loving feelings, like all decent daughters did. If only—

"Eleanor?"

"Oh, darling, is that you? Come close, so I can see your face."

Dee pulled a chair up by the bedside. "Here I am."

"Why are you smiling?"

"You're all right, you're fine."

"If I'm so fine, why am I in a hospital?"

"You'll be home in a day or two."

She sighed. "At home alone."

"That's nonsense. Friends will come to visit; you'll be up and out in no time."

"Dee?"

"Yes, Eleanor?"

"I wish you'd call me Mother. You're the only person in the world who can."

"I know."

"When you were little, I was Mommy. You remember?"

All too well. "Of course I do."

"Give me your hand."

Dee nearly said 'What for?'

"It's such a sweet hand. Do you know how much I love you, dear?"

Dee knew exactly, to the ounce. "I know."

"And you love me. I know that, too."

Dee felt like screaming, but she nodded.

"Let me hear you say it. It would mean so much."

What did it matter? It was only words. Dee closed her eyes and played a scene. From *Anastasia*. That great moment when Helen Hayes finally acknowledged Ingrid Bergman was her grandchild. Dee had done the Bergman part on stage. Hugs, kisses, tears; it was a killer. "Yes, I love you."

Van was leaning back against his locker, towel across his lap, watching drops of shower water dry away and disappear. He had been placing mental bets; which would go first, the knee one or the tummy one? It had absorbed him for a while, but it was starting to wear thin. There was a dull ache in his stomach and another in his head. If good things came in threes, where would the next one strike? He raised the towel, looked down and nodded. There.

Ron Storke passed by, beet red and sopping wet from tennis. In this heat? The man was crazy. Playing golf was bad enough; which took him instantly to Marcie. He had thought about her till it hurt. He heard a nearby locker open, turned to look.

"Hi, Sandy."

"How's it going, Van?" Not very well, if you believed in body language. Sandy took his jacket off. The textbooks had it right: don't mix your practice with your friends. It didn't work; your feelings kept on getting in the way. The last thing in the world to do was mention seeing Van last night.

Van straightened up. "If you want my advice, stay off the golf course. It's an oven."

"I'm no fool, I'm going swimming. Just had lunch, but what the hell, you can't drown in the shallow end."

Decision time. To talk or not to talk. Van struggled with it, back and forth. An easy chat, a few words in the pool; no harm in that. It wasn't like a session, sitting there in Sandy's office. "Tell you what. I'll join you."

There were people by the pool, some in the water, others under awnings having drinks; an early kickoff to the holiday. It offered little in the way of privacy, but there was music, pop stuff playing over speakers. It was safe enough to talk.

Van dived in. He had graceful strokes, just like his golf game. Sandy took the steps and waited chin deep by the pool's edge. What else could he do? Run out on Van? Besides, his boys and Alice would be coming any minute. So would Van, when he was ready.

"Sandy?"

"Yessir?" With a smile.

Van put one hand on the gutter, shook the water from his hair. "You have a little time?"

"I'm in here for the afternoon. What's on your mind?"

"Don't drop your teeth. I quit my job."

"At Steuben Motors?" Stupid question, but the information staggered him. What in God's name had driven Van to do this?

Van nodded. "I resigned."

"That's quite a move to make."

"And then some."

"Have you had it on your mind awhile?"

"I don't know." Van frowned. "I must have. Yeah, it must have been there."

Sandy nodded. "That makes sense." It didn't yet. "When did you do it?"

"Last night. You know, every week we have this poker game and—Sandy, I still can't believe it. I just blew apart. I yelled, I threw my drink in Ed's face, broke a window, packed my trophies—"

"Just a sec, you've lost me. Packed your trophies?"

"At the office. Packed 'em up and brought 'em home. It's my home, too, you know."

"Who says it isn't?"

"I don't know; I guess I never feel it's mine. Ed gave it to us, more or less. I've paid him back, though. Every dime. I'm even, I don't owe him anything."

"How do you feel about it all?"

Van frowned again. "All what?"

"My fault. Dumb question. One thing at a time. You're glad you quit? No second thoughts?"

Van grinned ear-to-ear. "How do I look?"

In dire need of Librium. "It's good you feel that way. What does the family have to say?"

Van shrugged. "I don't much care. Dee thinks I'm right. I haven't checked with Ed and Harriet. Why should I, all I'll get is crap. The two of them can fry in hell."

"I hear you." It was tempting just to leave it there. The man was high on rage. Why bring him down, what did he stand to gain? "You haven't mentioned Marcie."

Van looked blank. "I haven't?"

"Nope."

"That's funny, she's the most important."

"Have you talked with her about it?"

"Yeah. We've batted it around."

"What did she have to say?" He watched Van tighten. Pay dirt. "You don't have to tell me."

"You can save your shrink tricks. I don't have to tell you fuck-all."

"Fair enough. You know I wish you luck." He gave Van's arm a squeeze. "I'll see you."

"Wait, God damn it."

"Sure, O.K."

Van swallowed, looked around. "I didn't mean to shout at you."

"It's what I'm paid for. Take your time."

"I don't know what I want to say."

"Whatever's on your mind."

Van couldn't look at him. "I'm scared."

"All right. That's something, that's a start. What are you scared of?"

"Marcie."

"Why?"

"I need her."

"She's your wife. Of course you do."

"What if she isn't there for me?"

"We're all afraid of that sometimes. What makes you think—"

"This morning, I'm out playing golf. No caddy; I'm alone. I like that, all the grass and trees, it's peaceful. I'm not playing very well, I've got this problem with my hand." Van held it out. "You see?"

"I see."

"Next thing I know, there's Marcie in this golf cart. Ran into a fountain, like the kids did. You remember? No, of course not, you weren't there."

"Did you two have a fight?"

"Yes. No. I don't know what it was. She told me . . . what's the matter with me?"

Sandy looked at Van and shared his pain. You couldn't treat a patient if you didn't get inside. "What did she say?"

"You want it word for word? Here goes. 'Stand on your own two fucking feet for once.' O.K.? What have you got to say to that?"

"Why does it scare you?"

"Are you dense? She doesn't care. It doesn't matter what I do. Hell, I could sell insurance, drive a bus. That's what she said. She doesn't give a damn about me."

"Or she does."

"Oh, stuff it. I can stand up to the others, take them all on. But without my Marcie . . ."

"Shut up." Twenty years of training out the window. "Listen. Pay attention. Maybe what she wants is what you want. You ever think of that? Just maybe what she's telling you is, it's your life, it's your decision. Do what makes you happy."

"That'll be the day."

"How do you know I'm wrong? Van, look at me. What makes you so damn sure?"

"God, Sandy, I don't know."

"Why don't you ask her when you see her?"

"Ask her?"

"Listen to me, Van. You want the bottom line? I can't read Marcie's mind, but there's one thing she's right about. She's right about you standing up. Do what you need to do. There's no peace for you if you don't."

Van looked at him a long time. Someone dived in over them; his kids were waving from the terrace. "Van? It's important. Do you read me? Am I clear?"

Van hadn't understood a word of it. "Thanks, Sandy. You've been great."

Talker slowed down near the Service area, stopped by the gates, and took it in. All auto dealerships of any size were basically the same; he could have found his way around it in his sleep. Used cars, the trade-ins, stood in rows off to his left. The finished jobs, all waxed and polished, waited to be picked up near the entrance. The garage itself was big. Its doors were open: half-a-dozen grease pits, cars on lifts. Mechanics in neat uniforms were busy, moving slowly but methodically; the good ones always had that pace, not fast but never standing still.

"Not bad." Weller had been right. The place impressed him. Marcie's old man was house-proud, he'd spent money on the back. Most dealers never did.

He turned in, drove across the lot to the garage, and got out. He didn't have to wait long. Put the T-bird near a bunch of car nuts or mechanics and it always drew a crowd. One man looked up, then two or three. They started drifting over, talking softly: "duo-carbs . . . twin pipes . . . how many horse, three-twenty-five?"

"Three-sixty," Talker said.

"What do you get a gallon?"

"It depends."

They saw the scratches now. "Good God almighty . . . how'd that happen? . . . It's a crime."

"I know. Look, here's the thing. What can you do for me and how fast can you do it?"

Mumbles, frowns, discussion. "Dan, what do you think?"

"Well, I don't know." Dan was a black man, tall and getting on, hair flecked with white. He turned to Talker. "First off, mister, it's a Ford car, you should take it in to Ford. This here's a Chrysler shop."

"I know that. Sheriff Weller sent me here. He tells me you're the best in town."

Dan grinned. "One man's opinion."

"Can you help me?"

"I don't know, I'd have to ask. Besides, there must be six, eight coats of paint on her at least."

"It's more like twelve."

Dan puckered up his forehead. "I'm not sure we want to take that on."

"I understand, but could you maybe buff it down, touch up the scratches?"

"Well . . ." Dan shrugged. He moved around the car, bent here and there to touch the finish, then looked up and beckoned. "Mr. Steuben? Come and take a look at this."

Ed glanced up. He had just come back from lunch, and in the showroom everyone was sullen. Ed knew why: the weekend holiday. They wanted out, but no one closed up early when he was a kid, and they would damn well stay till closing time. The boys in Service were different; no complaints, they did a day's work for a day's pay. So did Ed. He started ambling over.

Talker watched him. Coming here, he'd known he might run into Van, he was prepared for that. But Marcie's father? Working on a Friday afternoon when half the town was closed? How was he going to handle this?

Ed's eyes were on the car. A '65, a great machine, and Chrysler should have made one like it. More than once, he'd written to Detroit and told them so. The owner of the car was looking at him. Ed gave him a smile, held out his hand.

"Ed Steuben."

Talker took it. "Paul McBride."

Ed was not what he expected, nothing like it. Marcie's father was a rich man, and the ones he'd seen—he'd even met a few—all had that look; superior and smug, like someone in the near vicinity was cooking cabbage. Marcie's father looked like he could lift an ox; and wouldn't mind it.

"McBride." Ed had a feeling he had met the man; or seen him someplace. It would come to him. He turned, looked at the car. "Somebody did a job on you." He shook his head and grinned. "They left *cocksucker* out."

"It's on the hood, you missed it."

"Vandals."

"More like religious bigots, if you're asking me. You've got a bumper crop out here."

"I know." Ed didn't like them, either. "Where'd it happen?"

"At the Fair."

The world was changing. Five, ten years ago, you'd never see this kind of thing. "How do you like that."

"Not a lot. I parked it by the Midway; there's a place there for Concessionaires. You know it?"

Know it? Hell, Ed knew it all. The barker from the girlie show. What was he doing here? Was this a hustle? One coincidence—Annie at Marcie's house—was bad enough. McBride made two. Were they in this together? There were ways of finding out.

Dan spoke up. "He wants to know if we can buff it, take the scratches out. I told him we're a Chrysler shop."

"Who cares? How long to do the job?"

"Well, sir . . ." Dan frowned. "We're closed tomorrow, Monday. Maybe Tuesday afternoon."

"O.K. with you, McBride?"

"No problem."

It struck Ed there should have been a problem. "Don't you people leave on Sunday when the Fair shuts down?"

"I'm staying on in town awhile."

Whatever that meant. "Do you know . . ." Ed peered at him. "I've got the damndest feeling—that's it. You're the fella from the strip show."

Talker nodded. "Guilty."

"Not in my book. Dan, you boys get busy. Right away. How's that, McBride?"

"I'm going to need another favor. This weekend, there won't be a rental car in town."

"You need a loaner? Here's my deal. I've never met a fellow in your line of work before. You tell me some about the show, you've got yourself a set of wheels."

A chance to talk to Marcie's father, find out things about her? It was too good to be true. He shrugged. "I've got a little time."

"Come on inside, we'll beat the heat." They started in. "I caught your show, you know. First night it opened."

Talker grinned; the old man couldn't wait. "Well? How'd you like it?"

"Frankly, it's a little tame."

"You know the rules here?"

"Hell, I'm on the Board of Governors, I wrote them."

Talker laughed and followed Ed across the showroom floor.

"In here." They kept a room for cozying the customers: big chairs, big bar, big deal. Ed started toward the bar, then paused. "How come you brought your car to us?"

"The Sheriff sent me."

Maybe so. It could be true. "Weller's a good man, knows his place. What are you drinking?"

"Is there beer?"

Ed got two bottles, took the caps off. He was feeling easier. If there was one thing he was great at, it was judging character, and there was something decent about McBride. Ed liked his eyes; they looked right at you. On the other hand . . .

He took two glasses, poured the beer. "I'll call you Paul, you call me Ed."

"O.K. by me."

"I've got to tell you, there was one girl in your show who really caught my eye. She wore a harem costume."

"Annie."

"Pretty thing. You don't mind if I'm blunt?"

"I'm used to blunt."

Ed handed him a glass. "I'd give a lot to get my hands on her."

The old man screwed around. At his age. Good for him. "So would a lot of people."

"Everybody has a price."

"You think so?"

"Paul, I've been in business donkey's years. I know it."

Talker shrugged. "You'd have to ask her."

Ed sat down and crossed his legs, relaxed and casual. He'd laid the groundwork. "What's her story?"

"I don't know that much about her."

"Where's she from?"

"Some town in Pennsylvania."

"How long has she been a stripper?"

"Four, five days."

Ed laughed. "You're kidding me. What got her into it?"

"You ever run away from home?"

Ed nodded. "Once or twice." If Annie was a shakedown artist, he was Betty Boop. The same went for McBride. He took a long, long swallow. "So you're staying on in town."

"That's right."

"Mind if I ask you why?"

Far from it. It was just the opening he'd been waiting for. "Well . . ." Half the truth was better than none. "I like it here. The fact is, Ed, I've quit the show. It's great when you're a kid, there's all that tail—you know exactly what I mean." He grinned.

Ed couldn't stop from grinning back. "I guess I do."

"Don't get me wrong, I'm not against a good lay, but there comes a time when what you want is one girl and a home to keep her in."

"I know. I'm a married man myself. Same woman, forty years."

"You're lucky."

"That's debatable." Ed took a swallow, wiped his lips. "You've got me on the wrong day. Yes, I'm lucky."

"You have children?"

"One. I've got a daughter."

"What's she like?"

"Hands off. She's married."

"Is she anything like you?"

"Oh good God, no."

"Tell me about her." Talker watched his eyes light up.

"She's something." Ed felt drawn to him. The fellow sounded as if he cared, he made you want to talk. Ed smiled and leaned back. "Marcie's what they used to call a pip. One time, you won't believe this, she was five years old—" The door flew open. "I'll be damned, speak of the devil."

"I've been hunting you all over town. I've got some things to—" Marcie stopped dead in her tracks. She didn't scream, but it was close.

Both men stood up. Ed was beaming. "Paul McBride, my daughter, Marcie."

Talker made a little bow. "We've met."

She felt herself go numb. What was he saying, was he crazy? She produced a sound like, "Oh?"

"Don't you remember?"

If they lived through this, she'd kill him. No words came. She shook her head.

"On Monday, when I registered. You rented me a space."

A space. What space? It came to her. "That's right. I did."

"It's nice to meet officially." He offered her his hand.

"Your father was just telling me about you." Marcie's hand was trembling. Talker didn't want to let it go.

Zack stepped in. "Ed, you've got a phone call in your office."

"Now?" He made a face. "Who is it?"

"I don't know."

"You didn't ask?" Zack's days were numbered. Ed turned in the doorway. "I'll be right back. You two get to know each other."

Talker closed the door. His heart was pounding. "Marcie—"

"Ohmigod, I damn near died."

"I'm sorry, if I'd known—"

"What are you doing here, for Jesus' sake?"

"I brought my car in."

"Brought it here? You're fucking crazy. Don't come near me."

"No one's watching."

"Talker, please . . ."

"When you stop shaking, I'll let go. I've got to see you, Marcie."

"Not today. I can't."

"I meant to give you time, I didn't mean to rush you, but you're here, I'm holding you, and Jesus, Marcie . . ."

"Stop it!"

"O.K., sure." He stepped away. "When can I see you?"

"I speak English, what do you speak? Not today. It's too much, I can't deal with . . . Do you want to hear what I've been going through? You want a list?"

"I'll match you."

"I've been up all night, I've had no sleep, I've had my mother, I've had Van—"

"You want to hear about the Sheriff?"

"No. I haven't finished. I've got many miles to go before I sleep. I tell you, I could slit my wrists. They're coming at me from all sides."

"Can I do anything to help?"

"Don't be ridiculous. What could you do?"

"There must be something. You're the only thing I've got."

That caught her. "Please. Don't talk like that."

"You're all there is."

"Oh Christ." She closed her eyes. "Tomorrow. At the Lodge."

"When?"

"How do I know? When I get there."

"Do you know I love you?"

"Shut up. Yes, I know it. Afternoon—and keep your distance, Dad could walk in. Cool it down."

"I'm cool. You want a beer?"

"That's brilliant."

"It beats screaming."

Marcie folded up, collapsed into an armchair. "I'm not doing very well."

"You're doing fine."

"I'll never make it."

"Yes, you will; and so will I." What would he give to hold her? Then and there, that second?

Ed moved in. "Look, Marcie, that was Dee just now."

"To talk to you?"

"No. She's been phoning for you everywhere. She's at the hospital."

"That better be a joke."

"There's been an accident."

"Oh God." Somehow, she got up from the chair. "Is Dee all right?"

"She's fine, she needs to see you, but it's Eleanor."

"It's Eleanor?" She started laughing. "Is she dead?"

"What's *wrong* with you?"

"I'm sorry, Dad. It isn't funny. Nothing's funny. See? I'm serious." A final giggle burst out.

"Marcie." Ed looked really worried. "What's the matter?"

"I'm O.K. You know what girls are like, sometimes they get hysterical. It doesn't mean a thing." She turned to leave.

Ed stopped her. "Look—are you in shape to drive?"

"We'll soon find out." She turned to Talker. "Pleasure meeting you."

27

ANNIE WENT WHIZZING out of Sunset Crescent, skidded on the turn and headed toward the Fair. Her heart was thumping. Holy shit. That look on Ed's face when she passed him by just now; what was he so hysterical about? Small change to what she felt. She'd almost fallen off her bike. What was he going to say to Betsy? What would Betsy say to him?

She scanned the possibilities. Suppose he asked who Annie was and what she had been doing there? Was Betsy going to tell him she was hot for Denny and had wanted her advice? Would Ed say Annie was an evil influence and stay away from her? How could he, he had taken her to Pussy Point. All they could do was tell each other lies, make small talk. There was nothing they could say.

She felt a whole lot better—and what kind of family were they, anyhow? Gramps takes a teenage stripper to the woods and pops her cherry. And his daughter Marcie goes down for a strip-show talker, screwing every chance she gets; a married woman with a family. And her daughter, Betsy, all of four-teen, playing cocktease with her boyfriend, wanting him to stick it in. Were they all sex-crazed? Was it in their blood or something?

She had kept her head with Betsy, played it cool enough. She didn't want the girl to know the truth. Why hurt her? So she had been careful with her questions when they talked about the photos. She knew Marcie's name now. Simpy name. She had expected something special, like the house was special. And she knew who Ed was—Steuben Motors—and that Betsy's father worked for him. That was all. Not much to show but—

"Wow." That's when it hit her. Annie was the Keeper of the Secrets. As if there were a *Who's Who,* and she had the only copy. What to do with it? Great scenes raced through her mind. She'd go to Marcie, tell her, 'Listen, lady, keep your hands off Talker or I'll spill the beans.' And Marcie would go chalk white and say, 'Please. I'm at your mercy, anything you want.'

Not bad. Or she could go to Ed and pull the same thing in a different way. 'Now hear this, Mr. Ed. Your daughter's screwing my man. You either call her off or I'll go public.' That would get some action.

Or there was Marcie's husband. Van. He'd stop things if she told him. Blam-o, on the spot. And there was Talker, too. Suppose she told him what she knew and threatened to blow everything apart? She had him by the short hairs. How about that? She had all the keys, and lots of doors to open.

She was whistling when she turned into the Fairgrounds, stopped to flash her ID; getting in was free. The only trouble with these scenes was they meant hurting someone. On the other hand, if she did nothing, she'd end up with nothing. Someone wrote, "All's fair in love and war." The ball was in her court. Or, more exactly, Talker's balls. She wanted them, she wanted him. She'd spent her whole life on the losing side. Not anymore. Not this time.

Laurel's car was in the lot; it wasn't three, the girls were early. Betsy would be passing by with Denny later for the bike. She propped it up beside the ticket booth. They couldn't miss it there, and it was safe enough.

She waved to Norma, who was sitting on the tree stump in the shade and moved into the van. The girls were there, all three of them, and packing; putting costumes into wardrobe trunks.

"What's going on here?"

"Golly Moses, Orphan Annie, what's it look like?"

"You're a riot, Skipper. All I asked was—"

"Where the hell have you been?"

"That's my business."

"Children, children." Laurel glared at both of them. "What we don't need is small displays of petulance."

Pauline looked up. "What's petulance?"

"Pauline, you're a scientific miracle: a living biped with no brain." Laurel flopped down on a cot. "I don't know why we bother stripping. We could put you on exhibit, make a fortune."

"Fuck yourself." Pauline was bright red to begin with, sweating in the heat. "I'm just as good as you are."

"Better. When it comes to lard, you've got me ten to one."

"Will everybody stop it!" Annie shouted.

"Yes, M'am." Skipper tossed her a salute, turned to the others. "May I speak for all of us?"

"Why not?" Laurel leaned back. "You'll do it anyway."

"Dit-dit-dit." Skipper sounded like a telegraph key. "Latest news from Fulton. Hot flash. Time is running out for Annie. If she wants to get in Talker's pants—"

"Who says I do?"

"Come off it. You've been drooling since you met him. Everybody knows it. We've been in his pants, too, one time or another, and I'm here to tell you, it's not bad. But—"

"Zip it, Skipper." Laurel sat up. "Why be such a bitch?"

"Comes natural to me." Skipper shrugged. "Look, Annie, we've played by the rules here, we've been good girls. You know what we get for that? They've closed us down."

"They've what?"

"Tonight is it. We're out of here tomorrow, on the road. We're going to play a few more weeks—and that's O.K. But Talker isn't coming."

"Sure he is."

"He's given us the kiss-off, kid."

"I don't believe you."

"Ask him when he gets here."

Annie couldn't take it in. "You're lying to me."

"Wish I was. You'd better pack your things up."

Annie stood there, couldn't move. This time tomorrow, there would be no Talker. Was it possible? Or were they joking, playing games? They had to be. She turned, went out the curtain, spotted Norma. Norma was her friend. She jumped down from the stage and hurried over.

"Norma? You know what they've just been telling me?"

"Not for a fact, but I could guess." There were a lot of

things she needed right then, but a scene with Annie she could do without.

"I don't believe them." Annie's eyes were stinging. "I don't understand. I'm always nice to them."

"Look, Sweetcakes, if you want a grown-up conversation, fine. But otherwise—"

"What's wrong with everybody?"

Norma shrugged. "A dose of righteous indignation. Even scum like us have feelings."

"We're not scum."

"I know that. We're just feeling scummy."

"Are we really closing?"

"Yup."

"And moving on tomorrow?"

"Yup again."

"And Talker . . . ?"

"No, he isn't coming."

Annie sat down on the dust. The bottom had just fallen out. Of everything.

"Look, honey—are you listening?"

"What?"

"You never had a chance with Talker."

"Never?"

Norma shook her head. "Forget about him."

"How?"

"Like you forgot about not flying. Every kid of three or four thinks they can fly. What happens? They fall down, go boom. You with me?"

Annie wasn't, but she nodded.

"Good. You know what should be on your mind? I'll tell you. When we go tomorrow, are you coming?"

"No." The word came instantly, it just popped out.

"You're sure about that? Have you thought it over?"

Annie stared at nothing, shook her head. "I guess not."

"Well, you'd better." Norma knew she'd said enough. What happened to this little farm girl didn't matter; there were millions like her. "Kid, if I were you, I'd think about what's coming. Like next month, next year. How do you see it?"

"I don't know."

"Well, no one's going to see it for you. You're not made for this life, that's for sure; but I'd stay with us for a few more weeks. It means more pay, a bigger cushion." Norma got up from the tree stump. "Think about it. Me, I'm going for an ice cream. Want to come along?"

"No, thanks."

Norma looked at her. She had a hunch that Annie's no was going to stick. Where would she be a year from now? Hell, where would any of them be? She turned away and shuffled off to the Good Humor Man.

Marvin was bouncing down the road toward Carthage Lake in Donny's Jeep. He had intended to return it, but the day had been a little much. In fact, too many things were starting in to be a little much.

For a fellow who usually slept like an angel, he had spent a hellish night. He had dropped Lucy off at her place—hugs and kisses, whispered promises—then driven home. No sign of Dad, so he had trudged upstairs and fallen into bed. He was too young to be a father, and he prayed to God he wasn't. Lucy wasn't all that late, the thing could come to nothing. Sure. But if it didn't, he'd be there for Lucy. He was not the dummy that he knew she sometimes took him for.

He turned out the light, rolled over, and had nightmares all night long. He kept on waking up in sweats; he'd lost his job, no money for the rent, and Lucy and the baby crying. It was after two when he heard crashing noises downstairs. Dad was drunk again and stumbling into furniture. The old man would be murder in the morning.

And he was. He'd made it to the kitchen where he'd passed out on the floor, which was where Marvin found him, lying on his back, a lump high on his forehead like a hen's egg. And when Marvin tried to lift him, drag him off to bed, his dad had opened bloodshot eyes and told him to fuck off.

So Marvin did the morning chores alone, and when he came in later for a drink of something cold, his dad was sitting at the kitchen table.

"Hi, how are you?" Marvin asked.

"How do I fucking look?"

"What happened to your head?"

Walt glared at him. The fact that some old bag had demolished him with one blow—and in front of all his buddies—boiled his blood. "I had a little accident."

Walt took his mug of coffee, left the room. Marv saw him

next an hour later, moving to the truck. He looked transformed, all cleaned up, with his Sunday suit on.

"Where you going?" No reply. "Dad, where you off to?"

Walt got in the truck and slammed the door. He had his date at noon with Barney Lovell, and if Barney didn't show, he'd kill him. "What's it to you, kid?"

Marv watched him drive off in a cloud of dust, went back to work. The working helped; you grunt and sweat enough, you don't have strength to think. But Marvin went on thinking. He was broke. Except for fifty dollars that he'd stashed away. How far could he and Lucy go on that? Two tickets on the bus to nowhere.

Marvin threw the pitchfork down, went to his bedroom, got out his suitcase. He wasn't going to pack it; it just helped to make things real. That's when the phone rang.

"Marv?"

"Hi, Lucy."

"Watcha doin'?"

"Nothin' much."

"Let's drive in to the Fair."

"You mean now?" They had plans for going that night.

"What's wrong with now? You're doing nothing, and I'm bored. Dad's off somewhere, he isn't going to yell at us."

"But, Lucy—"

"Make it soon. I'll see you."

Marvin put the phone down. Something didn't sound right. If he knew one thing, he knew his Lucy. What was up? He turned onto the drive to Carthage Lake. He'd find out soon enough.

Lucy was sitting on the porch steps, waiting for him. He was late, as usual. She ran a damp hand through her hair and tried to calm herself. It was a big step, leaving home, and she was never coming back again.

She had held nothing back from Norma, if you didn't count her age. She had a driver's license saying she was twenty-one. Some friend of Marvin's made them up; you couldn't tell them from the real thing. Marvin had one, too. Aside from that, she told the truth and nothing but. Her life was hell, she'd missed her period, her boyfriend loved her, he'd stick by her, but they needed money to get started, and she had to join the show or die.

"I've got a future, Mrs. Cusak, but I'll never have it staying here. Besides, my dad'll kill me if I have a baby. You know what he's like."

"I know."

"I'm just as pretty as the other girls. I tell you, Mrs. Cusak . . ." Lucy let the tears well up. "I'm desperate." She rubbed her eyes, then peered at Norma, couldn't tell what she was thinking. Nothing showed.

"You ever strip?"

"You mean in public?" Lucy asked her.

"Pull yourself together, honey. Where the hell else would I mean?"

"It's not a problem, I can do it." Lucy meant it, and if Norma asked for proof, she would have peeled it all off on the spot and done a number on the picnic table.

Norma frowned. "I'll tell you what. Come in today, we'll see if you can do it. If you can—"

"Oh, thank you, thank you."

"Don't thank me yet."

Norma went back to her map and Lucy raced upstairs, called Marvin, packed her bag. A small bag, she was traveling light. Some clothes, her diary, the photo of her mother. All the rest, she left behind without a blink. Except the cross she'd gotten for first Communion. Just in case; you never knew if God was watching.

She heard an engine grinding up the drive, reached for her bag, and left the porch. She had a strong hunch Marvin would go crazy if he knew the whole truth, so she planned to fudge a little. Anyway, she really didn't have the job yet. Once she did, she'd call him next week from wherever they were working and he'd join her. He'd be used to it by then.

When Marvin saw her with the bag, his heart sank. Was she leaving now, this minute; was she taking off without him; did she want him to go with her? What? He was afraid to ask.

"Hi."

"Hi." She got in, closed the door, bag on her lap. He had to notice it, he'd asked her what was up, she'd tell her tale.

"You all set?"

Lucy nodded.

"O.K., here we go."

He turned the Jeep around and started off. She glanced at him. What was he thinking? "You look nice, Marv."

He had washed and changed. "Thanks. So do you." He paused. "Well, everything's the same, I guess."

"What everything?"

"That everything." What did she think? "Your period."

She shook her head.

No luck today. Maybe tomorrow. Marvin turned onto the county road and gave the Jeep more gas. They drove in silence for a while.

"Marvin, honey?"

"Yeah?" He knew that tone of voice.

"You haven't asked about the bag."

"Oh, that." He braced himself. "Well, what about it?"

"Don't you want to ask me what it's for?"

He shrugged. "You'll tell me when you're ready to."

"Well, it's like this. You know the Moulin Rouge, right?"

"Yeah. The place I got my teeth kicked in. I know it."

"I've been talking to the girls. They're staying at our place, you can't help running into them."

"So?"

"Marv, you know how much they make?"

"I'll bite."

"A thousand bucks a week or more."

He whistled.

"That's what I think—and what I've decided is, I'm going to ask them for a job."

"*What?*"

"Shut up and listen. Marv, I'm leaving home. I don't care anymore if I'm knocked up or not, I'm getting out. The show is going on for two, three weeks. You know what that would mean for us, you want to count it up?"

"I don't care. You're my girl. You understand? I'm taking care of you. You get to strip for me—but no one else, and if you think—"

"You're jumping. I don't have the job. I haven't asked, they haven't said O.K."

"It's out. You can forget it, Lucy Lovell."

He was such a fool; and so was she for loving him. "It's just a show, that's all it is. It doesn't make me cheap or something."

"How'd you feel if it was me up there?"

She saw her opening and she took it. "You? I'd come to

watch." She reached out, zipped his fly down. "Hell, I'd even pay admission."

"Cut it out, don't joke around."

"Well, will you look at that." She smiled, then put a finger in her mouth and licked it.

"Lucy . . ."

"You're the only man for me. How often do I have to prove it?"

"Did you get the flowers, dear?"

"Oh, Harriet, you shouldn't have. They're absolutely beautiful." In point of fact, the nurse had put them by the window and she couldn't see them.

"I'm so glad. I've been at the Pavilion all day long, Ed called me there. I just this minute got home." Harriet kicked off her shoes and plopped down in her favorite armchair. "Are you in much pain?"

"It comes and goes."

"Well, that's a blessing."

"What's a blessing?"

"That it goes, dear. Anyway, first thing I did was call up Sunshine Florists—they're the best in town, I always think. Don't you?"

"I much prefer McPherson's."

"I'll remember that. In any case, they promised me two dozen perfect roses."

"They sent daisies and carnations."

"Eleanor, who can you trust?" She'd ordered daisies and carnations. "It's the thought that counts. Would you like company?"

Not Harriet's, thanks very much. "That's sweet of you, but I've had company all afternoon. Our darling girls were here with me."

"They were?"

"For ages, dear." Let Harriet try that one on for size.

"Ed's coming in, I've got to go. I'll drop by first thing in the morning."

"Would you, Harriet? I'd love to—" Eleanor gasped sharply.

"What was that? Are you all right?"

"I'm ringing for the nurse. Good-bye." She put the phone down, settled back. All day at the Pavilion? Some excuse. And

Sunshine was the cheapest place. She knew; she used it, too. She sighed and wondered whom to call; she had so many friends. Or maybe she should ring up Dr. Stone. He thought he was so smart. It might be nice to tell the man there were more ways than one to skin a cat.

"God help us." Marcie slumped into the hall and looked ahead. The stairs were mountainous, she didn't have the strength. She glanced at Dee and headed for the den. "You want a drink of anything?"

"Make that a double anything."

"Well, help yourself." The carpet looked too good to miss. She let her knees go, sank, rolled over on her back. "Oh God . . ."

"I take your point." Dee sank down close beside her, being careful with her shoulder. It had taken all the impact, and it hurt. She closed her eyes and sighed. "'O Death, where is thy sting?'"

"Don't ask."

They lay there for a while, merely breathing. Breathing was enough.

"Dee . . . about your mother . . ."

"Any other subject."

Marcie shifted to her side and looked at her. "Oh, you poor baby."

"What about yourself?"

"You mean my so-called life?" She nearly smiled. "I tell you, Dee, when I saw Dad and Talker in the same room . . . if I live to be a hundred . . ."

"Wish I'd been there."

"You're some friend."

Then, as they did when they were kids on those occasions when the world was clearly ending, they wriggled closer, put their arms around each other. Unspoken questions swirled around them, memories drifted in the air.

"Dee, do you ever wish . . ." It trailed away.

"I do a lot of wishing. Be specific."

"I don't know, would it be fair to say that we're among the privileged few?"

"Depends on what you mean."

"What everybody means. We're young, we're healthy, we have money, we're intelligent, attractive—"

"Damned attractive."

"And we do things. We're not parasites. We work, we pay our dues. O.K.?"

"Sounds realistic and objective. What's your point?"

"What's wrong with us? Why aren't we happy?"

"Oh, grow up."

"I did grow up. Remember how we couldn't wait? We'd run our own lives, we'd be free—and look at us."

"You want to change your life? What's stopping you?"

"You want a list?"

They heard the front door open, footsteps. Marcie sighed, rolled on her back, gazed at the ceiling. "Van?"

"I'm home."

"We're in the den."

Van turned and plodded toward the room. He had been driving; aimlessly, as usual. And thinking. Bits and pieces of what Sandy said had stuck. Like his response to all Van's agonizing, what had Marcie meant: "Why don't you ask her?" Tossed it off as if it were nothing, just a snap. And he got paid for asking crap like that. The man should lose his license.

Van moved through the door, looked down. "Are you O.K.? What's happened?"

Marcie shrugged. "We've died and gone to heaven. How've you been?"

As if she cared. "Delirious." Or did she care? He'd known her almost half his life, he'd seen her through a lot; and vice versa. Didn't he know anything? That fucking Sandy; left him twisting slowly in the wind, that's what he'd done. "Is Betsy home?"

"I haven't looked."

"Don't you think someone should?"

"Van, at this moment, I don't care."

Why had he asked? To pick a fight? What for? There was enough hostility around. Besides, she looked exhausted, vulnerable. What was he so afraid of? All Sandy's question meant was, was she for him or against him? "Marcie, can I ask you something?"

"Only if it's easy."

"It'll keep." He could have kicked himself. Wrong time, wrong place. Wrong question, too. Did she love him? That was it. The phone rang.

Marcie groaned. "Van, will you get it—and if it's for me . . ."

"I'll deal with it." What did she think? He couldn't deal with anything? He picked it up and snapped it out. "Yes?"

"Van?"

The Witch of Endor. "Hello, Harriet."

"How are you, dear?"

It was the "dear" that got him. "I'm in a meeting." Expletives flashed through his mind. What was the point? He slammed the phone down to applause and cries of "Bravo." Were they laughing at him?

"O.K., Marcie, what's all that about? Did I do something funny? What's the joke?"

"Oh, Van . . ." For just a minute there, she thought he'd joined the club. Had she been feeling stronger, she'd have wept. "It's nothing."

Ed put his briefcase down and heaved a sigh. The thing was heavy, filled with loan agreements from Jack Morgan, everything in triplicate. He had all weekend to go over them. He checked the living room for Harriet, moved to the bar, and poured a stiff one. There was no ice in the bucket, never was, he didn't bother looking. Harriet was fond enough of strong drink for herself; but not for him. "You're getting on, Ed, and I worry." It meant trudging to the kitchen if he wanted ice. It used to stop him now and then, until he learned to take it neat.

Harriet was in the bedroom, trying on things for the dance at Longview Saturday. It was, along with New Year's Eve, the major party of the year, and though appearances always mattered, there were times they mattered more. She turned as Ed came in. "How do I look, dear?"

"Well . . ." The blue brought out the color of her eyes; she looked quite beautiful. "Like a sack of potatoes." Sometimes irritating her gave him a big kick.

"I mean, really."

"So do I."

She knew what he was up to. Two could play. "You didn't speak to Van, I don't suppose—and don't deny it."

"Why deny it?"

"When you left today, did I or did I not—"

"I heard you, Harriet. You'd have to be a deaf man not to."

"Am I due an explanation?"

He was really getting to her. "There's no hurry, what's the rush? I figure I'll run into him tonight."

"You want to hear what he just did?"

Ed sat down on the bed and shrugged. "You know, I met an interesting guy this afternoon."

"I'm talking to you, Ed."

"This fellow owns a Thunderbird—"

"Van just hung up on me."

"What if he did?" To his surprise, he wasn't teasing anymore. "Show some compassion for the man."

"Some what?" Her eyes flashed. "After what he's done?"

"You know what's wrong with you?" Ed felt his temper rocket. "You're a selfish woman."

"Me?"

"I ought to know. I live with you."

"I want what's best for everyone, and if you think that's selfish, Edgar Steuben, you can—"

"Do you really want a fight?"

"You started it."

It was too fine a point to pick. "O.K. You look great in the dress, we're all on edge, I'm sorry."

"You don't mean it."

Ed got up. "Come here."

"What for?"

"Do what I fucking tell you."

He looked really angry. "Yes, dear."

"Here's the thing. We've got a shit heap to be thankful for. You understand, or do I have to spell it out?"

"I understand."

"I see the kids aren't happy. I don't like it, either."

"I know that."

"Stop worrying."

"I'll try."

He put his arms around her. "That's my girl."

"I always count on you."

"That's why I'm here." He stroked her hair. "Just you remember, nothing wrong that we can't fix." Then, bending close, he whispered in her ear, "Come on, I'll take you out to dinner."

*   *   *

Talker parked the loaner in the lot. A dark blue four-door something; Ed had picked it out for him. No form to sign or anything; the man just handed him the keys.

"Just bring it back on Tuesday, and don't rack it up."

"Don't worry."

Talker got out, locked the car, and started up the road. Ed was a hard guy not to like. He still believed in first impressions, trusting strangers, handshakes—and he loved his daughter. After Marcie left them, she was all he'd talk about. She didn't get her looks from Ed, but he was where her spirit came from.

It was crowded, hot and noisy. Talker stopped and looked around. It wasn't much as Midways went, but even so, he felt a twinge. He saw the Moulin Rouge ahead. How many years? It made you stop and think. One last night on the bally stage. That's all there was, there wasn't any more.

Enough of that, no second thoughts. He moved on, spotted Norma standing by the stage, bent forward, writing something. She had found a piece of wallboard, and was working with a magic marker. Big, bright letters you could see for half a mile: CLOSING TONIGHT—LAST CHANCE TO SEE THE SHOW.

She glanced at him. "You like?"

"What's not to like?"

There was a hammer and some nails beside it. "Tack it up on your way in. And by the way, we're going to play a few more weeks."

"Since when?"

"Since I decided. Don't feel bad. Nobody's going to miss you."

"Thanks."

"De nada."

Talker watched her walk away. He didn't blame her; not for being sore at him and not for going on. She wanted to? Why shouldn't she? He nailed the sign up, banged his thumb.

Inside the van, the atmosphere was like an acid bath. The girls kept nailing him for ducking out and leaving them: ". . . swell knowing you, you rat fink . . . thanks for nothing . . ." There was even crap from Annie, kept addressing him as "Mr. Dick." And what's-her-name from Carthage Lake, the old fart's daughter, bare-assed, trying costumes on. Was Norma nuts? They had four girls; who needed this one? Not his problem. None of what went on here was his problem any-more.

He checked his watch, four on the dot. Three shows an hour, seven hours; twenty-one more spiels to make. A bagatelle. No reason not to start. He turned as Skipper tapped his shoulder.

"Let's get going, dildohead."

"Get off my back."

"You want to see my pussy for the last time?"

"No."

"Kiss it good-bye." She spread her legs, then moved away.

She was entitled. They'd worked seven years together, never lovers but they'd made love. How would he feel? Not so hot, but there was just so much he owed her. Norma was an-other matter. How was he supposed to deal with that one?

"Fuck it," Talker said, and walked out on the bally stage, surveyed the crowd, picked up his mike.

Twenty-one and counting.

28

THE SUN WAS down, the lights were on, and crowds were streaming through the gates. How many people? Harry Weller wondered. They'd been pouring in now for an hour. Eight, ten thousand? All of them on holiday, damn-all to do till Tuesday—and a lot of it would start tonight. The bulk of them just now were moving to the grandstand. Johnny Cash was singing, and he always drew a mob. The show went on at eight, not long from now, assuming it began on time. He shrugged, went into his Command Post, closed the door, sat down, and waited for the calls to come.

In the grandstand, Denny thanked the usher for the programs, followed Betsy past the roped-off benches to their places down in front.

"Where's everybody?" Denny asked.

"Beats me." No sign of Mom or Dad or Gram or Gramps. "They're staying home, I guess."

"You hungry?"

Betsy shook her head.

"Me neither." It had been a funny afternoon. They'd had a swim at Betsy's, then he'd perched her on the handlebars and cycled to the Fair, picked up her bike, and goofed around, not talking very much. The time had come to broach the subject.

"Bets?"

"I just love Johnny Cash. Don't you?"

She knew he did. She'd been like that since lunch. Evasive. "I've been wondering, what went on?"

She frowned. "What went on when?"

"With you two girls?"

"Oh. You mean me and Annie?"

"Well?"

"We talked, that's all."

"I figured that much. I know when I'm not invited. What did you talk about?"

She had been dreading this, and now that it was here, it seemed so easy. "Girl talk. You know, clothes and makeup, diets, dating, boys . . . just stuff like that."

"You mentioned me?"

She grinned. "Oh, I don't know."

"What did you say?"

"What do you think?"

"Oh, come on, Bets."

"I told her how I feel about you. Who else have I got to tell?"

He smiled, edged closer, slipped an arm around her waist. "What did she say? I want it all."

Her breath caught when he touched her—and it shouldn't. She believed what Annie said; she knew it to be right and true. They had to wait. "We've got to wait."

"I'm sorry." He looked puzzled. "Wait for what?"

She poured it out. "We're too young, can't you understand that? And don't tell me Juliet was only twelve—"

"Hold on, Bets."

"I'm not Juliet and you're not Romeo. We're waiting."

"I know that."

She blinked. "You do?"

"Of course I do. I know things went too far last night. I'm glad it happened, but I wouldn't dream of—"

Betsy threw her arms around him. "Do you know how much I love you?"

Denny swallowed hard and nodded, and the floodlights went on, lit the field. The show was starting. People whistled, howled, and clapped. A cheer went up.

It carried to the midway, you could hear it in the van in spite of all the noise outside. The crowds were huge so far, the tent jammed full for every show. It was exciting. Even Talker felt it, but the girls were something else. Eyes bright and faces flushed, they rushed about like they were opening on Broadway. Even Annie seemed caught up in it.

For Lucy, it was heaven. She'd been nervous, really scared before she stepped on stage the first time. It was more than just the stripping. Anybody could be out there: friends of hers or Marvin's, God knows who. This was home territory. It was not just 'So long, Fulton County.' It was 'Screw you,' too. Then she went out and felt the eyes of every man, and nothing mattered anymore. She was dressed in something shiny with an open midriff, and their eyes were on her tummy. When she moved it, every eye moved right along. No matter what she moved—her tits, her ass—they followed her. She had them.

In between shows, she could not sit still. Her heart was pounding. She had never taken drugs, but she had read about the rush you got from some of them. That's how she felt. She couldn't think of anything but going on again. It made her wet. She didn't have to touch herself; she knew it.

Talker looked at her and shook his head. A crazy girl. If her old man could see her, it would blow his mind away. He peered out through the curtain at the crowd. It stretched back almost to the road. The cheer meant it was eight o'clock. How many more spiels did he have to get through? Twelve and counting.

Talker moved out on the stage, picked up his mike. A hush fell. They were really ready for him.

"Men and boys. What brings you here, all pressed together in the heat, tongues hanging out? You're curious, you're horny, you don't get enough at home, or all of the above. You've got your expectations and your dicks up. Am I right?"

He waited for the hoots and hollers to die down. "Well, men and boys, you're in for a surprise. If this were any place but Fulton, you'd see all the pussy you could eat. But you've got rules and regulations here. The law says it's not good for you to look at snatch in public. Maybe you're not old enough. Or you'd get too excited and go home and fuck your wives."

He got a lot of noise on that one. "That's the bad news. Here's the good. You've got imaginations. Use them. Hell, what's better in this life, reality or dreams? For just two bucks, you get to see some flesh and dream away."

The music started. Laurel came out in her golden dress.

He switched the mike off, watched the crowd. They stood there silent, riveted, eyes wide, mouths slightly open. What was going on? He glanced at Laurel just behind him.

She was smiling and her hips were moving, just like always. Only, she had one hand on her crotch, where it was rubbing up and down.

He moved to her and whispered. "Jesus Christ, what are you doing?"

"I believe they call it public masturbation."

"Are you crazy?"

"Would I be here if I wasn't?"

Marvin watched them from across the road. He'd given in to Lucy, more or less. He'd seen the show, they didn't really strip, not all the way; you could see more of Lucy on a public beach. Besides, he had believed her when she told him she was leaving, job or no job; and for damn sure they could use the money. Only, what the barker said just now got to him. And the things that girl was doing, rubbing cunt in front of God and everybody—Jesus, what was Lucy getting into? Did she know?

To hell with waiting. Marvin started forward, shouldering his way through all the gawkers to the ticket booth.

Laurel flashed a grin at Talker, curtsied to the crowd, and glided back in through the curtain. She was glowing. She had planned that moment since her night in jail; she sure as hell owed Fulton something. And those faces in the mob, that glassy-eyed amazement. Had they never seen a woman—or were ladies here brought forth without their genitalia? She loved it.

"What the hell was that about?"

She turned to Talker. "Oh. I take it we are not amused."

"I asked a question."

"What do you care? You're long gone, you're history."

"What's happened?" Skipper hurried over.

Laurel smiled and demonstrated. Skipper broke up.

Talker's fuse was getting shorter. "What so funny?"

"You are." Skipper sat down, wheezing. "I've got news for you. There's no way they can close the show. We're closed already."

"Skipper's right." Pauline stood up as rhythmic clapping starting in the tent. "It doesn't matter what we do. Not anymore."

"Look, ladies." Talker held his hands out, palms up. "Peace. Let's just get through the night, O.K.?"

Laurel nodded. "I'd like nothing more. You want to start the music, or shall I?"

"I'll do it," Talker snapped. "I'm still here."

"More or less."

He let it pass, turned on the tape. Pauline was the first to dance. She moved almost majestically toward the curtain. Then she turned to face them all and, in a simple, fluid gesture, took off her bra.

Pauline's breasts, unlike the rest of her, were perfect. Firm and shapely, far too vast to stand up—but they did. She tossed her bra to Talker, turned, and went on stage without a word.

Talker started after her, then stopped. Too late. He balled the bra up, threw it hard against the wall. The girls were looking at him, grinning.

"Got a problem?" Skipper asked him.

"You're a fucking riot."

Talker took off, out the curtain to the bally stage. There was a crowd already waiting for the next show. What a night. He slowed down, crossed the stage, leaped off, and headed for the entrance to the tent.

Norma looked up as he passed the ticket booth. There was a lot of whistling from the tent now, more than usual.

"What's up?"

"Don't ask."

He moved in, saw the two cops at the back. On duty, like marines: *Semper fidelis.* All he wanted was no trouble.

"Listen, boys." They turned. He saw their faces. They were grinning. "I just came to say—"

Tom, the huge one, looked down, clapped him on the shoulder. "Talk about great knockers. Jesus. Never in my life . . ."

"Me neither." Ozzie wiped his forehead. "What I'd give to tie my string to those balloons."

It took him by surprise. "You like the show?"

"What's not to like?"

"I know it's not the deal we made, but—"

"Weller made it." Ozzie shrugged. "If it was up to me, I mean, what's wrong with flashing boobs? You see 'em in the movies, don't you?"

Talker breathed a sigh. "Just checking in." He turned to go. "Enjoy yourselves."

"Don't worry."

Marvin stood beside a tent pole, feeling plenty worried. This was not the show he'd seen. The stripper with the giant cans, real number tens, was swinging them around. In opposite directions. One went left and one went right. Incredible. It must have taken years of practice, and no decent girl would put the time in. Only sluts would flash their tits in public. Not his Lucy. Never. Sweat was trickling down his neck. If Lucy showed up topless—Marvin watched and waited.

Lucy came out next. "Oh, thank you, God." He wished she'd kept her midriff covered, but she did look beautiful. She started dancing. Steps they did together. What had he expected? That was all she knew. Some dickheads started shouting "Take it off," but Lucy didn't. Marvin felt a burst of pride. He didn't mind that men were drooling; they thought she was a knockout, too. He even felt like saying, 'That's my girl.'

About a minute in, her dancing started changing. She began to swing her hips from side to side. He frowned, but he could live with that; kids did it on the Dick Clark show. He felt O.K. till Lucy's hips changed their direction. Back and forth, like she was screwing, thrusting out her privates toward the crowd. And she was smiling. Marvin closed his eyes; he couldn't watch. Then people started shouting, clapping, and he had to look.

Her top was off. She held it in one hand. Her tits—his tits, their tits—were swinging in the wind for all the world to see. He felt like screaming, but he didn't. He'd have charged the stage and dragged her off, except he'd tried that once and knew what happened. Had they forced her into this, had someone like the prick who kicked him made her do it?

Marvin turned, went plunging, shoving through the crowd. He knew exactly what to do. He rushed out past the entrance toward the bally stage. Talker, at the ticket booth with Norma, watched him go.

He jumped up on the stage. He heard applause; at least she wasn't dancing anymore. He headed for the curtain, whipped right through, the way he'd seen the barker do. The place was hot and smelled of sweat and powder, makeup, food. Half-naked girls were everywhere. The one with the giant cans was watching television. Where was Lucy?

Taking bows. She came in through the curtain. She was floating, couldn't feel the floor. "I did it, how about that."

"Lucy." Marvin stared at her.

"For godsake, Marv, what are you doing here?"

He rushed across the floor and grabbed her. "Jesus, Lucy—"

"Let me go."

"I saw you, I was out there."

All the girls were on their feet now, moving toward them: ". . . lay off . . . who the fuck are you . . . ?"

Marvin felt crazed. "They made you do it, didn't they?"

"The hell they did. I wanted to."

"We're getting out of here."

"You're hurting me."

"We're going home."

"Oh no, we're not." She wrenched free. "I told you stay away, I told you—"

"Lucy!"

Talker grabbed him by the shoulders, twisted hard, spun him around. "Look, kid—"

"Lay offa me."

"We don't want any trouble here."

"Go fuck yourself, you prick."

"I don't know what your bitch is, but you take it somewhere else."

Lucy moved in. "Don't hurt him."

"I'm not going to hurt him." Talker stepped back. "I just want him gone."

"Go home, Marv. Wait for me. I'll call you."

"Sure." He turned and glared at Talker, then went racing out.

"Well . . ." Talker turned to Lucy. "What was that about?"

"You want to know, I'll tell you." Annie's eyes were blazing. She was on next, she already had her top off. "It's not hard to figure out. That's got to be her boyfriend. He's in love with her and he thinks what we do here is a pile of shit. You know what love is, you're the fucking expert. How'd you like it—" She was shaking. "You want Marcie down here with her tits out? What would you do? Buy a ticket?"

Annie turned, went through the curtain. Skipper flipped

the music on. Laurel softly clapped her hands. "I didn't think she had it in her."

Talker stood there frozen. Marcie: Annie knew her name. It wasn't possible. How had she found out? What the hell else did she know? And then, the big one: if she knew it all, what would she do about it? He had never seen her like this. She was capable of anything.

Pauline was giggling. "Boy, she told you where to get off."

Talker took a deep breath. "Look, girls, let's just get through this alive, O.K.? You want to use my head for target practice, hold off till the show is over. And just take it easy with the bumps and grinds. Is it a deal?"

He looked across their faces. No one nodded.

As they stood there, Marvin was already past the Midway, running hell-bent toward the grandstand, tears of rage and outrage in his eyes. He'd seen her face when she came through the curtain; it would haunt him, but he didn't care. She'd come around, get over it. He'd die before he let her turn into a stripper. She was coming home with him, he'd damn well get her out of there. The only thing he needed was some help.

He saw the grandstand way ahead. He could hear Johnny Cash now, belting "Folsom Prison Blues." "You tell 'em, Johnny." Marvin didn't care what happened, fuck it if he broke a few heads, saving Lucy's ass was worth some time in jail. His legs were cramping on him; he slowed down a little. Even from this distance, he could see the mob outside. His friends were sure to be there; they loved Johnny. It might take a while to find them. He had time.

Midevening, Talker always called a break. You couldn't ask the girls to put in seven hours nonstop; you had to have a breather. He announced it from the bally stage. "Ten minutes, gentlemen. Our ladies have to rest their brains."

It got the laugh it always did. He switched the mike off, turned to face the curtain. He had Annie on his hands. He wasn't going to shake it out of her, but short of that, he had to know what she knew. All of it. Not much depended on it; just his life.

He started toward the curtain, noticed that his fists were clenched. He stuffed them in his pockets, moved in, cool and casual. The girls, as always, lay spread-eagled on their cots, eyes on the ceiling.

"Annie, do you have a minute?"

Annie nodded. "Talk away."

"In private."

"Why? I'm not ashamed of anything. Are you?" She turned to Skipper. "You think he's ashamed of anything?"

"Uh-huh. I think its name is Marcie."

Pauline giggled. "Marcie, Marcie, Marcie." Singsong, like a child on a playground.

Talker stiffened. "Let's just take it easy now."

"I've got to ask you." Laurel sat up. "What is Marcie short for? Maraschino?"

"Very funny."

"'Cherry ripe, ripe, ripe, I cry.' That's Robert Herrick."

"Fuck you and your college education."

"Any time."

He moved to Annie. "O.K."

"O.K. what?"

"Let's go outside." She shook her head. He took her arm. "Come on."

"What for? You want to know what I've been telling them? The same thing you've been telling me. Zip, nothing, fuck-all."

"Why should I believe you?"

"Why?" It cut her like a razor blade. "You think I'd lie to you?"

He'd told his share of lies. Who didn't? "Hell yes."

"Jesus, Talker." Wasn't losing him enough? She'd been so sure he cared for her, at least a little. And the man believed she'd hurt him. "You're the pits." She pulled her arm free, gave him one across the face, as hard as she knew how.

He raised his arm to strike her back.

The girls moved in.

The whites of Skipper's eyes looked red. "You want to take us all on? You just say the word." She shoved him hard with both hands.

Talker looked at her, at all of them. He'd played it wrong, he'd lost his head. "I'm sorry."

"Sorry gets you dickshit."

What else could he say? "I'm really sorry. Annie, look at me."

"I've seen you."

Laurel touched his shoulder, smiled. "You know what you

can do for us? Just get your rat's ass out of here. And keep it out."

"O.K., O.K."

He went to the bally stage. He'd done a lot of lousy things, and this one ranked up near the top. He switched the mike on. From the distance, he could hear applause. Just nine to go.

Walt listened to the clapping. Intermission. He was lolling on a bench outside the grandstand, listening to the show with Barney Lovell. Barney was his new best friend. The man had shown up with the money, paid the fine for both of them. Walt had felt like celebrating, so they'd had a beer or two, then visited a cat house west of Dwaynesville, had some food, more beer—and suddenly the sun was going down and here they were.

Walt got up. "Want to stretch your legs?"

"I don't mind if I do."

He heaved himself up from the bench and belched. They weren't drunk, either of them. They were buzzed, no sense denying that: but shit-faced? Nowhere near it. They started ambling up the walk when four, five high-school kids brushed past them, moving past.

"Watch where you're going," Barney grumbled.

Walter took a second look at them. "Hey, Marv." The kids stopped. Marvin turned. "Say, how you doin', boy?"

Marv told them.

Barney's eyes went dark. "You're lyin'. Not my little girl."

They moved out toward the Midway, all of them.

By then the girls were on again. Pauline had twirled her gifts around, to everyone's delight, and Lucy was about to finish. Skipper's turn was next.

She turned to Laurel with a grin. "Come here."

"What's up?"

"I was just wondering, you remember Cartersburg?"

Laurel laughed, "Hell yes," then did a double take. "What are you thinking?"

"What you're thinking. How about it?"

"Screw it," Laurel said. "Why not?"

Lucy came bouncing through the curtain; every time got better.

"'Scuse us," Skipper said. The two girls went out, hand in

hand. The music started. Whistles, cheers. Then everything went quiet, not a sound except the tape.

"What's going on?"

The three girls in the van moved to the curtain, parted it, peered through. "Wow," Lucy whispered. "Holy shit."

Skipper and Laurel stood pressed together, face-to-face. Their hips moving in and out—and they were kissing. Mouths wide open. Tonguing, you could see their tongues. And then, in perfect unison, they stepped apart and, moving to the music, took their panties off.

"It's pussy time, boys." Laurel spread her legs and started rubbing.

Skipper moved out toward the crowd, crouched down, and spread her knees apart. "Hot pussy. Get it while it's hot."

The crowd was still stunned, watching wide-eyed. Lucy came to life. If they could do it, she could do it. Annie grabbed her as she took her panties off. "Leggo of me, I'm going on."

Lucy went on. She'd give them something to remember. She was wet already. In her middle finger went. Just glided in. She thought of Marvin doing it and closed her eyes.

The roof came off. The crowd surged forward, shoving, shouting, struggling toward the stage.

Ozzie stood watching from the back, mouth open, penis on the rise. Tom blew his whistle, turned, and shook him. "There's a fucking riot here. Get on the walkie-talkie."

"Right."

Tom started bulling forward, nightstick in his hand. "Show's over, clear out, let's get moving."

Talker was already running toward the tent. He shot by Norma, who was moving toward the entrance, went on in. The fucking girls were working strong, he damn well should have seen it coming. Men were fighting for a chance to get at Skipper. Laurel had her shoes off, one in each hand, using high heels like a set of dildos. Lucy looked like she was coming.

Talker flew. Back out the entrance, up across the bally stage, into the van, then through the curtains out on stage. He got his hands on Lucy first, spun her around, and shoved her toward the van. Then Laurel. "Get off! You give me shit, I'll knock you flat!"

She laughed and tossed her shoes out to the crowd.

He grabbed her, shook her hard. "You *hear* me?"

Skipper next. She had three guys all over her. She'd gone too far; the place was crazed. He kicked one in the face. The others backed off when he screamed. Skipper looked scared for once. He took her shoulders, raised her up and dragged her to the van. The girls were standing in a clump. They looked scared. They had reason to. Inside the tent, it sounded like a free-for-all. He had to yell above the noise. "You're getting out of here! And fast! You hear me?"

Lucy started toward the bally stage.

"Not in the raw, for Jesus' sake!" He grabbed a robe and threw it at her. "All of you! Get something on!"

He darted to the curtains, took a look outside. The crowd around the bally stage was milling, like the mob inside. The fucking thing was like a fever, catching. In the distance, cops were coming on the run. He had to get the girls out somehow. It was going to be a bitch.

He turned. The girls were covered now, with robes and shifts. "Come here." They grouped around him. "Listen. It's a mess. We're going to make a run for it. Stay close to me, whatever happens. Got that? Once we're in the clear, we tear ass for the lot, you get in Laurel's car and go. O.K.?" They nodded. "Here goes nothing."

Talker turned, plunged through the curtain, tore across the bally stage and jumped down, right into the crowd. He heard the girls behind him. He could only hope to hell they kept close. "Move it!" Talker yelled. He bent his legs and hunched his shoulders, like a fullback. Knees high, pumping hard, he charged. A lot of people fell away. He took some shoves and punches, mostly on his back and shoulders. "Are you there?" He screamed; he couldn't turn to look.

He broke through to the road. It didn't take forever; it just seemed that way. There was a mob here, too; just not as dense. He stopped, looked back. He'd cleared a path. It closed up fast. The girls were coming, moving through it. Three, four, five; he had them all. Their robes were torn, but what the hell, they looked to be in one piece.

"This way." Talker turned, tried moving up the road. It was like salmon swimming upstream; not impossible, just damn hard. There were people pouring in from all sides. Nothing like a good old-fashioned riot to attract a crowd. He veered off toward the edge. The thing to do was leave the road and move along the boundary fence.

He was about to when a great voice bellowed, "You!" Just one word, filled with rage. He looked up. Just ahead were Lucy's boyfriend, old man Lovell, several teenage kids, and one enormous giant of a man. The giant pointed at him and let out another bellow. "You, there!"

"Me?" He knew a fight was on its way. Who was this mastodon?

"Are you the prick who kicked my kid?"

"Gee, I don't know." He gave a nod toward Lucy's boy. "If that's your kid, then I'm your prick."

He saw the punch a mile away. No problem, easy apple pie. He feinted with a left, way high, just to attract the man's attention. Then he pivoted and threw a right hand to the gut. It sank in halfway to the elbow.

All the air went out of Walt. He would have fallen on his face, except for all the people passing by.

"I've got more," Talker told him. "Do you want it?"

All Walt could do was gasp and glare. He couldn't speak. And Marv had seen it. Taken out with one blow; first last night by the old whore who ran the show, and now by this guy. It was too much. Someone had to pay for it. He turned and let himself be carried by the crowd.

"Kid." Talker turned to Marvin. "She's your girl, it's your life. I don't give a shit, you work it out."

He was about to go when Barney came to life. Till then, all he could do was stare at Lucy. He was breathless, bubbles of saliva flecked his lips. He choked the words out. "Lucy Lovell."

She had seen his face this way before. It was like you could see the hate; those bubbles were a part of it. She straightened up. "That's me."

"Are you a whore?"

"What's it to you?"

"Your mother was a whore. It's in the blood. One slut begets another. Filth breeds filth."

"I'll kill him," Marvin muttered.

Lucy heard him. "No, you won't. You'd go to jail, he isn't worth it."

Barney stumbled closer to her. He was trembling. "Slime and filth, scum of the earth."

"Takes one to know one." Lucy drew her lips back, bared her teeth. "You're always drooling after me. I see you. Have yourself a look." She threw the bathrobe open wide.

He started making choking noises. He was reaching for her throat when Marvin grabbed him. "You don't want to do that, Mr. Lovell."

"Touch me and you'll fry in hell."

"You've got yourself a deal."

"Don't do it, Marv."

Her warning came too late. Blood flowed from her father's nose. She threw herself into Marvin's arms. "Oh God . . ." He'd only made things worse.

"Don't cry, Luce; you know I love you."

"That and twenty cents buys bubble gum." Her father's hand was on her shoulder. All the fight went out of her. "I'll see you, Marv." She drew the bathrobe tight around herself.

They stood there—Talker and his girls and Marvin and his buddies—watching Lucy and her father move away. Poor dumb girl, Talker thought; the way some people screw their lives up. Then it struck him; he should talk.

He turned to Marvin. "Sorry, kid."

"You're sorry?" Marvin kept his voice firm. "Thanks a bunch."

"Here." Talker found a twenty in his pocket. "Go get drunk."

"Aw, go to hell."

The crowd still streamed by on the road. "Well, ladies . . ." Talker turned. He found a path between the concession stands and led them to the boundary fence. "From here, it's clear and easy. You just follow it along until you hit the parking lot." He glanced at Laurel. "Can you drive?"

"I'm fine."

"I've got to go find Norma and take care of things. I'll see you later at the lake."

Skipper looked up. "Talker, thanks."

"That was some fucking stunt you pulled. Get moving."

Off they went in single file. They'd be all right. He turned and started moving fast along the fence. There'd be a mess when he got back. If anyone got seriously hurt, he'd have some tall explaining; Tom and Ozzie knew what happened. He imagined Sheriff Weller . . .

Voices up ahead were shouting. Talker stopped and listened. "Fire!" They were shouting, "Fire." For an instant, it was funny. One kick in the nuts too many. Then he started running.

29

NORMA WAS THE first to spot it. Actually, she smelled the smoke before she saw the flames.

When the trouble started, she had followed Talker to the tent. They both took one look at the stage and moved out fast. He moved out faster. By the time she was outside again, she saw him tearing to the van. She knew what he was doing; going for the girls. He'd get them out, she'd just be in the way; and someone had to hang around. Mobs liked destroying property, they tore things up, and no one, no siree, was going to lay hands on her show and get away with it. Not if she could help it.

So, cash box in her arms—she took it when she left the booth, it always went where she went—she had struggled through the crowd and made it to her tree stump. One big step and she was up there, like a sentinel in a sentry box.

Below her, it was chaos. Men and boys were streaming from the tent—those two cops knew their job. The mob outside was surging back and forth, and when the groups collided, things got out of hand. What did they have to fight about? She'd never understand it. Talker called it "crowd psychology." A lot of good it did to name it. Everywhere she looked, it was a donnybrook; men yelling, swearing, pushing, punching.

And the crowd kept getting heavier, a mass of people streaming up the road. What were they coming for, what drew them? There were more cops on the way. She counted four or five. They'd need a whole platoon to clear this mess away.

And then she smelled the smoke. She looked around. It could be anything; grease catching fire at a food stand, or a match dropped in the cornfields where the kids were screwing; it was dry as tinder out there. Then she saw it; little tongues of fire licking at the grass along the tent and starting up one side. She spotted Ozzie in the crowd. She waved her arms and yelled his name. He heard her, shoved his way along.

"Hey, Norma—"

"We got fire."

"Where?"

"Get up here."

Ozzie hopped up on the stump. She pointed. "Christ," he said, reached for his walkie-talkie.

"Is the tent clear?"

"What?"

She had to shout above the noise. "Is anyone still in the tent?"

"We got 'em out." He raised the walkie-talkie. "Come in, come in, pick it up, for Jesus' sake." He waited. "Sheriff? Ozzie. There's a fire up here on the Midway. Got that?" Ozzie nodded. "Right. We'll do our damndest."

"What's he say?"

"What I need is a fucking bullhorn." Ozzie blew his whistle, started shouting, jumped down off the stump, and started shoving people toward the road.

Talker saw the smoke, faint trails of it. It had to be his show; it couldn't be the Bingo tent, they had God on their side. He dug in, running full out, saw the flames as he came near the Moulin Rouge. The fire started at the back. The flames were shoulder high here, lower as he tore along. He pulled up when he hit the crowd. The cops were struggling, pushing everybody back. He spotted Norma, circled round the mob, made good time.

"Norma—"

"Oh, thank God."

"I got the girls out. They're O.K."

"It's going, Talker. Up in smoke."

"I hate like hell to see it go."

She knew he meant it; it was part of his life, too. "Kiss it good-bye."

He had the taste of bile in his mouth. Five days in Fulton, and more shit had come their way. It felt like something snapped inside. The show was more than just an old truck and some canvas. He was God damned if he'd lose it all. "Wait here."

"Where are you going?"

Crazy, probably; he'd analyze it when he had the time. He flung himself into the crowd. A lot of them were moving back now on their own. The whole world loves to watch a fire, but it's no fun getting burned. The ground around the bally stage was clear. He leaped up, bolted through the curtain. There was smoke inside the van. He kept low, moved out on the stage.

It was a picture. Up above him, everything was orange. The tent was still intact. Flames crept across the canvas, like the ceiling of a planetarium on fire. It was hot. Damned hot. He had to find the pegs. He moved along the back edge of the stage, where it connected to the van. His eyes were streaming, it was hard to see them, but he'd put the fuckers in for twelve years, he knew damn well where they were. Four, five, six. There were ten in all. The smoke was thicker, he was coughing. Seven, eight, nine. Chunks of burning canvas started falling. Screw the stage.

He made it back into the van and closed the side door. It was hot. He shook his hands. The van had twenty gallons in its tank. At what degree did gas explode? Did it need contact with a flame, or was high heat enough to do it?

Talker wiped his eyes, moved forward to the cab. He rolled across the seat back, sat up. Did he even have the key? Which pocket, left or right? He found it, jammed it in and turned it hard. The engine wheezed and died. He tried again. This time, it caught, began to cough and fade—and then it held. He listened to that old familiar rumble: it was music.

Talker gunned it tentatively, let it rest, gunned it again. The van was pointed toward the boundary fence. All clear ahead. And all he needed was a real jackrabbit start. He had to get the van free, shake the tent loose, and the bally stage. If he dragged them along . . .

He slipped the clutch and shifted into first. Too much gas and he'd kill the engine dead. Too little, he'd go up in smoke. He rarely prayed. He didn't now. The Fates were with him or against him.

Vroom.

The van shot forward like a rocket, tore right through the boundary fence. He stopped it in the cornfield, leaned back, closed his eyes. He wasn't in the clear, not yet; not if he'd dragged the tent along. He fumbled for the handle, got it, all but fell out of the cab. He held on to the fender, turned, looked back. One whole side of the van looked black, some paint had bubbled from the heat. But he had left the fire behind, he'd done it.

Standing made no sense. Besides, the ground was tilting on him. It came up to meet him. Talker lay there, closed his eyes. He'd left the motor running. In the distance, he heard sirens. They were coming closer. Fire engines? Did he care? The sound of them grew fainter. Talker let it drift away.

"Are you all right?"

It was a voice he recognized. He'd place it in a minute.

"Talker?"

It was Norma. Kneeling on the ground beside him. "Hi," he said. She looked like death warmed over. "I'm O.K."

"You're sure about that?"

Parts of him felt sore, his lungs still ached, his vision could be clearer. "Sure enough."

She heaved a sigh. "You know, I've seen a lot of smart things in my time, but you just won the Einstein Prize. What did you do it for?"

"I had an impulse."

"Don't get smart with me." She nodded toward the van. "The damn thing wasn't worth it."

"I know that. You think I'm stupid?"

"You're a fool."

"What else is new?" He sat up. He'd felt better, he'd felt worse. "How long have I been out here?"

"For a while."

"What's left?"

There wasn't much. A field of ashes where the tent fell in, charred timbers where the stages used to be. Pale smoke hung in the air. There were two fire engines on the road. And people, kept back at a distance by a line of cops. What were they watching for? There wasn't anything to see. The painted flats were gone, too; all those gaudy dancing girls were dust. Or mud, to be exact about it. There was water everywhere, the ground was soaked.

Talker shuffled through the muck, hands in his pockets. Norma stood by watching. She was dry-eyed. She was tough.

"Hello, son."

Talker turned. "How's it going, Sheriff?"

"Strictly so-so."

"I know what you mean." He held his wrists out, close together.

"What's that for?"

"You're going to cuff me, aren't you?"

"Son, it's God damn tempting, let me tell you. Bob and Ozzie filled me in. I give you one last night, you pull a piece of shit like this on me."

"I lost control. O.K.? I couldn't keep the girls in line."

"You swore to me you could."

"I did my damndest." Talker shrugged. "There was no way; and you can take that as the truth or lock me up."

Weller rubbed his forehead. "Son, I told you when you came: not in my town. What you do in other places, I don't like it, I don't think it's right, but—"

"Sheriff, if you want to say we caused the riot, you're entitled. But we didn't torch our own show. You're not hanging that on us?"

"I wish I could."

"You know who started it?"

"No rain for weeks, it could have been a cigarette. I'll never know."

"Was anybody hurt?"

"That's where you're lucky. Black eyes, broken noses, busted teeth." He shrugged. "They did it to themselves. So far as I'm concerned, they had it coming."

"That's damn fair of you."

"Don't stroke me, son. I'm beat down to the ground, that's all. Now here's what you can do for me."

"It's yours, just name it."

"I want your women out of my life and out of my county. That's not much to ask, now is it?"

"It's a little late tonight."

"I'll settle for tomorrow morning." Weller moved to go. "And get that van the hell out, too."

"Can I say something, Sheriff?"

"No."

"It's complimentary."

"Keep it to yourself." He walked away.

The three of them were sitting in the blue light by the pool. It had been a desultory evening. Van had tickets for the concert, but it wasn't worth the effort. There had been no dinner, not to speak of; after which they drifted off their separate ways, then came together, drifted off again.

They sat there now, not saying much, avoiding what they felt. Tomorrow would be on them soon enough. The screen door closed. They looked up. It was Betsy.

"Well, young lady," Van said, "do you know what time it is?"

"Eleven-thirty."

"Isn't that a little late?"

"I know, but—"

"Let it go, Van." Marcie sighed. "Just let her go to bed."

"There was a fire at the Fair, that's why I'm late. We went to watch it." Betsy sounded calm about it.

"You and Denny?"

"Yes, Mom. On the Midway." They had seen the fire engines and gone racing after them.

"Was anybody hurt?"

"No, I don't think so, but the show burned down." She said it now so easily, but she'd been frantic at the time. She'd raced around searching for Annie, looking everywhere. Then some policeman told her everyone was safe.

"What show, dear?"

"With the dancing girls." She knew she'd seen the last of Annie. No good-byes.

Dee put her hand on Marcie's arm and dug in with her fingernails.

"Oh, that show." Marcie glanced at Dee. Her mind was racing, what to say or not to say? When Dad saw Van, would

he bring up McBride? If she said nothing now, would Van
think—

Betsy saved her. "'Night, all."

"Where's my good-night kiss?" Van asked her.

Betsy blew it to him.

Ed moved out of the bathroom, switched the air conditioner to low, and turned to Harriet. "Nice evening."

She was in her nightgown, sitting on the bed. "It really
was." She smiled. "We needed it."

"I ought to take you out on dates more often." He'd enjoyed it, too. She was an interesting woman. She could talk his
ear off, drive him crazy, but she never bored him. He sat
down beside her. "We should spend more time alone."

"I think so, too."

"I like it when you flirt with me."

"Ed Steuben, I am many things, but not a flirt."

He grinned and reached for her. The phone rang. "Hell.
I'll get it." It was on her bedside table. Making sure he rubbed
against her on the way, he picked it up.

"Yup?"

"Ed, it's Harv. I hope I didn't wake you up. I just got a
call from Weller, and I thought you ought to know. We had a
fire at the Fair tonight. No casualties, but—"

"What got burned?"

"The girlie show."

Ed's pulse went up. "No kidding. How'd it happen?"

"God knows, Weller doesn't. Anyway, for what it's
worth . . ."

Ed kept things businesslike. "You think we're liable for
anything?"

"I doubt it."

"We should check it out. Harv, thanks for calling." There
she went, his Harem Girl. A memory now. It struck him how
entangled he had gotten with that show. A glory day on Pussy
Point, McBride; and Marcie knew him, too. Paths had a way of
crossing.

He hung up, glanced at Harriet. "You know, it's funny.
Just this afternoon, the fellow I was mentioning . . ."

"What fellow?"

"With the car."

"Ed, all you think about is cars."

"Not all the time." He turned the light out, lay beside her.

Marvin paced around his bedroom, fists clenched. Was there anything that wasn't all fucked up? He'd laid one on the old man's nose. It felt great when it landed, but he'd made an enemy for life. He stopped and kicked the wall.

Who cared about the old man? Small potatoes. It was Lucy who was killing him. It wasn't enough she'd flashed her tits. The whole show had gone up in smoke. So much for leaving home and starting up a new life. But what really cut him up was some creep who had seen the last show told him all about her finger. Marvin told the jackoff he was lying, but he knew it to be true. She'd done it. Any girl who flashed her father . . .

Marvin leaned his forehead on the wall and closed his eyes. His Lucy. Maybe carrying his child. Nine months from being someone's mother. God, how could she do these things? Expose herself, get off in public. And he loved her anyway.

Downstairs, a door slammed. Dad was home. Sometimes he wished the two of them could talk. Not just about the farm or slicing off a piece. Real talk. A mother was fine for certain things; they hugged and kissed and made it well. But for the shit that he was in, what Marvin needed was a father. And he didn't have the one he needed.

Barney marched his daughter to her bedroom. He was seething. On the way to get the car, some people pointed at her, jeering, shouting what they'd seen her do. Barney believed them. Lucy was as great a whore as—he went racing through the Bible, couldn't find a whore that low.

They stopped outside her door. "Get in there."

"Yes, sir." She had never seen her dad like this. It scared her. She was used to screams and insults, and she prayed God that was all she'd get. She heard the door close.

"Look at me."

"Yes, sir."

"Don't call me that, you piece of sin. Yes, Father."

Lucy got it out. "Yes, Father." There was dried blood on his nostrils, and his nose was swollen.

"Take that robe off."

"What?"

"You heard me. Take it off."

This was a first. How far out was he? "No."

"I'll tear it off you if I've got to."

Lucy turned her back to him. She had the belt tied with a bow. Untying it might be the hardest thing she'd ever done. She got it loose. The robe hung open. That was it, as far as she was going. Barney grabbed her shoulders from behind. He tore the robe away. She heard him breathing, but he didn't speak.

He stood there glaring at her back, her buns, the crack between them, and those legs of hers. She was too beautiful. The Lord had marked her for perdition. Slowly—he felt calm now, in no rush—he took his belt off, doubled it, and moved it up and down to get the feel. Then Barney set himself, feet planted firmly, well apart.

"Are you listening to me clear?"

"Yes, Father."

"Say what I say. 'God forgive me.'"

"God forgive me."

Barney raised the belt as high as he could reach and brought it down.

She gasped and cried out as the pain shot through her. More was coming. She was going to get a beating; every year or two, she got one.

Barney cleared his throat. "'Forgive me for my sins.'"

"Yes, Father." Lucy braced herself. She wasn't going to scream again. No matter how it hurt. She'd die before he got that out of her. "Forgive me for my sins."

The belt whipped down. "'And rescue me from hell.'"

"And rescue me—"

He didn't wait. The belt came down. Again, more times than she could count. Across her back, her thighs, her bottom. Lucy bit her lips until they bled; no screams. She kept on standing till she couldn't. Then she toppled forward, face-down on the floor.

She waited for another blow. It didn't come. She lay there gasping. Silence in the room. She heard him breathing. Heavy breathing. Then she felt it. Something warm and wet, like porridge, just a drop, had splattered on her back. More drops came down.

She turned, looked up. He stood above her, straddling her, his belt in one hand and his sausage in the other. Jism kept on spurting out of it. She screamed. She couldn't help it now. The screams kept coming. Even when she heard him leave and close the door, she couldn't stop. Her stomach churned and tightened. Was she going to vomit? Lucy didn't care.

30

TALKER WAS A firm believer in a good night's sleep. Things had a way of looking better in the morning. Given last night's capper, they would have to.

It had been almost two when he had reached the lake with Norma and the van to find the girls and Lovell outside screaming at each other in the moonlight.

"Christ almighty, what now?" Talker cut the engine, hopped down, started over. The girls were in their scanties, Lovell must have dragged them out of bed. The man was at full throttle, both arms waving up and down like semaphores.

"Out, out! I want you out of here!"

The man's eyes were demented. Talker chose his words with care. "Is there a difficulty, Mr. Lovell?"

"Out! I want you off my property."

"We're leaving in the morning. All of us have had a hard night, sir, and I appreciate—"

"I ought to throw your filthy ass in jail."

"Now, Mr. Lovell—"

"You seduced my child, corrupted her. You made her do the thing she did."

"Just hold your horses." It was Norma. "Lucy came to me and begged for work. She told me what her life was like around this place."

"She lied."

"And no one made her do a thing."

"I know my daughter, I'm her father. Give me shit, I'll call the Sheriff."

"I've already spoken to him." Talker sounded calm and firm. "The man knows everything that happened, and he's given us till morning to clear out. You want to wake him up and verify that, you go right ahead."

It didn't stop there, but eventually Barney backed away. He cursed them and went stumbling to his house.

"You know what I think?" Norma sounded thoughtful. "Death is too good for guys like that."

"Forget about him," Talker said. "Let's hit the sack. We'll need it if we're clearing out at dawn."

The sun was up and they were going to make it. Talker took his bags out to the loaner, stowed them in the trunk. He had already carted Norma's and Pauline's things to the van. Pauline was driving south with her as far as Spartanburg; she had some family there. The other girls were moving out with bags and boxes, stuffing them in Laurel's car. Skipper and Annie had decided to go east with her; to where and what he did not know.

Norma was in her cabin at the table, counting out the wages, so much for each girl. She put the bills in Ziploc bags, stood up and looked around. Was there a single thing about this place she wasn't glad to leave? She picked up the money and went outside.

The girls and Talker stood around, not saying much of anything. In other years, she always gave a party when the season ended; food and drink and lots of laughs and 'See you when the summer comes.' There would be other summers, sure; but would there be another show?

"Well, boys and girls . . ." She smiled and handed out the bags. It was a silent ceremony.

Annie took the money, stuffed it in her bag along with the few things she'd come with; jeans and T-shirts, underwear, her Journal and her *Almanac*. The only new thing was the brass bed. It was time to say good-bye to Talker. Scenes of parting had been playing in her head for hours. All of them were true, they came from what she felt: rage, envy, disappointment, sadness, fear—she didn't know where she was going now—and love. He'd never kissed her, and she longed to hold him in her arms and feel his lips. Just once.

She almost threw herself at him. Why not? She wanted something for her memory book. He was the best man in the world; at least the best she'd ever meet. But when the moment came, she simply held her hand out, gave the firmest hand-shake she knew how, and looked him dead-straight in the eye. "I won't forget you." That was all she said. No tremor in her voice, no sign of anything she felt. He said, "So long," or something equally inspired. She turned and slipped into the back of Laurel's car and didn't look at him again.

He watched her go, and for an instant wondered if he'd miss her. Doubtful. Annie might remember him, but in a week her face would fade, and by the fall he'd have to strain to find her name. Had it been Sarah, Sally—he had known a lot of Sallys.

He had the other girls to deal with. Something rough for Skipper: "Keep your buns warm." "Just for you," she said, and kissed him. Something erudite for Laurel: "Have a nice ma-triculation." And for Pauline, something dumb: "Take care." "I will, I will, I will, and you, too, Talker."

Laurel came down on the car horn, loud enough to wake the dead, gave the Lovell house the finger, drove off spinning gravel, kicking up the dust.

He looked at Norma. "Good kids."

"Good kids grow on trees. Come on." She moved on quickly to the van. She'd store the thing in Tallahassee, the way she always did. They'd put it up on blocks for her. But would she ever have them take it down? She had the winter months to figure that one out.

She stopped beside the cab and looked at Talker. "You're some dope," she said.

"Could be."

"They'll hang you from the highest tree in Fulton County."

"It's one way to go."

"I know of better ones." She got the cab door open, climbed in, sat, looked down at him. "You know my number."

"And your street address."

"Don't come. Just call me."

Talker had to grin. "Collect?"

She slammed the door. She loved him like the son she'd never had. "Just watch your ass," was all she said.

                              *   *   *

Marcie was in the kitchen, drinking bitter herbs. She was alone; no Mrs. B. today. She'd taken sleeping pills at three, and by the time she came down, everyone was somewhere else. She found a one-word note from Dee. In big black letters: MOTHER. Bets was gone, as usual; out at the Fair again with Denny, she supposed. You'd think the two of them had nothing better in their lives than watching Ferris wheels go round. And Van, of course, was nowhere to be seen. How did that song go? "Mr. Cellophane." You could look right through him, walk right by him and never know he was there. Or something.

Why she couldn't sleep was Talker. Come this afternoon, she had him on her hands. She'd made that date to meet him at the Lodge. What would she say to him? Was that the right verb? Would, could, should. She knew the answer to the last one. What she should say was good-bye. She tried imagining the scene. It kept ending with their clothes off. Why, of all the Seven Deadly Sins, why was hers Lust? Why couldn't it be Gluttony? Or better, Greed. Greed had an upside, it was socially acceptable. Dad's poker crowd was filled with Greed; they gobbled it for breakfast and excreted it at night, and everyone looked up to them.

She put her elbows on the kitchen table, let her head rest on her hands. It was becoming her characteristic position. If Rodin were alive, he'd sculpt her—

"Hello, honey."

Marcie jumped. "Oh God, you startled me."

"I'm sorry." Ed moved in. "I rang."

"I didn't hear, I guess. You want some coffee? It's revolting."

"So's your mother's. Van around?"

"Uh-uh."

"You know where I can find him?"

Marcie shrugged. "The man's a mystery to me."

"I don't know why." Ed had him figured inside out.

"You try living with him."

"Count your blessings, I've got Harriet." He pulled up a chair, sat beside her. "Listen, baby—"

"If it's going to be a lecture, I may throw up."

"What's the matter?"

"Nothing much. You ever feel like everybody wants a piece of you?"

"Sure, all the time. I'm popular. What kind of trouble are you in?"

"You mean how deep?" She raised a hand above her head.

He nodded. "What can Daddy do to help?"

"I'm not a child," Marcie snapped. "Daddy can keep his trap shut."

"Pay attention." Ed leaned close. "There isn't much I wouldn't do on your account." He took her hand. "In fact, if I could get away with it, I think I'd kill for you." He'd gone a little far. He eased up, grinned. "You have a list?"

She shook her head.

He kissed her cheek. "It's loose talk, but you know the way I feel."

"I know."

He looked into her eyes. They were like Harriet's, but softer and more beautiful. He slapped the table with his hand. "Enough said, honeylamb." He stood up. "See you at the dance tonight."

"Oh God. The dance." She made a face. "Somehow, it slipped my mind."

He turned to go. "You may not recognize me. I'll be in a tux."

She smiled. You had to give him "A" for effort. He was with her all the way, but he was bulling in her china shop. A sigh came out of her. The dance was all she needed; making nicey-nice with Van in public while they danced on quicksand.

She stood up and wandered to the percolator for another cup of hemlock. It was her life, and what was she doing with it? Letting other people run it. Dad and Mom and Van and Talker, they were playing tennis doubles, using Marcie for the ball. They served her up, they stroked her, knocked her out of bounds.

Her cup was running over. Marcie put it on the counter. "Dammitall." The stuff was hot. She turned the tap on, put her fingers in the cold—and then it came to her. The single thing she had to do. The one and only course of action.

Marcie rushed upstairs, threw on some clothes, dashed to her desk, and scrawled a note. She jammed it in an envelope, went flying out the front door, racing to her car. She gunned it, backed it out the drive, and sped away.

Lucy woke up with a start. She'd slept where she had fallen; facedown on the carpet. Sleep was long in coming; there was so much pain. She'd been awake to hear her father screaming at the girls. She couldn't catch the words; she didn't really try. He never stopped. She hated him.

She didn't know what time it was. The sun was way up, shining on the carpet, and she couldn't stay like this forever. It was tempting, but she had to move. There was a table near her. Good idea. She reached for it. Sharp pains shot through her everywhere. She bit her lip—she'd cried enough, no more of that. She grabbed the tabletop with both hands, made it to her knees. She had to keep on; falling down was worse than standing up. The day would come when she'd get even; tear his heart out, kill him, anything.

She made it to her feet. How badly had he hurt her? Were there cuts, would she be scarred forever? What would happen to her future? Norma and the girls, they were her future.

Lucy inched her way across the room. The sun was in her eyes, she had to squint. She saw the cabins just across the yard. Their doors hung open. Laurel's car was gone. The van was gone. All gone, all gone away, and she was left here with her father and her baby.

Lucy held on to the windowsill. It wasn't fair. Maybe she had gone too far last night. That made her foolish, naughty, even bad. Not wicked, though. She wasn't what her father said. She couldn't stay here. "Marvin." Lucy nodded. Marvin was the answer after all. She'd call him and he'd come and get her. All she had to do was leave the bedroom, make it downstairs to the phone—

The door was locked. She pounded on it with her fists, then stopped. The noise would bring her father back. He'd come. What would he bring this time? A whip and chains? He had them in the toolshed; old horsewhips and tire chains. He wouldn't really do that, would he? Was she going crazy?

Lucy pulled herself together. In a day or two, when she felt better, she'd escape. Tie bed sheets, make a rope, go out the window in the middle of the night. And never come back to this place.

How badly was she hurt? She craned her neck, but couldn't see. The bathroom had a mirror. Lucy moved in, braced herself. Her front looked fine. She had to turn. She didn't want to, but she did it. There were welts all over, like red ropes. And sticky spots of foulness where his stuff had dried.

She opened the medicine cabinet. There had to be some cream, Noxzema, something good for what she had. Her eyes fell on her razor and the pack of blades. She took a blade, unwrapped it. It was blue, except along the edges, where it shined. She moved it to her wrist, just lightly touched it to her skin. It was a possible solution. People said it didn't hurt too much. All you did was fill the tub with nice warm water and lie back until you fell asleep.

She thought about it for a long time. It was worth considering.

Talker had to have a room in town. It wasn't easy, but he found one. At the Robert Fulton, on the little park that faced the County Seat. The place was old and full of atmosphere; high ceilings, creaky floors. They had a single in the back, but he was lucky finding anything. He took it for a week.

They didn't seem to have a baggage trolley, and it took the bellboy two trips to get all his things upstairs. He traveled the way turtles did; his home was on his back. Two duffels and four battered leather cases; he had won them in a dice game, they held everything he owned.

He did his living out of two of them; the rest stayed packed for months on end. But he had time to kill, and putting things away beat thinking.

He found things he had forgotten that he owned: a dark gray business suit, a summer tux, a silver cigarette box with some woman's name engraved on top. Felicia. Who had she been? And a batch of neckties from Burdine's and Rich's, Neiman Marcus. Vulgar, most of them, or out-of-date. He dumped the worst offenders on the floor; he'd pitch them later on.

It wasn't helping. All he thought about was Marcie. Everywhere he looked, he saw her face. He checked his watch. The time was crawling. When should he get out there? All she'd said was afternoon. That could mean anything from one to five. It made no sense to drive out now. The house was locked, she had the key, he'd end up sitting on the dock and being lunch for the mosquitoes.

Just one more duffel bag to go. He opened it and spilled the contents on the bed. More junk. Next week he'd throw it all away. By then he would be living in a real home, some place with a permanent address. You needed new things for a new life.

Talker moved across the room and started going through the closet, fingering his things. It mattered how he looked this afternoon. He wanted to be perfect.

"My dear, you're looking so much better."

"How would you know, Harriet? You didn't see me yesterday."

"I asked if I could come—and what I meant was better than I had expected."

"What did you expect?"

There was no pleasing Eleanor. "You scared me half to death, you know. That cry of pain, and then your line went dead."

"Oh, that." Eleanor was sitting in an armchair. She had done her hair and face, and looked nothing like an invalid. "They gave me something for it."

"Morphine?"

"I suppose. I didn't ask."

"I hope you're being careful. Morphine is addictive. Harvey Yaeger's wife got hooked, you know. They had to send her to an institution."

"That was years ago."

"She's never been the same, if you ask me. You'll tell me when it's time to go?"

"You just came in."

"I wouldn't want to tire you." It was a bold-faced lie, of course. She had a luncheon date.

"You're sweet to worry, but I'm going home tomorrow if I have the strength. Dee's at the house now, getting things all ready for me. Isn't she an angel?"

"Absolutely."

"And not only that, I think she's going to stay with me, at least until I'm well again. Where's Marcie, what's she doing?"

Harriet looked blank. With Ed and Van and the Pavilion on her mind, she hadn't made her morning call. First time in years. "Well, you know Marcie." There were endless fibs that she could tell. She was debating which when Dee breezed in.

"Good morning, one and all."

"Oh, darling. You look radiant."

Dee kissed her mother's cheek. It was the perfect word for how she felt. "I'm sorry if I'm late. I've been so busy, haven't had a minute."

Harriet stood up. "Come take my chair, dear. I was leaving anyway." She gave Dee's hand a pat. The day that creature was an angel was the day that pigs got wings. "And take good care of your mother. She's on drugs."

"I am not."

"Eleanor, that's what they all say. I'll come by tomorrow when you're home again."

"Call first, I may be resting."

"Yes, of course, dear."

Dee watched Harriet give Eleanor a big kiss on the cheek, the kind of wet smack you could hear a block away. She waited until Harriet had clattered from the room, then plopped down in the vacant chair and beamed.

"Well, have I had a morning."

Eleanor leaned forward. "Tell me everything."

She asked for it, she'd get it. Right from the beginning. "When you called last night, you left me with a lot to think about. I have to tell you, Mother—"

"You just called me Mother."

"So I did." And not by accident. "I didn't get much sleep. I kept on thinking, all she wants from me is just a few days' time, a little company until she's on her feet again. What kind of daughter would I be if—"

"Are you staying?"

"It's my story, let me tell it."

"I'm in such suspense, that's all. It means so much . . ." Her eyes were brimming.

"Yes, it does. To both of us. So, bright and early, I got dressed, I didn't even take the time to shower, I just drove straight to the house. The girls were still asleep."

"They do that when I'm not at home. You can't get proper help these days." The truth was, Millicent and Rose had worked for her for years now, but complaining never hurt.

"I got them up and told them you were home tomorrow, and I started airing out the house." It had old-lady smell, but Dee left that out and hurried on. "Then I drove to McPherson's, bought out half the flowers in the shop, went back, picked out the vases that you like—"

"You're such an angel."

"I arranged the flowers, every one of them, and put the vases where you'd see them; in your dressing room, your bedroom, in the sitting room upstairs."

"I can't believe my ears."

"There's more. I made your bed. I picked out the sheets, cheerful colors, tucked them tight, no wrinkles, fluffed the pillows. Then I found your slippers and the bed jacket with all the lace, and laid them out."

"Oh, Dee, my precious baby."

"After that, I took a breather, sat down in the bedroom bay, and looked around. The room was almost perfect. There was only one thing wrong."

"My goodness, what could that be?"

"I was in it. Mom, you almost had me. After all, what did a few days mean? I've got the time, there's no job waiting in New York. A few days would turn into weeks. And weeks would—"

"Dee—what are you saying?"

"God, I came so close to falling for it. You're not proud of me. Hell, you don't even like me, and the truth is, Mom, I'm not so hot on you. I'm getting out."

"Oh no, no." Eleanor let out a gasp and clutched her chest.

"You've got your signals mixed, Mom. It's your neck, it's not your heart."

"You're breaking it."

"Come off it. It's not there to break." Dee got up from her chair.

"Please God, don't go."

"Don't worry, I'm a good girl. I'll drop in tonight and say good-bye. And I'll be back in Fulton someday—but it hasn't been eight years by accident."

"Don't leave me, Dee."

"I left you twenty years ago. When Dad went, I went with him." Suddenly, her eyes were full, and she was biting back the tears.

Eleanor was wheezing, struggling to her feet. "Ring for the nurse."

"Hell, I'll do better, Mom. I'll pass the word when I go by."

Dee moved into the corridor and wept.

One of the boys had brought a chair, and Ed was sitting underneath a shade tree by the eighteenth green, a fresh Tom Collins in his hand. He had selected the location with some care. It was important that he stop whatever gossip was circulating at the Club, and there was certain to be some. The diners on the terrace and the drinkers in the Paddlewheel had full views of the green. He wanted witnesses to see the scene he was about to play.

He had been waiting half an hour for Van, and he could make him out now, halfway up the fairway, getting set for his approach. He watched the ball go up, only to lose it in the sun, then saw it drop pin-high a little to the left. Whatever else, the fool could play. He got up, ambled to the green, and waited till Van saw him. Then he waved.

Van waved back. He had been expecting this since yesterday, and he was ready for whatever line of crap Ed handed him. He wasn't nervous in the least. He had examined every gambit, and he had his answers ready. You could push a man around, manipulate him, use him, get away with it for years. But finally, there came a day.

His caddy handed him his putter, dropped the bag, and went to get the flag stick. Ed raised his glass, sent him a smile.

"How's it going?"

Van shrugged. "Fair to middling. I'll be with you in a minute."

"Take your time."

Van did. He checked the putt from all sides, lined the shot up, stroked it firmly. In it went, like it had eyes. Was it an omen? One more par. Four over for the day. Not bad, considering his hand still hurt.

The caddy grinned. "Nice shooting, Mr. V."

Van thanked him, signed his card, and turned to Ed. The ball was in the old man's court. "What's up?"

Ed's eyes were on the green. "Looks like they did a first-class job."

Van nearly asked, 'On what?' Not good; he wasn't being quick enough. He nodded. "When it comes to ground crews, they're the best."

"You'd never know this thing was chewed up just a week ago." He raised his eyes. "It goes to show you. Give things time, they heal right over."

"Some things do."

"And some things don't. I know. It all depends. Look, son—"

"I'm not your son."

Ed sighed. "You're right. My problem is, I tend to think of you that way. I've always wished I had one, but we had to stop when Marcie came. We damn near lost *her* as it was." He shook his head. "Poor Harriet, she went through hell. You take what God gives and say thank you. Right?"

Van wondered where in hell all this was leading to. Ed wasn't one for leaving things to God. He nodded. "I suppose."

Ed looked down at the green again. "You know how much it cost to fix?"

"I've got the figures, but I haven't checked. You want me to? They're in the manager's office, I won't be a minute."

"Fuck the figures. I'm just floundering around. The truth is, Van—" He broke off, looked away. He'd planned to hold this off till later, but the thing was playing well. "The truth is, it's damned hard for me."

"What's hard?"

The perfect question. "I don't like to say I'm sorry, and I like it less to say I'm wrong."

"You've lost me, Ed."

Eye contact was important now. Ed faced him squarely. "All my life, I've made my own decisions, lived the way I wanted to. It's why I'm happy, and it's why you're not. You've never made your choices on your own. That's not a weakness, son. You've never had a chance. I've always been there crowding you, I've shoved them down your throat." He paused to let it sink in. From the look on Van's face, he might need a little time.

"Just what exactly are you saying?"

"It's your life, Van. Sure, I'd love you back with me, I'd give a lot to see that happen. But you have to want that—and you don't. I'm saying, go your own way, find the thing you want to do. And take your time, don't rush yourself." He put an arm around Van's shoulder; it was safe to now. "You want to start up on your own? I'll back you if you want that. Or I'll keep my distance. You don't need my money. Hell, Jack Morgan thinks the world of you, he'll lend you anything you need. And that's without me calling him and asking for a favor. Do you understand me, Van?"

Van's mouth was slightly open. He'd expected anger, threats, bribes—anything but this. The man was backing off completely. "Yes, I understand—and it's damned decent of you."

"None of that. Don't thank me. Hell, the way I've treated you—I should have done this years ago. If you're not happy, what's that do to Marcie?" Time to look away again. "The two of you are all I've got."

"I don't know what to say, Ed."

"Don't say anything." He gave Van's shoulder one last squeeze, then turned and walked away. He felt a little guilty. Van was Silly Putty in a pair of hands like his. But still and all, what he had done was for the best. He took a swallow of his drink and wondered how long Van would take to realize he'd been strung up by his thumbs.

31

"HELLO?"

"It's Marvin, Mr. Lovell."

"If you're calling to apologize—"

"I am, sir. That's for sure. I had no business hitting you. I'm really sorry, and I'd like to talk to Lucy, please."

"She isn't home to you."

"I've got to, sir. There's things I need to say—"

"You're not to talk to her, you're not to see her."

"Listen, Mr. Lovell . . ." Marvin wiped his forehead. He'd expected trouble, and he didn't want to lose his temper. Not again. He'd lost it once, and look what happened.

"I don't want you near my daughter. Ever."

"But, you see, sir, we're in love."

"Your kind of loving got her in that strip show. You knew damn well she was in it. Hell, you even drove her there."

"I know, sir. That was wrong of me. I never should of—"

"You come near my girl again, I'll take a shotgun to you." Barney slammed the phone down. "Little bastard."

Barney stood there till he cooled off. Then he started toward the kitchen. Lucy hadn't eaten; even strumpets had to eat. Some water and a crust of bread, that's what she ought to get. But why should he be cook and bottle washer? Let the girl come down and feed herself.

He started up the stairs. There was one thing about last

night that didn't sit well. Not the beating; that was right and just. The only way to save a sinner was to drive the lessons home. But he had spilled his seed all over her. The sin of Onan. That was wrong. The Catholics had it easy. They could go into those little rooms of theirs, confess it all. Cheap absolution, but it worked for them.

He stood outside her bedroom door. He felt increasingly uncomfortable. He didn't really want to face her. If she brought up what he'd done, he'd shout her down, he had no choice. Besides, he'd have to face her sometime. If not now, tomorrow.

"Lucy?"

No reply. He said it louder. "Lucy, *Lucy?*" Little bitch; she damn well heard him. Being sassy, was she? Begging for another lesson?

Lucy heard him, all right. She'd been waiting for him. She had actually used the razor blade, drawn it across a fingertip to find out if what people said was true. They lied about the pain. It hurt. In fact, it hurt like hell.

She pitched the blade, put on a bandage, stuck a washcloth in some water, wiped off her father's droppings, then got some cream and rubbed the welts that she could reach. It hurt to sit, so she kept moving, feeling better all the time.

"I'm coming in," she heard him say.

"Don't try it." Lucy knew he would. She was prepared. Her bedroom had a standing lamp. She'd taken off the shade, removed the bulb, unscrewed the base, which left her with a steel rod four feet long. She took up her position, set herself.

She saw the door come open, saw her father's face. "You come in here, you piece of shit, I'll tear your fucking head off." Saying which, she swung the rod back like a baseball bat. "You think I'm bluffing? Try me."

Barney closed the door.

"You lock it and I'll bust it open."

Barney turned and went downstairs.

Talker hit the Lodge at one and left a little after two. He'd spent the time with Marcie's note, just sitting on the doorstep, thinking. What exactly did it mean? The envelope was Scotch-taped to the front door. No name on it, but he knew it was for him. By now he had it memorized. "Not com-

ing. Don't know what to do. Can't see you. I need time." No
signature.

He turned onto the county road and headed back toward
town. What was she telling him? What did she really mean to
say? For certain, not good-bye. Would it have mattered if she
had? No way. A lot of girls said 'no-no,' but last time he'd seen
her, there'd been 'yes-yes' in her eyes. Besides, he couldn't
give her up now. Things had gone too far. If Marcie wanted
to be rid of him, she'd have to say it to his face. And that she'd
never do. She loved him.

"I need time." He wished to hell she'd been a little more
explicit. Time for what? To sort her feelings out? He knew
her feelings; so did she. She had her troubles facing them, he
knew that, too—but there was so much he didn't know. How
shaky was her marriage? Were there problems with her family? It could be anything. How much time did she think she
needed? How much should he give her?

That was tricky. Should he wait around for days? If he
did, how could she get a message to him? Maybe it was all a
test; to see how much he cared. The male pursued the female,
that was how the game was played. Was he supposed to ride
upon a white horse, take her in his arms, and gallop off into
the sunset?

"Damn." He didn't know. The note was giving him a
headache, and he missed his car. He even missed the show.
He thought of going to the Midway, taking one last look.
What would he see? A lot of ashes on the ground. The holiday
ahead looked endless, everything shut tight till Tuesday. He'd
go crazy. What was Marcie doing now, this minute?

He pulled up at the Robert Fulton. Go back to his room
and climb the walls? He couldn't face it. Minutes later, there
he was on Pleasant Avenue. Maybe Ed would be there, maybe
Marcie, anyone who knew her, who could talk to him about
her. It was closed, of course. He took the turn and pulled up
by the Service area. There was a man inside. He honked his
horn.

Van turned. He had been agonizing. All he did these days
was agonize. He was a free man, Ed had opened all the doors,
and what was his reaction? He'd come back to take a look, see
how it felt. As if he didn't know by now. He shook his head,
moved to the gate. Some fellow in a loaner.

"Hi, what can I do for you?"

The husband. Talker thanked his lucky stars. "My name's McBride. I left my car here for some work. I'd like to take a look at it. If that's O.K."

Van nodded, worked the combination lock, drew back the gate. The car drove in, the man got out. He looked familiar. "Don't I know you?"

Talker grinned. "You've got a memory for faces. At the Fair. We talked about your cars." They started off toward the garage. "So what's it like to work for Ed?"

"You know him?"

"Just to talk to. He's a character."

"And then some."

"You been with him long?"

"Too long, I think." Van bent and pulled up a garage door. "Which one's yours?"

"The Bird." He looked around and spotted it. "I've met his daughter, too." They moved across the floor together.

"How'd you meet her?"

"At the Fair. She's something. What's she really like?"

Van smiled. "I'm not the one to ask, I'm married to her."

"No. They tell you it's a small world, Mr.—"

"Van. Just call me Van."

"I'm Paul. Don't take me wrong, Van, but I've got to say I envy you. I'm single, but I'd give a lot to have a wife like you do."

"Here's your car."

That meant a lot. No smile and 'Thank you for the compliment.' "How long have you been married?"

"Look, what is all this?"

"I'm sorry, people interest me, I'm always asking questions." Talker shrugged. "Guess I'm alone too much." He turned and focused on the car. The men had done a lot of work. They'd buffed out the scratches. In some spots, they had gone through all the paint right to the body. There were patches of bare metal. Not a pretty sight, but nothing that he couldn't drive.

"I'd like to take her out and bring her back on Tuesday. You know, have her for the weekend."

"Help yourself." Van had had enough of Steuben Motors, and he wasn't that much keener on McBride. No reason why. He watched the man get in his car and back it out, then moved to close the door. McBride was smiling at him out the window.

Talker felt like singing, but he tried to keep it cool. "Nice seeing you again." He waved and zipped away.

Van reached up to get the door. He had the evening to live through, let alone the rest of his life. He grabbed the handle, pulled it hard, and slammed it down.

Dee, in her bikini, all but skipped across the terrace toward the pool. She had done everything she had to do. Packed up her things, phoned Akron-Canton Airport, booked a seat, and called the local taxi for a cab tomorrow morning. She'd have left tonight, except she'd promised Eleanor she'd come to say good-bye.

The house was empty; no one home. She reached back and undid her bra, then stopped dead. There was Marcie, floating facedown in the pool.

"Hey, Steuben."

Marcie looked up, glad to see her. "Come on in, the water's wet."

Dee jumped up, made a big splash coming down. Just like a kid, which was exactly how she felt. She'd graduated, school was out, and she was on her way. She surfaced, paddled over, making waves.

"Well, Miss MacFarlane, what's with you?"

"I did it, Marce."

"Congratulations. Did what?"

"Freed the slaves and cut the cord. I told my mother where to stick it."

"You've done that before."

"Not like I did it this time."

"Did she hear you?"

"Loud and clear." Dee ducked and somersaulted underwater, came up grinning. "Oh God, Marcie, I'm a person. Does it show?"

"Around the edges."

"Give it time. What are you doing here?"

"Relaxing, counting blessings, contemplating suicide; I don't know which."

"At least you're smiling. Aren't you going to the Lodge?"

"I've come and gone."

"Well, that was fast. What happened?"

"Nothing."

"Good. I knew he wouldn't show up. Men like that go in and out. That's all they want."

"You've got that backwards. It's what I want." Marcie's face began to crumple. "Oh my God, Dee. I went early, left a note. I couldn't face him."

"Great. That's really coping."

"Dee, I don't know what to do."

"Well, shaking isn't going to help." Dee put her arms around Marcie. "Listen, dummy. It's an itch, that's all you've got. It goes away."

"It doesn't. It gets worse and worse. I'm so ashamed."

"It happens in the best of families."

"Not like this. Oh Jesus, Dee—"

"Hold on, hold on, I'm right here. Listen—try this on for size. A few weeks in New York. Why don't you come? I'm leaving at the crack of dawn."

"You're leaving me?" She sounded like a child.

"I'm leaving here, Marce; there's a difference. Come along."

"How could I?"

"Easy. Pack a bag and buy a ticket. Give yourself some space."

"What would I say to everybody?"

"Anything, who cares? I'll say it for you."

Marcie closed her eyes and swallowed hard. "You really think I should?"

"I'll tell you this much. If you don't, you'll fall apart, and I don't want to see that. I won't have you breaking into little pieces."

Annie looked around the room. It wasn't much: a bed, a chair, a window, and a dresser painted yellow. It was what fifteen dollars bought you in a rundown boarding house. Plus breakfast. Bed and breakfast. Annie wasn't interested in either one. She couldn't sleep, she couldn't eat. She didn't care. The single thing that mattered was, she was in Fulton. She'd come back. She had to.

Laurel drove like Talker did; not recklessly, just on the edge. She sat alone in back, half listening to Skipper, who was on a high and babbling on about her winter plans. Annie had none. She was not a happy person. She felt lost and lonely and confused, but all these things took second place to anger. She was angry with herself.

She'd always been a fighter. All her life, she'd struggled for whatever came her way. With Aunt Maria and Uncle Emil and their pinhead kids, with school and after-school jobs, friends, a piece of territory in that house, a room that measured six by nine; she'd paced it off enough, she knew. And when the first thing in her life worth fighting for appeared, what did she do? Just shake hands and say, 'Nice knowing you,' or some fool thing, and walk away.

They were a little east of Mansfield, turning onto U.S. 30, when she heard herself say, "Stop the car." She had to say it twice before they heard her.

"What for?" Laurel asked.

"I'm getting out."

The rest was history. She had left the car, her bag in hand, said, "So long" to the girls, and thumbed her way to Fulton, found the boarding house. No way was Talker going to disappear without a battle. She had never really told him how she felt, or even made a play. Oh no. Just Little Orphan Annie pining in a corner, bleeding quietly. To hell with that. She had a lot of plans to work out, not the least of which was finding him. Not knowing what his real name was presented problems. He had left the lake, he had to be in town, there weren't that many places, but she couldn't call and ask for someone nameless.

She was not without resources, there were moves that she could make. She had a good mind. All she had to do was use it.

Annie sat back, closed her eyes, and got her brain to working. You could almost hear the gears engage.

"Hot damn." Ed was standing by the full-length mirror in the bedroom, posing in his silk tuxedo. Harriet, all dressed and ready, sat across the room, still on the phone with Eleanor.

He left the mirror, crossed the room. "Get rid of her, for godsake."

Harriet looked up and mouthed, "I'm trying to." She'd spent the afternoon at the Pavilion, giving orders, closing down. She felt a little frayed. Then, full voice, into the receiver: "Yes, dear, and my heart is breaking for you. It's a tragedy. You've had so many. You're a tragic figure."

Eleanor, tears coursing down her cheeks, sat up in bed. "Oh, Harriet, you are so right. The crosses that I've had to bear . . ."

"I know. I'll think of you all evening, and I'll come by after Church tomorrow."

"Would you, dear?"

"I wouldn't miss it for the world. 'Bye now." She hung up and sighed. "That woman."

"Why in hell you bother with her beats me."

"You're a man. You wouldn't understand." She stood up, started fiddling with her gown.

"Why don't you try me?"

"If you really want to know . . ." She hesitated, trying not to smile. "It's not the least bit nice, Ed. It's like pulling wings off flies."

"Like what?"

"I knew you wouldn't understand. How do I look?"

He told the truth for once. "Just like a movie star."

She felt herself begin to blush. "Which one?"

It was a choice between Claudette Colbert and Myrna Loy. He told her so.

"Can I tell you a secret, Ed?"

"Why not?"

"I'm still in love with you."

He took her in his arms. He felt sensational. He'd solved the family problems, everything would work out, Marcie would be happy, and his wife of forty years still loved him. "You remember our first date?"

She nodded.

"You remember how it ended?"

"Ed, if you pull that on me—"

"Not now, but when the party's over, watch out." He stepped back and slapped her bottom. "Let's get going."

Van was fidgeting. His tux was on, and there was Marcie in her slip, debating what to wear. At least the choice was down to two: a red gown and a blue one.

Marcie turned and held them up in front of her. "Which do you think?"

"They're both terrific."

"You decide."

"The blue."

She frowned. "You're sure the red one isn't better?"

Why ask his opinion if it didn't matter? "I don't care, whichever you feel pretty in."

She felt about as pretty as a toadstool. "Van?" She took the red dress and began to slip it on.

"Uh-huh?"

She hesitated. "I've been thinking—would you mind it if I took off for a little while?"

His heart sank. Was she leaving him? "What do you mean, take off?"

"Dee's leaving in the morning, and she asked me if I'd like to come along."

"What did you tell her?"

"Nothing, yet. I'm asking you."

"For how long?"

"Just a week or two."

It sounded like forever. "You don't like New York. At least I always thought—"

"I need some time alone, that's all."

"How come?"

"No special reason. I just need to get away."

"Away from me, you mean?"

"No—yes. You're part of it."

"That's nice to know."

"Oh, look. It's everything I want to get away from. Mom and Dad and home and Fulton: all of it."

It was the same thing as the dress. "You've made your mind up, haven't you?"

"No. Honestly. I haven't. Would I ask you if I had?"

Damn right she would. And some swell fucking time to pick, with his life in the air. His future. Wasn't she involved? Was it of no concern to her what happened to him—or was all this Dee stuff just a cover? Did she have another man? Was that what this was all about?

"What do you think, Van?"

There was only one thing he could say. "Do what you have to do."

"That's not much help."

"I'll wait downstairs."

She sat down when he left the room. What was he think-

ing? Why be angry? All on earth she meant to do was save
herself. And save a marriage.

The sun was going down. The house was quiet. Mom and
Dad had left for Longview, Aunt Dee had just driven off to
see her mother, Bets and Denny were alone. The two of them
were watching television in the den. Or trying to. It wasn't
easy, not for either of them.

There they were in shorts and T-shirts—they had worn
them to the Fair and hadn't changed—and Denny's eyes kept
shifting, roving up and down her legs. All the way up. Her
skin was golden tan and perfect, and they beat the game show
on the tube. He knew that she was right; they had to wait. For
years. He'd even settled in an armchair, nowhere near the
sofa, not a chance of touching her. But she kept shifting,
stretching out. He looked away.

It was no picnic for her, either. He had such a pretty
body, and she'd never seen it, not the whole thing. He'd seen
hers. It wasn't fair. She caught him looking at her now and
then; it wasn't hard to guess what he was thinking. Waiting
was a lot like Church; no fun, but right.

And then their eyes met. Silence. It was awful.

"Denny?"

"Uh-huh?"

"I've been thinking . . ."

"Thinking what?"

She sat up straight, looked serious. "You know the saying,
'What's sauce for the goose is sauce for the gander'?"

Denny nodded. "Sure."

"You think it's right?"

He shrugged. "I've never thought about it. I suppose so."

"So do I." She knew that she was blushing, but she didn't
care. "I want to look at you."

"*What?*"

"Just the way you looked at me."

"That's crazy."

"No, it's not. It's only fair. You just now said so."

"You want me to take my clothes off?"

Betsy nodded.

"Here and now? In front of you?"

"I did it."

"That was different."

"How?"

"It's different, that's all."

"Tell me why, just one good reason. I won't touch you, nothing's going to happen." Denny looked away. "I think you're scared."

"Weren't you?"

"Sure. And embarrassed, too. It didn't kill me."

Denny felt his member rising. "Come on, Bets, give me a break."

She grinned. "I'll close my eyes. You say when it's O.K. to look." She closed them tight. "I'm waiting. I don't hear you moving."

Denny got up from the armchair. He was sweating. It was wrong, he'd hate himself tomorrow, but he did it. Off the T-shirt came, the shorts, the underwear. He looked down at himself. It stood there like a rock. He cleared his throat.

"O.K.," he said.

Bets opened up her eyes and gasped. Some weeks ago, she'd found a copy of *The Joy of Sex* tucked in a corner book-case, hidden. She had seen drawings of it, but they didn't do it justice.

Betsy swallowed, got up from the sofa, took a step in his direction.

"Hey, come on, what are you doing?"

Betsy felt a little dizzy. "Coming for a closer look. That's all."

She kept her word, stopped a good yard away from him, just staring at it. What a miracle. Fantastic. Boys were lucky, girls had nothing to compare. She went down on her knees.

"What are you doing now?"

"I want to see it from below." It looked enormous; and so pretty. Suddenly, it started twitching. "Denny—?"

"Watch out, Bets."

"What's wrong, what's happening?"

"It's going off." He turned away from her. She watched, mouth hanging open, as small squirts of white stuff started shooting out. They arched up through the air and landed on the armchair. Denny staggered back.

"Are you all right?"

He could have died. The damn thing went off by itself. "I'm sorry, Bets, I couldn't stop it."

"So that's how it works." It was incredible. She got up, careful not to touch him. "Wow."

"Bets—come here." His eyes were on the armchair. There were spots of sperm all over it. "Look, will you look at that?"

"Oh boy." Mom's new upholstery. "We've got to get it off."

"You're telling me?"

"What do you do, just wipe it up?"

He shook his head. "The stuff leaves spots."

"There's got to be a way."

"It washes off of bed sheets."

"That's a help, we'll put the armchair in the Bendix. If the folks come home and find it—soda water." On the bar. They kept some on the bar. She started for it when the phone rang.

Both of them stood stock-still, staring at it. It kept ringing. What to do? The family knew she was at home.

"I'll get it." Betsy picked it up, and in a voice she scarcely recognized, she said, "Hello?"

"Are the Van Burens in?"

"Who's calling, please?" It was a man.

"I'd like to speak to Mrs. Van Buren. Is she there?"

"She's out." She shook her head at Denny, who had gone to get the soda. She knew how to do it.

"You know where I could reach her?"

"At the Club." She hung up, turned to Denny, grabbed the bottle. "Get a towel. A Turkish towel. And fast."

He took off for the powder room. She looked at the chair. Her hands were shaking, but she wasn't sorry. She had seen a prong in action. She'd remember it forever.

Talker slowly put the phone down. Longview Country Club; that's where she was. It was a dumb stunt, calling at her home. Not altogether rational, he knew that, but he longed to hear her voice.

32

THE MANAGEMENT WENT all out. No expense was spared. The Clubhouse was awash with flowers, candles, buckets filled with French champagne. No end of hot or cold hors d'oeuvres were served by Club Staff sporting boutonnieres. The dining room had been transformed. Each year, it had a special theme. Tonight it was New Orleans: Bourbon Street, the Garden District; there were little touches everywhere. The buffet featured crabmeat flown in from the West Coast; lobsters, clams, and oysters from the East; and jumbo shrimp— not frozen, fresh—from Mobile Bay.

Ben Burbidge and His Boys came early. There was dancing on the terrace from six-thirty till whenever. Bits of patriotic bunting had been tastefully arranged around the bandstand, all the tablecloths had white stars on a ground of red and blue. And there were special paper lanterns striped with foil, gold and silver.

The sky was shot with sunset colors, glorious, when Van and Marcie pulled up at the portico. They'd scarcely spoken on the way. She glanced at him. Say what you will, he was a handsome man.

"How do I look?" she asked.

"Terrific."

"Well, here goes."

They put on their party faces, got out, exchanged a bright

word with the valet boys, and went inside. The place was busy, filled with members, faces suntanned from the summer, eyes bright, glasses in their hands.

"I'll see you," Marcie murmured as she headed for the powder room.

Van nodded, wandered toward the terrace. There were hands to shake on all sides, greetings to exchange. He managed well, a smile for everyone and casual remarks, even when he stopped to chat with Jack and Harvey. If they harbored secret thoughts about the blowup at the poker game, it didn't show. Van wondered, did Jack really think the world of him? What would the man say if he asked him for a bank loan? Now was not the time to ask. Besides, Van wasn't ready yet.

He reached the terrace. There were Ed and Harriet, like lovebirds, dancing cheek-to-cheek. He waved to them, turned to a waitress for a drink, and ran smack into Sandy Stone.

"Well, how's it going, Van?"

"Just fine—and if you've got more questions, keep 'em to yourself."

"How come?"

"What is it to you, can't you stop? I said I'm fine. I had a dandy talk with Ed."

"I'm glad to hear that."

"Aren't you going to ask about it?"

"Nope."

"You'd like to, wouldn't you?"

"I'm out, I've said my piece." He smiled. "See you."

"Not so fast." Van grabbed his arm. "I'm sick of your advice."

The man was in deep water. "I don't blame you, Van."

"You got me into this. You know what Ed said?"

"You don't have to tell me. There's no reason to."

"He said he'd back me. Any way I go is fine with him."

"I see."

"That's all? Don't you have anything to say?"

"I'm looking for my wife. She wants to dance."

Van felt like shaking him. "I don't know what to do."

"You can't ask me."

"I don't have anybody else."

"Look, Van, I want to help you. Why not come and see me?"

"Once was plenty, thanks."

"Where's Marcie?"

"Someplace, I don't know."

"Why don't you talk things out with her?"

"I can't."

"That's O.K., it was only a suggestion." Sandy couldn't press it; Van looked too close to the edge. "You know my office number; or drop over to the house." Enough. "Give Marcie a big hug for me, and if you stumble into Alice, tell her where I am."

Van let him go, the man was useless. "Miss?" The waitress stopped. He took a goblet of champagne and went inside to look for Marcie.

She was just outside the powder room with Pam. Pam was a friend, but not a Friend; not Dee. Still, there were things she had to say. "Let's go someplace where we can talk."

Pam grinned. "In this mob? You could holler 'fire' and they wouldn't hear you."

Fire made her think of Talker, Talker made her think of— "This way." Marcie led her toward the Paddlewheel. If it was crowded, there were french doors to the outside. "How've you been?"

"A little lonely in the shop." Pam said it lightly, but it meant a lot. There weren't that many people in the world she cared for.

"Oh God, I don't blame you. Haven't I been awful?" Marcie made a face. "I don't know what's been wrong with me." The Paddlewheel was jammed. They moved across it toward the doors. "I'm sorry, Pam."

"I've missed you, that's all. And I've been a little worried."

"Cash flow? Have I screwed up the accounts?"

"No, that's all fine." Pam hesitated. "Are you all right, Marcie?"

"Me?" Was she transparent? Did it show? She drew a door back, moved outside. "What makes you ask?"

Pam made a little gesture with her hands. "Let's put it this way. There's a lot I miss, I don't like seeing trouble, but when someone wears it like a shroud—"

"Is that what I've been doing?"

There were many things that Pam might mention. Like the country gentleman with the antiques who never rang quite true to her; or what she'd sensed on coming back into the office after lunch the other day; or how she'd felt about the

man who bought the brass bed early in the week; or the anxiety that streamed from Marcie now. She chose the safest
course. "Are things all right at home?"

"You've heard about the poker game?"

"A little."

Marcie saw an opening. She went for it. "I know it's selfish, Pam, but I've been thinking . . ." Marcie's hands were
clasped together, knuckles white.

"Go on."

"Dee asked me if I'd like to spend a few weeks in New
York."

"I see." She looked at Marcie. Things were worse than she
imagined. "Are you going?"

"I don't know. A lot depends on how you feel."

It was the other way around. The question was how Marcie felt. Pam took a flyer. "You don't have to answer this. I've
got no business asking, but . . . are you having an affair?"

"What?" Marcie's heart stopped. "Good God no."

Talker found the lot and parked the car himself. He'd
seen the valets, but he didn't trust the kids; he knew the way
they handled cars like his. He got out, tugged his jacket,
snapped his cuffs, and took a quick look in the sideview mirror. He looked fine. The summer tux was wrinkled, but he'd
steamed it in the shower. The tuxedo shirt was totaled out, he
hadn't worn the thing for years. He found his black bow tie, a
crisp white shirt; you keep your jacket buttoned, no one
knows the difference.

He squared his shoulders, started briskly for the Clubhouse. Brisk assurance was the key. He'd crashed a lot of clubs
far fancier than this one. Even places with Security. If they
had guards inside the entrance, he knew how to handle them.
And if he happened to bump into Ed or Van, and chances
were he would, he was prepared for that. No problem. Everything was cool.

Himself included. Granted, when he called the house, he
felt it wasn't rational. But afterward, the more he thought, the
better sense it made. There was a risk in giving Marcie time.
He wasn't altogether dense; the girl was torn 'twixt love and
duty, as the poets said. He'd seen it with his own eyes, it was
why she ran away from him their last night in the Lodge. In
certain ways, a love affair was like a business deal: not all that

hard to set up, but the trick was closing them. The great successes in this life, and he had met a few, knew how and when to move and close.

Cars were arriving at the portico. He waited, stepped between them, nodded to the valet boys, and strolled inside as if he lived there. Nothing, no Security, it was a breeze. The entrance hall was filled with people. Talker checked them out and felt distinctly unimpressed. This was Ohio, not Miami, what had he expected? O.K., where was Marcie? Everybody had champagne, so Talker got a glass and wandered to the bar.

The place was like a sardine can with paneling. He moved inside, leaned casually against the wall, checked all the faces, took his time. No luck. He shrugged, moved back out to the hallway, paused to get the layout of the place. The dining room was on his left, music drifted from his right. He opted for the music, started strolling. Someone said, "McBride?"

He didn't jump, just turned his head, put on a smile, held out his hand. "It's nice to see you, Van."

Van hesitated, took his hand. "I've got to tell you, I'm surprised. What are you doing here?"

He had expected that one. "Ed invited me. The other day, when we were talking in his office."

"Oh?" It might be true.

"Yeah." Talker didn't like the "Oh"; he laid it on a little thicker. "I was saying I had nothing on all weekend, and he told me to come by if nothing better came along." He grinned. "So here I am. Is Ed around?"

"Last time I saw him, he was on the terrace."

"That way?" Talker pointed toward the music. "I'll go and say hello."

"You do that." What was there about the man he didn't like? What did it matter?

Talker took a step or two, turned back as if on impulse. "Is your missus with you?"

"Somewhere."

"When you see her, say hello for me."

Well done. He strolled on past the people, smiling left and right, to faces that he didn't know. It was amazing what a little friendliness could do; most of them smiled back.

The band was strictly cornball, but the terrace was O.K. The night was clear, the sun was down, a faint glow lingered in the sky. There were a lot of people dancing. Marcie wasn't one of them, but there were cocktail tables all around the edges of the place. He'd have to circle round the dancers, check them all. He stopped a waitress for another glass, stuck one hand in his jacket pocket, started ambling.

Ed was in the Men's room, at the urinal. Beer he could hold for hours, but champagne went through him like a rocket every time, and he'd already had a few. He finished, shook the last drops off, then tucked it in and zipped up. He was moving toward the sinks when Van walked in. Ed wondered if Van knew he had him where the hair was short. He had to find out, it was irresistible.

Ed clapped him on the shoulder. "Good to see you, son. How are you?"

Van kept his composure; Ed knew damn well how he was. "Just fine, thanks."

"Only way to be. You had a chance to think about our little talk?"

Some little talk. He shrugged. "Not much."

"Do like I said, son; take your time. You're forty soon, and that's a turning point in every man's life. Make the wrong move now . . ." Ed slowly shook his head from side to side. "There's no way back."

Van felt like getting even. "I just ran into a friend of yours."

"Who's that?"

"A fellow named McBride. He tells me you invited him."

Ed didn't bat an eye. "That's right."

"What for? You hardly know the man. Besides, you know the rules; no guests on Labor Day."

"I make my own rules. Are you filing a complaint?"

"I'm only saying—"

"Look, I like the guy. You know where I can find him?"

"On the terrace, maybe. He was going to look for you."

Talker stood just gazing at her. She was at a corner table talking to the woman she worked with in her shop. She hadn't seen him yet. Her hair, the way her hands moved when she talked, or how she held her shoulders; was there anything about her less than perfect? When she saw him, what would her reaction be? Surprise, of course. She couldn't say much, not with people watching; but they'd take a long walk in the dark, and everything would happen then.

He moved on to the table, bent, and softly said, "Good evening."

Marcie gasped out loud. Was she hallucinating? Breaking down? He wasn't really there. She turned and looked. She couldn't move, she couldn't speak.

Pam glanced at Marcie, saw it all. The whole thing fell into place. But she would never talk of it, she'd never tell; not even Jerry. She put on a smile, looked at Talker. "Oh. Hello. Nice seeing you again." He nodded, smiled back. She reached across the table, squeezing Marcie's hand. It felt limp, icy cold. "Don't you remember, Marcie? He's the gentleman who bought the bed."

"The bed. Oh yes, of course."

He'd scared her half to death; he hadn't wanted that. "I didn't mean to interrupt. I'm sorry. I was only passing by."

"It's quite all right." Pam got up from her chair. "I've left my husband somewhere; he gets sulky when I do." She smiled at Marcie. "You know Jerry. See you later."

Marcie's lips were dry. She ran her tongue across them. "Well?"

"I had to see you."

"Now? You've lost your mind."

"I couldn't wait."

The way he said it, she believed him. "Sure as hell, we can't stay here." She got up. She felt steadier. He reached to take her arm. "Don't touch me. Are you crazy?"

"Sorry."

Marcie turned, moved from the terrace, started off across the grass. He walked beside her, careful not to be too close. "O.K., let's hear it."

"Just like that?" It wasn't possible. "It's not a simple sentence, Marcie. There's so much I've got to say."

She looked at him. It was like a disease. He was a carrier, and even with his tux on, walking nowhere near her, she could feel it. Or was she the carrier? She was the one who wanted it, she'd said as much to Dee just hours ago. She turned away. She had no self-control left, she was so ashamed.

"This way," she said.

"Where are we going?"

Marcie shrugged. "You'll see."

Ed watched them from the terrace. He was curious, to put it mildly, but he kept his head. He waited till they'd almost disappeared into the dark, then started following. They passed the eighteenth green, the swimming pool, then veered off toward the practice tee. He stopped and swore. He knew where they were going now. He'd used the place himself when need arose. He felt like rushing in and tearing them apart. He even started for them. Then he stopped. If Marcie knew he knew, their lives would never be the same again. This thing would always lie between them. There was fuck-all he could do but wait.

The next ten minutes were the longest of his life.

"We're nearly there now." Marcie wasn't all that sure which way to turn. There was a spot Dee and her boyfriends used to use when Dee was young and crazy. If it still existed, it was somewhere near. She saw the bushes up ahead. God willing, this was it.

"Come on," she said.

"Where are you taking me?"

"Duck down." She bent, moved through the shrubbery. There it was, just as Dee said: a clearing in the middle, bushes all around it. Like a private room. She waited till he reached her.

Talker had a puzzled look. "Why here?"

"Why do you think?" Her arms went out, she raised her lips and kissed him, rubbed against him, ran her fingernails across his back.

His thoughts were spinning. "Marcie . . . listen."

"Later."

"There are things we've got to say."

Her hand was on his zipper now. She pulled it down. "They'll keep." She reached in, found it, brought it out.

"This isn't what I came for."

Marcie grinned. "The hell it's not." She drew her gown up, went down on her knees.

"Please, Marcie. Don't . . ."

She wrapped her lips around it, let her eyes close.

"Jesus, Marcie." He could feel it sweeping through him. Yes, he wanted her. But there were things he wanted more. He drew himself away.

"What's wrong?"

He went down to his knees beside her. "I'm in love with you."

"I know." She found it with her right hand, started rubbing.

"I can't talk to you like this."

"You want to help me take my dress off?"

"No."

The gown zipped up the back. She pulled it down and started wriggling out of it.

"I want to talk about our future."

Marcie got the gown off. "We don't have a future."

"Yes, we do." Her hands were on her bra straps. Talker took her hands and kissed them. "Listen to me. I'm a different person, Marcie. Nothing like the guy you met. I want a home, I want a—"

"I don't want to hear about it. Can't you understand that?"

"All you've done is change my life. I'll get a job, a good job. I can do it. God, I've wasted so much time. I took my SATs and scored high, did I ever tell you? Got accepted too. A good school. I could start all over, if you want that."

"Fuck me."

Talker didn't hear it. "I want to take care of you, that's all I want. I'd make a decent husband."

"I've already got one. Fuck me."

"Jesus, Marcie. Don't. Don't talk like that."

She lay back, spread her legs wide. "Do it."

"Stop it. That's not what I want you for."

She sat up. "Are you kidding me?"

"I swear to God. I want to live here, make a decent home for you."

"A decent home." She choked up, tears and laughter, both at once. "That's funny. Are you going to work for Dad, sell cars?"

"You want me to?"

"Another salesman in the family." There was nothing she could do about the tears now. She stood up, gown in one hand. "You know what you've done to me?"

"I've loved you."

"Torn me open, that's what. I've done things with you—" Her head began to shake. "I've come apart, found things inside myself that have no business being there. And you know what I get to do now? Help me with this God damn dress."

He got up from the grass and zipped his fly. "You're wonderful. If you don't know that—"

"Shut up. What I get to do is kill the things I found. Pretend I never found them. I could die. Don't touch me, I took off this fucking dress, I'll get it on."

"You love me, Marcie."

"No, I don't."

"I know damn well it's in you. Say it."

"You know what I've got to say?" She had the gown on, more or less. "Stay back, I'll get the zipper. You're not going to like it, Talker."

"Johnny."

"O.K., Johnny. All I've got to say—" She choked up, then she got it out. "Good-bye."

He took her in his arms. She didn't mean it.

"Let me go."

"I never will."

"It's over, Johnny."

"No, it's not. I'll love you till the day I die."

"That's not my problem. Let me go."

"Why should I? You're in love with me."

The truth came out. "What if I am?" She brought one knee up sharply. Talker gasped and staggered back.

Her hands went to her cheeks, her eyes looked huge. "Oh Christ, look what you've made me do." She started to say more, but nothing came. She spun around, plunged through the bushes, disappeared.

It couldn't be. He sank to one knee, held his groin. She hadn't meant to hurt him. Not his Marcie.

Ed stood hidden in the shadows, watching while his Princess fled the bushes, rushed away into the dark. McBride had stayed behind. Just what the doctor ordered. He remembered telling Marcie that he'd kill for her. He wondered if he would. He started forward.

Talker made it to his feet and wiped his eyes. A grown man had no business crying. Down was down. That's how the gamblers said it. He had rolled his dice and come up empty. All he felt was emptiness; a space inside that you could drive a truck through. From the distance, he could hear the cornball music. It had been some party.

Suddenly, he stiffened. Rustling in the bushes. Marcie. She'd come back. He felt a swelling in his chest: it was his heart.

"What's new, Paul? How's it going?"

"Ed?" What was he doing here?

"Van tells me I invited you."

"I thought you did."

"Could be. I'm getting on, you know. You get to be my age, you start forgetting things. But I'll remember you, McBride. And you'll remember me." He drew his fist back.

Talker saw it coming. He just let it come. It got him high up on the chest. The old man packed a punch.

"O.K., you scum bag, put 'em up."

"Forget it. I'm not going to fight you, Ed."

"Get this. A gentleman. He's half my age. That's what you call respect." He choked with rage. "You fucked my little girl, you filthy prick."

That's when the punches started flying. Talker didn't raise a hand. He dodged the head shots, no sense getting all cut up. But all the other ones he took. Ed swarmed all over him. He staggered, grunting from the punishment. He kept his feet, arms by his sides, until he couldn't anymore. His knees went, he slumped forward on his face.

Ed gasped for air. "Get up, I haven't finished."

Talker made it to his knees.

"Get up, you gutless wonder. Fight me back."

"I love your daughter. I'm not going to hit you, Ed. How could I?"

"Love my daughter? Scum like you?"

"She loves me, too, for all the good it does."

"You lie!" Ed moved one leg back. He could punt like hell in high school. Talker took it on his chest, cried out, and toppled forward. Ed kept kicking. Talker curled up, arms across his face. He thought he heard a bone crack. After that, things hurt him less and less. Light faded. He was losing contact.

Ed looked down at him. The bastard wasn't moving. Had he killed him? "Holy shit." He knelt down, put a hand on Talker's neck. The pulse was strong and steady. Talker shifted, groaned. Ed straightened up. The prick was fine, he'd be O.K.

Ed turned and left the bushes, started toward the Club-

house. He was panting, soaked with sweat. His knuckles hurt
like hell. He changed direction, headed for the locker room.

The door was open, but the place was dark. He switched
the lights on, made it to his locker, flopped down on the
bench. His heart was pounding, thudding in his ears. His
knuckles were a mess; no blood, but red and sore. His hands
were steady. Not a bad performance for a man of sixty-eight.

He had to reappear upstairs and look as if nothing had
happened. When he could, he stood, took off his jacket, hung
it carefully. His shirt was damp, the armpits soaked. Hair dry-
ers. Ed went to the washroom, took off the shirt, blew it dry,
then soaked a towel in water, good and cold, and wrapped the
thing around his neck. He'd saved the family honor, that was
something. He would never say a word to Marcie. Neither
would McBride. You had to hand it to the man; he'd had his
brains kicked out for love. He'd lick his wounds and go away.
They'd seen the last of him.

Ten minutes later, he was dressed and polishing his shoe
tips; he had scuffed them on McBride.

"Hi, Dad."

Ed looked up sharply. "Hello, son. What brings you here
this time of night?"

Van might well ask the same of him. He'd seen Ed from
the window of the Paddlewheel as he went to the locker room.
It struck him odd enough to pay a visit.

"Me?" Van shrugged. "I've got a match tomorrow, I just
came to check my golf shoes."

"Sure." Van had been selling cars for all these years and
couldn't tell a decent lie. "What's really on your mind?"

"I looked for Marcie, looked for you. What's going on?"

"I took her for a long walk."

"Oh?"

Ed tossed the shoe cloth down, got to his feet, and looked
Van squarely in the eye. "We had a lot to talk about. You're
not the only one these days who has a pack of trouble."

"I know that."

"I've seen how she's been acting."

"So have I."

"You want to know the truth?"

Van wasn't altogether sure he did. "Of course I do."

"She loves you very much and she's been worried sick
about you, Van. She wants you back with me."

"She told you so?"

Ed smiled. "At least a million times."

Talker saw the parking lot ahead. It wasn't easy getting this far, and his breath caught as the pain swept over him again. His ribs were killing him, he had to keep his breathing shallow, and his right arm wasn't working. It hung limply by his side. Not broken, he had checked for that. Nor was it damage to a nerve; his fingers moved. The trouble was his shoulder. Something there was all screwed up.

He willed his feet to move, kept shuffling till he reached the car, then sagged against it. He'd just had some going over. In an odd way, he had no regrets about the beating. If some sideshow barker had been screwing with his daughter, what would he have done? What Ed did.

It was clumsy doing everything left-handed, but he managed to take out his key, get in, and close the door. How did left-handed people make it through the day in this right-handed world? He reached across himself to get the key in the ignition, turned it, heard the motor come to life.

He sat still for a minute, let it idle. Then he worked the shift, backed out, drove slowly through the parking lot. He took the driveway past the portico for one last look, then drew up at the Fallsburg Road. He had no love of doctors, but he knew he had to see one.

Talker took the right toward town. Someone would tell him how to find the hospital.

Marcie was sitting on the terrace, faced out toward the darkness, looking at the ruins of her life. Somehow, she'd made it to the powder room without attracting stares, and managed to repair herself. She had to do her lips how many times, her hand kept shaking. In the end, she got it right, and her exterior was perfect. Nothing showed.

Her insides were another matter. She had done the right thing. Ghastly as the scene had been, it had to end the way it did. She couldn't have him, not on his terms. Or on hers. How long could she have hoped to go on seeing him in secret? Someone had to find out someday. Someday soon. The consequences were unthinkable. If Dad or Van or Pam or anybody had the least suspicion, what would happen to her life?

Was it a crime to save herself? Of course not. Any decent woman with responsibilities would do what she had done. Then why, dear God, why did she feel like such a criminal? She'd hurt him. Hell, she might as well have ripped his throat out. And her own, while she was at it. She could feel his pain. She shared it. And tomorrow, would the hurt be any less? In time, it had to be. It had to fade and disappear. If not, how could she possibly go on? She knew what Dee would tell her. 'Get your act together, Steuben. Tough it out.'

"Is this dance taken?"

"What?"

Van stood there, smiling down at her. "A penny for those thoughts of yours."

"You wouldn't want them."

"It's all right. I know. Ed told me everything."

Her hands went to the chair arms, holding tight. "What did he say?"

Van wanted to believe what Ed had told him. Knowing Marcie's thoughts and feelings was like having burdens lifted. Heavy weights. If it was true. It still left a lot of questions unexplained, but sometimes you were better off not knowing everything. Van did his best to push his doubts aside. He bent and kissed her cheek.

"You know I love you, don't you? Ever since our first date. I just wanted you to know that. And I'm going back with Ed." That was what she wanted, wasn't it? He took her hand. "O.K.?"

It had to be O.K. Her life was here, around her on the terrace; she was looking at it. And he loved her in the only way he could. She smiled at him. "Did you ask me to dance?"

"That's right."

"I thought you did." He bowed and took her arm. She smiled again. "I'm going to stick around, you know."

"You are?"

She went into his arms. "I've never liked New York. It's nicer here."

They started dancing. Every move he made was perfect. She felt lighter. Couples all around were smiling. Dad and Mom danced by. She grinned at them. Van twirled her, and she spun around as if she knew what she were doing. Everything was spinning, all the candles and the lanterns, all of it in rhythm to Ben Burbidge and His Boys. Life had its recompenses.

"Van?"

He bent close. "Yes?"

She had to say it, so she did. "I love you, too."

33

LUCY WOKE UP with a start. It wasn't dawn yet. She felt sticky. From the heat? The room was cool enough. She sat up, touched her back; maybe a welt had opened up. Her skin was sore but dry. What could it be? She looked down at herself and saw it. Blood. Dark, sticky, gorgeous blood. She touched it with a fingertip. The stuff was really there, she wasn't dreaming.

"Oh my God." She sat there staring at it for the longest time. That such an ordinary thing could mean so much. She felt the pressure lifting. It meant no more desperation. She had time to breathe. She lay back, took a pillow, put the thing across her face and just let go. She'd get up later, put a pad on. Right now, all that mattered was to let the feelings flow.

About the same time, Annie bolted out of bed. "You dummy." What in hell took her so long? She flung her robe on, grabbed her purse and took off like the wind. There was a wall phone in the hall downstairs.

She rifled through the phone book, found the number, jammed a coin into the slot and dialed. She was grinning, couldn't wait. She had some wham-o things to say.

Ed groaned. The fucking phone was ringing off the fucking hook. Let Harriet take care of it. His head ached, and his temples throbbed. He'd had enough champagne last night to float a battleship. The ringing stopped.

"Ummm?"

That was Harriet. He felt like death, rolled over on his side and started drifting off.

"Ed, it's for you."

"Who is it?"

"Some girl from the Sheriff's office."

"Screw it, take a message."

"Why me?" Harriet reached out, stuck the receiver in his hand. The cord was short, he had to lean half over her.

"Uh-huh?"

"Good morning, Ed. You know who this is?"

Some fool secretary playing guessing games. "No."

"Pussy Point, Ed."

Holy shit. His eyes flew open. Was she crazy, calling him at home before the sun was up?

"You there, Ed?"

Harriet lay right beside him. "Yes, miss."

"Place me now?"

"That's right, miss." He was sweating.

"Wonder why I'm calling?"

Little bitch, she had him trapped. "That's true, miss. Yes, I am."

"I need a favor, Ed. I've lost my man. You're going to find him for me."

"Am I?"

"Yes, indeedy, Ed. Damn right you are, or I'll call Marcie, tell her what you did to me. Or Betsy or—why don't you put your wife back on?"

"That isn't necessary, miss."

"O.K. His name is Talker. You gave him a loaner for his T-bird. I don't know what name he used. Just find him."

Life was funny. Annie's man was Marcie's man. The guy sure got around. "I'm not sure how I'd do that, miss."

"Come off it. You're important. Call the Sheriff, how do I know? You've got thirty minutes. Here's my number. Got a pencil?"

It was out of reach. "One moment, please." He staggered out of bed. The pad and pen were by the phone. He made his way around it. Harriet was going to ask him questions. What he needed was a story.

"Got the pencil, Ed?"

"I have it, yes."

"Five-five-five, three-three-oh-five. I'll be waiting."

"Thank you, miss. It's been a pleasure."

"You know, Ed, you're really not a bad guy. I'll remember you."

The line went dead. He hung the phone up. "Harriet?" She'd drifted back to sleep. He could have kissed her. What a world. He took the number, went downstairs, called Harry Weller from the kitchen.

A little after that, a taxicab pulled into Van and Marcie's drive. It had instructions not to honk; no reason to wake up the neighborhood. The girls were downstairs, waiting for it, talking softly. It was miserable for both of them.

"Oh God," Dee said, "it's here." She felt so good. And felt so rotten. She had done it, broken free—so it had taken thirty-eight years, what the hell, who counted. She was out, and Marcie wasn't. All Dee wanted at that moment was to drag her out the door, take her along. It wasn't going to happen. Now or ever.

"Are you going to be all right?" Dee asked.

"Are you?"

"I'll call you once a week and let you know."

"You promise?" Marcie knew she wouldn't; didn't really want her to. It hurt too much. She envied Dee. Dee had no man, no family, no great career. It didn't come to much, why should it seem like everything?

The driver stood outside the door. They let him in. He took the cases, went away.

"You'll say good-bye to Van for me?"

"Of course."

"And Betsy, too. I never got to know her."

"Maybe next time." Marcie smiled.

Would there be a next time? Sure. Once you were out of jail, it was a cinch to visit. "Any chance you're coming East?"

"You never know."

They left the house, moved down the walk. It seemed important not to cry. They had their looks, their health, and almost everything a girl could want. They stopped beside the cab and faced each other.

"Love you," Dee said.

"Love you always."

One quick hug, and Dee got in. The taxi pulled out. Marcie watched and waved, then turned, walked quickly to the front door. Home. Whatever that meant, it was hers; to live and die in and absorb whatever came between. She knew she should have thought "enjoy" but it was much too soon for that. "Absorb" would do for now. She softly closed the door and went upstairs.

Talker needed help to dress. He managed most of it himself; but shirt buttons and shoelaces were beyond him. From his navel to his armpits, he was taped up like a mummy, and they had his right arm in a sling. The X rays showed two cracked ribs and a hairline fracture, and his shoulder had been dislocated. He had orders not to move the arm for days.

He had orders not to move himself much, either, but no way on earth was he not getting out of Fulton then and there. He had to go. Like stepping out of boiling oil, it was not a thing you questioned; you just did it.

Where to go and what to do were questions of another kind. He couldn't deal with them at all. His aches and pains—there wasn't much of him that wasn't black-and-blue—were incidental. They would go away with time. But Marcie wouldn't.

How and why and where had it gone wrong? Love crossed all borders, didn't it? Priests left the cloth for belly dancers, millionaires and waitresses got married, Lana Turner and a gangster nearly tied the knot. Why wouldn't Marcie have him when she loved him? Would he ever understand it?

He rang the buzzer for the nurse. She came and tied his shoes, buttoned his shirt and tucked it in, then helped him put on his jacket. She tucked the empty sleeve into the pocket of his tux, then stepped away and smiled.

He took a quick look in the mirror and came close to smiling, too. He looked like someone from a thirties movie; Ronald Colman, Robert Donat, coming back to England from the War. An old-time hero. Something he would never be.

He thanked the nurse, went down to the cashier, and paid his bill. There wasn't much that still remained: pick up his bags and go. That summed it up. He left the building, started at a good clip for the parking lot, then slowed down. Moving fast was not a good idea. The sun was bright, he had to squint. His shades were someplace, maybe back at the hotel.

Annie heard him coming. She was sitting on the curb beside his car. Her bag was close beside her. She had been there for an hour or more, since Ed had called her back. The man delivered. Annie even knew about the injuries; not how he'd gotten them, but what they were.

She wondered who had beaten him and why it happened. Something had gone very wrong—and when she saw him in his tux, she knew. The damn fool, he had gone to Marcie at some party, Ed or Van had caught on. One of them had smashed him up. It had to be. Her guess was Ed.

He stopped dead when he saw her. "What's this?"

Annie stood up. "What's it look like?"

"I thought you left town."

"I did. I changed my mind, that's all."

"How come?"

"It dawned on me that I'd left something valuable behind."

How was he going to handle this? An eighteen-year-old farm girl was a prize he didn't need. True, she was beautiful, she even had a mind—and she looked changed in some odd way he couldn't name. "So you came back for me, is that it?"

"On the nose. I knew the thing with Marcie couldn't last." She'd seen her home, she knew the world that Marcie lived in. "It just ended sooner than I'd thought."

"And you're here to pick the pieces up." He shook his head. "As you can see, I'm fine."

"I see more than you think I do."

"How did you find me?"

Annie grinned. "I've got connections in this town. You'd be surprised."

"You want to tell me—"

"No. The deal is, we don't ask each other questions. There's a lot I'd like to know—but you don't ever have to tell me."

"Fair enough." The more he looked at her, the less she seemed to be the kid he'd met a week ago. "I don't know what it is," he said, "but you look different."

Annie nodded. "That's because I am. In some ways, Talker—what's your real name?"

"Johnny."

"There are ways that I'm as old as you are, Johnny. Even older."

"You don't say." He smiled, turned toward the car. "Where can I drop you?"

"That's not how it's going to work." She held her hand out, palm up, open.

"What's that for?"

"The keys. You need a driver, and I'm it."

"The day comes I can't drive myself—"

"It's here. Shut up, give me the keys."

He stared at her, then brought the keys out. What in God's name was he doing?

Annie took the keys, unlocked the door, and slipped behind the wheel. "Get in." He stood rooted to the spot. "You heard me. Are you deaf or something?"

Talker did as he was told. She watched him settle on the seat beside her, close the door.

"Where to?"

"I've got to get my bags."

She drove the car out like a man. "Just tell me how to get there."

Talker told her, sat in silence, watching every move she made.

Lucy sat beside her father as they drove to Church. She felt as if the world had changed, and she'd changed, too. Not just the fact she wasn't pregnant. Much, much more. She had the time to plan and save before she ran away. Except she wasn't running now, not like her mother did. And she had Marvin. He'd surprised her. Loved her, stood beside her, tried to save her—right or wrong—from stripping in the show. And punched her father's face in. Not what you'd call kid stuff. Marvin was a man worth having.

Lucy hadn't spoken to her father, not one word since yesterday. The Church was up ahead, and she had things to say before they got there.

"Dad?" She started quietly. "I've learned a lot these last few days."

"Well, thank the Lord."

"I have. I want to thank you, too. The whipping, spilling cum all over me—you taught me things."

"Amen." He'd long since prayed his guilt away. "You giving up your sluttish life?"

"Yes, Dad. I am."

"The Lord moves in mysterious ways His wonders to perform."

She nodded. "Dad, I've tried to take Mom's place for you. Not anymore. I'm saving up my money and I'm leaving home with Marvin when I'm good and ready to." He started sputtering.

"Just you hold on, young lady."

Lucy smiled. "And if you come near me, touch me—hell, you even just look at me cross-eyed, you know what I'm going to do? I'll wait till you're asleep some night, I'll creep into your bedroom, and I'll cut your balls off with a bread knife."

Barney looked at her. "You wouldn't."

"Swear to God," she said. "By all that's holy."

He believed her.

Marvin saw them drive up. He was standing by his father on the Church steps. He'd been dreaming of his Lucy, had their future all worked out. He'd marry her and bring her home and have the baby. If his father didn't like that, he could choke. Since Friday, when he'd seen him taken out with one punch in the belly, he had started looking smaller. Ever since, he'd kept on shrinking. He was stupid, gross, and clumsy. If the old man bitched about the wedding or the baby, he could run the fucking farm himself. He'd go broke in a month. The man would either learn to value and respect him or he'd find himself without a son. Marvin didn't care which way it went.

He moved toward Lucy, who was running to him, smiling, threw her arms around him.

"Marv, guess what. I've got my period."

"You do?"

She thought she knew the answer, but she had to ask him. "Marv? That lets you off the hook, you know."

"The hell it does." He kissed her lips, right there in front of everybody. She was his. He put an arm around her waist, and they walked into Church together.

Harry Weller stood by his Command Post watching all the trucks and vans move out. The Fair was over, God be thanked. He'd had a bellyful. He'd had Ed Steuben, too, at six o'clock. He'd wondered why Ed gave a damn about McBride, and how the man had gotten beaten up. He knew his place, he didn't ask. He found him, called Ed back, and shrugged it off, just let it slide.

He checked his watch. Ten minutes and he'd go pick Martha up for Church. After that, he had a mind to pay a visit to Walt Greener. He had seen Walt at the fire, watched his face. He knew as sure as God made apples Walt had started it. No proof, he'd never hang it on him, but he wanted Walt to know he knew. Walt was a no-good troublemaker, and he couldn't wait to tell the man that if he ever caught him doing anything, he'd throw his ass in jail so hard it bounced.

He lit a cigarette and smiled. Being Sheriff wasn't all bad. There were parts of it he loved.

The bags were in the back, and they were starting out of town. He wasn't sure which way to go, but Fulton was a pinprick on the map, and all roads led to Rome. He listened to her chattering. She had him smiling now. The way her eyes glowed when she looked at him . . . he wasn't worth it.

"Would you like to know how Labor Day began?"

He shook his head.

"In New York City. I was reading all about it in my *Almanac* last night. 'A holiday in honor of the working man.' That's word for word."

It got another smile. "I'm impressed."

"You want to guess what year it was?"

"Why don't you tell me."

"Eighteen eighty-two, when Garfield was the President. That's something, isn't it?"

He was about to answer when he spotted something. "Stop the car."

"What for?"

"Just stop it."

Annie put on the brakes, drew up to the curb. A half-block ahead of them, there was a church. People were strolling down the sidewalk, moving in. She took a second look, saw Betsy. All dressed up. So pretty and so innocent; high, lacy collar, low-heeled patent-leather shoes with straps. She felt like dashing out to say good-bye, but she knew she couldn't. It was over; what connected them was gone.

And there were Van and Marcie, too. And Ed. The woman with him had to be his wife. A battle-ax. She grinned, then looked at Talker. Poor dumb bastard; it was torture.

"Can we go now?" Annie asked him.

"In a minute."

Marcie, Marcie. He began to see her for the first time: beautiful, desirable, and miles out of reach. He'd been a fool to think there was a place for him among those people, on that sidewalk. He imagined strolling with them, Marcie on his arm. Ridiculous. He felt like laughing, but it hurt too much. He'd known her for a few days, that was something to be proud of. And he ached for her. He knew what she had felt for him, how much it had cost her to let go. If he had never come to Fulton . . . but he had, and both of them had found where love could go and where it couldn't. She was precious to him, always would be, like a diamond he could never own. He'd seen enough. He cleared his throat.

"Let's go."

Matthew Larkin moved out to his pulpit, gave a nod to Charlie Spofford, waited for the air conditioner to die away. Another week. Time, at his time of life, was seamless. Days sped into days, one Sunday blended into the next one.

Matthew gazed out at his flock. It was the continuity that moved him most; the lack of change. There were the Brinkers and the Steubens and Van Burens sitting where they always sat and looking the way they always did.

The youngsters in their pews were all embarking on a new year. School was starting soon, which was the basis for his sermon of the day: how endings and beginnings meld together. There was nothing old in life, and nothing new. What mattered was the steady flow.

"My children . . ."

Marcie couldn't pay attention. He was gone. She'd driven him away. Their scene last night kept haunting her. Sometimes the things you said in desperation were the truest. She would have to kill the things she'd found inside. If only she knew how. She saw his body, saw him in the melon patch, felt the cool juices of the fruit running across her breasts. That moment, as if she were naked now and laughing in the noonday sun.

She dug her nails into her palm. This had to stop. She had to stop it. There was no one else to do it. She was Marcie. Marcie had her place, her home, her family. It had to be enough. She looked at Van, then took his hand and squeezed it.

Van squeezed back. On cool consideration, it had been a hellish week. But he'd survived, crossed all the barriers and come out at the end a better man, a better father, better husband. He felt sure of it. He even knew the reason why. There was no other way to feel. He'd faced his choices, he had made them, and the road ahead was clear and straight. Ten years from now, he'd run the Agency, they'd still be living where they were on Sunset Crescent. It might seem a little big by that time. Betsy would be married, gone. He looked at her. She was his special blessing. Children were the future; they held all the hope.

Betsy wriggled on the pew. Her thighs were damp. The heat was stiffling, and the thought of Denny last night didn't help. Old Reverend Larkin mumbled on about the coming year. They would be sophomores, she and Denny. Fifteen soon, both of them. Was fifteen old enough? She closed her eyes and saw his thing as it jerked wildly up and down. It still held many mysteries for her. When would she unravel them? She didn't know, and like a good girl, she tried not to think about it.

Harriet was dozing off. She rarely drank too much, but by the time they left the Club her snoot was full. Ed grinned and jabbed her lightly in the ribs. He'd had a Bloody Mary for his breakfast; he was feeling fine. Life had its winners and its losers. Why he always won, he didn't know. There was a law of averages, but he was an exception. Bad luck always passed him by. He'd had his Harem Girl, saved Marcie's marriage, got his son-in-law back where he wanted him. He'd even laid his wife last night. She really let loose when she wasn't sober. Always claimed she had no memory of it in the morning. He knew better.

Harriet was wide awake now. Ed was grinning at her. She knew why. She could remember every single thing last night, but that was not for him to know. She kept a stony face and thought about the afternoon, the pins she'd stick in Eleanor. It was a wicked thought, not worthy of her, so she straightened up and listened to the homilies that flowed from Reverend Larkin. That was what Church was for.

*   *   *

The Thunderbird was roaring down the open highway. Sunlight glinted on the patches of bare metal where the paint was stripped away. He'd have to get a paint job somewhere, once they knew where they were going.

There was a golden oldie playing on the radio. "The Fifty-ninth Street Bridge." The rhythm bounced along. He shifted on his seat and looked at her. She had a whole life waiting. For that matter, so did he. It was a puzzle. What was either of them going to do with it?

"It's coming up," he heard her say.

There was the state line just ahead, a big sign right beside it. FAREWELL GREETINGS FROM THE BUCKEYE STATE. WE HOPE THAT YOU ENJOYED YOUR VISIT. COME AND SEE US SOON AGAIN.

They whizzed on past it. Pennsylvania.

"Johnny?"

"Ummm?"

"Where are we headed?"

Johnny didn't know. He had to tell her something, so he said the one thing he was sure of. "No place where we've been before."